MIKE HOLLOW

LION FICTION

Published by Lion Fiction
an imprint of
Lion Hudson plc
Wilkinson House, Jordan Hill Road
Oxford OX2 8DR, England
www.lionhudson.com/fiction

ISBN 978 1 78264 186 5
e-ISBN 978 1 78264 187 2

First edition 2016

Acknowledgments
Extract p. 7 taken from "Burnt Norton" in *Four Quartets* by T.S. Eliot,
copyright © 1940 T.S. Eliot. Reprinted by permission of Faber and
Faber Ltd.
Extract p. 9 taken from *Daily Digest of Foreign Broadcasts*, No. 399, 21
August 1940, copyright © British Broadcasting Corporation. Reproduced
by permission of the British Broadcasting Corporation.

Back cover photo of Mike Hollow taken by Stephen Crockford.

A catalogue record for this book is available from the British Library

Printed and bound in the UK, February 2016, LH26

For Margaret, my wife, friend,
and most faithful editor in art as in life

Footfalls echo in the memory
    Down the passage which we did not take
Towards the door we never opened
    Into the rose-garden.

"Burnt Norton" (1937), from T.S. Eliot, *Four Quartets*

"Churchill and his fellow liars have deceived us on every phase of this war, and it is typical that they should have assured us that Germany had decided to abandon her air attack [on Britain] just before the biggest raids of the war… A more sinister example of mendacity was the official denial that any parachutists had landed, whereas in fact they did land, and are now being sheltered by the Fifth Column, and are probably receiving regular coded instructions from Germany."

From a broadcast by the New British Broadcasting Station, a German propaganda radio station purporting to be British, at 9.30 p.m. on 20 August 1940. Reported in the BBC Monitoring Service's *Daily Digest of Foreign Broadcasts*, No. 399, 21 August 1940.

The Essex County Borough of West Ham, 1940

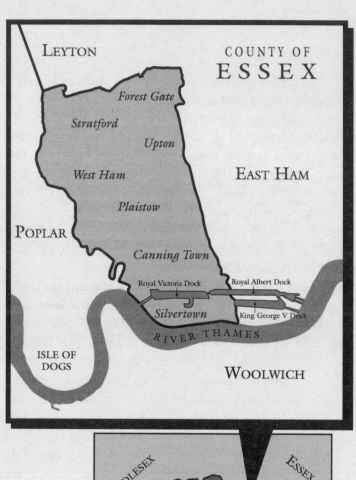

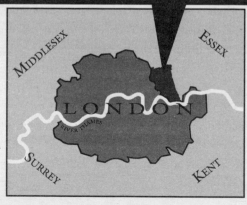

CHAPTER 1

The Anderson shelter had guarded his life for another night, but it felt like a grave. Only the thin sheet of corrugated iron at his side separated him from the cold earth in which he was lying. He drifted in and out of a restless, shallow dream. Now he was in France again, in a dug-out lined with sodden planks of wood, waiting for the day's shelling to begin. Then the picture shifted, and he was twelve years old, a Boy Scout stirring in a canvas tent as a chorus of birds heralded the start of day. Their song began to fill his ears, with one note soaring louder than all. It wailed on and on, and his body jolted. He was awake.

His eyes opened, and he was back in the present. It was Friday morning. He wasn't a Boy Scout and he wasn't a soldier, and the dawn chorus was the monochrome blast of the all-clear siren.

Detective Inspector John Jago was chilly despite being fully clothed, and his joints were stiff. He tugged the worn blanket up under his chin and shifted his aching body carefully on what passed for a bed in this cramped metal box as his mind cleared.

What a way to live, he thought. He'd spent twenty-five shillings – not to mention elevenpence postage – on Selfridges' promise of a purpose-made "shelter bed", but that decision was beginning to feel like a triumph of hope over experience. The wooden frame and webbing ("comfortable even without a mattress") were sturdy enough, but the thing was only five foot nine long and a miserly twenty inches wide. The simple act of turning over was now a delicate manoeuvre that risked pitching himself onto the damp floor, bedding and all. Tonight he would fetch his old eiderdown from the house and lay that on top. At least being warm might help, although the air raids of late had pretty much put paid to any chance of a decent night's sleep.

A lady in the newspaper, well-meaning no doubt, had advised that the best antidote to a sleepless night in a shelter was to undress and go to bed "properly" as soon as the raids were over. All very well if you didn't have a job to do, he supposed. And as for her other helpful suggestion – having a sleep after lunch – well, that was just another way to make a policeman laugh.

He checked the time on his wrist-watch. Eight minutes past six. Just five minutes or so until the blackout ended, then another half-hour till sunrise, but there was nothing to be gained from staying on this paltry shelf of a bed. He hauled his reluctant body out from under the blanket, tied his shoes, slipped on his coat and clamped his crumpled grey fedora onto his head. One final stretch to get his limbs working and he felt at least half ready to face the world. He unlatched the door he'd cobbled together a year before from salvaged wood – wondering then, as now, why the government had decided to supply the shelters with no means of sealing the entrance – and climbed out.

His house was still there: a good start to the day. At least he should be able to go to work. No signs of fire in the immediate vicinity, but half a mile away the first of the dawn light revealed smoke curling above the rooftops, marking the points where random destruction, and no doubt death, had befallen the unlucky.

He trudged along the few yards of uneven path to the back door of the house. A cup of tea would perk him up if the gas was still working, and if there was power he'd make a bit of toast to keep him going until he could get some proper breakfast in the station canteen – if not, it would be bread and margarine with a scraping of jam again. He opened the door, went in, and closed it behind him. With the blackout curtains still in place it was darker inside the house than it was outside. He searched for the light switch with his fingers and flicked it down, and was pleased to see the bulb that dangled from the ceiling glow into life – he had electricity.

The brown enamel kettle was already full – he tried to remember to fill it every night in case the Luftwaffe hit the water main. He turned the knob on the stove and heard the hiss of gas, followed by a dull pop as his lighted match ignited it. He placed the kettle over the flames and reached for the teapot – and then the phone rang.

With a sigh and another glance at his watch he put the pot down and walked through to the narrow hall. At this time of the morning there was no mystery about who might be calling. He lifted the receiver.

"Jago."

"Good morning, sir. Tompkins here, at the station. Sorry to disturb you at this time of day, but I've just come on duty on early turn and I've been asked to call you."

"Don't worry, I was already up. And it's always a pleasure to hear your dulcet tones, Frank."

"That's not what my missus calls it."

"Well, far be it from me to intrude on private grief, Frank. So what is it that needs me to turn out at this ungodly hour?"

"A body, sir."

"Lots of bodies around these days, Frank. What's special about this one?"

"Possibility of suspicious circumstances, apparently. That's why they want you."

"Where is it?"

"Down in Canning Town, sir. Tinto Road, near the bottom end of Star Lane. On a bomb-site on the right-hand side as you go down the road. They say you can't miss it."

"I dare say. Have we got anyone down there?"

"Yes, sir, young Stannard. He's waiting for you to arrive. He's got reinforcements, too – one of them War Reserve constables."

Jago noticed the dismissive tone in which the station sergeant referred to PC Stannard's recently enrolled companion. That was Frank's way of signalling his opinion of the government's solution to the wartime shortage of police officers, he thought, but now was not the time to rise to his bait.

"Very well," he said. "Get hold of DC Cradock and tell him I'll pick him up at the station in about twenty minutes. And see if you can get the police surgeon down to the site pretty smartish."

Detective Inspector Jago put the phone down, returned to the kitchen, and turned the kettle off. A cup of cold water would have to do for now.

***

His estimate of twenty minutes proved to be optimistic. The Riley started first time, and he was on his way promptly, but the roads were still clogged with fire hoses, and twice he had to find a way round streets that had been cordoned off because of bomb damage.

It was five to seven by the time Jago reached West Ham Lane. He could see the police station ahead of him, its front door screened against blast by a wall of neatly stacked sandbags and the windows to the side of the entrance protected by horizontal wooden slats. On the pavement in front of the station stood Detective Constable Cradock, awaiting his arrival.

Jago pulled up beside him. The young man looked as though he'd dressed quickly, and his hair was dishevelled. He eased himself carefully into the passenger seat with a quick "Morning, guv'nor", and Jago nodded a wordless greeting to him in return. Cradock looked as bleary-eyed as Jago felt.

"You getting enough sleep with these air raids every night, Peter?"

"Not too bad, sir. They wake me up, of course, but I try to get back to sleep when the noise stops. How about you, sir?"

"I seem to have lost the knack. Every time I think I'm going to doze off again Hitler drops another bomb just to spite me, and the anti-aircraft guns make so much noise I wonder whether he's slipping them a fiver just to keep me awake. Last night I don't think I got to sleep until it was nearly time to wake up. I must be getting old."

Cradock raised his eyebrows and opened his mouth as if he'd just realized something important.

"It could be night starvation, sir. Maybe you should try a cup of Horlicks at bedtime."

"Tommy rot," said Jago. "I haven't quite reached that stage, thank you very much. It's morning starvation I'm suffering from – I didn't even have time for a piece of toast before I came out. And in any case, if I need anything to drink before I go to bed, I'll stick to a tot of whisky. Now, if I can stay awake long enough we're going to Canning Town to see a man about a body."

Jago slid his left foot onto the gear change pedal, then with a glance over his right shoulder and a light touch on the accelerator he eased the car back into the sparse early morning traffic.

CHAPTER 2

"Morning, sir," said PC Ray Stannard as Jago swung his legs out of the car. "Sorry to drag you out first thing in the morning, but I thought you ought to see this."

Jago looked the young constable up and down. So much had changed in the last few weeks. It was no surprise now to see an officer in such a state at the end of a night shift. His tunic and trousers were streaked white with plaster dust, his boots were scuffed, and his hands and face were daubed black with soot. Not so long ago, thought Jago, Stannard would have spent the night quietly patrolling silent streets, rattling the doors of shops to check they were locked and watching out for any evidence of petty crime. But now it could reasonably be assumed that in the last few hours he and his colleague had been scrambling over scorched wreckage, helping to pull the living and the dead out from under ruined buildings, and taking on any and every task that needed doing in the wake of the latest air raid.

The detective turned to the War Reserve PC, who was in a similar state. He knew Stannard, but this other somewhat shorter man he didn't recall. He gave a sideways glance back at Stannard and raised his eyebrows.

"Oh, sorry, sir," said Stannard, "this is PC Price; he's a War Reserve. Volunteered when the war started, but he's been on nights a lot, so you may not have met him." He leaned a little closer to Jago and lowered his voice. "Not as bad as some, sir. Old soldier. Quite resourceful, considering they get thrown out onto the streets without any training."

Jago nodded.

"Right, tell me what we've got here, then."

"A woman, sir, found dead just back there."

Jago followed the direction of Stannard's pointing finger. The neat row of small, late-Victorian terraced houses was punctuated by a gaping space where two, three, perhaps even four dwellings had been reduced to a straggling heap of matchwood and rubble by at least one high-explosive bomb. Those still standing either side of the gap had lost all their windows and most of their roof tiles. At the far end of the wreckage he could see part of a front bedroom that remained attached to the neighbouring house; a wardrobe leaned drunkenly against the wall where what was left of the floor was sagging, the ragged stumps of its joists exposed to the air. Seven untidy-looking men were standing in a huddle on the pavement, smoking. There was no other sign of activity on the site.

"So what's all this about suspicious circumstances?" said Jago.

"Well, it's just that this woman, she wasn't here when she should've been – if she'd been dead, that is – but then she was when she shouldn't have. I've told the men who found her you'll want to talk to them, so they'll explain."

"All a bit quiet here now, isn't it?"

"The ARP warden says everyone's accounted for, sir, and there's no sound of anyone trapped. The people who've been bombed out have been taken to the rest centre in Star Lane. I thought it best to stop the work until you got here, so nothing would get disturbed."

"Good man," said Jago. "Do we know who she is?"

"I'm afraid we don't, sir. There's no identity card on her, no sign of a handbag or purse, and the warden says he doesn't recognize her."

"And you've had a thorough look over the site?"

"Yes, sir. Price and I looked all round for anything that might identify her, and got the rescue squad involved too, but there was nothing." Stannard paused, since Jago seemed to be thinking, then said, "The police surgeon's here too, sir, just on the other side of that pile of wreckage there. That's where the body is – you can't see it from here."

"Very good. DC Cradock and I will go and take a look. You show us the way."

The two detectives followed Stannard and Price, clambering up the unsteady heap of bricks, tiles and timbers littered with the shattered furniture and belongings of the unfortunate people whose homes this had been only hours before. When they reached the top they saw the grey-haired portly figure of Dr Hedges, the police surgeon, crouching beside the body of a young woman. She was a redhead, wearing a green coat that was unbuttoned, revealing a grey suit and green blouse. She had a black shoe on her left foot, and a matching shoe was lying near her right. Hedges hauled himself awkwardly to his feet as they approached.

"Morning, doctor," said Jago. "What have we got?"

"Good morning, Detective Inspector. Young woman, mid to late twenties, I should say. Your constable seems to suspect foul play, but she could easily just have been caught by the blast of a bomb. No obvious signs of interference, but I expect you'll want to get the pathologist to look at her. A proper examination in the mortuary will tell you more than I can from crawling round on my hands and knees in this mess, but I'll leave that decision in your capable hands. In the meantime, I've certified her dead, and if you don't mind I'd rather get back to my breakfast. I'm getting a bit too old and creaky for these early morning calls."

With that he snapped his bag shut, dusted his trousers down with his hand, and made his way cautiously across the sloping debris towards a black Rover saloon parked on the other side of the road.

"Short and sweet," said Cradock.

"Indeed," said Jago. "A man with his mind on his pension, I suspect."

He turned to the pair of police officers. Stannard's expression was attentive, as if he were waiting for his next instruction, but Price looked uncomfortable.

"Are you all right, Constable?" said Jago.

"Yes, sir, thank you, sir," said Price. "Just feeling a little queasy."

"Not your first body, is it?"

"Well… It's just… a young woman like that, sir, lying there dead. It was just a bit of a…" His voice trailed off, uncertainly.

"PC Stannard," said Jago, "I suggest you take your colleague for a cup of tea. I expect you've both had a demanding night. But two things before you go." He turned to Price. "First, you go and find a phone that's working, call the station and tell them to get Dr Anderson the pathologist down here as quickly as he can manage – immediately, if possible."

Price set off, scrambling back down the mound of wreckage towards the road.

"And second, sir?" said Stannard.

"Second, tell me: who are these men who found the body?"

"That lot over there, sir – or two of them, anyway, the ones on the right," said Stannard, gesturing with his thumb in the direction of the group of men standing on the pavement. "They're part of the heavy rescue party that's been working here during the night. They told the ARP warden, and he found me and Price pretty sharpish and brought us down here. Shall I fetch them over?"

"No," said Jago. "Just tell the two who found her to come up here, then go and get your cup of tea when Price comes back. We'll manage."

"Thank you, sir," said Stannard, and headed off in the direction Price had taken. Jago saw him speak to two of the men. The constable pointed back up the heap, and they began to clamber up it.

Both of the rescue men were clad in blue dungarees and flat caps, so filthy as to make the departed police constables look relatively respectable. Jago scrutinized them as they approached. He estimated the taller of the two to be almost six feet in height and in his late forties. The second man was shorter and looked a little younger.

It was only when they drew close that the bigger man's face became clearly visible. Jago stepped forward to stand squarely in the man's path, his arms crossed.

"Well, well," he said. "Now look who's turned up like a bad penny. The Good Samaritan himself, eh? Fancy seeing you here." He peered into the man's face. "Just happened to find a body, did you? Simple as that. If anyone else had told me, I'd believe them. But nothing's ever simple with you, is it? Can you think of one good reason why I should believe you?"

CHAPTER 3

Jago looked round to see where Cradock was and beckoned him to his side.

"Let me introduce you. Detective Constable Cradock, you may not have come across this gentleman before, but he and I have spent a considerable amount of time together over the years, one way or another. Mostly in the nick. Isn't that right, Harry?"

The man's only response was a look of what Cradock took to be pained incomprehension.

"Henry Parker, Esquire, of this parish," said Jago. "Commonly known as Harry."

He took a close look at Harry's clothing, as if inspecting him on parade.

"Well, I never. I have to say, Harry, you're the last person I'd expect to see out here rescuing people. I thought you had better things to do at night."

"Oh, please, Mr Jago," said Parker. "That was a long time ago. You must know I gave all that up years back. Straight as a die, I am, so help me."

"I had heard rumours, Harry, but you'll forgive me for being sceptical. Policeman's habit, you know. So how do you make your living nowadays, if it's not climbing in through the windows of the unsuspecting public and relieving them of their valuables?"

"I clean them, don't I? The windows, I mean – I'm a window cleaner. Least I was, till old Adolf started going round smashing them all. Things've gone a bit slack in the window-cleaning business of late. I still do some, mind – proper regular work, but it's mainly for businesses, the ones who have to keep looking smart. Anyway, I've got involved in this heavy rescue lark now. It pays a bit, and

I'll have you know, Detective Inspector, I'm saving people's lives. Repaying my debt to society, you might say."

"Very noble. You must be putting in some pretty long hours if you're repaying your debt to society." He looked Harry up and down. "Looks like you've put on a bit of weight since I last saw you, too."

"Yes, it's my wife's cooking."

"So you're not the one who goes crawling through cellars and wreckage to rescue people, are you?"

"No, Mr Jago, I leave that to the skinny blokes. I may not be quite as fit as I used to be, but I'm still good with ladders and with lifting and shifting. I can drive too – got a lorry licence six years ago when they first came out, and I'm the only one in the squad who's got one. So it's my job to drive the truck."

"Man of many talents. And where are you living now?"

"47 Hemsworth Street. And before you ask, the furniture's all paid for, and I'm up to date with the rent too."

"Very good. Now perhaps you could introduce me to your colleague."

The shorter man standing a few feet behind Parker pinched the short remainder of his cigarette between the forefinger and thumb of his right hand and slowly took it from his mouth, blowing a lazy stream of smoke upwards into the air. Jago wondered whether this was something the man had picked up from a movie.

"No need, Harry," said the man. "I can speak for myself."

"By all means," said Jago. "Could you give us your name, please?"

"Jenkins. Stanley Jenkins, but my friends call me Stan."

"Thank you, Mr Jenkins. And you're a member of this rescue party too?"

"Yes, I'm in the same boat as Harry, really. Before they decided to have this war I was a roofer, but the government's pretty much stopped people building anything now, so it's all gone a bit quiet in my line of work too."

"You'll be good with heights and ladders then, like Harry, if you're a roofer. Am I right?"

"Oh yes, definitely. But I don't drive. Never had enough money to run a car, and never had occasion to drive a truck."

"Thank you, Mr Jenkins. Now perhaps one of you would be good enough to tell me what happened here. How did you find the body?"

The two men exchanged a quick glance. Harry Parker spoke first.

"We were called out at about eight o'clock last night, not long after the air raid started. These houses had been hit, so we were sent down here to dig out anyone who might be trapped and generally tidy the site up a bit, make it safe – prop up dangerous walls and such like."

"And was anyone trapped?"

"Yes, we got a couple of old dears out from the first house that isn't there any more, if you see what I mean. They were the only people the ARP warden knew were unaccounted for – until we found them, that is – but we had a good look round after that in case there were any passing strays that had got caught out in the raid. You can easily miss someone, you know. Sometimes these days all you find is a few bits."

"Quite. So what happened next?"

"We got a message telling us to go and help at another site."

"What time was that?"

"Just before ten, as I recall. Is that right, Stan?"

"Yeah, I think so," said Jenkins.

"And what did you do then?" said Jago.

"We went, of course," said Harry. "It's not up to us where we go and what we do. We just go where we're told. And we have to be quick about it too. We don't spend half our time standing about doing nothing, like your lot."

"All right, Harry. But you haven't told us about the body yet. What happened?"

"Well, that's just it. That's what I couldn't understand. When we left, there was no sign of her. No sign at all. I call that fishy."

"Fishy? If what I know of you's anything to go by, things only start getting fishy when you turn up, Harry."

"Oh, come on, Mr Jago, that's a bit harsh."

"I wouldn't trust you as far as I could throw you. That was true twenty years ago, and nothing's happened since to make me change my mind. In fact the only thing I can see that's changed is your waist measurement, so I probably couldn't even throw you that far now. Why should I take anything you say as gospel?"

"But I told you," said Harry. "I've changed. Honest day's work for an honest day's pay, that's me."

"I'll give you the benefit of the doubt, then," said Jago. "Now tell me what makes you think there was something fishy going on."

Harry drew himself up straight, like a man vindicated in court.

"Well," he said. "It was like this, you see."

He turned to Cradock.

"You going to write all this down?"

"Yes," said Cradock. "Don't you worry about that. Look – pencil, notebook, all ready."

"Good. I expect this is going to be crucial evidence."

"Get on with it, Harry," said Jago.

"All right, all right," said Harry. "So anyway, we get the call and off we go to the other place – down Beckton Road it was, about half a mile away. Nasty business – there was this woman who'd decided to ignore the siren and stay in the house. She'd got a bed downstairs, thinking it'd be safer. As it was, of course, the house was hit and collapsed on top of her. We had a job clearing the stuff away so we could get to her – the whole upstairs and the roof had fallen in. But she was one of the lucky ones – the blast had blown a wardrobe across the bed, and that'd kept most of it off her, and she survived. Different story next door, though. The family who lived there had gone down into their Anderson shelter and copped it – the whole lot of them. Mum, Dad and three nippers, all dead. Very messy, it was. So that kept us there quite a while, you see."

"And then what?"

"As soon as we'd finished there we shot back up here to finish off tidying things up, like I said. And before you ask, I know exactly what time we got here, because I was wondering how close we were to knocking-off time. It was ten past five this morning. We'd only been on the site a few minutes when we came across the body – it must've been twenty past five at the latest. That's when we started thinking there'd been some funny business going on."

"Funny business?"

"The thing is, I know for a fact that that woman wasn't there when we left this site at ten o'clock last night. So how come she's suddenly there dead at five o'clock the next morning?"

"Could she have been killed by a bomb that fell after you'd gone?"

"That's what I thought at first, especially on account of there being that debris on her."

"What debris was that?"

"There was a bit of wooden rafter lying across her legs and a couple of bricks on top of her arm –"

"There wasn't when I saw her," Jago interrupted.

Harry shrugged his shoulders.

"Probably that doctor feller moved it so he could get a better look. I don't know. Looked to me like he was in a hurry."

"Carry on," said Jago.

"So anyway, I'm standing there looking at this corpse and thinking the same thing as what you said – there must've been another bomb. Only I'm thinking there couldn't have been, because the site looks just the same as it did before. She was lying there, like she is now, with that bit of wall still standing behind her, and everything all around looked the same as it did when we left it. In other words, the place was all blown up, but no more blown up than it had been at ten o'clock last night."

"So what did you do?"

"We went to find the warden, told him what we'd found. We checked with him about bombs too. He says the last bomb that fell here was at five-and-twenty past seven yesterday evening. Categorical, he was – he has to fill a form in, you know, and report the time."

"Yes, I know."

"So I'm thinking if the body wasn't there when we left at ten o'clock last night, and there'd been no more bombs here since, but here she is dead at five in the morning, there's definitely something fishy going on. I told Stan here to go and find a copper, pronto, which he did. Those two lads of yours turned up pretty quick, and I suppose they're the ones who got you down here."

Jago was about to conclude the conversation when he saw a familiar figure approaching from the direction of the road.

"Thank you, gentlemen," he said to Parker and Jenkins. "You've been most helpful. Detective Constable Cradock will make a note of your details. We'll need a statement from you later."

Jago left them with Cradock and began to walk back across the bomb-site to meet the new arrival.

"Good morning, Dr Anderson. Good of you to get here so quickly."

"Morning, Inspector," said the doctor. "I'm told you have a body for me."

"Yes, I'm afraid so," said Jago. "A young woman. Witnesses' testimony suggests it wasn't the air raid that killed her, so I'd like to know what did. She's just up there."

"Very well. I'll take a little look at her and the surroundings, then I'll have the body taken to the mortuary for examination."

"Thank you. I'll just check whether DC Cradock has finished with the witnesses and then we'll join you."

Jago turned back to see Cradock standing alone, writing in his notebook. The two rescue men had already left.

The heavy rescue unit's Austin three-ton lorry was parked on Tinto Road. The other members of the squad had loaded their ladders, wheelbarrows, baulks of timber and tools onto the truck's open back, coiled their ropes and hung them over the ladder rack behind the cab. Half a dozen of them were now sitting on the wooden benches that ran along both sides of the back, while two others stacked the baskets used for moving debris and loaded them into a corner of the truck.

One of the two turned round as he heard Harry Parker and Stan Jenkins approaching.

"You took your time gassing to those coppers," he said. "Thought you were never coming back."

"Sorry, lads," said Harry. "Wasn't much we could do about that. Still, all done and dusted now. Back to the depot?"

"I should think so."

"Off we go, then. Should be there in two ticks."

"About time too," said the other man. He tossed the last basket onto the back of the lorry. "I want my breakfast."

Harry walked round to the front of the truck and climbed into the driver's seat, while Stan got in on the passenger side. Their two team-mates clambered over the tailgate into the back of the truck and found themselves room to sit amidst an assortment of shovels, picks, and crowbars.

Harry started the engine and prepared to move off. As the vehicle began to move he leaned forward slightly and felt beneath his seat with his right hand. His fingers came into contact with a package wrapped in sacking. He smiled to himself. It was still there.

CHAPTER 4

"Here you are, dear," said the woman in the familiar navy-blue serge uniform. Her face was tired, and she brushed away a wisp of greying hair that had escaped from under her bonnet. She looked down with a smile from inside the Salvation Army mobile canteen at the dishevelled pair of police constables standing on the pavement and placed a mug of hot tea on the fold-down counter that hung from the side of the vehicle. "Busy night tonight for you, eh?"

"Not so quiet for you either, I should think," said Stannard. "And you're not getting paid to be out here, are you?"

The woman laughed as she poured a second mug from the urn.

"I don't think I could do your job, even if I was."

"Not your cup of tea, then, as you might say?"

"Most definitely not, officer," she said. "Now, would you like a couple of currant buns too?"

"Thanks, love," said Stannard. He gave an appreciative nod and moved away, holding the two mugs with one hand and the buns with the other. It hadn't taken long to find the mobile canteen. The Salvation Army volunteers tended to head for where the trouble was, and tonight they had parked just a few streets away, in a turning off Barking Road. He'd told Price to take the weight off his feet while he went to fetch them something to drink: the War Reserve constable looked as though the night's work had taken it out of him.

He headed back to where he had left Price sitting on the kerb. A nice cuppa should put him right, he thought. And now that there was the prospect of getting a bit of rest, he began to notice how tired he was himself.

He picked his way carefully through the clutch of exhausted-looking ARP workers and bombed-out residents who had gathered near the mobile canteen.

"Ruddy air raids," he said. Out of habit he moderated his language in the hearing of the public, although the dazed faces of those made newly homeless suggested they would neither notice nor care if he turned the air blue. He found Price and led him farther down the street, to a spot where they would not be overheard. "I reckon we're off duty now, so we're entitled to a bit of peace and quiet."

They perched side by side on a low brick wall, and Stannard passed a mug of tea and a bun to his colleague. Price took them, but his mind seemed elsewhere.

"These air raids," said Stannard. "I can't be doing with them. Get on my wick, they do. And the perishing blackout. I nearly did myself a mischief last week. Did you hear about that butcher in Plaistow who had a light on in the flat over his shop in the middle of an air raid?"

Price nodded slowly, as if making an effort to catch up with the conversation.

"Like a lighthouse, it was," Stannard continued. "And he'd gone out somewhere and locked it up after him. Nothing for it but to break in – nearly caught my wrist on the broken glass, I did. People like that should be made to do compulsory roof-spotting duties. See how they like it with incendiaries landing all round them. They might think twice then about lighting the street up and leading the bombers in."

He was surprised to hear a quiet laugh from Price. The tea must be doing him good, he thought.

"Was he done for it?" said Price, sounding more himself now.

"The butcher? Oh yes, fined thirty pounds at the magistrates' court, he was. More than six weeks' pay for a copper, but not for the likes of him, I should reckon. Probably making a bit on the side, putting a pound or two of best beef under the counter for his favourite customers – the ones who don't mind slipping him a few bob extra to get a treat for supper. Sometimes I wonder why we bother."

"Hanging's too good for them: that's what I say," said Price. Something about Stannard's story seemed to have spiked his interest and brought his mind back from wherever it had been. "I mean, is that what we fought the war for?"

"Exactly," said Stannard. "Mind you, I was too young for the last one." He did a quick mental calculation of how old Price had probably been during the Great War. "Were you in it, then?"

"Yes, I was in the Army. Two and a half years I did – terrible times. Biggest mistake we ever made, that war."

"What do you mean?"

"Fighting Germany, that's what. I mean, look at it: they're like us, aren't they? Hard-working, serious people, civilized. How did we end up on the same side as the French and the Russians? We should never have let ourselves be talked into getting involved in a European war in the first place, and certainly not a war against the Germans."

"Yes, that's what my mum says. My dad was in the war too, but he was killed at Passchendaele. I don't remember him at all – I was only two when he went off, and he never came back. Three hundred thousand casualties on our side in that battle, they reckon. My mum says it was all a stupid waste."

"It was. They said it was a war for civilization, but I think we'd all have been better off if there'd never been a war. And now look where it's got us: sitting here in the gutter while everything people have worked for all their lives is burning around us."

"So do you reckon we've gone and made the same mistake again?"

Price didn't answer immediately. He sipped his tea, as if thinking about the question.

"That's not for me to say. I'm not saying that's what I think, but I know there's plenty who do."

"My mum says we've only got ourselves to blame after the way we treated them at Versailles. She says we tried to ruin them and now we're suffering the consequences."

"Reaping the whirlwind, some might say."

"You can say that again. We've seen a bit of a whirlwind tonight, all right."

"Yes. Whatever people say about this war, I can't help thinking it could all so easily have been very different."

"Certainly couldn't have ended up much worse," said Stannard. "I mean, they've beaten us in Norway, beaten us in France, and now it looks as though they're doing their damnedest to beat us here too."

He downed the last mouthful of tea from his mug and brushed a few crumbs off his tunic in a futile gesture towards tidiness.

"Still, won't do to sit around here feeling sorry for ourselves, will it? Time for you to get home to your wife, and for me to try and bag a hot bath at the section house."

"I'll take the mugs back to the Sally Army," said Price, picking them up from the wall as he got to his feet.

"Thanks," said Stannard, peering up at him. "Feeling a bit better now, are you? You didn't look at all well when we found that poor girl's body."

"Yes, I'm all right, thanks. There's nothing to worry about."

"Good. Glad to hear it. Got to keep your pecker up, haven't you? Mind you, I'd have thought you were used to seeing dead bodies, what with being in the Army in the war and all. Wouldn't have thought it would affect you like that."

"Yes, well never mind. I just felt a bit ill, that's all. Is that all right?"

"Of course," said Stannard. "Just being curious. Sorry I asked."

CHAPTER 5

Jago did not enjoy these times. The post-mortem room at Queen Mary's Hospital always seemed to carry the chill of the grave. The stone floor and the white glazed tiles that lined its walls were cold and unwelcoming, and the stark electric light exposed its emptiness. There was no hope here: it was like walking into a tomb.

He thought of the crypt at St John's Church, where the dead, their spirits having flown who knew where, were abandoned to decay slowly into dust. This place had the same feel. The only difference was that here they were allowed neither burial nor decay until the due process of medicine and the law saw fit to release them.

During his first spell at the front in France there'd been a Catholic in the platoon. A gentle and dutiful man, he used to talk about purgatory – sometimes he'd seemed more concerned about that than about dying. As Jago sat in the trench listening to him explaining the word, it had seemed like a kind of lostness, a hovering mid-way between life and death. Even then he didn't like the idea, didn't like things being unresolved – and it was the same now, he realized. He liked the case to be closed, the matter resolved one way or the other. No loose ends.

This mortuary was supposed to be part of the process of settling the uncertain, but it seemed to him more than anything another place of lostness. The young woman whom he had not met until she was dead was lost to life, lost to her family, to her lover if she had one. Right now she didn't even have a name. Whoever she was, all that remained of her was the mortal flesh she had once animated with tears, laughter, a smile, a sigh, now laid out in this municipal crypt, this repository of the dead that was as cold and lifeless as she was.

He followed Dr Anderson into the room and his nose caught

the familiar mingled odours of death and disinfectant. He stopped short. Facing him were two shelves loaded with ranks of naked bodies, each with a label tied to its big toe. Anderson turned and caught the surprise on his face.

"First time you've been here since the air raids began, isn't it?"

"Yes," said Jago.

"Things have got a bit busier, as you can see. Nearly all of these are casualties of the raids. We don't even have enough shrouds to cover them. Just having to make do, like everyone else."

Jago composed himself and followed the doctor to the post-mortem table. His boss, Divisional Detective Inspector Eric Soper, was already there, standing silent and sober-faced, with Cradock looking uncomfortable alongside him. Probably worried the DDI might ask him a difficult question, Jago thought.

With a brief nod to Cradock and a "Morning, sir" to Soper he took his place beside the table. One small mercy, he thought: at least the mortuary assistant had found a sheet to cover the corpse. By the time Jago was nineteen he'd seen enough mutilated bodies for a lifetime; twenty and more years on he had no desire to examine whatever injuries this poor woman had suffered in more detail than was necessary for his investigation.

He hoped Anderson's findings would be brief. To his relief, the doctor began his report.

"Not a lot to say about this one, gentlemen," he said. "As you know, the body was found on a site in Canning Town that had been bombed overnight –"

"Yes, yes," the DDI interrupted. "But is there any evidence of foul play?"

"If you'll bear with me, Mr Soper," said Anderson with a smile that Jago thought was more generous than his chief deserved, "I'll come to that in a moment."

"Get on with it, then," said Soper. "Some of us have got a lot of work to do today."

"I imagine so," said Anderson.

Jago suppressed a smile. He was surprised that a doctor as young as Anderson, who looked not a day over thirty, should be so composed under fire from Soper. But perhaps there were Sopers in the medical world too, he surmised. The man had probably had his own tartars to contend with. Or maybe you became a bit philosophical about power and rank when you spent your days fishing around in dead bodies. He reined his thoughts in as Anderson resumed his report.

"The first thing I would note," said the pathologist, "is that there's very little sign of injury on the body. The main wound is to the back of her head, and I found particles of brick and small splinters of wood in it. Given the fact that she was found on the ruins of a bombed house, much of which consisted of brick fragments and smashed timbers, this in itself is not conclusive. I understand the police surgeon who first attended the scene suggested her death could have been caused by a bomb blast, and this would indeed be possible. Since the air raids began we've seen a number of casualties found dead without a mark on their bodies – they've died because the blast has effectively suffocated them. Such a blast could have thrown her back onto the rubble, where she could have injured her head on landing."

"So are you saying it was a bomb that killed her, not murder?" said Soper.

"No. I'm saying that would be a reasonable deduction, were it not for my next observation, which is a second wound to the left side of the head. This one has some splinters of wood but no brick, which is curious but not something from which one can draw any reliable conclusion."

"But if you can't conclude anything from it, how can that mean it's murder?"

"I'm sorry. I should have said that my second observation is about other injuries, and that there are two parts to it."

"Good grief."

Jago was finding the scene unexpectedly entertaining, but thought it prudent to try to steer the conversation in a more fruitful direction, if only to save Dr Anderson from possible injury to his own person.

"And would part two be the part that suggests the possibility of murder?" he asked.

"That's for you to decide, Inspector. The second part of my observation concerning other injuries is that I find on the body a particular pattern of bruising which I believe is not inconsistent with strangulation."

"Can you explain?"

"There are fingertip bruises in the muscles on both sides of the voice box, and the upper horn of the hyoid bone is fractured."

Anderson reached a hand out towards the sheet.

"Would you like –"

"No," said Jago quickly, "I don't want to see, thank you very much. You don't need to show me. I'll take your professional word for it."

"This damage would be consistent with her having been strangled, and from the front rather than from behind. That in turn could indicate that the victim was lying on her back at the time, particularly since there is bruising on her upper body consistent with the application of pressure by a knee, together with more bruising on her back that I would expect to see if she'd been lying on a pile of loose bricks and other debris, as she was, when that pressure was applied."

"So the murderer knelt on her while she was lying on her back on the rubble, and strangled her?" said Jago.

"So it would seem."

"And how does the wound to the back of the head tie in with that?"

"The bleeding from the wound would indicate that she suffered that injury before death, so you might choose to infer that the assailant knocked her to the ground before attempting to strangle her, but I cannot be certain of that."

"And is that all?"

"Just one other thing. There are more bruises on the left of her neck than on the right, which would suggest that whoever strangled her was right-handed."

"That narrows it down, then," said Cradock under his breath.

"What was that, Constable?" said Anderson.

"Nothing, doctor. Just thinking out loud."

"Before we go," said Jago, "was there any indication that she'd been interfered with?"

"Interference of a sexual nature, you mean?"

"Yes."

"I found no evidence of sexual violence, but there is evidence of sexual experience."

"Would that be recent activity?"

"Not so recent as to have been part of the assault, but beyond that I can't tell."

"And what's your estimate of the time of death? At this stage that's more important to me than knowing precisely how she died."

"Judging by her body temperature and the fact that she'd been lying outside on a September night for some time, I would estimate that death occurred at some point between nine o'clock and midnight last night."

"Thank you," said Jago. "That's very helpful. Isn't that right, sir?" he added, turning to Soper.

"Yes, very good, doctor, very good," said Soper. "I think that concludes our business here. We'll leave you to clear up while I have a word with the detective inspector. Come along, John, let's get some fresh air."

***

Jago headed straight for the door and stepped outside, but found himself waiting for Soper, who he assumed was giving some parting advice to the pathologist. For once, he was pleased at the prospect of further conversation with the DDI, if only because it got him out of the mortuary. It was not a place he liked to be. It brought back memories – being taken at the age of fourteen to see a dead body for the first time when his father died. The shock of witnessing death where he had always known life had left a deep mark in him. He knew it was his dad, and yet it wasn't – he was there and yet not there. Within another five years Jago had seen men ripped open and torn apart by bullet, shell, and shrapnel, and knew more than he'd ever wanted to know about the raw and bloody detail of human flesh. Ever since those days he'd had no difficulty picturing a heart that no longer beat, lungs that no longer breathed, a stomach that would never again be gripped by fear. But the departure of life from a body he could not understand.

He had a vivid childhood memory of an aunt who'd shocked him by talking about the fires of hell as the destination of the dead. But the mortuary he'd just been standing in, he thought – that was where they really ended up, and nothing could be farther removed from the picture she'd painted. For him now, fire and brimstone meant the savage insanity of battle, that devil's playground where the evil one man can do to another was loosed from all restraint. That was hell. He wondered whether the room he'd just left was a more accurate picture of the lostness of death – a cold and empty eternity of regret.

The click of the mortuary door interrupted his train of thought, and the DDI appeared at his side.

"So, John, you've no idea who this woman is?"

Jago reeled his mind back to the case.

"No, sir. No identity card on her, and nothing else to identify her. If she had a handbag, that's gone missing too."

"Could it be a robbery, then? A robbery that went wrong?"

37

"I really couldn't say. We've got nothing to go on yet."

"And strangled, that doctor says. That sounds a bit more deliberate."

"Quite possibly, sir, yes."

Soper appeared to ponder Jago's words for a short while, then continued.

"I've been meaning to ask you about this Dr Anderson. A bright chap, judging by what some people say. Is that right?"

"Yes, sir – a rising star, by all accounts."

"Hasn't made a proper name for himself yet, though, has he?"

"Only a matter of time, sir, I should think."

"Hmm, I'm still not sure about him. He looks too young. Are you sure he knows his stuff? You know what it'll be like if this gets to court and it turns out he doesn't – counsel for the defence will tear him apart."

"I could imagine him giving them a run for their money."

"That's as may be. But when it comes to pathologists giving evidence in a murder case, juries like to see a big name from one of the London hospitals blinding them with science."

"Judges too, I believe," said Jago. "Put an eminent pathologist in the witness box and some of them treat him like Moses down from the mountain, that's my impression. Pity the poor defendant if a professor's decided he's guilty."

"At least we get a conviction. With this young Anderson we can't be sure. He just doesn't look the part."

"Perhaps justice would be better served if we told him to wear a top hat and spats in court."

Soper looked askance at Jago.

"What? Of course not. That's not what I mean, and you know it. All I'm saying is we need a pathologist who can put together a cast-iron case, or we'll be laughed out of court."

"And a true case, sir. If you want my opinion, I'd rather put Dr Anderson up for the prosecution than some of those big names you were referring to. I've heard he's very highly regarded by his peers, and from the little I've seen of his work I'd be happy to stake my reputation on his evidence. He may be only at Queen Mary's Hospital now, but I think he could run rings round some of those old buffers. Besides, there's a war on, and we should be thankful we've got him just up the road."

"Well, I just hope he knows what he's doing, that's all."

Soper looked at his watch. "Time we were on our way, I think. Let's walk back to the station."

He set off in the direction of West Ham Lane, with Jago falling into step beside him.

"There's something else I wanted to ask you," said Soper. "How are you getting on with that American?"

"The journalist, sir?"

"Yes, the newspaper woman. Are you telling her what she needs to know? And more to the point, telling her what the Ministry of Information needs her to know? That fellow from the ministry who brought her down here said it's essential to the war effort to paint the right picture for the American public."

"She certainly seems interested in telling the truth, sir, if that's what you mean."

"What do you mean, 'If that's what I mean'? Of course we want her to tell the truth – it just needs to be our truth."

"She's a clever lady, sir: I'm not sure she'd fall for it if I tried to pull the wool over her eyes, especially when she's here and can see for herself what's happening."

"Just watch your step, that's all I'm saying. No spreading alarm and despondency, especially to her. What sort of things is she asking about?"

"Well, I haven't seen her or heard anything from her for a few days – I believe she's gone to Liverpool to report on the effects of the bombing there. I dare say the censors will only let her talk about 'a town in the north-west of England' or 'a north-west coastal district', but I suppose to American readers that might not sound as absurd as it does to us. I did get a note from her yesterday, though."

"And?"

"She said she wants to write something about the effects of the blackout on the level of crime – the fact that it's gone up since the war started. She's arranged to come and see me next week to talk about it."

"Fine. No doubt you can reassure her that we're coping with the challenge."

"She also said she's interested in all the talk of a Fifth Column. Wants to know if we've seen anything like that going on since the air raids started. Anything we can talk about, of course. After what happened with Quisling in Norway when the Germans took over I imagine the Americans are wondering how many similar characters might be waiting in the wings here. I'm supposed to be having lunch with her tomorrow, so I might find out more then."

"Fifth Column? Good Lord! You be careful what you say about that. And don't go treading on Special Branch's toes: they won't take kindly to having a detective inspector from West Ham quoted in the American press on a subject like that."

"I don't think I'll get on the wrong side of the Branch, sir."

"Yes, of course, I was forgetting. You've got a foot in the door there, haven't you? When was it you did that secondment?"

"In 1936, sir, during the fighting in Spain. Liaison with the French police, to do with arms smuggling."

"Yes, yes. Don't tell me any more: I don't want to know. It was because you had the lingo, wasn't it?"

"I like to think it wasn't just because I speak French, sir, but yes, that was part of it."

"A policeman who can speak French. Who'd have thought of it, eh? Personally, I've always found the King's English is all I need. I don't hold with foreigners: you can't trust them. Especially the French – nothing but trouble, if you ask me."

"Yes, sir."

The DDI fell silent and said no more until they reached the entrance to West Ham police station, where he halted.

"By the way," he said, "how was it you came to speak French? You did tell me once, but I've forgotten. Family connection, wasn't it?"

"My mother was French, sir, so I suppose I couldn't help it."

"Ah, yes, your mother. Quite. Well, I can't hang about chatting. Just make sure you don't tell that journalist anything you shouldn't. I don't want to find out she's part of the Fifth Column herself."

CHAPTER 6

"Morning, sir... Morning, sir." Sergeant Tompkins greeted Soper and Jago in turn as they entered. The DDI replied with a brisk grunt and strode on towards his office. Jago stopped at the station sergeant's desk.

"Morning, Frank. Thanks for the early call – very kind of you to make sure I didn't oversleep. How's things with you today?"

"Mustn't grumble. A little spot of trouble with the missus in the night, though."

"The joys of marriage," said Jago. "The things I miss. Dare I ask what was the matter?"

"It was the cold, that's all. That shelter of ours was freezing, and she's been complaining about it. The thing was, I splashed out ten and six on a paraffin heater last week to try and keep us warm at night, but when I went down the oil shop to buy some paraffin, they'd sold out, and she was none too pleased."

"Maybe you should borrow a few blankets from the cells."

"Not likely. Have you smelled them?"

The door opened, and Cradock breezed into the station.

"Hello again, sir," he said. "All sorted out down at the mortuary. Morning, sarge – hope I'm not interrupting anything."

"Not at all, Detective Constable. I was just discussing some operational matters with Mr Jago. Isn't that right, sir?"

"Yes," said Jago. "Important matters, but nothing to detain us now. I fancy we've a busy day ahead of us."

"Too true," said Tompkins. "I hear you've got a body to get your teeth into."

"In a manner of speaking, yes," said Jago. "Bad news travels fast, I see."

"Young Stannard told me. Said it looked like there may have been foul play. Is it murder?"

"It looks that way, yes."

"Well, that'll be nice for you, sir. Something to take your mind off things."

"What things are you thinking of?"

"Oh, nothing special. Just things, you know – like the small matter of the Nazi hordes massing on the other side of the Channel and getting ready to invade us at the drop of a hat, that's all."

"Not the sort of thing to worry an old soldier like you, Frank, surely?"

"Quite right. Especially not now we've got those Local Defence Volunteers to protect us."

"The Home Guard, you mean – they changed the name weeks ago."

"Yes, that's the one. I tried to join up, but they said I was too young." Tompkins laughed at his own joke and continued. "I preferred the original name. You know what they say: LDV – 'Look, Duck, and Vanish'. Not a good name for a crack fighting force."

He leaned on the desk and gave another wheezy laugh.

"No, the only thing worrying me is what'll happen to my pension if the German storm troopers somehow get past them and that Hitler sets up shop in Whitehall."

"Now that's something I hadn't thought of," said Jago. "The effect of an invasion on police pensions."

"You can laugh. It'll be your turn one day. And in the meantime, I nearly forgot – there was a message for you. I think it could have a bearing on this case of yours."

"Oh, yes? Who was it from?"

"It was a Miss Hornby, phoning from a company called Everson Engineering in Fords Park Road. She sounded the prim and proper sort – said she was their head of personnel, or something like that. She called about an hour ago to say one of their employees hadn't turned up for work this morning and wasn't at home."

"A bit soon to start phoning us, isn't it?"

"She said this was the sort who's very reliable, never late. She also said this particular employee is a young woman who lives alone in a flat in Canning Town. This Miss Hornby was phoning to check whether she might be on the casualty list from last night's raid. That's when I thought there might be a connection with your body on the bomb-site."

"Name?"

"Mary Watkins. Miss."

"And did you ask for a description?"

"Of course. She's twenty-something, height about five foot four, slim build, and red hair. Cut quite short and not permed, apparently – she gave me all the detail. Said this Mary was the only woman in the office without waves, but was the kind of girl men seem to find attractive all the same. The old bird sounded a bit sniffy about it, too. Probably jealous, I shouldn't wonder."

"The description fits," said Jago. "Come along, Peter. We're going back to Canning Town."

***

Jago drove the Riley south through Plaistow towards Canning Town. He had the roof down and hoped the cool breeze would keep him awake, but in the passenger seat beside him Cradock seemed to be dozing off already – he probably wasn't sleeping as well as he'd claimed, Jago reflected. Didn't want anyone to think he couldn't take it.

That's what we're all supposed to say, he thought: "We can take it." To judge by the newsreels and the papers, and what they said the American reporters were writing, that was the watchword of all Londoners now that the city was taking such a hammering. It struck him that he hadn't seen anything that Dorothy, the only American reporter he knew, had written for her paper about them. Did she too make it all so simplistic? He was growing tired of the cheerful optimism he read everywhere in the press, the jaunty tone of the newsreel announcers. The whole thing was a damn sight more complicated than that.

He found himself wondering what Dorothy might be doing right now, in Liverpool, if that's where she really was. The feeling had crept up on him, but it was a fact: he missed her. She was definitely intruding into his thoughts more than she should, he thought. That was complicated too. He'd spent twenty years making a life for himself, building habits, weaving patterns of existence like a cocoon around him, and now this blasted war was unsettling everything. Nothing was in its right place any more, and he didn't like it.

He saw the turning for Fords Park Road and yanked the steering wheel round. Cradock gave a little jump, as if waking.

"Must be nearly there," said Jago. "Keep an eye out for Everson Engineering."

"Will do," said Cradock, stifling a yawn.

Jago drove past the rambling 1890s factory complex that formed the Paragon Works. That was a big place, impossible to miss. He doubted Everson's premises would be quite so conspicuous. He slowed the car.

"There it is, guv'nor," said Cradock, pointing ahead and to the left.

Jago spotted the company's name in large letters on the front of a more modern two-storey building, behind which he could glimpse the roof of a larger structure. It looked like the usual arrangement – a front block in brick, designed to impress, which would be where the management had its offices, and a much larger and cheaper factory area behind, where the employees made whatever it was the company sold. After the distinctive towers and tall chimney of the Paragon Works it looked very ordinary. There was a parking area in front, so he pulled in and stopped.

Jago and Cradock were soon met in the entrance hall by Miss Hornby. Prim and proper might be a fair description, thought Jago. She was tall, thin, and bespectacled, and wearing a black dress which to the best of his limited knowledge was not the fashion of the day, certainly in its length. She looked in her forties, although perhaps the style of her hair, pulled back into a neat bun, and her formal stance with hands clasped before her made her look older than her years.

"Good morning, Miss Hornby," he said. "I'm Detective Inspector Jago and this is my colleague Detective Constable Cradock. I understand you're the head of personnel here."

"Head of personnel and administration," she corrected him.

Yes, thought Jago, prim and proper. Spot on, Frank.

"And what is the business? Clearly engineering, judging by the name, but what sort of engineering are you involved in?"

"We are indeed an engineering company, and our work is light engineering, both mechanical and electrical. Before the war we did specialist projects for bigger companies, things like electrical motors, parts for machine tools, and so on. Now it's mainly war work: components for aircraft control systems and communications, and other things which I'm sure you'll forgive me for saying I can't talk about."

"Quite. Now, I've received your report about Miss Watkins; thank you for informing us. I'm sorry to have to say this, but the description you gave us does appear to coincide with that of a young woman who was found dead at a location which was bombed during the night, but she was carrying no identification and wasn't known to the local air-raid warden. It's quite possible that she is not your missing employee, so I'm sorry if what I've said is distressing, but we need to find out who she is."

Jago noticed that there was not a tremor of emotion on Miss Hornby's face.

"Can you tell me a little about Miss Watkins?" he continued. "I'd particularly like to know who her next-of-kin is, but anything else you can tell me could be useful."

Miss Hornby took a pale blue folder from under her arm.

"I brought her file down with me in anticipation of such a question," she said. "Shall we sit?"

She led the two men across the lobby to a small seating area partially screened off by a couple of large palms in brass pots. It looked like the kind of spot where visitors would be asked to wait until a representative of the company came down to escort them in. She invited them to take a chair and then sat beside Jago and opened the file. He noticed, however, that the way she held it ensured he could not see the contents.

"Mary Watkins," she read from the file. "Born in Canning Town, 12 August 1912, so she's twenty-eight years old. She left school at fourteen and joined us as a junior clerk. She was very capable, and worked her way up to her present position, which is staff welfare and clerical officer in the welfare and personnel department."

"So she works for you."

"She works for Everson Engineering, Inspector, but I am her manager, so she comes under my direction."

"I see. What more can you tell me? Her address, for example?"

"Let me see now... yes, here it is. She lives at 17 Hudson Road. It's only a short walk from here."

"And next-of-kin?"

"Under next-of-kin we have her sister, Miss Susan Watkins, with an address in Forest Gate: 21 Banham Road. But I'm afraid that may not be up to date. I suppose with these air raids now we ought to put more effort into keeping our next-of-kin records accurate, but things have got so busy there never seems time. Anyway, all I'm saying is she may not be there any more."

"Don't worry: we'll check. I'm anxious to confirm her identity, though, as soon as possible. Would you be willing to come and identify the body for us at Queen Mary's Hospital as soon as we've finished here? We'll run you over there in the car and bring you straight back."

"Yes, of course. But tell me, is she – is the body badly damaged?"

"No, there's nothing to worry about. You'll be all right."

For the first time since arriving, Jago saw a crack appear in her carefully constructed façade. She took a small lace handkerchief from her sleeve and dabbed her eyes.

"I'm sorry, Inspector, but this is all such a terrible shock. The idea that Mary, Miss Watkins that is, could be dead – it's too much to take in."

"Were you close to her?"

Her expression suggested she found the question curious, and she resumed her previous composed manner.

"Miss Watkins was a valued member of staff and had become very dear to all of us. I don't know what we'll do without her."

"What else can you tell me?" said Jago. "How would you describe her?"

"Experienced, efficient, and reliable. She seemed to put her whole life into her work: the sort that would stay on and work late to get the job done. As you may have worked out for yourself, she's been with us for fourteen years, and we've seen her grow from a mere slip of a girl into a responsible and reliable member of staff."

"And outside of work?"

"That I wouldn't know. I only saw her in working hours, and she didn't talk about her life outside those hours. I would say she was a private person – she didn't bring her personal life to work with her."

"Right," said Jago. "Do you know of anyone here who did see her outside working hours?"

Miss Hornby removed her steel-rimmed glasses and held them in her right hand, tapping them against her lower lip. After a few seconds' thought she jabbed them towards him.

"Yes, there's one girl I believe she sees socially from time to time. Angela Willerson – she's one of our workshop supervisors."

"Could we see her? It will probably have to be tomorrow."

"Yes, she'll be here tomorrow morning. We start at eight o'clock and finish at one on Saturdays, so come any time between those hours. I'll tell her you want to talk to her."

"Thank you. But to get back to Miss Watkins – when was the last time you saw her?"

"She was here at work yesterday. I was talking to her just before she went home."

"And did she seem worried about anything, preoccupied?"

"No, she seemed quite happy, actually. What a dreadful loss: I can't imagine we'll never see her again."

"I'm sorry to ask you so many questions. I realize this must be very distressing, but can you tell me, please: what was she wearing?"

"If I recall correctly, it was a grey jacket and skirt and a green silk blouse. I remember telling her I thought the blouse was very fetching on her, although it's not the sort of thing I'd wear myself."

"That's what the body was wearing."

"Oh," said Miss Hornby. Her voice was dull, subdued.

"Please excuse me, Inspector," she said after a pause, "but it's beginning to sound as though the person you've found is Mary, and there's a question I have to ask you. Were any keys found on her?"

"No, but if she had them in her handbag they're missing, because we haven't found one. I assume these are important keys?"

"Yes, and I expect they would be in her handbag. She always used the same one for work, quite a large black leather one. Mary was a keyholder for the premises, so they were very important keys, giving access to most of the building. I should explain that we also do some classified research work which I can't discuss, so we'll have to get the locks changed, but if those keys get into the wrong hands in the meantime, it would create a serious risk for us."

Miss Hornby looked over her shoulder at the sound of heavy footsteps rapidly descending the stairs behind them. She rose from her chair abruptly and smoothed her dress.

"Excuse me, gentlemen: this is Mr Everson, founder and managing director of the company."

A large-framed man in a black suit strode over to them. He looked about forty-five, well-fed, and confident.

"Mr Everson," said Miss Hornby, "this is Detective Inspector Jago and Detective Constable Cradock. They've come about Mary – Mary Watkins. They've asked me to go and identify a body they found in the air raid last night. They think it could be her."

"I see," said Everson. He fell silent, as if taking in what she had said. When he continued, his voice was quieter. "That's serious news indeed. I'm very sorry to hear it. I'm sure Miss Hornby will have given you all the help you require, gentlemen, but if there's anything you need from me I'll be only too pleased to assist."

"No, thank you," said Jago. "Not at this stage. Miss Hornby has been most helpful."

"Nothing less than I would expect," said Everson. "I bid you good day, then."

He took a few steps towards a pair of large doors at the back of the entrance hall, but then turned back to them.

"Actually, Inspector, since you're here, there's something I'd like to have a word with you about."

He placed a hand gently on Jago's elbow and steered him to one side.

"It's a small private matter," he murmured. "For your ears only, if that's all right with you."

Jago nodded and pulled a key ring from his pocket, then gave it to Cradock.

"Take the car, Peter," he said. "Drive Miss Hornby to the mortuary at Queen Mary's and see if she can identify the body, then bring her back here as soon as you can. I want to get this business wrapped up. I'm not in the mood for complications."

CHAPTER 7

Mavis Price was in the kitchen, dusting. The only sound she could hear was the ticking of the Bakelite mantel clock. Slowly ticking her life away. The hands showed ten past eleven, and she wondered whether Gordon was still awake. It wasn't like him to stay up after a night shift. Straight to bed it was, normally, when he got home, but today he'd taken the *Daily Mail* into the parlour and said he was going to read. Since then she'd neither heard nor seen him.

She wiped her fingertip through the dust on top of the mantelpiece and tutted. There was definitely more of it in the air these days – probably to do with the bombs. No matter how often you wiped things down, it was always back the next day. That was the worst thing about cleaning. Of course, some women had people to do it for them, and all the washing and ironing too. Fat chance of that on what Gordon earned, though.

It wasn't what she'd imagined when she was a girl – rich husband, big house, and a maid to run around for her while she read magazines and painted her nails. She could almost laugh at the memory of it. Getting married had soon cured her of fancy notions like that. And what a year to choose for your wedding – 1929! Hardly back from their cold and windy weekend's honeymoon in Great Yarmouth when all that financial jiggery-pokery in America put Gordon out of work overnight. She was just a kid of nineteen then and couldn't have explained what the Wall Street Crash was all about to save her life, but she was smarter now, and well aware of who was to blame. Financiers and speculators, they were called, but she knew a shorter word for them.

She turned her attention to the wireless. It was a Mullard, a good, solid-looking set that stood two feet tall on a small table next to the fireplace, confident and elegant in two-tone wood veneer. They'd bought it five years ago after months of scraping the money together, and now she was glad they had. The evenings were lonely when Gordon was out on duty, and it was her only companion. Tonight she was going to stay up late to listen to Ambrose and his orchestra on the Home Service at eleven o'clock. She must have a word with Gordon, though – there was something wrong with the tuner, and she'd be wanting to change stations before that. There weren't many things he was good at, but fiddling with machines seemed to be one of them.

She wiped the little window on the front that showed the stations it could be tuned to, and thought of faraway places. She wasn't happy. She wanted to know what was up with Gordon, and she wanted news from the kids. That was another thing she couldn't have imagined when she was nineteen – how it felt to be without your children, even if it was for the best.

Can't start thinking about that too, she told herself. The scullery floor won't scrub itself. She reined in her roaming thoughts, put the duster back in the cupboard and closed the door.

She was about to go through to the scullery to fill a bucket with hot water from the copper when Gordon appeared in the doorway.

"Hello," he said.

Mavis turned to see her husband of eleven years. He looked tired. He was thirteen years older than her – when she first met him that had just made him seem more mature, but now it made him look old. He was clearly preoccupied too. She was the first to admit he was never exactly the life and soul of the party, but now his voice sounded as though he were carrying all the woes of the world on his shoulders. He always seemed to be weighed down by some great burden, but sometimes she felt she was the one who had to carry it.

"Hello, love," she replied, putting on a cheerful voice. "Finished the paper, then?"

"I couldn't concentrate. I should be sleeping, but I don't feel like it."

Mavis moved closer, scanning his face to gauge his mood.

"Something up?"

"Just a bad night, that's all."

"Shall I make you a cup of tea?"

"Yes, that'd be nice."

"Sit yourself down, then, and I'll put the kettle on."

He sat in the old armchair that filled one corner of the kitchen. Mavis came and perched on the arm while she waited for the kettle to boil.

"The air raid, was it? What happened?"

Gordon cleared his throat and paused for a moment before speaking.

"There was this body. A woman."

"Oh, I'm sorry. Was she badly... you know?"

"No, it wasn't that. There was hardly a mark on her. It was just, I don't know, just that she was dead. I came over all queasy and didn't know what to do."

"It's only natural."

"Not if you're a policeman. You're supposed to cope with all that, even if you're only a War Reserve for the duration. Now I feel like a fraud and I'm worried what Ray Stannard thinks. He's younger than me, but he's a real copper."

"You reckon he thinks you're a fraud?"

"I don't know. I told him I'd been in the Army in the Great War and he said he was surprised, thought I'd be used to bodies. I didn't know what to say."

"That's all right. He'll probably think no more about it."

"I hope so, but I'm still worried."

The kettle boiled, and Mavis went to make a pot of tea. She returned and put it on a mat on the kitchen table.

"I keep thinking about the children too," he continued. "I couldn't get them out of my mind in the night, when I was out hearing those bombs going off. I'm still not sure we've done the right thing."

"Of course we did," said Mavis. "It's getting far too dangerous here, and we had to get them out of it. They'll be having a whale of a time. Best for them to be somewhere safe until the war's over. It can't be long."

"Who's to say it can't? And who's to say they'll be any safer where they're going?"

"Look, we both know what's happening. This war's all Churchill's fault, but he can't keep it going much longer. Germany's so strong, and we're so weak. We're the only ones left fighting them now. The papers make Hitler out to be a fool, but he's the one sitting in Paris, isn't he, and we're the ones who got driven into the sea at Dunkirk."

"We're not beaten yet, though."

Mavis poured two cups of tea and took one to her husband, placing it firmly on the shelf beside him and looking him straight in the eye.

"There's only one way it can go now, Gordon. Hitler's bombing us to pieces and he's going to invade at any moment. It's as clear as day." She returned to the table and sat down. "If only people had listened to Mosley. He was right: we should've had a referendum with a straight question, do you want war or do you want peace, and let the people decide. But the government wouldn't risk that, would they? They never had a mandate for war and they knew we'd all vote for peace. And now they're going to have to sue for peace anyway – if we keep resisting it'll only make things worse for us. It might only be another week or two before it's all over."

"I know, but that's why I keep thinking we should have kept the kids here where we could look after them until it finishes," said Price.

"No. I don't like it any more than you that we've had to send them away, but we've got to face it: this is no place for children at a time like this. They can come back when it's all over. People aren't going to put up with that dictator Churchill for much longer. We could have come to some arrangement with Hitler long ago if it hadn't been for him. Now we're not going to get rid of him until Hitler does it for us. But at least then we'll have peace, and a chance of a better life. Look at you: in and out of work for ten years, and all because of an economic system that doesn't work, that can never work. But no one's unemployed in Germany. Look what Hitler's achieved – six million people with no job when he came to power, and now everybody's got one. Once we get an armistice and a decent government, there'll always be a job for you, and we can give the children the future we want for them."

Price seemed uncomforted by her air of confidence.

"I keep thinking we should have just sent them out into the country, somewhere away from the bombing, away from London," he said.

"But who's to say where the bombing will be next?" said Mavis. "At the moment it's round here because of the docks, but this time next week it could be anywhere in the country. We did the right thing. The Luftwaffe is never going to bomb Canada: it's too far away. The kids'll have a wonderful time there, with all the food and fresh air they need, and they'll grow up without fear. Then when it's all over they can come back here and take their place in a new Britain. It's hard for us to let them go, but their safety has to come before anything else. You don't want them to be in danger, do you?"

"Of course not, but I don't feel happy about them being on that ship. I'd rather have them here where I can look after them and know what they're doing, that's all."

"Well, it's too late anyway, whatever we think – they must be nearly there by now."

"Yes. I suppose it's all for the best. I just wish I could stop worrying."

"Trust me," said Mavis. "We've done the right thing. I'm sure we've done the right thing."

CHAPTER 8

"We'd better go to my office," said Everson. "The government keeps telling us careless talk costs lives. I'd prefer to speak to you in private."

He led Jago up a flight of stairs from the entrance hall to the first floor and into an unadorned corridor with offices on both sides. The third door on the right was open, and they entered to be greeted by a woman whom Everson introduced as his secretary before showing Jago into the adjoining room, his office. He closed the connecting door behind them and sat behind a large mahogany desk, motioning Jago to take the seat opposite.

"Now, then," he began. "Mr, er…"

"Jago. Detective Inspector Jago."

"Quite, quite. I know Winifred – that's Miss Hornby – told me your name but I'm afraid I have rather a lot on my mind these days. I won't detain you for long: I'm a busy man and I'm sure you are too."

"Not too busy for a word, sir. Is it about Miss Watkins?"

"In one sense it is, yes. Miss Hornby told me she was going to contact you – the police, that is – when Miss Watkins failed to arrive for work this morning. It was so unlike her, you see: in many ways she was a model employee. And you think this body you've found may be hers?"

"I'm afraid so, Mr Everson."

"Where was she found?"

"In the wreckage of some houses that had been bombed in Tinto Road."

"Not far from home, then."

"You know where she lives?"

"Well, I know she lives in that area. It's quite close to here too. And may I ask when she was found?"

"Certainly. It was early this morning. We think she was killed overnight."

"In the air raid?"

"Possibly."

Everson nodded slowly, as if not sure what to say next.

"It was a bad one, wasn't it?" he continued. "I was at a meeting of the Horticultural Society yesterday evening and we had to abandon it when the bombing started."

"Keen gardener, are you, sir?"

"Not really – my wife was the gardener. She loved her plants."

"I'm sorry. Is she –"

"No, it's not what you're thinking. I don't mean she's no longer with us. My wife is an invalid – she contracted tetanus some years ago and almost died. She's been confined to a nursing home ever since. I originally became involved in the society through her, and I continue to help as its secretary. Of course nowadays plants hardly feature in our discussions – the Dig for Victory campaign has rather pushed our traditional activities to one side, and our members concentrate almost entirely on cultivating vegetables. Do you have a garden?"

"I have a small patch at the back of the house, but it's hardly worthy of being called a garden. I've neither the time nor the knowledge for flowers."

"Then you should think about growing a few carrots, perhaps."

Jago found himself hoping Cradock would soon be back with the car.

"I don't suppose you asked me in here to talk about carrots, did you, sir?"

"Ah, yes. I mean no, indeed. It's, er, it's just that there's something I was intending to contact the police about, but it's rather a delicate matter. You see, we've noticed some materials going missing from

57

the factory, and I'm concerned. It could be pilfering plain and simple, but because of the work we do here it could be something more sinister."

"I understand from what Miss Hornby said that some of your work here is classified, but of course she didn't give me any details."

"Ah, yes. Winifred is the soul of discretion. I'd trust her with my life."

"Can you give me any idea of what it is, without breaking confidentiality? If it's any reassurance, I have signed the Official Secrets Act."

"No, I can't tell you anything. All I can say is that we're engaged in certain aspects of research and manufacturing for the War Office."

"Can you tell me what's going missing? It would help me to know what I'm looking for."

"Yes. It's mainly electrical components: valves, batteries, switches, all quite small things. And chemicals too."

"Is that valves as in wireless, or as in plumbing?"

"As in wireless. What the Americans call tubes. The bits that get hot."

"And what kind of chemicals?"

"Sulphuric acid and hydrogen peroxide."

Jago listed the missing items in his notebook.

"Do you suspect anyone in particular?"

"No, but whoever took these things knew what they were looking for and where to find it. The valves, for example, weren't on open display – they were behind some big wooden crates, so he'd have had to move those out of the way first."

"You say 'he': you've ruled out your female employees?"

"No. I say 'he' just because the crates were heavy, not easy to move. It could have been a woman, but it would be difficult, I should think. It could be more than one person of either sex, of course: there's no way of knowing. It may be just that we have someone light-fingered on the staff who wants to make a bit of cash on the side, but it could be something much more worrying, and we can't take that risk."

"How well do you know your staff?"

"That's just the problem. I mean, identifying something is missing is one thing; establishing who took it is quite another. The thing is, since the war started we've been working flat out and we've had to take on a lot of extra employees. I trust our old staff – many of them, like Miss Hornby, have been with me for fifteen years or so and are utterly loyal and trustworthy – but I can't be so sure about all the ones who've joined us recently. And of course if someone had some kind of malicious intent, this is the time when they would try to join a company like this."

"When you say 'malicious intent', you mean someone who might be a bit too interested in this classified work you're doing?"

"Well, yes."

"So are these missing items connected with that work?"

"I can't answer that question."

"I see. What sort of scale are we talking about?"

"Not huge amounts. But what's worrying me is that if someone on the staff is prepared to steal from us, they might also reveal information about our work. We don't know how many spies Hitler may have in this country, but we certainly know there are people here who are sympathetic to him."

"So you'd like me to see what I can find out?"

"Exactly. This must be handled very carefully, so I hope you won't mind if I say it might be best if it were not entrusted to an inexperienced police constable."

"I understand. I shall have to share what you've told me with Detective Constable Cradock, though, as he is my assistant."

"Yes, of course. I would appreciate it if you could make some discreet enquiries yourselves. I don't want anyone here to know they're being investigated."

Jago closed his notebook and rose from his chair.

"Very well, Mr Everson, I'll look into it. I'll let you know how I get on. And now I think I'd better see if DC Cradock has brought Miss Hornby back, so we can be on our way."

CHAPTER 9

Canning Town didn't feel like home to Flo Parker, even though she'd lived there since 1921. Before seeing it she'd imagined a proper town, like the ones she knew in Scotland, a higgledy-piggledy patch of buildings hugging the shore around a small port, or a cluster of houses in all shapes and sizes nestling together among the heather and the hills. But Canning Town was very different. At first sight it seemed to her another world – a sprawling mass of tightly packed streets that all looked the same, full of people who hadn't two ha'pennies to rub together, their grimy, ragged children playing on cobbled roads. She'd moved there for work and stayed for love, but as a home it wasn't much of an improvement.

It lay in the lower part of the Borough of West Ham, bounded to the south by the docks and merging to the north into the identical streets of Plaistow, without any of the open space she thought you always got separating one town from the next. She'd asked people why it was called Canning Town, but no one seemed to know. When she first heard of it Flo had imagined a place full of factories canning fish, because it was near a river – or canning beans, for that matter. Since moving there she'd discovered it certainly had plenty of factories, but whether any of them were for canning she still had no idea.

In 1921 there'd been plenty of older people who remembered the open sewers, so at least there'd been some progress. The little house she and Harry rented in Hemsworth Street only had the one tap and an outside toilet, but it had proper drains. People didn't get ill as often as they had in the old days, and she and Harry both still had their health, touch wood. She looked around for the nearest wooden item, moved to the kitchen table and touched it with her right hand, her train of thought continuing uninterrupted. She heard the front door slam. That must be Harry home for his lunch, she thought. It was the first she'd seen of him today – she'd been out at work from seven in the morning, as usual, before he got in from his night shift, and then by the time she got home he'd gone out somewhere.

Ever since she moved south the only work she'd been able to get was as a charwoman, cleaning offices and anywhere else that would pay her. She always seemed to feel tired these days. Harry, however, never seemed short of energy. You wouldn't think he'd been up all night to look at him, she thought.

"Hello," he said as he came into the kitchen. "And how's my darling little Flo today?"

She didn't like being called Flo, not even by Harry. People down here had always called her that, but she'd never asked them to. They seemed to think her name was Florence, and Florences were always called Flo. She'd given up trying to explain she was Flora. The days when she'd been Flora MacLeod were long gone. She sometimes wondered who she'd be today if she hadn't moved away. Not that she missed her old life. Charring in West Ham might be hard work, but it was better than gutting herrings in Stornoway any day. There was many a day when she missed the Isle of Lewis, though. She gave Harry a weary smile.

"Morning, dear," she said. "I hope you behaved yourself last night. I don't like to think what you get up to when you're out in the middle of the blackout."

"Never you mind what I get up to in the night," said Harry. "Serving my king and country, that's what I'm doing."

He made an amorous lunge towards Flo, who stepped neatly to one side to avoid it and then winced as her body reminded her of her age.

"Get away from me, you silly old fool," she said. "My knees are killing me. If you spent half your day scrubbing floors you wouldn't be so full of the joys of spring."

Harry stood behind her and slipped his arms round her waist.

"If you must know, I've been up to nothing," he said. "Not much, anyway. Digging round in rubble trying to find out if anyone's got a house fallen down on top of their head, mainly."

"Not digging round for anything else, I hope. I know what you're like with your little bits of treasure."

"Now don't start on about that, Flo," he said. "Harmless bit of tidying up, that's all it is. If I do happen to pick something up it's only stuff that people don't need any more."

"Because they're dead, or bombed senseless, you mean."

"It's only things that'd get carted away with the rubbish. They might as well do someone a bit of good as be taken off to the dump. What use will they be there?"

"You've always got an answer, but I'm worried."

"What's up, then?"

"I saw a magpie."

"So what? I saw a couple of pigeons myself."

"But it was on its own. You know what that means – bad luck's coming."

"Stuff and nonsense."

"I'm serious – you need to watch your step, Harry Parker."

"Look, love, you don't need to tell me that," said Harry. "You know me – squeaky clean, that's what I am. I do an honest day's work for an honest day's pay – or an honest night's anyway. I'm rescuing people from bombed buildings, I'm demolishing dangerous ruins, getting plenty of good exercise, and getting paid three quid a week into the bargain."

One or two other perks came to mind, but he didn't mention them. There were risks, of course, in being out during air raids while everyone else was tucked up safe in their shelters, but there were more important things in life than keeping safe. All things considered, Harry reflected, he was enjoying the war.

***

Mavis Price poured her husband a second cup of tea. He sipped it and gave a sigh that he hoped would sound appreciative. He tried to sound more cheery than he felt.

"What are you planning to do when I'm out tonight, then?" he asked.

"You asked me to mend the turn-ups on your old trousers," said Mavis, "so I was going to do that, but the treadle on the sewing machine doesn't seem right. Can you do something with it before you go out?"

"Yes, that should be easy – probably that new belt I put on has stretched. I'll shorten it when I've had a bit of sleep. What else are you going to do?"

"Listen to the BBC, I think," she said. "I want to hear the news at nine o'clock, and they've got some nice music on later, with Ambrose, and Evelyn Dall singing."

"Is that the American woman?"

"Yes, that's the one. Good of her to stay here, I thought, instead of running back to America when the war started, like some people I could mention. They've got that new kid singing too, Anne Shelton. Lovely voice – and she's only sixteen. I think there's something wrong with that wireless, though – when I was trying to change to the other station last night it wouldn't tune properly. It sounded all crackly and kept breaking up. Can you have a look at that too?"

"Yes, of course," said Gordon. "It might be just the tuning condenser contacts that need cleaning. Only takes a couple of minutes to clean them up with a drop of spirit, but it's the devil of a job getting to them. I'll try and do it later on if I'm not asleep."

"Thanks, love. Sounds like double Dutch to me, but if you can fix it that'd be really nice."

"And the other station you were trying to tune in to – would that be what I'm thinking?"

"Maybe," said Mavis. "It was Hamburg, if you must know. The

64

BBC's hopeless – it only says what the government allows. You know I like to switch over after the news of an evening and hear what the other fellow has to say."

"Switch over to Lord Haw-Haw, you mean?"

"Yes, and why shouldn't I?"

"You need to be careful, Mavis."

"Why? I think he talks a lot of sense. I reckon people listen to him to find out whether our government's telling the truth. And he's British, so he understands how we think. He says the war's pointless, and I agree with him."

"But he fled the country as soon as he could see we were going to declare war, didn't he? He's working for the enemy now, and that makes him a traitor. You must be careful, Mavis. If people find out you're listening to him there could be all sorts of trouble, especially in our situation."

"I don't care."

"Well, you should care. What are we going to do if I lose this job? It's a miracle I got it in the first place – why they didn't ask me any questions about my past I don't know. If they start nosing around and finding out what we used to be involved in, I'll be out the door before you can say Jack Robinson. Look at all those people who got arrested in May. Do you want the same to happen to us?"

"I'll tell you what's going to happen to us: nothing, that's what. No one knows about your past – you were just rank and file. And anyway, the police were so desperate to get extra men when the war started I reckon they'd have taken on Jack the Ripper as long as he didn't mind doing nights. You're sitting pretty there, Gordon, and there's nothing for us to worry about."

"Sitting pretty? Sitting on a time bomb, more like. Look here, Mavis, if I lose this job we're in Queer Street, and no mistake."

"We'll be in Queer Street before long anyway, with you on three pounds a week. I think I ought to get a job. We need the money, and with the kids away I've got the time."

"No, I don't want you going out to work. I don't hold with it. I'll fix everything, don't you worry. But you've got to watch what you say, or you'll drop me right in it. If I end up on the wrong side of the bars you'll be next, and where would that leave the kids? As long as I'm a WR I'm respectable, and if I keep my head down no one's going to come round asking awkward questions. I'm worried enough as it is. I said some things to Ray Stannard this morning that I shouldn't have. I was tired, you see, but I should've been more careful."

"I still think you're getting all agitated about nothing," said Mavis. She rose from the table, picked up the empty tea cups and started towards the sink.

"I just don't want any trouble, that's all," said Gordon. "And now that woman's gone and messed it all up."

Mavis stopped and turned round.

"Woman? What woman?"

"The one I told you about – the one we found dead on the bomb-site this morning. I can't get her out of my mind."

"What do you mean?"

"Ray Stannard says he reckons she might have been murdered."

"So what's that got to do with you?"

"Nothing, in one sense. But the thing is, I think I know something about her. I ought to tell the detective who's investigating the case, but then he might start digging around, and I don't want that."

"Don't tell him, then."

"But you don't understand. Suppose I don't tell him and it comes out anyway. Then I'd be in bigger trouble for not reporting it – I'd be obstructing the investigation. I tell you, I don't know what to do. I wish I'd never seen her."

CHAPTER 10

Jago steered the Riley away from the Everson Engineering building, heading north. By the time they were halfway through Plaistow he had briefed Cradock on what the owner had told him.

"All clear, then?" he said.

"All clear, guv'nor," said Cradock. "Discretion."

"That's right. And you know what discretion means?"

"Of course, sir. It's what I'm the soul of."

"Quite," said Jago. "How did you get on at the mortuary with Miss Hornby?"

"Nothing unusual to report. She identified the body as Mary Watkins, and that was that."

"Good. And what did you make of Miss Hornby herself?"

"She's no oil painting," said Cradock.

"I was thinking more of her character."

"Right, yes. Bit of a dark horse, I reckon. Did you see the way she was looking at Everson? Those big eyes? I thought she was going to swoon. It was like that look Ruby Keeler used to give Dick Powell in the films. I was thinking, any minute now she'll be going into soft focus and the music'll start."

"Come, now, I think you're exaggerating a little."

"Well, yes, maybe, but I definitely saw something there that wasn't just a personnel manager reporting to her boss."

"I thought she seemed a very professional woman."

"Yes. Still waters run deep, though, eh, sir? She's very neatly turned out, too, isn't she? Some of these working women can be quite dowdy, but she hasn't let herself go."

"You make her sound as though she's some old dear about to kick the bucket. The poor woman can only be the same age as me, if that. You'll be telling me next I'm looking a bit frail and ought to sit down."

"Oh, no, sir, you're still very spritely."

"Spritely? You can't tell a man who's barely turned forty that he's spritely. Sixty is spritely, not forty."

"Yes, sir. My mistake. I'm sure Miss Hornby's still in her prime. Definitely a case of sheep's eyes, though, if you ask me."

Jago turned a corner and swerved to avoid a bomb crater that had swallowed up half the width of the road. He could see workmen hunched over what must have been a broken water main, judging by the flood that was spilling across the street. He braked sharply to avoid showering them with spray, causing Cradock to grab the dashboard and brace himself.

"So where are we going now, sir?" he said, steadying himself as the car swayed on and hit dry road again.

"We're going to see whether Miss Watkins' next-of-kin is at home."

He continued driving north through Plaistow and beyond, until they came to Forest Gate. The address they'd been given by Miss Hornby turned out to be an imposing semi-detached house from late in the last century, standing back from a broad and tree-lined road. He parked the car outside it and stopped the engine.

"A bit more money up here than there is round Canning Town, I should think," said Cradock. "Big bay windows and a few extra feet of front garden. Makes all the difference, I'm sure."

"You're just jealous," said Jago. "Let's go and knock on the door."

Cradock followed him up the tiled path and was still adjusting his tie in the reflection of the front door's stained-glass windows when it opened.

The woman before them was younger than Jago had expected – in her early twenties, he would have guessed, younger even than Cradock. She looked like the kind of woman who took care over her appearance – with his first glance he took in a carefully made-up face, neat brunette hair, an expensive-looking lime-green two-piece dress, sheer silk stockings, and a spotless pair of dark green shoes.

She stood in the doorway, with one hand still holding the door. She said nothing, evidently waiting for them to identify themselves.

"Good afternoon," said Jago. "I'm sorry to disturb you."

He pulled his identity card from his pocket and held it before her.

"I'm Detective Inspector Jago, West Ham CID, and this is Detective Constable Cradock. Are you Miss Susan Watkins?"

"No, I'm not. That is to say, not any more. I'm Mrs Susan Fletcher. I used to be Watkins, but Fletcher is my married name."

"I'm sorry: the information we've been given must be a little out of date. It's you we've come to see, though. May we come in?"

"Of course," she replied, opening the door wider and standing back so they could enter. "What's happened?"

"Perhaps we could all take a seat," said Jago.

She showed them into the living room, gestured to a choice of comfortable-looking seating, then sat in an armchair by the fireplace. Jago and Cradock took the sofa.

"I'm afraid we have some bad news for you, Mrs Fletcher," said Jago.

Her mouth tightened.

"It's not George, is it?"

"George?"

"My husband. Has something happened to him?"

"No. But I'm sorry to have to inform you that the body of a woman was found early this morning in Canning Town, on the site of a house that had been bombed during the night. The body has been identified as that of your sister, Miss Mary Watkins."

"Are you sure?"

"Yes, a representative of your sister's employer accompanied my colleague to the mortuary earlier today and confirmed it was her."

"Oh." Susan said nothing more, but sat in silence, not moving, as though trying to digest this information. Eventually she spoke.

"But why are you here? Why two detectives? Shouldn't it just be a police constable in uniform?"

"It's because we have reason to believe your sister was not the victim of an air raid, Mrs Fletcher," said Jago. "I'm afraid we're investigating a suspected murder."

He watched her face for a reaction – surprise, shock, or even mystification, all responses he'd seen when notifying someone of the death of a sibling. But not a muscle moved. Whatever feelings she might have, it didn't look as though she were going to give way to them. She simply stared ahead, seemingly at nothing.

"Could you tell us a little about your sister?"

She ran a hand through her hair and seemed to be forcing herself to concentrate on his question.

"She's – she was older than me, five years older. We grew up here together and then she got a job and left home. You know where she worked. What else is there to say?"

"I understand she was unmarried."

"Yes."

"Do you know if she had any close male friends? Was she walking out with anyone?"

"I've no idea. And if she were, I doubt whether she'd have told me."

"Is there any other family?"

"No, it was just the two of us. Our parents died three years ago, and we had no other brothers or sisters."

"When did you last see her?"

"I don't know – not for a while, anyway. Mary's always busy with her work and we don't run into each other very often. I don't think I've seen her since before the wedding."

70

"Which wedding was that?" said Jago.

"Mine," she replied. "It was at the end of July, so that's nearly a couple of months ago now."

"So how was she at the wedding?"

"She wasn't. I'm sorry, I didn't put that very clearly. I didn't see her at the wedding. She wasn't able to come."

"I see. Now, there's a small matter you may be able to help us with. Do you have a recent photograph of your sister that you could give us?"

She thought for a moment and slowly shook her head.

"No, I'm afraid I haven't. We weren't the sort of people who'd take pictures of each other."

Jago nodded.

"Very well," he continued. "I'm sorry to have to ask you this, Mrs Fletcher, but can you think of any reason why someone might have wanted to kill Mary?"

Susan gave a faint shudder.

"What a horrible thought. The answer is no. As I said, we didn't see a lot of each other, and I have no idea what kind of people she mixed with. I wish I could be more helpful, but she was a very private person. She always kept herself to herself."

"Can you tell me where you were yesterday evening?"

She drew herself up straight in the chair and looked affronted.

"Are you asking me for an alibi?"

"It's purely routine, Mrs Fletcher."

"I see. In that case, if you must know, I was here, with my husband."

"And later, during the night?"

"Here, of course. We were in bed all night, together."

"In your Anderson shelter? If you have one, that is."

"No, we've got a cellar here, so we shelter down there during the raids: it's a bit cosier than those horrible little Anderson shelters. My husband shored it up, and it's got electric light. Does he need to confirm that I was here?"

"No need for that, thank you. Will he be able to get home if you need someone to look after you?"

"Yes, that won't be a problem. He's a typewriter mechanic, so he's out and about in his van all day, but if I need him I can ask the company where he is and get hold of him. But there's no need for you to worry: I'm perfectly fine."

"Could you give me the address and telephone number of your husband's office for me, Mrs Fletcher? We may want to speak to him."

She crossed the room to a bureau that stood in the far corner, wrote on a piece of notepaper and handed it to him. Jago folded it and put it into his pocket.

"One last question," he said. "We've already had your sister's body identified by her employers, as I said, because we didn't even know if we had the right address for you. But would you like to see her body? We can drive you to the mortuary. People sometimes just like to say goodbye to their loved one. Would you like to go?"

"Thank you, but no," said Susan. "I don't think I shall."

***

Jago and Cradock got into the car, and Jago turned the ignition key.

"What do you make of that, then?" he said.

"Mary was a private person who didn't go to her sister's wedding," said Cradock.

"Yes. Now in my experience it's usually the neighbours who say the deceased was a very private person, and all it means is they could never be bothered to talk to him or take enough interest to know anything about him. But the sister? You'd expect her to know a bit more, wouldn't you? But then again, if you walked down this street and knocked on fifty doors you'd probably find there was some kind of family feud going on in every other house."

"She didn't seem very upset at the news."

"You can't always tell. It takes people differently. Did you see that look on her face when we told her it was suspected murder?"

"Yes, she just stared, didn't she?"

"Correct. I've seen that sort of stare before, more times than I'd like to remember. Soldiers, in the war. Shell shock. Men who've seen more than they can cope with. They never said anything about it – they just stared at nothing."

"It can't be the same with her, though; not a young woman like that. Maybe she's just a goldfish."

Jago turned to face Cradock with what he hoped was a patient expression.

"Cold fish, Peter."

"Sir?"

"A cold fish is a person who doesn't betray their emotions. A goldfish is what the rag and bone man gives you for your mum's old clothes."

"Sorry, sir."

"Don't worry. Whatever kind of fish she is, her reaction may mean nothing. Perhaps Mrs Fletcher's a private person too."

"And she cares more about her husband than her sister."

"That's common enough. You can't choose your family."

"Looks like she's chosen a husband who can keep her in a smart house and new clothes, at any rate."

"Ah," said Jago, "but that depends on who chose whom."

He pressed the gear change pedal, and the car's engine rose to an eager growl as they set off for the police station.

CHAPTER 11

There wasn't much greenery in Canning Town, but Beatrice Cartwright's walk home from Everson Engineering took her past the recreation ground, which to her was an oasis of peace. On sunny days she liked to stop there and sit for a while to enjoy the smell of the grass and the sight of the horse chestnut trees, so refreshing after a day cooped up in an office full of cigarette smoke. Today the light was just beginning to fade, but it was still a pleasant enough evening for her to linger, as long as she was home before the blackout. She was pleased to find she had the park to herself – it was deserted.

She sat down on a wooden bench facing south across the recreation ground, leaned into the backrest and closed her eyes, letting the declining sun warm her skin. Her mind drifted to bank holiday trips to the beach just ten years ago. Beatrice was still a child then, and she remembered her heart and imagination straining for some magic to make this the longest day of the year – anything that would enable her to squeeze out just ten minutes more to perfect her sandcastle, one more game of ball with her mother. Now she did not want to think about those beaches. They would be scarred with barbed wire, mines and tank traps to fend off the approaching invasion. Any day now the sand could be soaked in the blood of unimaginable battle.

She opened her eyes to dispel that unpleasant image and felt a slight downward movement in the slats of the bench beneath her. It made her jump. She turned to see what had caused it. A man had sat down beside her, silently. He was wearing a dark coat and had a cap pulled down over his eyes. She didn't recognize him.

Before she could say anything, he addressed her.

"Beatrice Cartwright?"

"Yes. I mean, who – what do you want?"

"I want you to stay right where you are and keep quiet."

"What are you talking about?"

"I told you to keep quiet. I'll do the talking, and you'll speak when I tell you to."

She looked around for help, but there was no one in sight. The man kept his eyes fixed on her.

"And if you're thinking of trying to run for it, I should think again if I were you. Not in a lonely place like this."

Beatrice felt as though she were physically shrinking into herself.

"What… What do you want?"

"I want to have a little chat with you, that's all – as long as you behave yourself."

"A chat about what?"

"About your work, my dear – at Everson's."

"Who are you? And how do you know where I work?"

The man spoke quietly. His voice was low and even, with none of the tension she could hear in her own.

"It's my business to know," he said. "In fact I know quite a lot about you. I know, for example, that you're twenty-two years old and that you passed your Matriculation Examination and left West Ham High School for Girls in the summer of 1934. I can tell you every job you've done since then. And more importantly, perhaps, I know where you live."

"What's this about? You've no right to pester me like this. My husband is a police officer – I shall report you."

She moved her handbag to cover her ringless left hand, but realized she was too late.

"I dare say it would be very nice if you had a husband who was a policeman," said the stranger. "But unfortunately, Miss Cartwright, we both know perfectly well that you're not married. It's pure fantasy – perhaps like your fantasy of England living under a German flag."

"What? That's outrageous! Who's told you that? Whoever it is, they're a liar."

She made a move to get up from the bench, but the man placed his hand firmly on her arm and held it down.

"There's no point running away, Miss Cartwright. I just need to ask you a few questions, that's all."

"Stop it. You're hurting me."

He eased his grip, and as he did so she took her chance. She twisted away from him and jabbed backwards with her elbow into his chest. She heard him give a grunt of pain as she sprang away from the bench. But before she could get to her feet he had already lunged forward. She felt his arms close round her from behind and stop her escape. She pushed against them with her hands but could not dislodge his grip. Her shoes skidded on the path as he dragged her sideways and slammed her back onto the bench. In one movement he whirled round and pinned her against the back of the seat, his forearm across the top of her chest.

"Keep still, Miss Cartwright, and keep quiet, otherwise I shall have to force you to."

She wrestled her right hand free and aimed a punch at his ear. He darted his head to one side and the blow seemed to have no effect.

"I told you to keep still," he said.

He stood and leaned over her. She felt his hand close around her throat, and he began to squeeze. She could not push him back, so she tried again to hit him. Her arms were restricted, but she could reach the sides of his trunk. She pummelled him as best she could, but it had no effect. She felt the panic beginning to paralyse her mind.

Then she remembered what her father had told her when she turned fifteen. She was not far off leaving school and would soon be starting a new and unknown experience. Entering the world of work – the world of men. She'd been surprised by the advice he gave her, but now she knew why. She couldn't move her head, but from the corner of her eye she could see that the man had planted his feet about twelve inches apart to keep his balance. She wriggled as best she could until she thought she was in the right place. Then with every ounce of strength she could muster she thrust her knee upwards in a vicious jerk and caught him between the legs.

What happened next astonished her. Her dad was right – the man screamed in a way that she did not know men could. He let go of her throat and clutched his groin. Now, she thought: run! But she couldn't move – the injured man had slumped across her knees. She pushed at his weight, but it seemed that despite his pain he was determined not to budge. She could not dislodge him. His initial howl had now given way to something more like whimpering, and when he wasn't groaning he was cursing. She made one last effort and pushed him off with both arms, sending him sprawling on the path.

She leaped from the bench and ran, heading away from him and towards the nearest gate. Glancing over her shoulder she could see he was already on his feet and setting off after her. She thought she had disabled him, but he seemed to be still capable of running, and he was tall – one of his strides might be worth two of hers.

The thought of screaming went through her mind, but no one was likely to be coming into the park now. People didn't hang around waiting for the dark these days. They hurried home to fix their blackout curtains. No – better save your breath for running, she thought.

She tried to put on more speed, but could not. It was her shoes. Her favourite Lilley & Skinner black courts with a two-inch heel – slip-ons that she could discreetly ease off behind the modesty panel on her desk and give her feet a break at work. But slip-ons meant loose on the instep and round the heel, and now that seemed like a fatal flaw. Ideal for the office, but not for the park.

She pressed on as fast as she could manage. She was desperate to take her useless shoes off, but that might give him time to catch up. But if she didn't, they'd just keep slowing her down. She decided the risk was worth it. She stopped and quickly pulled off first one shoe and then the other, keeping one in each hand – their heels were the only weapon she had. She glanced back. He was getting closer. She sped off again, barefoot now save for the rayon stockings that offered no protection to her feet. She felt the rough path cutting into her soles and winced at the pain. She swerved onto the grass, hoping to make more speed on a softer surface.

She was breathing hard now, and could feel a stitch developing in her side. She tried to force it out of her mind, but as she thrust her left foot to the ground a piercing agony shot through it – she'd trodden on something sharp. She cried out at the shock of the pain but ran on, the foot of her stocking growing wet with her blood. She willed herself forward, but it was no good – she knew she was slowing, and in an instant the man was upon her.

He grabbed at her arm and she fell to the ground, her shoes tumbling away on the grass. He pinned her hands roughly behind her. She was caught.

His breath was coming in rasping gulps. It was some moments before he could speak. To her surprise, he eased his grip on her arms.

"I'm sorry I had to restrain you forcibly, Miss Cartwright," he said. "I can assure you I had no intention of harming you, but I couldn't afford to have you running away and causing a commotion."

Beatrice shook herself free of him and turned to face him.

"You were choking me," she said.

"Only to stop you attacking me. As you may recall, it was you who hit me first. I was speaking to you on official business, and I still have some questions to ask you. Once you've answered them, you'll be free to go. It's as simple as that. Now, shall we find somewhere quiet to sit to finish our conversation, or do you want to cause another scene?"

Keeping his eyes on her, he crouched down and picked up her lost shoes. He held them out to her.

"Here," he said. "You can put these back on – just don't try any more tricks."

She slipped both shoes on.

"What do you want, then?" she said.

"First I want you and me to go and sit on the bench under that tree," he said, pointing to his right.

She nodded and went with him to the bench.

"Sit down," he said.

She sat. He joined her, sitting at an angle on the seat so that he was facing her.

"Let's start again," he said. "As I was saying, it's my business to know a lot about you and what you've been doing."

"And I suppose it's my business to know nothing about you," said Beatrice. "You haven't told me who you are. What's your name?" She tried to sound officious, but knew before the words left her lips that it was futile.

"My name is Smith," he said.

"I don't believe that for a moment. Show me your identity card."

"Showing you my identity card is neither here nor there," he said. "For someone in my position it's not always appropriate to disclose personal details, and while the government requires every British subject to carry an identity card, that requirement is of course subordinate to the broader national interest."

"So you're not necessarily called Smith."

"I couldn't comment."

"What do you want, then?"

The man glanced to his right and to his left down the length of the path, but Beatrice already knew there was no one to help her. He lowered his voice.

"Does the name Radio Security Service mean anything to you?"

"No. Why should it?"

"Because you're in trouble, and that's who you're in trouble with."

"I don't know what you're talking about."

Beatrice was finding it impossible to inject any trace of confidence into her voice. Smith was taking no notice of her protestations.

"Come, now," he said. "There's no need to be so modest. You've been under observation for some time. My colleagues and I are investigating certain attempted breaches of national security, serious offences under the Defence Regulations 1939. You speak German, don't you?"

"Yes, but –"

He leaned closer, and his tone became harsh again.

"So was it your political allegiance that got you into it, or just money? It must be tempting to think you can make a bit of cash out of what you know – and of course working at Everson's, you'll know some things you're not supposed to talk about."

She felt like a prisoner under interrogation.

"Nonsense – I'm just a secretary."

"I'm not talking about secretaries; I'm talking about spies – people who'll betray their country for a pocketful of cash."

"I'm not a spy – I'm British."

"You don't have to be parachuted in with a suitcase and a German accent to be a spy. We're well aware there are plenty of British subjects willing to serve a foreign master. With some, of course, it's just a case of misguided naivety. Perhaps that's how it started with you. But when we find people are sending wireless communications to the enemy it's a much more serious matter."

"I've never done that. I wouldn't have the faintest idea how to do it."

"If you'll pardon my frankness, that's exactly what I'd expect you to say. You see, my job is to intercept those signals to Berlin – yes, we are very capable of doing that – and to track down the people who are sending them. You're in serious trouble."

"Look, there must be some mistake."

The emotional stress of everything that had happened since she'd met this man who called himself Smith was taking its toll on Beatrice. She pulled a handkerchief from her pocket and dabbed at her eyes.

"I haven't done anything wrong. I need that job – I can barely make ends meet as it is. All this has got nothing to do with me. You have to believe me."

Smith moved back a little from her on the bench, and his voice softened.

"Trust me, Miss Cartwright, if there were anything I could do to spare you this unpleasantness I would."

She lowered the handkerchief and looked at him uncertainly. He paused, as if giving further consideration to what he had just said, then continued.

"You know, I almost believe you. But I have my job to do, and my own position could be at risk if I dropped my investigation and cleared you in my report. Having said that, of course, I did have a case only recently where a gentleman who came to my attention was able to reassure me of his innocence."

"How was that?"

"It was quite simple: he gave a pledge."

"What do you mean?"

"I mean, as an assurance of his good faith he entrusted a small sum of money to me. I took it as his personal guarantee that he was innocent of all the charges that would have befallen him if I had reported the evidence I had. Perhaps we could come to a similar arrangement."

Beatrice's eyes widened.

"You mean you want me to give you money to keep your mouth shut? That's outrageous!"

"A rather vulgar way of putting it, in my opinion, Miss Cartwright. I would call it a form of surety. Think of it as bail: a sum of money that can keep you out of prison. If you can imagine, heaven forbid, finding yourself out of a job and in significant trouble with the police, you might conclude that providing such a surety is a very attractive alternative to the cells."

"But that's extortion!"

"These are difficult times, and we all have to make difficult decisions."

Beatrice felt defeated.

"How much?" she said, her voice flat.

"I think twenty pounds would be an appropriate sum."

"Twenty pounds? Who do you think I am? I don't have that kind of money going spare."

"Well, I'm a reasonable man: I'll give you four days. I'm sure you'll find a way. You will meet me at nine o'clock on Tuesday evening and you will give me twenty pounds."

Beatrice fought to stop her voice trembling. When she was able to speak, her response was hushed.

"Where?"

"That's more like it. I shall contact you on Tuesday to tell you where to go. I don't want you to have to roam too far in the blackout, so I'll make sure it's somewhere near that nice little flat of yours."

She shuddered, but said nothing.

"There we are, then," he continued. "You just think for a moment about what it will cost you if I submit my report, and you'll soon see that twenty pounds is quite a bargain for your liberty."

Smith got to his feet and pulled the peak of his cap a little farther down.

"Good night, Miss Cartwright, and pleasant dreams. I shall see you on Tuesday evening. And now you'd better get along home before blackout time. I wouldn't want you to come to any harm in the dark."

CHAPTER 12

It was a few minutes before nine o'clock on Saturday morning when Jago parked the Riley outside Everson Engineering. There were wisps of cloud in the sky, but the air was still and the temperature agreeably warm. It looked like a promising day.

"Out you get," he told Cradock. "We've a lot to get through this morning, and I've got a lunch engagement to keep, so look sharp."

"Lunch, sir?" said Cradock. "That wouldn't be with the American lady, would it?"

"Yes, it would, as it happens," said Jago. "Not that it's any business of yours."

"Of course, sir."

"Although in actual fact on this occasion it is your business."

"Sir?"

"Miss Appleton has been away in the north for a few days but should be back today, and it seems she wants to quiz me about all this talk of a Fifth Column and whether we've seen any evidence of it locally. I'd like you to join us."

"As a chaperone?"

"Don't be impertinent. If I needed a chaperone I reckon I'd go in there and ask Miss Hornby, not you. This is purely out of the kindness of my heart – I thought you might like a change from the canteen."

"Thanks very much, guv'nor. Where will we be eating?"

"Miss Appleton has never experienced Rita's café. I think it's time she did."

"You're sure you won't need me as a bodyguard, sir? I'm not sure what might happen if Rita sees you with Miss Appleton."

"Don't talk nonsense. Rita and I are very old friends."

"Exactly."

"Your imagination's running away with you, lad. Now, let's go and meet this Angela Willerson."

"Very good, guv'nor."

They crossed the small parking area and Cradock followed Jago into the building, where after a short wait they were met by Miss Hornby. She showed them to an empty office and returned minutes later with a young woman.

"This is our employee Miss Angela Willerson," said Miss Hornby. "I'll leave you to talk, Detective Inspector, but please don't take too long – we have a lot of work on our hands this morning."

"We'll be as quick as we can," said Jago.

Miss Hornby nodded and left, closing the door behind her.

The room had a desk, two steel filing cabinets and a bentwood coat-stand, but didn't look as if it were in regular use. Three wooden chairs had been arranged facing each other a few feet apart in a kind of triangle in front of the desk – by Miss Hornby, Jago assumed, or on her instructions, in anticipation of their visit. She was probably used to taking care of details, he thought.

He motioned the young woman to one of the chairs, and when she had sat down he and Cradock took the other two. She looked about twenty-five, he thought, and was dressed in loose-fitting overalls, her fair hair tucked under a light cotton headscarf. He was struck by the contrast between the worn and grimy clothes and her neatly made-up face. No doubt she was following the constant advice in the newspapers and magazines for women to do their bit by keeping up their appearance despite the bombs and shortages, he thought – although he suspected that for some of these girls the reasons might be more personal than patriotic.

"Miss Willerson," he began.

"Miss Hornby's the only one who calls me that," she replied. "Everyone else calls me Angela."

"Very well, Angela. I understand you're a workshop supervisor here."

"That's right. I've been here for a couple of years. I was an assembly worker to start with, then got promoted when the workshop supervisor was called up. He's in the Navy now, poor soul, probably freezing cold out in the middle of some ocean while I swan around here in the warm. I dare say I'll be demoted again when the war ends, though: same thing happened to my mum after the last war."

"It might be different this time, though, don't you think?"

"Yes, and pigs might fly."

"Well, let's hope. Now, we've come to talk to you about Mary Watkins. I assume you've heard the sad news?"

"Yes, I heard yesterday. Miss Hornby told me Mary had been killed in an air raid, and she'd been to identify the body. It's so sad. How can I help you?"

"We're trying to find out more about Mary, and we were told you've spent some time with her outside of work."

"Yes, but not much. I can't say I know much about her."

"How long have you known her?"

"Since I started working here, really, although I'd met her once or twice before that. That's how I came to get the job. We were in the same keep-fit club for a while, before the war started. I didn't know her well then, just socially – you know, the odd chat now and then. Anyway, one day after we'd finished our keep-fit I must have said I was looking for a change of job, and she told me they needed people here, so I came along and they took me on."

"And how did you get on with her here?"

"Fine. I didn't see a great deal of her in the normal run of things from day to day, but she was always nice, and I suppose we just became friends. We'd go out together in the evening sometimes, go for a drink. Mary liked a drink – a pink gin was her favourite – and sometimes we'd go to the pictures or dancing. Not often, though."

"What kind of person would you say Mary was?"

Angela inclined her head to one side and pursed her lips.

"Friendly, I'd say – she took an interest in people. She even told me she did a bit of voluntary prison visiting in her spare time. She never gave much away about herself, but she was always good at listening. When you talked to her, she seemed to care, to want to understand you. I suppose that's why she worked in staff welfare. She was probably good at that – although I never had any need for dealings with her in that way myself."

"Do you know of anyone else she was friendly with?"

"Can't say I do, actually, now you come to mention it."

"Did you regard her as a close friend yourself?"

Angela hesitated. She looked a little distressed, and turned away for a moment to wipe her eyes before continuing.

"It's difficult to say," she said. "People don't always mean the same thing when they say 'friend'. I don't think I've had many real friends in my life, and I couldn't say Mary and I were particularly close – she wasn't the kind of person to share her secrets with you. But I reckon as far as it went she was a good friend to me, especially when I was new here and lonely, and I'll miss her. Please forgive me: this is all a bit of a shock."

"Yes," said Jago. "I'm sorry to have to ask you these questions, but it helps us to get a clearer picture of Mary."

"Don't mind me. I understand," said Angela. "What else would you like to know?"

"Anything you can tell me about her."

"Well, from what I could see – which wasn't much, you understand – I think she took her work very seriously, worked hard. She was always very proper at work – it was always Miss Willerson this, Miss Willerson that in the office, never Angela."

She paused and then smiled as if recalling something.

"Mind you," she continued, "when she'd had a drink or two in the evening she'd sometimes let her hair down a bit, and then she could be really funny, a bit indiscreet even. But I think she trusted me not to speak out of turn. She was clever, I reckon, and confident. The modern professional woman, if you know what I mean. It was just the odd thing or two she said when she was a bit the worse for wear that made me think she might have had a rather more colourful past than she usually let on."

"What sort of things made you think that?"

"Well, there was one time I can remember quite clearly. To be honest it was a bit of a shocker, really. I mean, if you saw her here at work you'd say she was every inch the confirmed spinster, dedicated to her job, no time for men – you know. But one night when we'd both had a bit to drink I asked her whether she'd ever been interested in men. I thought she'd say no, she had no time for them, but what she actually said was 'Never again'."

"What do you think she meant by that?"

"That's exactly what I was thinking, so I asked her what she meant and she gave me a sly sort of look and said, 'Once bitten, twice shy.' I pressed her a bit, but she didn't want to talk about it. In the end, though, it turned out that at some time in the past she'd had what the papers call a liaison with a man."

"Did she say when?"

"Not exactly, but it can't have been that long ago. Last year, from the way she talked about it – she said it ended when the war started."

"Do you know who the man was?"

"No, she never let on what his name was, or anything."

"Did she ever talk about her family?"

"I can't say she did, no."

"Not even after a pink gin?"

"Not particularly. I know she had a sister, but Mary never said what her name was. She only mentioned her a couple of times, and I think she just said 'my sister'."

"We've met Mary's sister: her name's Susan. She told us there were no other siblings, and that their parents died three years ago. Is that consistent with what you know from Mary?"

"Yes, that's right. She mentioned the mum and dad dying, because that's how they got the house."

"Which house?"

"The one her sister lives in, as far as I know. I've never seen it, but Mary said they'd both inherited it. But she said she didn't want to live there – she wanted to have her own place. I suppose it'll all be the sister's now. Susan, you say?"

"Yes, Susan. And do you know her husband?"

"What, Susan's?"

Jago nodded.

"No," said Angela. "I didn't even know she was married. Like I say, Mary didn't say much about her family. To tell you the truth, I don't think she got on with her sister. No love lost between them, if you ask me."

There was a knock at the door, and it swung open into the office. A timid-looking girl in a dark dress who looked no more than fifteen or sixteen came in, carefully balancing a tray on which were three cups and saucers and a sugar bowl.

"Miss Hornby thought you might like a cup of tea," she said shyly. She put the tray down on the desk and left the room immediately, closing the door behind her.

Cradock jumped to his feet and passed a cup of tea and the sugar bowl to Angela and Jago in turn, then got his own.

"Miss Hornby thinks of everything," said Jago.

Angela made no reply, but stirred her tea silently, her eyes looking down.

"Now, can you tell me whether anything was troubling Mary before her death?" he continued.

"She seemed the same as normal at work," said Angela, looking up. "But there was one thing that struck me as a bit funny – unusual, I mean. It was a week or so ago, and I thought Mary was acting peculiar. We went to a dance together at the RAF station in Hornchurch on a Saturday night – the Saturday before last, it was.

Mary was getting into the swing of it – she liked dancing, and we were both enjoying having some men to dance with for a change. But then something happened, and she seemed to change. It was like something had upset her – she got all moody and strange, not her usual self."

"What was it that happened?"

"It was after we got talking to a woman there."

"Who was this woman?"

"Can't remember her name. Hang on, it'll come back to me." She screwed up her eyes in concentration. "Yes, I remember now, or at least I think I do. I think it might have been Celia. Yes, that's it: Celia."

"And what was she? A WAAF?"

"No, she was nothing to do with the air force, as far as I know, and not in uniform. She was just ordinary, a civilian, same as me and Mary. Older than us, I should say, but not too old to be out for a good time with the boys in blue – she was certainly dolled up for the dance. She seemed to be on her own, like us, but I noticed she had a wedding ring on. Anyway, we were sitting at the same table as her and we got talking. She was friendly, but a bit cagey too: I asked her if she was married, whether her husband was away with the forces, as you do these days, but she didn't answer. I didn't want to tread on any toes, so I shut up. Fortunately then a nice young airman came and asked me for a dance, so I went. Ground crew, he was: tall, with lovely blond hair."

"Yes, quite, but what happened to upset Mary?"

Angela shrugged her shoulders.

"I haven't a clue. I didn't see anything happen, as such. When I left them at the table to go and have my dance they seemed to be fine. Just making small talk, as you do. I looked over once or twice from the dance floor and at one point I could see the other woman, Celia, getting what looked like a photo out of her handbag and showing it to Mary, so I thought they were getting on all right, showing snaps and what have you. But then when I got back from my dance it was like the atmosphere had changed. Mary seemed quite different – she looked cold, distant, as if her mind was elsewhere. She said she wanted to go home, she wasn't feeling well. I wanted to have another dance, so I persuaded her to stay for a bit, but in the end Mary insisted on going. I was miffed, to be honest – I'd taken a bit of a shine to that young airman, see, and I've always said you shouldn't let a good 'un slip through your hands. I wasn't in a hurry to leave."

"Did you see what was in the photo?" said Jago.

"No, I was too far away. I could just see it was a photo, that's all."

"And did anything else happen?"

"Well, that's just it, you see. When we got outside the hall, Mary was sort of brooding. I got the impression she was angry about something but didn't want to talk about it. When I asked what was the matter, all she said was, 'He'll pay for this. He's a traitor.' It was as if she was talking to herself. When I asked her who was a traitor, she wouldn't say any more about it. I could tell she was really upset, so I didn't press her any more, and we went home. She never mentioned it again. And now she's dead, and I suppose I'll never know."

Angela looked away and seemed lost in her thoughts for a moment, then snapped her attention back to the policemen.

"I'm sorry, Inspector. That's probably not much help to you, but it's all I know."

"Not at all," said Jago. "You've been most helpful."

Jago held out his empty cup and saucer towards Cradock, who got up from his chair and took it. He placed it on the tray that the girl had left on the desk, then collected Angela's and did the same. Jago kept his eyes on Angela.

"Just one other thing," he said. "Talking of photos, we haven't been able to get hold of a recent photograph of Mary. Do you have one by any chance?"

"Well, yes, I do, as it happens. A rather nice young man took a picture of us at a dance a few weeks ago – a different dance, that is – and he sent me a copy. I think I've got it here in my bag."

She rummaged in her handbag and pulled out a small photo which she handed to Jago.

"There," she said. "Do take it. See – it shows both of us together. We had a good time that night. But could I have it back when you've finished with it, please?"

"Yes, of course."

Jago put the photograph in the inside pocket of his jacket and stood up.

"We must go now," he said, "and let you get back to your work. But thank you – you've been most helpful."

Angela jumped up from her chair and looked at him nervously.

"Wait," she said. "Before you go, Inspector, can I ask you something?"

"Yes, of course."

"It's just that I'm puzzled. You say Mary's been killed in an air raid, but then you ask me all these questions about her private life. Why is that necessary?"

Jago gave her a reassuring smile.

"Actually, I think that's what Miss Hornby told you, not me."

"But that's what happened, isn't it? She was killed in an air raid?"

"No, Miss Willerson. I'm afraid we believe she was murdered."

Angela clapped her left hand over her mouth, her eyes staring wide. Two or three seconds elapsed before she slowly let her hand fall to her side.

"Murdered? No – it can't be true."

CHAPTER 13

Jago checked his watch as they stepped out of the Everson Engineering building into the pale morning sunlight.

"Ten past ten," he said. "Plenty of time to fit in one more visit before lunch." He took a folded piece of paper from his pocket and handed it to Cradock. "I think it's time we got to know Mr George Fletcher."

Cradock scrutinized the details on the paper.

"That's on the way back to Rita's too," he said. "Sounds perfect."

They got into the Riley and headed north in the direction of Forest Gate. Ten minutes later they were driving eastwards along Romford Road. As they passed the Gothic Revival flint and red brick of the Congregational church, Jago slowed the car so that Cradock could count down the numbers to Fletcher's office address.

"There it is," said Cradock. He pointed to a three-storey house on their left.

Jago parked the car at the kerbside. He and Cradock got out, crossed the pavement and mounted a flight of ten stone steps to the front door. So this was Fletcher's place of work, thought Jago. The black paint on the front door was scratched, and at the bottom it was chipped back to the wood. A dull brass plaque screwed to the wall to the right of the door was engraved with the words "Empire Office Services". He ran a sceptical eye over the building.

"Doesn't quite fit, does it?" he said.

"What do you mean, guv'nor?" said Cradock.

"The name and the place. 'Empire Office Services' – sounds like they sail off in pith helmets with vital supplies of carbon paper and typewriter ribbons to every last dot on the map that's coloured pink, but when you get here it's just a converted Victorian semi, and they don't even keep their brass polished."

Cradock looked the old house up and down. It had clearly seen better days.

"Yes, sir. Not what you'd call loved. Could do with a lick of paint on those window frames too. Maybe they spent all their money on the inside instead."

"We'll see," said Jago. He pressed the bell button beside the door, and soon it was opened by a young man in a cheap-looking suit who admitted them. Cradock was wrong: the inside of the building was as shabby as the outside. They were standing in a hallway where little daylight penetrated. The green dado running along the walls had a battered look, as if the victim of careless assaults during office furniture moves. The space above it was distempered white, while below it the wall was papered with heavily embossed Lincrusta that looked as though it had been painted over once every ten years since about 1880. A miserable place, he thought.

"Is Mr Fletcher here this morning?" he said. "We'd like to have a word with him. We're police officers."

He saw the surprise on the man's face.

"Don't worry, we haven't come here to nick him. We just need to have a word with him about something we're investigating."

"Yes, he's here," the young man said. "Come this way."

They followed him up a creaking staircase to the next floor and along a narrow corridor until they reached an open door that gave into a small office. Inside it a man was sitting at a wooden desk with his back to a window flanked on both sides by steel shelves loaded from floor to ceiling with cardboard box files.

"Visitors for you, George," said the man, and left them.

The man at the desk stood up and extended his right hand towards Jago.

"George Fletcher," he said. "How can I help you?"

"Detective Inspector Jago and Detective Constable Cradock,"

said Jago, shaking the hand offered to him. "We'd like to ask you a few questions, if you don't mind."

"Ah," said Fletcher, "this must be to do with Susan's sister. She told me last night that you'd called. Terrible business."

He was not as Jago had imagined him. Tall and slim, with a touch of elegance, he looked as though he might still be on the right side of forty, although only just. There was a relaxed and confident air about him. With a brief smile he reached into his inside jacket pocket and brought out a silver-coloured cigarette case, which he opened and held out towards the two policemen.

"Cigarette?" he said. "Turkish or Virginian?"

"No, thank you," said Jago.

Fletcher took one for himself and turned away while he lit it with a matching cigarette lighter. He drew deeply on the cigarette and blew smoke towards the ceiling. Jago caught the tang of it in his nostrils and was thankful that judging by the smell it was a common or garden Player's or Piccadilly. He didn't like the cloying, sweet-scented smoke of Turkish cigarettes, and his father had always said they weren't the kind of thing any self-respecting Englishman would smoke.

Fletcher slipped the lighter into his trouser pocket and waved his right hand casually towards a couple of simple wooden chairs.

"Do take a seat, please. I've got the room to myself today, and I'm just catching up on some paperwork. We won't be disturbed here." He returned to his seat behind the desk.

Fletcher seemed out of place in these surroundings, thought Jago as he sat down. Carefully tended black hair, oiled in a rakish and slightly foreign-looking way, and a well-cut suit, not the kind of off-the-peg job he'd expect to find a man wearing to work in a place like this. Handsome, too, he supposed – in the way that women seemed to find attractive but that tended to leave him feeling wary. The man's manner was certainly a lot more charming than the building he worked in.

Jago glanced at the coat-stand in the corner of the room and noticed a homburg hanging at the top – black felt, silk-brimmed, it was clearly a good-quality Anthony Eden, and no doubt expensive. Just what he would expect now that he'd met the man. Mr Fletcher was a regular Anthony Eden himself, although presumably achieving the effect without the benefit of the breeding – and salary – of the Secretary of State for War.

"I understand you work with typewriters, Mr Fletcher."

"Yes, I'm a typewriter mechanic. It may sound simple to the layman, but in fact there's more to it than meets the eye. A typewriter is a complex piece of machinery and it takes a pounding every day in a busy office. It needs to be properly maintained and adjusted, and then of course there's the huge variety of models that one has to be familiar with."

"I'm sure. How did you become a typewriter mechanic?"

"I suppose I just fell into it really. I was in the merchant navy in my younger days, during the war – a seafaring man."

"But not sailing the seven seas as a typewriter mechanic, I imagine."

"No, of course not. I was a wireless operator. It was all quite new then, and an important job. We had to learn Morse code, and how to take and send messages. It was revolutionary – all they had before that was flags and semaphore."

"You should join the police. Wireless cars are all the rage now. Not enough to go round, of course, now there's a war on, but it would certainly make our job a lot easier if we didn't have to find a police box or public telephone every time we wanted to contact the station, let alone if they wanted to contact us."

"I'm very rusty now – I've forgotten most of what I knew. But sitting in a car would be a damn sight more comfortable than when I last did it, tossing around in the South-West Approaches waiting to be sunk by a U-boat. I wasn't in at the beginning of the war, of course – I was too young. By the time I was sixteen, though, it was

1917 and they were crying out for wireless operators. The Navy had pinched all the merchant ships' operators, you see, when the war started. I was trained by Marconi at their place in the Strand, then went straight out to sea on one of Sir John Ellerman's freighters. Those were the days, I can tell you. Some people say that if it wasn't for us the Fleet would never have been able to bottle up the German Navy in port like they did."

"Yes, well I can see you had an exciting time of it, but I'd like to get back to the present."

"It wasn't all excitement, as I'm sure you'll know, Inspector, if you served your country in those days."

Fletcher reached across the desk to bring the ashtray closer to him. He caught Jago's eyes, which were focused on his left hand, and stopped.

"This?" he said, raising his hand before him. "Nothing to worry about. Can't say I miss them. Three fingers are as good as five for most things."

"A war wound?" said Jago.

"Yes, we had a run-in with the Imperial German Navy. One of their destroyers put a few shots our way and one hit the superstructure. Didn't sink us, and luckily some of our ships turned up and the Germans withdrew – but not before a shell splinter had taken these two fingers off. Lucky it was my left, not my right, otherwise it would have been the end of my signalling career, and I wouldn't be able to do the work I do now. But I'm a lucky man, Mr Jago. Why, only this week –"

"I'm sorry to interrupt you, Mr Fletcher, but as I said, I'd like to get back to the present. Tell me, how long have you been a typewriter mechanic?"

"Well, after the war I could see there was no future in the merchant navy…"

"I think we'll have to have the short version, if that's all right, Mr Fletcher."

"What? Oh, I see. Well, I went into manufacturing."

"With your own company?"

"No, working in a factory, making gramophones, telephone receivers and suchlike. Then I worked for a typewriter manufacturer."

"Doing what?"

"Making typewriters, in a factory. After four or five years of that there wasn't much I didn't know about them, so I went to work for an office services company as a typewriter mechanic. Been doing it now about nine years on and off."

"On and off?"

"Well, I've worked for a few different companies, with a bit of a gap now and then, as you do. I've been with my present employer for about a year. Nice people, and the job suits me – I cover a patch round here and East Ham, travelling from customer to customer during the day. The company give me a little van to get about in, so I'm my own master in a way. As long as I get through my list of appointments for the day, no one minds how much time I take for lunch."

"And I understand you and Mrs Fletcher are fairly recently married?"

"Yes, as a matter of fact we are. We got married on the last Saturday in July – the twenty-seventh."

"How did you meet?"

"Well, it was an interesting story. It was a blind date, you see, at a dance – at the Ilford Palais, in the High Road. Someone I knew through my work knew her and introduced us, and we just seemed to hit it off. We –"

"I'm sorry, Mr Fletcher, but time is pressing and I don't want to get in trouble with your employers for keeping you from your work. As you know, we're here in connection with the death of your sister-in-law. We've spoken to your wife already, of course, but I wondered what you might be able to tell us about her."

"About my wife, or about her sister?"

Jago wasn't sure whether there was a hint of sarcasm in this remark. Fletcher's air of charming bonhomie seemed to have faded, and he wondered why.

"About her sister, please."

Fletcher shrugged his shoulders.

"Next to nothing, really. I've never met her."

"I understand she wasn't at your wedding."

"That's right."

"Why was that?"

"I don't know. I just have the impression that for some reason Mary didn't like my wife. Susan made all the wedding arrangements, and it was only quite late on that I discovered she hadn't invited her sister."

"And why do you think that was?"

"I've no idea. I tried to ask once, but I got that look that women do: the one that means 'No further questions will be permitted'."

"You said your impression was that Mary didn't like your wife. Did you ever consider the possibility that it might have been the other way round, that your wife didn't like Mary?"

"No, that's not like Susan. I don't know what might have gone on between them, but I do know Susan's a gracious and gentle creature, and I can only assume Mary must have hurt her in some way in the past."

"Badly enough for Susan not to want to see her at her own wedding?"

"I don't know: I'm just guessing."

"Badly enough for her to want to hurt Mary back?"

Fletcher rose from his chair, an angry frown crossing his face.

"Now hang on," he said. "What are you suggesting? You're not saying Susan had anything to do with Mary's death? That's ridiculous. I've told you: Susan wouldn't harm a fly. In fact it's not just ridiculous, it's outrageous."

"I'm only asking questions, Mr Fletcher," said Jago. "That's my job."

Fletcher sank back onto his chair.

"Yes, yes, I understand. You're trying to dig up some dark secret, but I tell you you're digging in the wrong place. Haven't you asked enough questions yet?"

"I'm almost finished, Mr Fletcher. Just a few more. Now, I understand your wife and her sister jointly inherited the family home when their parents died. Is that correct?"

"I believe so. But you'd better talk to Susan if you want chapter and verse."

"I visited the house, and I must say it's a very fine property."

"Spacious enough for the two of us, yes."

"So presumably Mary's death means that now it will all belong to your wife."

"Yes, I assume so."

"That should ensure a secure future for both of you."

Fletcher gave Jago a quizzical look, as if surprised by the implication of his words.

"Wait a minute. What are you getting at? The house will be Susan's, not mine. Married women are allowed their own property these days, Inspector, or had you forgotten that? I don't like what you're insinuating."

"Just an observation, Mr Fletcher, not an accusation. Can you think of anyone who might have wanted to harm your sister-in-law?"

"Well, no, of course not. I've already told you: I've never even met the woman."

"And just one final question: can you tell me where you were between nine o'clock on Thursday evening and half past five on Friday morning?"

"At home, of course – and in bed for most of that time. In the cellar, to be precise: we go down there when the air raids are on."

"With your wife?"

"Yes, of course with my wife."

Jago rose from his chair, followed by Cradock.

"Well, that will be all for now, Mr Fletcher. You've been most helpful. If you do think of anything, please get in touch with me."

"Yes, I will," said Fletcher. "They may not have been close, but she was still my wife's sister. I'll do anything I can to help."

CHAPTER 14

"Hello, Mr Jago. How lovely to see you. And this is your Detective Constable Cradock, isn't it? Such a nice young man. You know, if I were twenty years younger… But hark at me – I'm getting carried away."

Rita's voice was warm and welcoming as they entered the café.

"And, er…" She leaned back slightly and looked askance at their companion, eyeing her up and down as if the woman in the smart grey woollen suit were applying for a waitressing vacancy. "I don't believe I've had the pleasure."

"This is Miss Appleton, Rita – Miss Dorothy Appleton. She's a journalist, reporting in London for her newspaper. She's from America."

"Charmed, I'm sure," said Rita, continuing her examination. Jago followed her gaze and noticed it seemed to be particularly focused on the fitted waist of Dorothy's jacket – a cinched look that he could not imagine Rita attempting.

Rita gave Dorothy a thin smile.

"It's not often we see a real American in here," she said. "In fact, come to think of it, you might be the first. Friend of Mr Jago, are you? I don't recall him mentioning you before."

Jago caught the subtle change in Rita's voice but wasn't sure whether Dorothy would. It was time to interrupt.

"Miss Appleton is a professional acquaintance, Rita," he said. "I've been instructed to assist her with her work, help her to find out what's happening round here, with all the bombing and so on."

"Well, dear," said Rita, smiling at Dorothy, "if you want to know what's going on in these parts you've come to the right place. I get all sorts in here, hear all manner of talk. See right through people, I do."

She led them to a table for four near what had once been the front window.

"Still patched up with plyboard, I see," said Jago.

"Yes," said Rita. "Can't see much point putting glass back in, just so it can get blown out again by the next bomb. Did you hear what the Home Secretary said?"

She turned to Dorothy with an understanding look.

"He's a bloke in the government," she said.

Dorothy smiled and nodded her thanks.

"Apparently he told the House of Commons that little strips of brown paper aren't much good at protecting your windows if a bomb drops outside," Rita continued. "Fancy that. Not just a pretty face, is he? Blinking genius. I just wish he'd told the rest of us before mine all got blown in. The time I spent putting those bits of paper all over them. What I want to know is why didn't they find out whether it worked before they told everyone to do it? You'd think they could've tried it out first – you know, just one little bomb outside a few windows, just to see."

"I think this table will be perfect, Rita," said Jago.

"Oh, very well, then. Sit yourselves down." She pulled a chair back from the table for Dorothy. "Here you are, dear. Take the weight off your feet."

Dorothy sat down and pulled the chair in towards the table.

"American, eh?" said Rita. "I don't know much about America myself, only what I see at the pictures. You know what I like best?" She didn't wait for an answer. "Those Fred Astaire musicals – him and Ginger Rogers. When he's dancing, it's like he's floating in the air. Lovely songs too – I only have to hear him sing 'The Way You Look Tonight' and I come over all funny. But those dances – they're just beautiful."

She gazed at the wall as if she were watching the film all over again, then seemed to wake from her dream.

"But that's Hollywood. All we've got here is the Lambeth Walk."

"The Lambeth Walk?" asked Dorothy.

"It's a dance, dear," said Rita.

"I see. Like the jitterbug?"

"The what?"

"The jitterbug. That's a dance too, very big in the States – fast footwork, lots of swivels, strutting and spinning, and the man throws the woman around in his arms. 'Swing the wing and whip the hip.' That's what they say."

"Never heard of it," said Rita. "Sounds a bit racy for here. The Lambeth Walk was just Lupino Lane strolling round the stage with a girl on his arm, like they were out in the park, with a load of other people doing the same thing behind them. It was in *Me and My Girl* – I saw it at the Victoria Palace just before war broke out, but the theatre's closed down now on account of the bombing. It was supposed to be about Cockneys, but the plays and the pictures never get that right."

"I've heard of the jitterbug, Miss Appleton," said Cradock quietly. "I read about it in a magazine."

Jago had almost forgotten Cradock was there. Was the young pup growing soft on Dorothy? His idea of a quiet and friendly lunch seemed to be getting complicated. He was already feeling awkward about inviting Peter to join them, but the truth was he'd been keen to make it clear to Rita that this was a working lunch, so that she didn't start getting ideas in her head about him and Dorothy. He didn't want to keep his friendship with her a secret from Rita, but neither did he want her to think it was anything more than a friendship. Right now he wasn't sure what impressions Rita was getting.

He glanced across the table at Dorothy, who was still smiling patiently at Rita. He didn't really know what he thought about her. He liked her, but then he imagined most people probably did. He admired her – her paper must think her more than capable if they'd posted her to London as a war correspondent. And in dirty old London, so set in its ways, she was like a breath of fresh air.

The fact was he enjoyed spending time with her and wanted to know her better. But on the other hand, women were undoubtedly a complication. Then again, if he tried to set aside the possible complications and look at it simply, she was one of the nicest people he'd met. Like her half-sister Eleanor. But that was another complication. He was still coming to terms with the fact that she was related to the woman whose path had crossed his so many years ago. It was all too confusing, and he wasn't going to sort it out now.

"What can you offer us for lunch today, Rita?" he said.

"Well, I can do you all the usuals – sausage, egg and chips, beans on toast, all that kind of thing – and I've got a couple of specials on. Beef and two veg and cabinet pudding and custard, or tripe and onions and boiled apple pudding. Oh, and I've got some nice pork chops in too."

"Excuse me," said Dorothy to Jago. "I've never eaten tripe; in fact I'm not even sure what it is. Should I try it?"

"I don't think so," he replied. "It's part of a cow's stomach, or a pig's – either way I wouldn't recommend it."

"Okay. Maybe I should go for something lighter. I think I'll have beans on toast."

"And you'll want a cup of tea with that?" said Rita.

"Of course."

Jago ordered a pork chop with boiled potatoes and peas, while Cradock opted for a more extensive combination of sausage, eggs, bacon, chips, and beans. Rita scribbled the orders on her small notepad, slipped it into her apron pocket and set off towards the door at the back of the café that led to the kitchen.

Dorothy leaned a little towards Jago across the table.

"Do you think I should have had the tripe and onions after all?" she said. "I know you've been trying to introduce me to British cuisine and culture, and it feels like I may have just missed an opportunity."

"No," said Jago. "I think it's best to take these things gradually. I don't want to endanger your health."

"So what other cultural experiences do you have lined up for me?"

"I don't have a list, I'm afraid. I'll have to think about it."

"How about your English football? Would I understand it?"

"The rules are simple – one side tries to kick the ball into the other side's goal while the other side tries to kick lumps out of them."

"Sounds just the right game for wartime."

"I suppose so. But I'm not sure whether you're ready for the cultural shock of a football crowd."

"I am a war correspondent, remember."

"Okay, I could take you to a match at the Boleyn one of these days, perhaps."

"At the what?"

"The Boleyn – it's the local football ground. It's Boleyn as in Anne Boleyn, but we say it differently round here: 'Bow-lin'. Don't ask me why – it's just what we do."

"She was one of Henry VIII's wives, wasn't she? What's she got to do with football in West Ham?"

"Not a lot, really. It's just because there's an old tower in the street where the ground is, and it's called Anne Boleyn's castle, though there's no evidence that it was."

"Did she get her head chopped off?"

"Yes. Henry wasn't very good with women, and especially with the Boleyn women."

"There were more than one of them?"

"Yes. He had Mary Boleyn as his mistress for a few years, but then he married her younger sister Anne, who became the queen – and as you so rightly said, had her head chopped off for her pains. I don't think there's any evidence that she ever lived in West Ham, but the football ground is still called the Boleyn. If you'd like to go some day I'll take you."

"Would Rita mind?"

"No – you mustn't take any notice of her. It's just that we're old friends and she can be a bit protective."

"I think she's sweet," said Dorothy.

"Yes, and if you don't get on the wrong side of her she can be very kind," said Jago.

"In that case I'll do my best."

"To business, then. What do you want to know about the Fifth Column?"

"I'd like to know if you have any personal experience of these people, whether there's been any activity locally that you could call Fifth Column. And does it even really exist, or is the government just talking about it to keep people on their toes?"

"That I wouldn't know," said Jago. "I do know that a lot of high-ups in various pro-Nazi organizations were arrested all over the country in May, but I'm not sure I can tell you whether any of them were part of some real Fifth Column in the sense of working actively to aid the enemy."

"Anyone from around here?"

"Yes, there was one. He was the local West Ham leader of the British Union of Fascists. A Welshman actually, but he moved over here sometime in the thirties. And as I recall, before that he lived in Texas for a while and served in the US Navy in the last war. So there's an American connection for you. He was going to be the Blackshirts' candidate for the general election too – we were supposed to be having one this year, but it was cancelled because of the war. I don't imagine he'd have won, though – there was a by-election in February in Silvertown, down by the docks, and the BUF man only got about a hundred and fifty votes. Labour got fourteen thousand."

"But I guess you don't need to be a fascist leader to be part of the Fifth Column," said Dorothy. "Surely that could be anyone who's sympathetic to the Nazis or who has some other reason to help an enemy."

106

"Absolutely," said Jago. "And that's presumably why the government rounded up all the German and Austrian men in the country and put them in camps when the war started. I can't say I agreed with it, but I suppose they couldn't tell who might be a spy and who wasn't, so they decided they were all enemy aliens and put the whole lot away just in case. Seems barmy to me when some of them had been here for donkey's years and were as loyal as I am, but that's government for you."

"I'm an alien myself, you know. I had to register with the police when I came to England and I'm required to carry an alien's registration certificate."

"Yes, but you're American: you'll be classified as a friendly alien."

"That's right. So there are aliens and aliens. But have any spies or enemy agents been caught around here?"

"To my mind all the talk about a Fifth Column is rather vague. When France fell in June there were rumours going round that German parachutists would be landing here and organizing local Fifth Column members and arming them, but I don't know where the weapons were supposed to come from. These Germans were apparently going to create panic and confusion and spread false news among the civilian population, but I don't know how. The papers say people who spread rumours are Fifth Columnists, but they might be just people who've heard something and are worried about it. Passing proper secrets or useful information to the enemy is a different kettle of fish, of course. There's been a few court cases around the country – people charged with doing that kind of thing – but none in this area."

"So you don't think there's much to it."

"That's not what I said."

Jago saw Rita approaching, followed by a waitress with a faraway look in her eyes. Both women were carrying trays of food and drink.

"Perhaps you'd better ask Rita," he said.

Rita arrived at their table.

"Here we are, Phyllis," she said to the girl behind her. "Yours is for the young lady over there." Phyllis deposited Dorothy's order on the table in front of her. "And these," Rita continued, putting her tray down and taking off a plate in each hand, "are for my two favourite policemen."

Jago smiled his thanks as she arranged his plate and cutlery carefully before him. She straightened up and gave Cradock a look that was kindly but that also clearly signalled he was to sort his own knife and fork out.

"Rita, Miss Appleton would like to know what you think about the Fifth Column," said Jago. "Can you spare us a moment?"

"Me? Of course," said Rita. "But eat up – don't let your food get cold."

She eased herself onto the fourth chair at the table, carefully folded the white cloth she was holding and put it down in front of her.

"I can't really say I know much about that. Why do they call it the Fifth Column anyway?"

Cradock had assembled a forkload of sausage and beans but paused before putting it into his mouth.

"Good question," he said. "I've been wondering that myself. Is it like a sixth sense – the one that doesn't really exist but might do? Do you know, sir?"

"Actually, Peter, I don't."

Cradock looked surprised. He couldn't remember Jago ever not knowing the answer to one of his questions.

"Perhaps I can help," said Dorothy. "I think I was there when people first started using the expression. It was in Spain four years ago – I was covering the civil war. General Franco was about to attack Madrid and said he had four columns of troops, but also a fifth one in Madrid."

"You mean he had troops hiding in the city?" said Cradock.

"Not troops, but sympathizers, and he reckoned they could be as much help to his victory as an extra column of troops."

"Right," said Rita. "That makes sense. The Fifth Column's doing the same job for Hitler here, then. I've heard rumours, you know."

"Maybe," said Dorothy. "That's why I think it's interesting. People are talking about a pro-German Fifth Column in America too, and we're not even at war."

"Well," said Rita, picking up her cloth and rubbing at a spot of grease she'd noticed on the floral-patterned oilcloth that covered the table, "interesting it may be, but to me it just seems it's another thing to worry about. I mean, if we're going to be invaded we all need to be on the same side, don't we? I think it's jolly good what the government did, interring all those foreigners."

Out of the corner of his eye Jago could see Cradock looking at him with a questioning expression, as if expecting him to explain to Rita the difference between interment and internment, but Jago ignored him. His job was to make a coherent and intelligible professional out of Cradock, not Rita.

"I'm more worried about being invaded," Rita continued. "Everyone who comes in here reckons it must be any day now, otherwise why would the papers keep telling us every day what the weather's like in the Channel and talking about the RAF going over to the French coast to bomb the invasion barges all the time? The Germans must be planning something really big."

She cast a cautious look to either side before leaning into the table. She dropped her voice, as if wary of being overheard.

"I got a letter from my sister-in-law who lives up in Nottingham – she's the one my Walter's brother married. Nice girl she was, and they moved north after the war; he survived the war, of course, unlike my poor Walter. Anyway, she said there's rumours going round up there that Hitler's already tried an invasion down on the south coast and failed – hundreds of dead German bodies floating about in the Channel, she says. Do you know if that's true, Mr Jago?"

"I haven't heard it for a fact, Rita, but I'm sure if any Germans had landed round here they'd have been arrested. Last time I checked the cells at the station there were no storm troopers in custody."

"There were a few nuns with jackboots under their habits, though," said Cradock with a chuckle that caused a piece of sausage to fall from his mouth.

Rita's face took on a pained expression.

"You're making fun of me, Mr Jago. That's not fair. It's a very serious thing, being invaded, and everyone knows the Germans are going to try. Who's to say they haven't had a go already? I'm not surprised my sister-in-law's worried – I know I am. Not to mention the thought of parachutists landing all over the place, whether they're dressed up as nuns or not. If Hitler can drop a bomb on the street out there he can drop soldiers too."

Rita pushed her chair slowly back from the table and got up.

"I'd best be getting along now. I'll leave you to enjoy your nice food." She sighed quietly. "Wars and rumours of wars – it's all too worrying. You don't know who you can trust these days, do you?"

CHAPTER 15

Lunch over, the two detectives walked Dorothy to Stratford station for her train back to central London. Cradock hung back several paces behind them, out of earshot. Whether this was evidence that the young man was developing a sense of tact, or whether he had simply been distracted, Jago did not know, but he appreciated having a little time alone with Dorothy. It was only when she looked at him with an expression of questioning concern that he realized he'd been lost in thought for several minutes, trying to understand what he felt about her. She flashed him a brief smile.

"Are you okay?" she said. "You look very serious."

"I'm terribly sorry," said Jago. "I was miles away." He hesitated, unsure what to say next. "So, was there anything else you wanted to know about the Fifth Column? Not that I'm a great expert, as you can probably tell."

"There is one thing, yes," she said. "I got the impression from what you said that you hadn't seen much of the Blackshirts here, but I was told they'd been very active in the East End. Is there really not much support for the fascists in this area?"

"It's actually difficult to say now, because they've gone a bit quiet since the arrests in May. The fascists certainly always used to be able to draw a crowd, and their message appealed to a lot of people. British first, that's what they used to say – look after Britain and the empire. But Labour's always been very strong in West Ham, you see – the borough had the first socialist council in England – and the communists did pretty well too, so there were plenty who'd have liked to run the Blackshirts out of town. I got the impression that the parts of the borough where more of what we'd call lower-middle and middle-class people live, like Forest Gate and Upton, were more pro-Mosley –"

"That's Sir Oswald Mosley, right? The leader of the BUF?"

"That's right. The Blackshirts used to call him the Leader, with a capital L, à la Hitler, but now he's sitting in Brixton prison."

"A bit of a comedown, I guess."

"Absolutely. So as I was saying, he had more support in those areas – the places where people tend to buy their houses rather than rent – but other parts of West Ham were very anti. The worst place for the fascists was Plaistow – the people there were very red."

"Did he ever come here?"

"Oh, yes – we had a big song and dance with him here in 1935. He came and spoke at a meeting in Stratford town hall. That BUF man I told you about, the Welshman, he organized it – bit of a fanatic, by all accounts. It was Mosley's first big indoor meeting in East London, and quite a crowd turned out to hear him. But there was some trouble outside – lots of people shouting abuse and so forth."

"A riot?"

"I wouldn't go so far as to say that. I wasn't on duty that night – it was a job for uniform and the mounted police – but it can't have been too bad, because if memory serves me right only five people were arrested and ended up in the magistrates' court the next day. Two of them were fined five shillings for the usual offences – obstruction, using insulting words and behaviour – and someone else got fined a pound for smashing the glass globe on top of a Belisha beacon in the High Street. Not exactly the storming of the Winter Palace."

"Did he ever come back?"

"I don't think so. The BUF carried on having propaganda meetings, though – they had quite a few in Canning Town before the war."

"Where's that?"

"It's another part of West Ham – just a couple of miles south of here as the crow flies. I remember they had some open-air meetings down there, in Hayday Road. I was there yesterday, actually, crawling over a bomb-site at the crack of dawn."

"Were you caught in a raid?"

"No, but someone else was. Very sad scene. A good-looking young woman, full of life one minute, gone the next."

He reached into the inside pocket of his jacket and pulled out a photograph.

"Here she is, look." He passed the photo to Dorothy. "She's the one on the left. Looks like she hasn't a care in the world, doesn't she? And now she's dead."

Dorothy peered closer at the picture.

"Wait a minute," she said. "That's extraordinary."

"What do you mean?"

"I mean I think I've seen these two women before. In fact I'm sure I have. Look – they've both got a beauty spot in the same place, on the lower left cheek."

"That's quite a coincidence, isn't it?"

"No – they're not real. They're make-up."

Jago looked baffled.

"Do many women do that?"

"It's the fashion. It's supposed to make you look kissable."

The word hit Jago like a punch. He kept walking – the last thing he wanted now was for Cradock to join them – but his businesslike conversation with Dorothy had been suddenly disrupted as an image of a kiss came into his mind, displacing every other thought. He had a strange sensation of fear and for a moment didn't understand why, but then he realized – he'd already admitted to himself that he liked and admired Dorothy, that he missed her when they were apart, and that she'd become a friend, but only in that moment had the truth become clear. What he felt was more than friendship – he'd been ambushed by an unexpected sense of attraction and attachment to her. He wanted to tell her that she was kissable, and he was shocked. How could he be so unprofessional? He brought his imagination under control and took a deep breath. He hoped she hadn't noticed his confusion, and tried to make his voice sound as flat as possible when he spoke.

"Right, I see."

He was alarmed by the intensity of his feeling for her and he determined to bury it. He couldn't bear to think of her knowing. He was relieved to see that her face showed no sign of having noticed anything untoward.

"These two were probably friends," Dorothy continued, tapping the photo. "They were having a night out and decided they'd both paint one on in the same place, just for fun."

"And you, er, you say you've seen them?" He was now Detective Inspector Jago again, professional, attentive, focused on the case.

"Yes, that's it – I saw them having a night out."

"When?"

"Quite recently..." Dorothy thought for a moment. "It was a Saturday night – not last Saturday but the one before that. I was at a dance at an RAF station – the one in Hornchurch."

"You were at a dance at RAF Hornchurch? What on earth were you doing there?"

Dorothy laughed.

"I've been there several times. I'm a journalist, aren't I? I have contacts everywhere."

"And a very good memory for faces, too."

"I guess so. But I remember these two particularly, because I saw something that looked a bit suspicious."

"Really?"

"Yes. This one on the left, the one you say has died, she was with two other women – this one here, who she seemed to be very friendly with, and another who's not in the picture. When the other two left the table to dance, your one – what's her name?"

"Mary."

"This one, Mary, looked around quickly as if she wanted to be sure no one was watching her, then took something out of one of their handbags and slipped it into her own."

"And then?"

"Then she just sat back as cool as a cucumber and waited for the other two to come back."

"And could you see what it was she took?"

"I wasn't close enough to be certain, but I'm pretty sure it was a photograph."

"Thank you, Dorothy," said Jago. "That could be a very helpful piece of information."

They were at the station entrance, and Cradock had caught up with them. Jago excused himself briefly to Dorothy and took the detective constable to one side.

"I'll see Miss Appleton onto her train, Peter. I want you to go straight to the nick. You remember Angela Willerson told us Mary Watkins got very upset when they were at a dance at the RAF station at Hornchurch?"

"When some woman showed her a photo or something, and then Mary got all cross and started calling someone a traitor?"

"That's right. It turns out that Miss Appleton was at the same dance, and she thinks she saw Mary and Angela – she recognized them from that photo Angela gave us. But the interesting thing is this: she says when Angela and the other woman were away from the table she saw Mary take something from one of their handbags – something that she thinks was a photograph."

"So that photo could have been quite important?"

"Exactly. Now, when you get back to the station, get on the phone to the RAF at Hornchurch. Find out if they've got a dance there tonight."

"Are we going? I wouldn't say no to that."

"No, I don't want us both turning up like a police enquiry in the middle of their dance. You just find out if there's one on tonight. If there is, get hold of Angela Willerson and tell her I want to take her to it. I have a sudden desire to go dancing at RAF Hornchurch."

CHAPTER 16

Gordon Price slept better on Saturday than he had on Friday. He'd gone to bed as soon as he came off his night duty and managed to stay asleep until nearly two o'clock. That was the only advantage of working nights, he reckoned – it meant he got his evenings at home, and a good part of the afternoons. All he needed was a little nap for about half an hour before he went back on duty, and that kept him going through the night. When he first started doing nights he'd worried about nodding off, especially after a War Reserve Constable in another division of the Metropolitan Police was found asleep on duty at five o'clock in the morning and forced to resign. That was a few months ago, of course, before the air raids started, when the nights could be a bit quieter. Not much chance of dropping off these days – the bombs, fire engine bells and anti-aircraft guns saw to that. Still, he didn't want to take any chances.

Mavis looked up from her knitting when he came into the kitchen.

"Hello, love," she said. "Had a good sleep? I'm just finishing off that little pullover I was doing for Tom. Shame I couldn't get it done before he and Gracie went off – they grow so fast I can't keep up. I suppose I'll have to post it to Canada now. Goodness knows how much that'll cost and how long it'll take to get there. He'll probably be too big for it by the time he gets it."

"He'll be pleased to know his mum's thinking of him, though," said Gordon, sitting down beside her.

"Shall I fetch you something to eat, dear?"

"No, not just yet, thanks."

"That's all right. All this night work must play havoc with your system. I mean, you're home from work but it's not tea time, you've

117

just got out of bed but it's not breakfast time, and it's dinner time now but you're not ready for it yet. Not to worry, though: it's in the oven. It'll keep."

"Thanks, love. How was the wireless last night? Did it work all right?"

"Oh, yes. Thanks for fixing it. I listened to Ambrose, like I said, and Evelyn Dall – they said she was a croonette. Have you ever heard such a ridiculous word? Maybe it's supposed to mean she's a brunette who croons, but you can't tell what colour her hair is on the radio, can you? Anyway, she's got a lovely voice."

"She's a blonde, actually," said Gordon.

"Ah, so you've been looking at pictures of her, have you?"

"No, not particularly. I just picked it up somewhere. Same as I picked up the fact that she earns fifty pounds a week while I'm out there risking my life six or seven nights a week for three – as you reminded me yesterday."

Mavis put her knitting down into her lap.

"I'm sorry, dear. I didn't mean to imply... Look, I'm sorry I got all aerated yesterday, too, about the government and everything. I know you were preoccupied – you were worried about Gracie and Tom. I was probably on edge too, thinking about them, but I was trying to stop you feeling so anxious."

"I know, love. Thanks. I was worried about that woman, too – the dead one we found. I'm going to have to go and see DI Jago about it; there's no two ways about it. I'll go on Monday and be done with it."

He got up and paced the floor to one end of the room and back.

"I need to get out," he said. "Get some fresh air and clear my head."

He took a step towards the passage, but as he did so there was a loud knocking at the front door.

He stopped, then strode briskly down the passage and opened the door. A man he didn't recognize was standing on the pavement, facing him. The caller looked odd, at least in the sense that he wasn't the kind of man Gordon would expect to see in Liverpool Road on a Saturday afternoon. It was his clothes – bowler hat, wing collar and black coat. He held a leather attaché case with both hands in front of him. He looked official, and he looked uneasy.

"Mr Price?" asked the stranger.

"Yes," said Gordon.

"My name is Jackson and I work for the borough council. May I come in?"

"Yes, of course," said Gordon. He led the man down the passage and into the kitchen. "Mavis, we've got a visitor."

Mavis stowed her knitting beneath the chair and moved quickly to the table to remove a pile of ironing, then pulled out a chair for the man to sit on.

"Sorry about the mess," she said. "We were just, er…"

She glanced at Gordon. He could see distress in her eyes.

"Good afternoon," said the man. "Mrs Price?"

"Yes," replied Mavis.

"I'm sorry to disturb you, Mr and Mrs Price. I'm a welfare officer with the council, and I've been asked to visit you by the local education authority –"

Gordon interrupted him.

"If it's about Tom and Gracie not being at school, it's because they've been evacuated. They've gone to Canada with the Children's Overseas Reception Board. It's all been done properly, so the council should already know."

"I'm sorry," said Jackson, "that's not what it's about. Do sit down, please, and you too, Mrs Price."

Gordon sat down. Mavis sat close beside him, clutching his hand with hers.

"I'm afraid I have some bad –"

Mavis gave a low gasp, her voice little more than a breath.

"No!"

"Some bad news," said Jackson. "The very worst news, and there's no easy way I can say this, but I must. It's been confirmed that the *City of Benares*, the ship on which your children were travelling to Canada, was torpedoed and sunk by a U-boat last Tuesday night when it was still about six hundred miles from land. There were a hundred and two children on board, of whom eighty-nine were lost. I'm very sorry to have to tell you your children were not among the survivors."

Mavis stared at him, her face at first numb and uncomprehending, then slowly breaking into a contortion of grief. Tears welled from her eyes, and a hushed wail seemed to rise from somewhere deep within her, growing steadily louder. She twisted round on her chair and threw herself onto Gordon's chest, her arms clinging to him. He could feel deep sobs racking her body. He felt numb too. He didn't know what to do.

Jackson shifted awkwardly in his chair, glancing around as if in search of more words to say.

"The authorities wanted to inform all the parents as soon as possible," he said, "and so they arranged for people like myself to bring the news in person. Letters would be too slow, and it was judged that receipt of a telegram would be too shocking. I'm afraid the details are likely to be in the newspapers by Monday morning, so we acted as quickly as possible to notify you. I'm so sorry."

"That's all right," said Gordon quietly. "You're only doing your job. It's not your fault." He stroked his wife's hair absently as she wept in his arms. "Are you sure this is right? There hasn't been some mistake? There are mistakes sometimes, aren't there?"

Jackson shook his head.

"I'm sorry: only thirteen of the children survived, and they've all been identified. Your children are not among them."

Gordon stared at him emptily, as though every shred of strength in his body had drained away.

"But Tom – he was only seven. He can't die when he's only

seven. We were going to play cricket together. I was going to teach him how to make things, how to mend cars. We were going to go out for a drink together when he grew up. I was going to see Gracie grow into a beautiful young woman and walk her down the aisle one day… She hasn't even had ten years… How could anyone do that to them?"

Mavis pulled herself away from him.

"Stop it!" she said. "There must be a mistake. The Germans don't kill children in cold blood – not my children. They wouldn't sit there and deliberately sink a ship with a hundred children in it. Tell me it's a mistake. Gordon, make him tell me it's a mistake!"

Gordon slowly shook his head.

"No, love. It's war. They wouldn't have done it in the old days, but I remember back in the last war when they sank the *Lusitania* – that's when all the rules got torn up. Now anything goes. A U-boat will sink anything it can, no matter who's on board."

"But look at what Hitler did for children – he made them strong and healthy, well fed, gave them hope and confidence about the future. You could see it in the newsreels. He loved them, and they worshipped him. This can't be his doing. It must be people lower down, bad men, like the captain of that U-boat. Hitler will punish him – you'll see."

"I don't think so, love," said Gordon. "Maybe we just never cottoned on that what we saw was what Hitler wanted us to see. There were probably plenty of other kids in Germany who didn't look all fresh-faced and eager like the ones in the films."

Mavis began to sob again.

"We should never have sent them. We should have kept them here and protected them. If we hadn't sent them they'd still be alive."

"We can't know that," said Gordon gently. "They might have been killed right here in their own beds. It was the right decision to send them away. We couldn't know what would happen."

"But at least we'd have gone together. It's not right for children to die before their parents. I'm so sorry, Gordon: I persuaded you they should go. It's all my fault. My babies…"

Jackson rose from his chair. His hands were tense as they gripped the handle of his attaché case.

"Yes, Mr Jackson," said Mavis, her voice now cold. "You'd better go home now. There's nothing you can do here, and nothing you can say. Just go away, please. You've knocked on my door, and I've lost everything that means anything in my life."

CHAPTER 17

Jago picked his way through the chattering crowd with a drink in each hand: a gin and tonic for Angela and a pint of mild and bitter for himself. He saw she had found somewhere to sit – at one of the small tables scattered around the perimeter of a large hall, presumably brought in as part of its temporary conversion into a venue for dancing. Someone must have taken some of the electric lights out, too, judging by how shadowy the room was – the kind of low lighting that people liked for a dance these days, he supposed. On the far side a dance band was playing "A Nightingale Sang in Berkeley Square" to an improvised dance floor packed with slowly dancing couples, the men almost all in the blue-grey uniform of the RAF and the women a mixture of WAAFs and civilians. He was surprised that the tempo wasn't more vigorous, given how young most of the dancers were – perhaps they'd had a few more energetic numbers before he and Angela arrived.

He'd picked her up in the Riley and driven straight over, but RAF Hornchurch was about a fifteen-mile journey from West Ham by road, and by the time they'd arrived the dance was already well under way. He'd not been to the station before, and was surprised to find how close it was to the little Essex town of Hornchurch, on the south side of Romford. Knowing what a pasting the airfields in south-east England had taken from the Luftwaffe in recent months, he wondered what the locals thought about having such a target on their doorsteps.

The light was fading as they'd approached, and all he could see of the station was the dark outlines of anonymous buildings, while in the fields that skirted it he made out the ghostly shapes of the disused cars and trucks that had been scattered across them to prevent enemy aircraft landing. He wondered whether the government would find enough rusty old Austin Sevens in the country to defend every potential landing ground.

He reached the table where Angela was sitting and placed the drinks on the table. Angela picked hers up immediately.

"Well, thank you, Inspector," she said. "Cheers."

"Cheers," said Jago, lifting his pint of beer.

"Very kind of you to bring me," said Angela, "although I must say the last thing I thought I'd be doing tonight was going to a dance with a detective."

"I appreciate your willingness to help at such short notice."

"You're welcome. But let me get this straight. You just want me to keep an eye out for that woman, Celia whatever-her-name-is, that Mary and I met here the other week, right?"

"Yes, that's right. I want to ask her one or two questions, and since we don't know her surname or where she lives, I'm just hoping she might come along this evening."

"Hoping she's a regular, like, yes?"

"That's it. So if you spot her, just let me know."

"I won't be getting her into trouble, will I?"

"No, it's just to help me find out something."

"And I won't get into any trouble myself?"

"No, not at all."

"That's all right, then. Cheers again."

Jago was already beginning to wonder what this evening might cost him in drinks – and for how long Angela would be in a fit state to recognize the mysterious Celia if she did turn up.

"How often do you come to these dances?" he said.

"Whenever I can, really."

"You're keen on dancing?"

"Yes, I love it."

"And I suppose it's a chance to meet some young men?"

"Yes, of course. The way things are these days, with them all being called up, a girl's got to take any chance she gets. All you find at work now is old men – the young ones are all in the forces, and there's no big Army or Navy bases round our way, so this is the nearest place you can meet them."

"How do they rate as dancing partners?"

"Well, I have to say I prefer dancing with officers – they wear shoes. Sometimes the other ranks have those heavy boots on, and what they can do to your feet when a bloke doesn't know how to dance properly is nobody's business. Still, they're always pleased to see us – most of them are on the look-out for girls. There's competition from the WAAFs, of course, but I reckon we can see them off if push comes to shove."

"And may I ask if you've met anyone special?"

"I've met some nice young RAF boys here, but no one that you'd call special – not in that way. They're very sweet, but some of them are just kids."

Jago was becoming aware that he was probably twice the age of some of the young men on the dance floor.

"Look," he said, "I don't want to cramp your style. I'll move over to the other side and find somewhere to sit quietly, and then you can get some dances. Just come and find me if you see Celia."

"Okay," she said. "Will do."

Jago headed to the far side of the hall as the dancing couples waltzed to a slow arrangement of "Love's Old Sweet Song". By the time he got there and looked back, he could see a young airman was already asking Angela for a dance. She was smiling sweetly and accepting. As they walked onto the dance floor together she gave a discreet wave to Jago behind the airman's back to signal that she knew where to find him.

He sat down in an empty chair and supped his beer. He was beginning to think this might prove to be a long and uneventful evening when he noticed another RAF man approaching. This one was older and had three blue rings on the cuff of his tunic, so Jago knew he was an officer, but what rank they signified he didn't know – in his own soldiering days the RAF had still been the Royal Flying Corps and its officers had Army ranks. The man seemed to be heading directly towards him, and when he got to within three or four yards he raised a hand in greeting.

"Jago!"

He strode up to the detective and shook his hand firmly.

"What a surprise to see you. It is you, isn't it? Why, it must be more than twenty years."

Jago searched the officer's face. To his relief, a name sprang from his memory.

"Roy Dyers," he said. "Well I never."

"It was just after Christmas 1917, wasn't it? I arrived in that hospital in France, and you were one of the old hands, I recall. You showed me the ropes, how to get on the right side of the nurses, and then you were sent back to your regiment and left me there to fend for myself. Well, well. I seem to recall you were rather sweet on one of those young American nurses – did anything come of it?"

"No, I'm afraid not."

"Bad show – still, plenty more fish in the sea, that's what I always say. Mind you, I've never managed to land one myself." He gave a hearty laugh. "How about you – are you a married man these days?"

"No, I've never married."

"Thought as much – you don't have that harassed look some of the married chaps seem to develop." He laughed again. "So what do you do for a living? Not still in the Army, I suppose?"

Jago smiled and shook his head.

"No, after the war I joined the police. Then later I decided I'd had enough of uniforms and transferred to the CID. Now I'm a detective inspector. But you were in the Army too when I last saw you. Fusiliers, wasn't it? How did you end up in the air force?"

"I transferred to the RFC after I'd got out of that hospital. They were desperate for pilots, as you no doubt recall, and I wanted to fly, so I did my training and became a fighter pilot. The war was nearly over by then, of course, but that probably saved my life – we used to reckon a new pilot would have about three weeks to live. When the war ended I decided to stay on, and by then they'd turned us into the Royal Air Force, of course, which is how I ended up in this blue."

"Are you still flying? It's been pretty hellish for the last few months, I should think."

"No: too old for that. My flying days ended eight years ago, more's the pity. These days I fly a desk. I transferred to the Administrative Branch – which curiously enough handles intelligence too, although I'm not involved in that myself – and now I'm head of the Administration Wing for the station here."

"Sounds pretty senior – a more exalted rank than when I last saw you, I expect," said Jago, studying Dyers' cuffs and looking puzzled.

"Trying to work out what my rings mean, eh?" said Dyers. "Let me translate – think of a pip and a crown."

"A half-colonel, you mean?"

"Yes, or the equivalent, anyway: wing commander. What it means in practice is that I'm up to my ears in paperwork and I wish I were up above the clouds again. On the positive side, I get involved in organizing things like this evening. Good for morale, and takes the poor chaps' minds off the nasty business of war for a while."

"They seem to be enjoying themselves."

"Yes, but this is nothing: you should have been here a few weeks ago. We had the Windmill Girls down from the West End."

"From the Windmill Theatre itself?"

"Yes, they came down on a Saturday evening and did some of their, er, exotic dances. Second time they've been – they did a show last Christmas too. Caused a bit of a stir, I can tell you."

"I should imagine it did."

"The young chaps all loved it. Not the WAAFs, though – they walked out."

"I can understand it might not be their cup of tea."

"Quite. Nice girls, the WAAFs. I'd do it again, though. Those pilots don't have much to look forward to. Since France fell, the Germans are only ten minutes' flying time away in a modern plane, and the Luftwaffe's got plenty of them."

"Do you have Spitfires here?"

"Yes, thank goodness. I don't like to think where we'd be if we hadn't. Trying to hold off Goering with Gloster Gladiators, I shouldn't wonder – top speed 250 miles per hour, totally out of date now. The Spitfires turned up only just in time, too – we didn't get our first ones here until February of last year, only six months or so before the blasted war started. I've heard pilots call them the perfect plane. They're a good hundred miles an hour faster than the Gladiator, and the Hurricane's not far behind."

"Faster than the German planes?"

"There's not much in it between the Messerschmitt 109 and the Spitfire, so it's pretty touch and go. We're going to have to keep making them faster, there's no doubt about it."

"But surely there must be a limit to how fast an aircraft can go?"

"I suppose so, but I'm sure we can still do a lot better. The bad news is that the Germans may be ahead of us on that front – they've been experimenting for years with ideas for some kind of rocket motor that would make planes much faster than anything we see today. The problem is that that kind of engine's difficult to control, but in the last couple of years their scientists have been having a crack at developing new fuels that could make it possible."

"But presumably not aviation spirit – we already use that, don't we?"

"Correct. These fuels would be different. There are still some big problems to solve, though – not least the fact that the main chemical used has to be highly concentrated, and that can make it blow up. So don't think about putting it in your car."

Dyers laughed at his own joke, and Jago gave him another friendly smile.

"Good advice. And what is the chemical?"

"H_2O_2," said Dyers. "Hydrogen peroxide to you."

Dyers picked up Jago's beer glass.

"I say, your glass is empty. May I get you another drink?"

"I don't think so, thanks very much."

"In that case you must tootle over here some other time and I'll stand you one in the officers' mess."

"Or you could come over to me – I'm based at West Ham police station. We could go out for an early drink before the blackout. How about tomorrow?"

"Jolly good idea," said Dyers. "I'll try to get over there by opening time."

"Good."

Jago looked over Dyers' shoulder and saw Angela approaching.

"Look, I'm sorry," he said, "I'll have to ask you to excuse me. There's someone I need to speak to."

Dyers turned to follow the direction in which Jago was looking and saw her.

"You sly old dog," he said. "You didn't say you had a popsy here with you."

"It's not like that," said Jago. "She's helping me with my enquiries."

"I bet that's what all the policemen say." Dyers grasped his hand and shook it, and gave him a hearty slap on the shoulder. "I'll leave you to it, then. Very good to see you, old man."

He strode away as Angela arrived, turning back briefly to wave farewell before disappearing into the crowd.

"Hello, Angela," said Jago. "Any sign of Celia?"

"Sorry, no," said Angela. "Do you want to go?"

"Not if you're enjoying it. We'll stay a bit longer. If you spot her, just come and tell me, or if you're with her bring her over to me. I'll either be somewhere in here or outside getting some fresh air."

"Okay," said Angela. "You're right – it is getting a bit hot and stuffy in here."

Jago thought he detected a hint.

"Can I get you another drink?"

"That would be nice. I'll have another G and T, thanks."

Jago headed off towards the temporary bar that had been rigged up at the end of the workshops. The dance floor was still packed with dancers, but as he skirted it the music stopped. The couples stepped apart and applauded the band. He glanced through a gap in the crowd and stopped dead. He didn't think she could have seen him, because she was some distance away. What's more, she wasn't paying much attention to anything else in the room – she was gazing into the eyes of a tall young man in the uniform of an RAF officer, with one ring on his tunic cuff.

Jago felt a stab of pain and then a confusion of guilt at having seen them, as if he were some kind of voyeur. He ducked back, closer to the wall, but kept watching them. The man put his hands gently on her shoulders, then leaned forward and kissed her on the top of her head. She responded by giving him a peck on the cheek, then hugged him, her head buried in his chest.

Jago didn't know the young officer, but there was no mistaking Dorothy. He felt his face flushing as he darted towards the exit.

CHAPTER 18

There was the sound of someone tapping on the passenger-side window of the Riley, and the beam of a flashlight shone through it. Jago looked round from the driver's seat. He could see by the light of the torch it was Angela, and she had someone with her. He got out of the car and walked round to join them.

"What happened to my drink?" said Angela. "You said you'd get me a G and T, and that was the last I saw of you. Some thanks for helping you out."

"I'm sorry," said Jago. "Something cropped up and I couldn't get back."

There was a hint of a slur in Angela's voice, and he had the impression that she'd not gone short of drinks this evening.

"Never mind," she said. "One of those RAF boys got me one instead. It was the devil of a job finding you out here in the blackout, though. You didn't say you'd be in your car, and if I hadn't had my torch with me I wouldn't even have tried to find you – and then you wouldn't have met Celia."

She turned and swung the torch in the direction of a woman who was standing beside and a little behind her.

"Watch it," said the woman. "You're not supposed to wave torches around in the air in the blackout. The Germans'll see it."

"I can't hear any planes," said Angela. "Can you? We're safe for the moment."

The woman stepped forward.

"She said you want to speak to me, Inspector. What's it all about?"

"I'd just like to ask you a few questions. It'll only take a few minutes – do sit in the car, please."

"All right if I go back for a last dance or two?" said Angela.

"By all means," said Jago. "Then I'll run you home."

Angela wandered back towards the building, her torch playing an erratic pattern on the ground as she walked.

Jago got back into the car.

"Good evening, Mrs, er…" he said. "I'm sorry, but I'm afraid I don't know your surname, and we haven't been introduced."

"It's Berry – Mrs Celia Berry. And you are?"

"I'm Detective Inspector Jago of West Ham CID. I understand you met Miss Willerson – the young lady who just brought you out to me – at a dance here the Saturday before last."

"That's right – she's Angela."

"Yes. And I believe there was also another young lady with her, called Mary. I'm particularly interested in anything you may remember about Mary."

"Why's that?"

"Well, I'm afraid it's because she was found dead yesterday morning, and we have reason to believe she may have been murdered."

"Oh, Lord. Not by one of those lads from the RAF station, I hope."

Jago continued without responding to her comment.

"I'd like you to tell me about Mary, please: anything you remember from that evening at the dance."

Celia was silent for a few seconds and then answered.

"Not a lot, to tell the truth. I remember meeting her and talking to her, but I haven't seen her since."

"Did she give any indication that she was out of sorts, or upset in any way?"

"I don't know as I could say. I mean, I'd never met the woman before. We just had a chat at a dance, so I don't think I would have known if she was out of sorts. She seemed pretty normal to me."

Celia opened her handbag and took out a cigarette case.

"Got a light?"

Jago struck a match and held it out towards her. She took his hand in hers and guided it to the end of the cigarette she held between her lips.

"Thanks," she said, drawing on the cigarette.

"I'll open the window for you," said Jago. He leaned across and pushed the hinged opening in the side screen.

"Ta," she said, and blew smoke out into the night. "Craven As – good for sore throats, they say. Want one?"

"No, thanks, I don't smoke," said Jago. "Now, Angela told me that at one point during the evening she saw you showing a photo to Mary, and Mary seemed to get upset. I asked Angela what was in the photo, but she said she was too far away to see it, so I wonder if you can tell me."

"Too far away? Are you sure? I may be mistaken, but I thought she was still sitting at the table with me and Mary when I got that photo out. Probably my mistake. Anyway, one of the two of them had seen my wedding ring and asked me if I was married, whether my husband was away with the forces. I laughed and said no, he's just away – he did a runner. I still wear the ring, but that's just because it keeps some of these boys' hands off me. Too much energy, some of them."

"And your husband?"

"What about him?"

"Tell me about him."

Celia stared ahead through the windscreen into the unbroken darkness of the blackout.

"What's to say? I haven't seen him for a year or more. We met in 1937 when I was up in the Midlands visiting my sister – we're both from Ilford originally, but she moved away. She took me to a dance in Wolverhampton – that's where he was living – and I met him there. Seemed a nice bloke, had some kind of factory job. Right charmer, he was, really. Anyway, I fell for him, and the following year we got married, in a lovely old church in Wolverhampton – St Luke's, it was – on the seventeenth of February 1938, the nearest Saturday we could get to Valentine's Day. It was very romantic. But then straight after the wedding we moved down here, because Richard got a new job. I should've known it wouldn't work when I first clapped eyes on him – he wasn't the settling down type. The Wolverhampton Wanderer, that's what I used to call him. After the football club, you know: Wolverhampton Wanderers?"

"Yes, I'm familiar with the football team."

"He had wandering hands, you see. And a roving eye, too – and I don't think that was all that roved. He had a tendency to go off somewhere without telling me, then come back a couple of days later with some cock-and-bull story. I don't know how he got away with it at work – probably just told them he was sick or something. Anyway, in June last year he went off again, and after a while I realized he wasn't coming back. We'd only been married sixteen months. I haven't seen him since, and for all I know he could be dead."

"Did you report this to the police? That he was a missing person?"

"No. What's the point? I was used to it, you see, and I suppose I just knew somewhere inside that he'd left me. He was too slippery to get into serious trouble, anyway: gift of the gab, you know, always had an answer for everything and could talk his way out of anything. For all I know he's probably talked his way into someone else's bed by now. All in all, I reckon I'm better off without him. I can look after myself. I've got a nice little job and I can pay my way, and I'm having more fun now than I ever did."

"Does your husband have any family?"

"Parents both died before I met him. He had two brothers, but both died in the war: one was in the Army and died at Mons, the other was in the Navy – he survived the war but then went to fight the Bolsheviks with the Baltic Squadron and died in 1919."

"And what about Richard – did he serve in the war?"

"Oh yes, he was a bit of a hero, or so he says. He was in the Navy, in a destroyer at Jutland. The ship was hit and he was nearly killed, but he rescued a wounded officer, even though he was wounded himself. He was mentioned in despatches, apparently. Mind you, he promised to love me and cherish me till death us do part too, but that never happened, so perhaps I should have taken all that heroics stuff with a pinch of salt."

She laughed with a throaty rasp and pulled on her cigarette, then tossed the stub out of the window.

"I mean, he might have just made the whole thing up, mightn't he?"

"And can you tell me about your own family?" said Jago.

"I haven't got much family, really," she said. "My parents are both gone now, same as Richard's, and we didn't have any children. My only family is my sister Vera, up in the Midlands, and I don't see much of her. She's not married."

"Thank you. Can we go back to that photograph now? I'm interested in why it may have upset Mary Watkins."

"That's the Mary who was at the dance, right?"

"Yes."

"Well, I'm sure I don't know. It was just an ordinary photo, and she didn't say anything at the time."

"Can you show it to me?"

"No, I seem to have lost it. I obviously had it in my handbag at the dance, but a couple of days later I noticed it wasn't there any more. I must have dropped it somewhere, I suppose. No great loss, though."

"Can you tell me what was in the photo, then?"

"Yes, that's easy. As I said to those two girls, if I'm getting a bit more attention than I want from any of the lads at these dances and I'm not interested I flash my wedding ring at them, and if that doesn't work I pull out the photo. It was a wedding photo, you see – my wedding."

135

"And what was Mary's reaction when you showed it to her?"

"Well, I haven't thought about it since then, but now you mention it, I suppose it was a bit odd, the way she reacted. It was like she was shocked or surprised or something. I didn't ask why, though, and she didn't say anything. She just sort of went quiet."

"Was there anything unusual in the photo?"

"No, it was just me in my wedding dress – a lovely white silk, it was. Lucky I got married before the war started, I suppose – I think they're using all the silk for parachutes now. And my husband was in it too, of course: wearing his black suit and looking like he wasn't sure he was supposed to be there. That's just my mind going back, of course: I don't recall thinking that at the time."

She turned in her seat to face Jago and looked him in the eye.

"To be honest, I suppose even then his mind was wandering, on his own wedding day. But he's still my lawful wedded husband, unless he's dead. If you find out he's dead you will let me know, won't you?"

Jago realized his mind was wandering too, at the thought of someone being betrayed in this way.

"Er, of course," he said. "You've been most helpful. Tell me: do you have any other photos of yourself and your husband at your wedding?"

"No, that was the only one. An incendiary bomb got the rest. Not that I minded much – the quality was terrible anyway. Richard got one of his mates to take some snaps with an old Box Brownie – that was all we could afford. The only reason why I still had that one was that I carried it round with me in my bag. All right if I go now?"

"Yes, but I wonder if you could just leave your address with me in case I need to ask any more questions."

"Of course. It's 357 Shrewsbury Road, in East Ham. I've got a cosy little upstairs flat now, with a nice view out the back window of Plashet Park. It's very quiet – just like living in the country."

"And where do you work?"

"Ilford."

"The town or the company?"

"I know. It's confusing, isn't it? I work for the company – Ilford Limited, the film people. The council tried to stop them using the name but didn't get anywhere, so now they just have to lump it. I'm in the sales department, but nothing grander than the typing pool, so don't ask me anything about photography. Anyway, that's all I can tell you about Richard, and it's certainly enough for me for one evening. I don't expect I'll see him again, but believe you me, if he does turn up he'll get a piece of my mind."

CHAPTER 19

It was Sunday morning. Jago had secured a table in the corner of the police canteen and was enjoying a spot of peace and quiet as he ate his breakfast. Taking the old eiderdown into the shelter had proved to be a good idea. At least he hadn't been so cold, although the night's violent noises had kept him awake for longer than he'd have wished.

He dipped a piece of fried bread into his fried egg and chewed on it. He wanted to do some calm thinking before the day got too busy, but his mind was agitated, and he knew why. It was about Dorothy. It wasn't just the bombs and artillery that had kept him awake – it was what he'd seen at the dance. He couldn't stop thinking about what he'd felt when he saw her in that man's arms, the look of contentment on her face, the kiss she gave him at the end. Nor could he stop thinking about his shocked realization that he'd wanted to kiss her himself. Don't be ridiculous, he told himself. You're getting carried away. We're friends, that's all, and pretty new friends at that. We barely know each other, and I'm acting as if I own her.

He thought back to their first meeting just a few weeks ago, and the apprehension he'd felt as he began to find himself liking her. It's asking for trouble, he thought, getting involved with a woman, especially a strong woman – and especially at my time of life.

What should he do? He had no right to ask her personal questions about men she chose to dance with. Besides, as far as he could tell she hadn't seen him – the place had been crowded and the lighting none too bright. Best to let sleeping dogs lie? There was nothing to be gained from digging deeper. Twenty years a policeman, and three-quarters of that time a detective, had left him an instinctive questioner. He must curb that instinct; he mustn't make the mistake of interrogating Dorothy on her personal life and alienating her for ever. None of your business, he told himself.

And yet he couldn't shake the desire to know who the man was, even though it was scary to think that if he tried to find out it could mean the end of his friendship with Dorothy. He tried to put out of his mind the affectionate scene he'd witnessed, but the confusing sense of pain wouldn't go away. His mind told him it was foolish and irrational, that she'd made no promises to him and he'd asked none of her, but there was a dark and secret place, deep down, where he couldn't suppress the feeling that in some way she'd betrayed him.

Get a grip on yourself, he thought. It's simple, you fool – you're a caveman. You've met a woman who's attractive, so you want her for yourself. Now you've seen her with another man and your primeval instinct says he's a rival. In fact you're not even a caveman, you're an animal: it's you or him, and your survival instinct wants to fight him off. But no, he thought, it's not as simple as that. I'm not driven by an urge to rush out and fight another man for a woman. What I feel is more like a bitter-sweet tenderness, a sad sense of loss.

He was still feeling tossed about by these thoughts when Cradock joined him.

"Morning, guv'nor."

"Morning, Peter. How are you today? You look as though you haven't slept a wink."

"Bit of a bad night, sir – didn't sleep well. All that noise. How did you get on at your dance?"

"It was crowded and noisy, and I felt old – but I did meet Celia, the lady with the photograph. I'm not sure whether it moves things forward much, though. The question remains: who would want to do away with Mary Watkins, and why? What do you think?"

Jago welcomed the opportunity to set his earlier reflections to one side. For once, the thought of trying to get DC Cradock to think intelligently and analytically about a case in the light of the evidence gathered to date was an attractive proposition. A chance to look at a problem objectively and dispassionately.

"What do we know about her, except that someone decided to strangle her?" he said.

"Well," said Cradock, as he shook salt onto his breakfast, "not much family to speak of. Didn't get on with her sister. Seemed to be good at her job. No problems at work, if that Hornby woman's to be believed. Just another hardworking spinster, except…"

"Yes?"

"Well, it sounds like she was partial to having a bit of fun on the side, doesn't it? Enjoyed a drink or two when she wasn't at work, and even had some kind of affair with a man. And then there was that business at the post-mortem – what the doctor said. Spinster she might have been, but perhaps not quite as respectable as she'd have had people believe."

Cradock reached for the bottle of HP Sauce that stood between them on the table, unscrewed the cap, then slapped the bottom of the bottle with the palm of his hand several times to send a quantity of the contents spurting over half of his breakfast. Jago paused until the ceremony was completed.

"She seems to have been a bit short on friends, though, doesn't she?" he said. "Angela's the only one we've been able to find, and if it weren't for their occasional drinks we'd know next to nothing about Mary's private life."

"Yes. So a bit of a loner, perhaps?" said Cradock. "She certainly seems to have been a private person, like Miss Hornby said. And Angela said she didn't share her secrets – although maybe that's just because Mary wasn't as forward as her."

"Forward indeed," said Jago. "She was even chatting me up in the car on the way to the dance."

"Really? What did she do?"

"Never you mind, Peter. I only mention it to put you on your guard – I think she prefers younger men than me if she gets the choice. But let's get back to Mary."

"Okay," said Cradock. "So Mary kept herself to herself. What if she had something to hide? It could be a reason for someone wanting to murder her."

"We haven't come across any evidence to confirm that, though."

"Right. So she's a bit of a puzzle. We haven't got much to go on on the family side either."

"No, just the sister, Susan," said Jago. "And I wouldn't exactly describe them as close, at least judging by what her husband and Angela say. Maybe they'd always been like that – sisters don't necessarily get on. Or maybe something happened between them to set them against each other."

"It certainly seems like Mary wasn't keen to talk about her," said Cradock. "She didn't even tell Angela what her sister's name was. And George did say he thought Mary must've done something to hurt Susan in the past, although I suppose that could've been just a guess, if it was before he'd met Susan. The only thing we can definitely say is that George likes a good chat. Doesn't strike me as the most reliable of witnesses, though."

"Yes," said Jago. "He seemed keen to talk, but not about what we wanted to know. I thought we were going to get his entire life story at one point. I didn't like his manner either, but I can't arrest him for that."

"And what about that photograph, sir? It's got to be important, hasn't it? Did you manage to find out anything more from Celia last night?"

"Yes – I told her Angela had said she thought Mary looked upset when she saw it. The way Celia described it, Mary looked surprised or shocked. I asked Celia what kind of photo it was and what was in it. She said it was her wedding photo: a picture of her and her husband."

"But Angela says that after Mary saw it, she said, 'He'll pay for this. He's a traitor.' Why would Mary say that if she was talking about Celia's husband?"

"We can't be sure who she was talking about. From what Angela said, it was later that Mary said that, not when she was looking at the photo. She could have been talking about anyone."

"Did Celia have the photo with her last night?"

"Unfortunately not. She said she'd lost it. The last time she saw it was at the dance, when she put it back in her bag, and then a couple of days later she noticed it wasn't there any more. Now, when we were walking from Rita's café to the station, Dorothy said –"

He noticed Cradock's eyebrows rise ever so slightly, and corrected himself.

"Miss Appleton said she'd seen Mary take a photograph out of either Celia's or Angela's handbag. If Celia says she put it back in her own bag after she'd shown it to them, it's possible that Mary stole it from Celia that evening. I wonder why she'd do that."

"Search me," said Cradock.

"Quite," said Jago. "Look, I want you to get over to Mary's place and see if you can find any photos that fit the description: a wedding photo of a bride and groom."

"Will do," said Cradock.

He returned to the task of finishing his breakfast. Jago watched him eating, hunched over his plate and loading food into his mouth – like a stoker feeding a furnace at Beckton gasworks, he thought.

"Peter, have you ever thought you might have a marshal's baton in your knapsack?"

Cradock suspended his eating project for long enough to give him a blank look.

"Sir?"

"It's what they used to say in Napoleon's army: even the humblest private might one day be a field marshal. Do you ever think one day you might get to be the Chief Constable of the CID?"

"Course not," said Cradock. "They're all retired colonels, aren't they?"

"How about the next job down, then – a CID area superintendent?"

"Can't say I have, sir, no."

"Someone's got to do the job, you know. So just in case you do consider that post sometime in the future, may I give you some advice?"

"Of course, sir."

"Learn how to eat. You look like a prisoner, wolfing it down before a fellow inmate can steal it off your plate. Eat like a free man, someone who's in control of his own destiny and his own dinner. Sit up straight, put your fork in your left hand and your knife in your right, and try to eat with a little grace."

"Sorry, sir, I don't think I had your upbringing."

"My upbringing? That's nothing to do with it. It was the Army – when they decided they needed me for an officer in the last war. I wasn't their first choice, you understand, but it got to the point where so many of the proper upper-class officer types had been killed off that they needed Other Ranks like me to plug the gaps. I knew all about fighting – rifle, bayonet, grenade or bare hands – but that didn't make you an officer. No, they sent us to an Officer Cadet Battalion and taught us the two most important things for an officer to know. What do you think they were?"

"No idea, sir – strategy and tactics?"

"No. It was how to be jolly positive about getting killed for your country, and how to use the right knife and fork. I tell you, if you want to get on, learn how to eat properly."

"Yes, sir," said Cradock. He pulled himself into a more upright position and fiddled with his cutlery. "Thank you, sir."

He put his knife and fork down again almost immediately.

"Talking of getting on, sir, what about that Everson fellow and his missing stock? I imagine he'll be doing quite well out of the war if he's got special contracts from the War Office, and he won't want them getting cold feet about him. What do you intend to do about that stuff that's been going missing? He seemed a bit worked up about it."

"It's difficult to know how significant it is. He'd obviously like it cleared up."

"What I'm wondering is: could there be some kind of connection with Mary's death? Maybe she'd found out something she wasn't supposed to know. She was part of the company administration, so she'd know about what was going on, what was where, how things worked. What if she'd found out who was doing it? What if it was something more serious than Everson's letting on? She might've found out something so dangerous that someone had to silence her. Or maybe she was involved herself – maybe there was some racket going on that she was mixed up in, and it turned sour."

"That sounds dramatic," said Jago, "but anything's possible, especially in times like these. At the moment we've no reason to think it's anything more than a coincidence, but we'll certainly have to look into it, and keep it to ourselves for the time being in view of what he said. This murder is our first priority, but we'd better take some action on his problems too. I want you to do some observation. If stuff's being pilfered from Everson's, chances are it'll end up being sold by some shady character in a pub. Have a sniff around, find out whether anyone can supply that kind of thing – tell them you're looking for a little present for your girlfriend."

"But I haven't –"

"Your imaginary girlfriend, Peter."

"Any suggestions where?"

"Try the Railway Tavern in Scott Street – I've heard it sometimes hosts a bit of informal enterprise, you might say."

"On my own, sir?"

"Yes. I'm sure I can trust you not to turn it into a pub crawl. You'll need a clear head and sharp eyes."

144

"Thank you, sir – you can rely on me."

"I know – that's why I'm asking you to do it. You don't need me to nursemaid you all the time. I suggest you go down there tomorrow evening or Tuesday evening – and that you get an early night tonight and try to catch up on some sleep."

CHAPTER 20

The telephone rang on Jago's desk, and he jolted in his seat. It had been a quiet Sunday afternoon at the station – so quiet that he must have dozed off. His mind was still foggy as he picked up the receiver and put it to his ear. The voice on the other end was Tompkins'.

"Sorry to disturb you, sir," said the station sergeant, "only I've got some visitors for you down here. Two ladies and a gentleman, to be precise. Would you like to come down for them?"

"Certainly, but I'm not expecting anyone. Are they together?"

"No, sir. At least, not the gentleman. The two ladies are together and he's not, if you see what I mean, but they all want to see you. The gentleman's called Wing Commander Dyers. From the RAF. Says you're taking him out for a drink. I reckon that's all they do in the RAF: lark about in planes and then prop up the bar. And chase the girls in between, of course."

"Ah, yes, thank you – I remember now. I am expecting him. And the ladies?"

"They're a Miss Hornby and a Miss Cartwright. Miss Hornby is the one who called from Everson Engineering on Friday morning, and I think the other one works there too, but I don't know her from Adam – or I suppose I should say from Eve. Anyway, I've put the two of them in an interview room, and the RAF chap's down here with me."

"Good. Ask him to be so kind as to wait, and tell him I'll be with him as soon as I've finished with my other visitors."

Jago put the phone down and made his way to the interview room. He opened the door and found the two women seated at a table. The older of the two he recognized as Miss Hornby, but the younger one was a stranger. He entered the room, and Miss Hornby jumped to her feet.

"Detective Inspector," she began. "I wouldn't normally visit a police station on a Sunday afternoon – in fact it's not my habit to frequent them at any other time either – but an extremely distressing matter has arisen. Miss Cartwright here is one of our employees, and she's confided in me about a most unpleasant incident – something that happened on Friday evening. It seems a man has been behaving in a disgraceful manner towards her. I insisted that she report it to the police, and she has agreed to do so. I hope you don't mind me troubling you personally, but your sergeant said you were here."

"That's fine," said Jago. He turned to the other woman. "Miss Cartwright?"

"Yes, Beatrice Cartwright. Would it be possible to speak to you alone?" She turned to her companion. "I hope you don't mind, Miss Hornby, but I think I'd rather speak to the inspector in private."

"Of course, my dear."

"In that case, Miss Hornby, I'll take you back to the station sergeant," said Jago. "Please wait here until I return, Miss Cartwright."

He led Miss Hornby down the corridor to the front desk.

"Sergeant Tompkins will look after you while I interview your colleague," he said.

Dyers was sitting a few feet from the front desk, leafing through a magazine. It struck Jago that in daylight and in calm surroundings he looked rather imposing in his uniform. The wing commander looked up with a hopeful expression when Jago appeared.

"Sorry, old chap," said Jago. "I must crave your patience for a short while. I have to speak to someone, but I'll be with you as soon as possible. In the meantime, I'm sure if you speak nicely to Sergeant Tompkins here he'll get you a cup of tea. Isn't that right, Sergeant?"

"Of course, sir," said Tompkins. "It would be my pleasure."

"I shall leave Miss Hornby here in your safe keeping, then." Jago turned back to Miss Hornby. "May I introduce you to my friend Wing Commander Dyers? As you can see, he's an officer in the air force."

Dyers got up from his chair and nodded to her.

"And this," said Jago to Dyers, "is Miss Hornby, who works for a local engineering company and has come in on an important matter. I hope not to keep you both waiting too long."

***

When Jago returned to the interview room, Beatrice Cartwright was sitting just as he had left her. He took a seat facing her across the table.

"So, Miss Cartwright, perhaps you could tell me exactly what this incident was. Take your time."

"Thank you, Inspector. To tell you the truth, there isn't a lot to say. It was a man – he accosted me in a park."

"When was this?"

"It was the day before yesterday."

"Do you recall the time?"

"It was about ten past six. I was on my way home from work, and I'd stopped to sit down for a while in the Beckton Road recreation ground. I do that quite often, but nothing like this has ever happened before."

"What did he look like?"

"He was wearing a dark coat and a cap, but it was pulled down and I couldn't see much of his face. He was clean-shaven, but that's about all I can say."

"And what exactly did this man do?"

"He came and sat beside me – without being invited, I hasten to add – and started to say all sorts of strange things. He seemed to know all about me, as if he'd been spying on me."

"Did he give a name?"

"Yes – Smith. But that's not likely to be his real name, is it?"

"Not if he was up to no good, it isn't. Carry on, please."

"I tried to get away – I was on my own and I was frightened, and there was no one else there apart from him. I pushed him and even punched him, but he was too strong for me. He got his hand on my neck and was choking me."

"You mean this man tried to strangle you?" said Jago.

Beatrice looked uncertain.

"In a way, yes – he certainly had me by the throat. But now I think about it, I don't think he was trying to kill me."

"What makes you say that?"

"I think he was just trying to frighten me, because later on, when he could have hurt me more, he didn't."

"Later on?"

"Yes, you see I managed to kick him and escape. I ran away, but he caught me again. But the thing is, he wasn't violent then – he just talked."

"Talked about what?"

"He started making all sorts of strange accusations – said I was spying, passing information to the enemy. He claimed he was working for something called the Radio Security Service. Do you know what that is?"

Jago had heard of it, but he also believed it was a department of Military Intelligence and therefore not for discussion with members of the public.

"What did he want?"

Beatrice shuddered.

"He may not have been violent, but he was still very menacing. He said I was in trouble, but he might be able to not file his report – as long as I gave him some money. He's blackmailing me, Mr Jago."

"How much does he want?"

"Twenty pounds. I'm to give it to him on Tuesday evening. And

149

before you ask, he didn't say where – he said he'll contact me on Tuesday and tell me where to go. I might just be able to scrape the money together, but I'm worried that he'll ask for more. What shall I do?"

She began to cry.

"Don't worry, Miss Cartwright. We'll deal with it. As soon as you hear from him on Tuesday, tell me where he's told you to go and what time he wants you to be there."

"I'm scared."

"I quite understand, but we'll be keeping an eye on you – and on him."

Beatrice wiped her eyes with her handkerchief and smiled at him.

"Thank you. Is that all you need to know?"

"It's all I need to know to sort Mr Smith out. But if you could spare me a few more minutes, there is something else I'd like to ask you about."

She looked puzzled, but nodded.

"Yes, of course. What is it?"

"It's to do with the death of your colleague Mary Watkins."

"Ah, yes, poor Mary."

"We're looking into it and trying to put together a picture of her from people who knew her. Did you have any direct dealings with her at Everson Engineering?"

The change of subject seemed to be a relief to Beatrice. Her voice became calmer, more businesslike.

"Yes, we worked on the same corridor. She was in welfare and personnel, and I'm a secretary in admin. I do some clerical work too. I suppose I knew her reasonably well."

"What was she like?"

Beatrice spent a few moments in thought before answering.

"If I had to sum her up in one word I'd say caring. I've only been working at Everson's for a couple of years, and it's always difficult finding your feet in a new company, but she took me under her wing and helped me settle in. She was the kind of person you could talk to. She certainly made a point of being nice to me and helping me through some tricky moments."

"What kind of tricky moments?"

"Changes in my job, mainly. Before I joined Everson's I'd had secretarial posts of one kind or another in three other companies, but here my role was more interesting. I've studied languages a bit, you see, but had never had much chance to use them in my work."

"Which languages?"

"Just French and German, but when I was eighteen I had a chance to go over there and work for a bit, in both countries, so I got quite good at them. When I came here, Mr Everson asked me to deal directly with some of his foreign clients. He had customers and various business links with companies in France and Germany, and I handled most of the correspondence with them. Unfortunately, of course, the German side of things came to a halt last September, and then the fall of France put paid to the French side too."

"And Miss Watkins was helpful to you?"

"Yes, she was very supportive. And before that, too. At one point I thought I might even lose my job, but she – well, she stuck up for me."

Beatrice stopped, as if uncertain whether to say more. She looked down and straightened the hem of her dress.

"In what way did she stick up for you?"

"It was all a little bit difficult," said Beatrice. "It was to do with Miss Hornby. I don't think she liked it when Mr Everson made me responsible for dealing with those clients in Germany and France. She said to me once that she thought perhaps I was too young to do a job like that."

"You mean she was questioning Mr Everson's judgment?"

"Oh, no, she would never do that. She just said something like it's unusual for a girl of your age to take on a role like that, reporting directly to the managing director, and perhaps we should have waited until you were a bit older. I got the impression she might have said the same to him too, because not long after that he came out with something similar. But then, like I said, that side of the business pretty much collapsed anyway, so it never came to anything."

"But Mary helped you?"

"Yes. I know she put in a good word for me with Mr Everson, because she told me. I think it might be thanks to her that I kept my job. And then when the war changed everything and there wasn't enough work for me, she made sure the company found alternative duties for me. It's thanks to her, really, that I'm still here. She got me transferred to general secretarial duties and record-keeping, which is what I do now."

"I see. So you were indebted to her."

"Yes, I was."

"Would you say you were happy in your work?"

Beatrice paused, as if weighing up how to answer the question.

"I suppose I am, on balance."

"Only on balance?"

"Well, you see, I've never felt I fulfilled my potential. I thought I'd have an interesting career and earn a decent amount of money, but somehow it's never happened. I've had a string of ordinary jobs, and now I'm in another one. All that's changed, I suppose, is that I've come to expect it."

"Is the pay not good at Everson's?"

"It's not bad for the kind of job I have, but it can be difficult to make ends meet. There's certainly nothing left over for luxuries at the end of the month."

"What's the record-keeping that you do?"

"It's in the stores. Stock in, stock out."

"I've heard that some things in the stores may have gone missing. Do you know anything about that?"

"No, I can't say I do."

"But these are items in the stores. Isn't it your job to know?"

"Not exactly, no. What I mean is it's my responsibility to check items in and out, and to maintain a ledger of deliveries and items signed out."

"So wouldn't you notice if things started going missing?"

"No, I wouldn't really, not unless it was a big quantity suddenly disappearing. My job is just to make sure everything's recorded and signed for. I don't do the stock control or reconcile the amounts coming in and going out: I just compile a weekly report and pass it to Miss Hornby. She expects me to keep careful records, but what she does with the information is her business, not mine."

"And how do you get on with Miss Hornby now? Has your relationship improved?"

Beatrice seemed to hesitate before answering the question.

"You won't tell her this, will you? Only I don't want to speak out of turn. But if you want an honest answer, I'd say no, I can't say it has. I still don't think she trusts me, and for that matter I don't trust her."

"But you confided in her about this incident at the recreation ground. Doesn't that suggest you trust her?"

"No. I only told her because she said she reckoned my mind wasn't on the job and she wanted to know why I wasn't concentrating. I thought I was heading for more trouble, so I told her what had happened. It wasn't out of choice. If I'd wanted to confide in someone I'd have chosen Mary."

"Mary trusted you."

"Yes, she did. Miss Hornby doesn't, and I'm pretty sure she doesn't like me either. But if you ask me why that is – well, I really don't know."

CHAPTER 21

"Good afternoon," said Dyers to Miss Hornby when Jago had left them. He accompanied the words with a slight forward inclination of his head, a form of residual bow and his habitual expression of formality.

"Good afternoon," she said. "I understand you're awaiting the detective inspector's pleasure. I'm sorry my colleague and I have taken up his time – and yours."

"Think nothing of it, my dear lady," he said.

He cast an appraising glance over her appearance – discreetly, he hoped. Soberly dressed, and with a no-nonsense look to her face. A little past the first bloom of youth, he thought – rather like himself, in fact. What people used to call a handsome woman. His few male friends who weren't in the RAF seemed to envy him his lot in life, surrounded as he was every day by immaculately turned out young WAAFs, but most of them were so flighty it could be – well, frankly, it could be tedious.

"I do hope it hasn't been too tedious for you waiting here," she said.

He was startled – how curious that she had just said the very word he was thinking.

"Not at all," he said. He held out a hand to shake. "Roy Dyers – call me Roy."

She took his hand and shook it.

"Miss Hornby – that's what most people call me, but my name is Winifred."

"Charming," said Dyers.

He closed his magazine and laid it down on the table beside his chair.

"Don't let me stop you reading," said Miss Hornby.

"Not at all. I was just leafing through it to pass the time. I thought I might have to wait around for Inspector Jago if I came to the station. I'm supposed to be going out for a drink with him once he gets away from his duties."

"Ah, yes. He said you were his friend. Do you have any connection to the police?"

"Good Lord, no. Jago and I were in the Army together in the last war. We haven't seen each other since 1918, so we're having a quiet get-together in a local hostelry."

"How nice. It's always good to meet up with old friends, isn't it?"

"Yes, indeed, although one doesn't get much time for that sort of thing these days."

"I could see from your uniform that you're in the RAF. A wing commander's quite a senior rank, isn't it?"

"Fairly senior, I suppose, but I've been in the RAF for a good many years – ever since the tail end of the war."

"When it was still the Royal Flying Corps?"

"Yes. You know something about it, then?"

"Not really. I had a fiancé, you see. He was a pilot in the Royal Naval Air Service."

"And was he transferred into the RAF like me, when we were merged in 1918?"

Her confident voice dropped to a softer, gentler tone.

"No. He died. In 1917 he was involved in some trials to do with landing aeroplanes on moving ships, in Scapa Flow, and there was an accident."

"I'm so sorry," said Dyers.

"It was a long time ago, and there were many others like me. We just had to carry on."

She shook herself and sat up straight, as if to shake off the burden of the past. She smiled at him and continued.

"Your work must be very interesting, especially at a time like this."

"Not as interesting as it was," said Dyers. "My glamorous flying days are over now, and I work in administration. It's the young men, the junior officers, who are doing all the important work."

"I work in administration too – personnel and administration."

"What a coincidence. Of course, it can be very interesting sometimes, can't it? A chance to make use of the lessons one's learned and the wisdom one's gained over the years, to make things run better for the benefit of others – that's what I like to think."

"Oh, absolutely. Keeping the wheels moving quietly in the background while others get the glory."

"Yes, but at least with the satisfaction of knowing they wouldn't have achieved anything without us."

"My sentiments entirely."

Tompkins arrived with two cups of tea on a small wooden tray.

"Here we are, sir, madam – with the compliments of the Metropolitan Police Service. Sugar's in the bowl there."

He put the tray on the table and returned to his desk.

"Thank you," said Miss Hornby to his back as he left. She smiled at Dyers.

"I would say 'Shall I pour?' but the sergeant seems to have done that already. I couldn't help noticing the magazine you were reading. It's *Picturegoer and Film Weekly*, isn't it?"

"Yes, that's right. Just passing the time, you know."

"Do you like films?"

"Yes, I do. Not as good as the stage, of course – you can't beat a live production in my book. But these days with all the theatres closed because of the bombing it's something one can only look forward to as a possible future pleasure. The last time I checked, the only theatrical show in town seemed to be the Revudeville at the Windmill Theatre, which is, er –" He stopped and made a sound as if clearing his throat, in an attempt at an expression of gentlemanly consideration. "Which is perhaps not the first choice of entertainment for a lady such as yourself."

"Indeed not," she said. "I understand the show features young ladies at considerable risk of catching a cold."

"Please excuse me. It was most indelicate of me to mention it. I hasten to assure you that I myself don't –"

"I'm sure you don't, Wing Commander. You were saying?"

"Yes, the theatres closing. A great tragedy. You can't beat a cracking good live performance with some foot-tapping tunes."

"You like musical theatre, then?"

"I should say so. Before the war, a show in the West End would have been my perfect night out."

"Mine too. What was the last thing you saw?"

"It was *Under Your Hat* – Jack Hulbert and Cicely Courtneidge. I saw it last November. Good plot, and some great musical numbers. Best five bobs' worth of entertainment I had all year, I should say – reduced wartime prices by then, of course."

"Where was it on?"

"The Palace Theatre, that beautiful pile D'Oyly Carte built on the corner of Shaftesbury Avenue and Charing Cross Road. When the show started its first run – the year before I saw it – the BBC showed some of the first act live from the theatre on that television service of theirs. Not that I saw it, of course – I don't own a television receiver and don't know anyone who does."

"It's all been closed down anyway, now, hasn't it?"

"That's right – a casualty of war. The government was worried the Germans could use the VHF signal as a beacon to guide their planes to London. Of course, if they had, they might have dropped every bomb they possessed on Alexandra Palace instead of on the rest of us, and that mightn't have been a bad thing."

Miss Hornby gave him a mock-reproachful look.

"I can't tell whether you're joking or not," she said. "But anyway, it all sounds a bit technical to me. I must confess I don't really understand things like radio frequencies and beacons. I suppose you have to in your work, though."

"Yes, it's all part of the flying business," said Dyers.

"Tell me more about the show. What was the plot?"

"Well, if memory serves me correctly, some foreign agents have stolen a secret carburettor and Jack Hulbert's a spy trying to get it back. Cicely's his wife, of course, as always, and she gets suspicious of Jack, so she starts spying on him too – and so on and so forth. Something like that, anyway. Jolly entertaining."

"I suppose for someone in your position that sort of thing's deadly serious too – I mean, we hear about new secret weapons to beat the Germans, but people like you must have to work hard to keep them secret."

"Well, yes, I suppose so, but one gets used to it."

"We all think you're wonderful, you know."

"Who do?"

"The public, I mean. The way you're fighting to drive the enemy from our skies. We think you're all heroes."

"Very kind of you to say so. But it's the young chaps that are doing all that, not the, er, slightly older ones like me."

"I'm sure they learned everything they know from men like you. And for you and your colleagues all this is real life, not just a play on the stage."

"That's certainly true. I must say, though, if you like a musical, that Jack and Cicely show was awfully good. Top-class entertainment."

"Yes, it sounds as though it was the kind of show I would have loved to see. But you know how it is – things got extremely busy at work when the war started, and most evenings by the time I'd got back to my flat and cooked myself some tea I was too tired to go out for entertainment. That's the trouble with the solitary life – it does have the advantage that one can do whatever one wants, but that doesn't mean one always has the time and energy to do so."

"Quite. One's never alone in the forces, of course, but I know what you mean. Anyway, let's hope it won't be too long before the theatres can reopen. Perhaps they'll put *Under Your Hat* on again – it was certainly having a great run back then."

"And may I ask your taste in films?"

"I like anything that's got a strong story and some action, where you know who the goodies and baddies are. I'm not one for weepy introspective stuff. I enjoy thrillers as long as they're not too violent, and westerns if they've got more in them than chaps riding horses and shooting guns at each other."

She gave a gentle laugh.

"Yes, I know what you mean. Something that doesn't leave you walking out of the cinema feeling depressed. We don't need that these days – real life is depressing enough. So what's in your magazine?"

Dyers flicked through the pages.

"I haven't read much of it. There's something about Paulette Goddard, although I don't know what she's in."

He found the page he was looking for and stopped.

"Here we are – this is the one I was thinking about seeing. It's called *The Westerner*, with Gary Cooper starring as a drifter in the Wild West. It's on at the Regal, Marble Arch – last showing at seven-twenty. That's a bit early if a chap wants to eat beforehand, though."

"They all have to finish by nine o'clock now, because of the air raids, don't they?"

"Yes, although I believe if you go east of here beyond Ilford they're allowed to stay open later. I suppose they assume there'll be fewer bombs that far out, although I can't say I'm convinced. In any case, Essex cinemas aren't a patch on the West End."

Neither of them spoke for a few moments, then Dyers closed his magazine and put it down on the seat beside him. He cleared his throat.

"I say, I hope this doesn't sound terribly forward, but I just wondered: would you possibly like to come with me to see it?"

"Well, yes," said Miss Hornby, "as a matter of fact that would be delightful. Thank you very much."

"Jolly good. Are you free on Saturday?"

"I believe I am. I shall look forward to it."

A fresh smile began to cross Miss Hornby's face, but it disappeared in an instant as she saw Detective Inspector Jago return, accompanied by Beatrice Cartwright.

CHAPTER 22

Monday morning. Jago tried to picture a million men and women from London's suburbs crowding into trains to make their way to the metropolis for the start of another working week. These days, of course, they might discover their regular line to Waterloo, Victoria or whatever other destination they had in the city had been bombed overnight. When they finally arrived, there was every chance of finding their familiar workplace obliterated by high explosives. The one thing that would be constant, however, was that when their alarm clock rang it would be Monday morning. They'd have had their day of rest and it would be the start of a new working week.

Jago wondered what it would be like to be a solicitor's clerk or an office manager, knowing that every Sunday was a day off. It wasn't that way in the CID – you simply worked the hours that the case required. True, he hadn't had to work all day yesterday, but even so, the days all seemed to merge into one. Maybe he'd get a day off next week.

Going out for the evening with Dyers yesterday had turned out to be a pleasant break from work. They'd spent a couple of hours or so catching up on past times and treated each other, as it now seemed to him in the harsh light of day, to perhaps just one or two more drinks than they should have done. That could have been what helped him sleep, but whatever the reason, today he'd woken a little later than he'd intended. That was his excuse for troubling Rita for nothing more than a cup of tea and a couple of rounds of toast for breakfast today, but he knew he had other reasons for not wanting too much of a conversation.

He knew the pose well. Rita had positioned the cup of tea carefully on the table before him and then arranged a plate, a rack of toast, a small dish of butter and another of plum jam around it, and placed a knife at right angles to the edge of the table. She'd nudged the sugar bowl a little closer, then taken one step back. Now she stood with her hands folded across her pinny, head cocked slightly to one side and chin drawn back, her eyebrows knitted in the stern, inquisitorial expression she would use with a naughty boy caught red-handed from whom an explanation was due.

"Well," she said, as if he should have confessed by now, "what is it?"

"What's what?" he said.

"You're not yourself. You look down in the mouth. Is something on your mind?"

"There's always a lot on my mind, Rita. It's part of the job."

"This doesn't look like the job to me. I've seen you sitting there thinking before, but not with that sad look in your eyes. That's a look that tells me there's a woman in it somewhere. You be honest with me: are you sweet on that American girl?"

"You don't beat about the bush, do you?"

"If your friends won't talk straight with you, who will?"

"I know, and I appreciate your concern. I'm not sure I can give you an answer, though."

"You don't give much away, do you? Sometimes I think you keep all the doors into your life locked and barred. You don't want to let anyone in."

"Perhaps you're right."

"You've been hurt, haven't you? I can tell. People change when they've been hurt – whatever it is, they don't want it to happen again, so they put up all the defences they can. Is that you?"

"I don't know, Rita, but it's kind of you to care."

"Of course I care."

"I think I've just had a bit of a shock – something's happened that I wasn't expecting. I can't tell you the details, but it's rather taken the wind out of my sails."

"That's all right, dear, you don't need to give me chapter and verse. I understand. I sometimes think I've understood everything everyone suffers in the whole world since I lost my hubby. There's some shocks nothing can prepare you for, and nothing can help you with."

"You know, Rita, I don't know if your Walter ever told you any stories about France, but I'll tell you one of mine. We'd been in a reserve area for a while but then we got orders to move up to the front line. This was when I was still a private, and over the previous few weeks I'd palled up with another lad in the same platoon. One morning we were standing in the trench, having a chat and a smoke – I used to in those days – and he was laughing at some joke he'd just cracked. We were waiting for the lieutenant to blow his whistle. Moments later we're over the top and advancing on the German line. Next thing I know, he's dropped to the ground just three feet to my left, lying on his back, not moving. I looked down. He was dead: shot in the side of his head."

"Walter only got home once on leave before he was killed," said Rita. "He didn't talk about it much: not one for stories, was Walter."

"Most of the things he saw probably couldn't be told, Rita," said Jago. "Do you know what I couldn't get straight in my head that day? It was that one moment he was a person, talking, laughing, thinking, and the next he was just a piece of dead flesh. He wouldn't ever do anything again. The thing that was inside him that made him a person had gone, disappeared somewhere, ceased to exist. I didn't really know much about him, but he was my pal, and I'd lost him."

"My mum used to say she sometimes wondered if it was better not to love anyone, then you wouldn't have to grieve when you lost them."

"Yes, but it wasn't as though I loved him: he was just a friend I'd known for a few weeks. There were plenty of men at the front who lost brothers; some of them more than one. I had none to lose, but

I had lost him. And the thing I couldn't understand was that he was gone, just like that, in the blink of an eye. It happened again lots of times later, but I think after that I never got close to anyone. I made sure I didn't get too friendly, because I didn't want the pain of that loss again."

Rita looked at him more gently.

"I know you don't want to tell me, and I don't want to intrude, but that American girl – she's all right, isn't she? Hasn't been caught in an air raid or something?"

Jago looked up and gave her a smile.

"No, she's fine. But there's more than one way of losing someone, isn't there?"

CHAPTER 23

The first face Jago saw on entering West Ham police station was that of Station Sergeant Tompkins.

"Not you again, Frank?" he said. "Haven't they got anyone else to do this job? You were here yesterday too. I thought I was the only one who never went home."

"Don't fret, sir," said Tompkins. "I had Saturday off. I thought I'd put my feet up with a nice bottle of ale to revive the soul and enjoy the last of the sunshine in the back yard."

"And did it?"

"Did it what?"

"Revive your soul."

"Not exactly. In fact I never got the cap off the bottle. It turned out the missus had a few plans of her own for me. Some little jobs that needed doing round the house, like. I came in yesterday to recover. How did you get on with that RAF mate of yours?"

"We had a very pleasant evening, thanks."

"Reviving your souls?"

"Yes, at the Royal Oak – they've got a nice saloon bar there. I always enjoy catching up with an old friend."

The side of Tompkins' mouth twitched into a hint of a grin.

"Well, in that case I've got a nice surprise for you. Another old friend of yours has just dropped in to see you."

***

Jago opened the door and saw the back of a seated man. He was wearing an old jacket that strained tight against his substantial form. The man rose from his chair and turned to face him, clutching a cloth cap in both hands.

"Well, I never," said Jago. "This must be a first for you, mustn't it? Something I thought I'd never see – Harry Parker enters a police station voluntarily."

"Come off it, Mr Jago," said Harry. "Don't get started. That's exactly what I've done. I've come here off my own bat, to support the police in their noble fight to keep crime off the streets."

"And off the bomb-sites?"

"What do you mean?"

"I mean I'm still wondering whether that dead body was the only fishy thing on that site in Tinto Road."

"Well, that's where you're wrong, see. I've come in because I think I've got something to help you with that."

Harry put his cap down on the desk and reached into his jacket. He pulled out an object about a foot long in a brown paper bag.

"I've just come off shift with the rescue party and thought I ought to pop in here with this before I go home for a kip."

He handed the package to Jago.

"I found it, like," he added.

Jago opened the paper bag and took out a woman's handbag. It was made of black leather and was dirty, dusty, and battered-looking.

"Where did you get this, Harry?" he said.

"I told you – I found it."

"Where?"

"In Tinto Road. On that site where we were working after the bombs dropped."

"When did you find it?"

"On Friday, when we were clearing up there."

"But it's Monday now. Why the delay in reporting it? We're investigating a suspected murder, and I'd like to know why you seem to have withheld a potentially important piece of evidence."

Parker took a step backwards and bumped into the chair. He reached out to steady it with his hand.

"Now look, Mr Jago, I've got nothing to do with no murder. I wouldn't be here if I did, would I? Don't forget, I'm the one that reported the body. I just thought this was a bit of lost property, and I was going to hand it in, only I forgot about it. Then I was thinking yesterday about that dead girl and I suddenly thought the bag might be hers. So here I am – to help you."

"All right, Harry, no need to get agitated. Just tell me exactly where you found it."

"It was on that pile of rubble where we found the woman. Not close to her, though – it was over towards the side near the first house that was still standing, about five or six yards away. I took it home for safe keeping, like."

Jago put the handbag back into its brown paper bag and looked him in the eye.

"I hope that's true, Harry. I'd hate to think you might have been meaning to keep it. That would be stealing, and that's a very serious matter nowadays, especially for someone in your position who's supposed to be helping people who've been bombed out. There's men who've got twelve months' hard labour for less. And if the court decided it was looting, you could be shot. I wouldn't like to lose an old pal like you just because he still couldn't keep his hands off other people's property."

"No, no," said Harry, "you've got it all wrong. It's not like that at all. Honest, Mr Jago, I'm not like that any more."

"I shall give you the benefit of the doubt again, Harry," said Jago. "Just don't give me any reason to regret that."

***

As soon as he'd sent Harry Parker on his way Jago took the handbag to the CID office, where he found Cradock reading the *Daily Mirror*.

"Morning, Peter," he said. "You got nothing better to do than read the paper?"

167

"Sorry, guv'nor," said Cradock. "I was trying to educate myself, keep up with what's happening in the world."

"Well, I suppose you've got to start somewhere. I'm not sure the *Mirror* is your best guide to world affairs, though. It's not that long ago it was telling us we all ought to join the Blackshirts."

"Doesn't say that now, though, sir, as far as I can see."

"No, well it would be a bit daft of them if they did, wouldn't it? But I'm probably being unfair – it must be five or six years ago they said that, and I'm sure they've changed their minds since. Back then they reckoned what the Nazis were doing in Germany was just 'patriotic enthusiasm', but I think we can all see where patriotic enthusiasm can get you now."

"It's not wrong to be patriotic, though, is it?"

"Of course not. But you can be patriotic without being stupid and vicious, that's all."

Jago put his brown paper package on the desk and pulled out his chair. He sat down and leaned back with his hands behind his head.

"So, how did you get on at Mary's flat?"

"No luck, guv'nor," said Cradock. "She kept it very tidy. No clutter anywhere – which was a mercy, I suppose, but I didn't find any wedding pictures. Perhaps she wasn't a wedding kind of person."

"Perhaps."

"In actual fact, I didn't find any photos at all – well, just one, to be precise. I thought with her being a spinster there might be family pictures or something, but no."

"Except one, you said."

"Yes, but I don't think that was important. It was a photo of an actor – one of those publicity shots, I suppose. It was signed – 'Sincerely yours, Hadleigh Crane'. That sounds like an actor's kind of name, doesn't it? He's probably resting, these days, what with the theatres being shut down. That's what they call it, isn't it? Resting – when they're out of work?"

"Yes. He'll be more than resting, though. He's very likely locked

168

up in Brixton prison or Wormwood Scrubs or somewhere like that with Mosley and his Blackshirt mob by now – he was quite pally with them, I believe."

"I'm surprised you've heard of him, sir," said Cradock. "He's the sort they call a matinée idol – not quite up your street, I would've thought."

"I keep my finger on the pulse," said Jago.

He leaned forward in his chair and pulled the brown paper bag towards him across the desk.

"Now I've got something to show you. Nothing to do with matinée idols, not by a long chalk. This has just been handed in by Harry Parker, former local window cleaner and now public hero, if we're to believe him."

He took the handbag from the bag and set it on the desk.

"I see," said Cradock. "You still don't think he's as straight as he says, then, sir?"

"Maybe he is, maybe he isn't. I just remember the days when he used to tell his window-cleaning customers he'd keep an eye on their place while they were away, and then when they came back they'd discover it'd been turned over and all their valuables had mysteriously disappeared."

"So there was a connection, yes?"

"Too right there was, and the connection was Harry's light fingers. But be that as it may, he brought this in this morning. Says he found it on the bomb-site where Mary's body was and meant to hand it in but forgot."

"Fits the description that Miss Hornby woman at Everson's gave us," said Cradock. "Do you believe Harry?"

"I believe he found it, but as for the rest – well, let's just say I'll keep an open mind on the subject."

"A leopard can't change its stripes, eh, sir?"

"Spots, Cradock. A leopard can't change its spots. Have you never seen a leopard?"

"No, sir."

"Not likely to, I suppose, round here. But they don't have stripes. You're thinking of zebras."

"Yes, sir."

Jago opened the handbag and emptied the contents on the table. He picked up a pencil and began to poke through the items.

"Let's see," he said. "An identity card in the name of Mary Watkins, which suggests it's her bag. A bunch of keys – could these be the ones Miss Hornby mentioned? And this. That's the one we've been looking for. What do you make of that?"

He used the pencil to push a photograph across the desk. Cradock took a clean white handkerchief from his pocket and used it to pick up the photo. He looked at it and felt an immediate sense of disappointment. It was a small black-and-white print, just two inches square, and it looked as though it had been taken either with a very cheap camera or by a very poor photographer, or both. It had a soapy look to it, and although it clearly showed a bride and groom in their wedding clothes, the faces were too small and unfocused to recognize.

"Not the sort of picture you'd put in the *Police Gazette* for a missing person or a suspect," said Cradock.

"No," said Jago. "I wouldn't be able to say who either of those people are. But if this is what upset Mary, she must have known the man well enough to recognize him."

"So we need to try and find out who that man is," said Cradock.

"I think so, yes," said Jago. "And there's another thing. Angela said she was away from the table dancing when Celia showed the photo to Mary, but Celia says she thought Angela was still sitting at the table with her and Mary when she got the photo out."

"Could that be significant?"

"It may or may not be significant, but it's certainly inconsistent. They can't both be right."

CHAPTER 24

The phone rang. Cradock jumped up and answered it.

"Yes, he's here. I'll tell him she's arrived." He put the phone down. "Miss Appleton's arrived, sir," he said. "Says she's got an appointment with you to talk about local crime."

Cradock noticed that Jago looked hesitant, as if he didn't know what to say.

"Is something wrong, sir?"

"No, no," said Jago. "Go and fetch her, but tell her I haven't got long."

Cradock departed, and within five minutes he was back with Dorothy in tow. He showed her to a seat in front of the desk and hovered, unsure whether Jago would want him to stay. He gave a sideways nod towards the door a couple of times, but Jago shook his head. Cradock sat down again.

"Thank you so much for sparing me a few minutes," said Dorothy. "I'll be as quick as possible. It's just for this article I'm researching on the way the crime rate has fluctuated since the war began. If you can give me some figures for this borough, that would be really helpful."

Jago pulled a buff-coloured folder from a wire tray on his desk.

"I, er, put a few figures together for you yesterday, and some other anecdotal information. You should find something useful in there."

He pushed the folder across the desk to her.

"Thank you," said Dorothy. "I'm interested in petty theft and what you might call the black market, too. For example, I've heard there's quite a lot of pilfering going on, now that there are shortages of various things, and I'd like to know how that kind of market

171

works. Do people take things for themselves, or are they mainly selling them on to strangers? How do they do it?"

Jago had promised to help her, but that was last week, and now he felt a reluctance to lengthen the conversation more than was absolutely necessary.

"Well, typically someone will sidle up to you in a pub and offer you something on the cheap."

"I'd like to see that, get a feel for the ambience of an East End pub."

"They're not necessarily good places for a woman to go on her own."

"I've told you before, I can look after myself."

"Yes, I know, but some of the men in those pubs – when they see a woman coming in on her own they can jump to the wrong conclusion."

"So it would be better if I were accompanied by a man?"

"Now wait a minute…"

"In that case it's a deal. Would tonight be convenient for you?"

"No, I'm busy tonight, and tomorrow too."

"Wednesday, then."

"I'm really not sure I –"

"But what would your divisional detective inspector say if he heard you'd been sending me into a pub without an escort? I'm sure I recall you saying he was expecting you to look after me."

Not for the first time, Jago felt outmanoeuvred by Dorothy. He could feel anger brewing inside him. If he had felt betrayed when he saw her kissing a young RAF officer at the dance, now he felt used. What was worse, she seemed to find it amusing. He was not best pleased that Cradock was within earshot and probably enjoying the whole scene.

He controlled his expression. He did not want to give any indication of what he was feeling. He wasn't a kid any more. He would be polite and self-controlled.

"Very well."

"Where shall we go?"

"There's a place called the Railway Tavern, in Canning Town. I've told Cradock to do some observation down there in the next day or two. If you get the train over here I'll meet you at the station at six o'clock or so and drive you down there. We might have time for a drink before the air raids start."

If Cradock's going to be keeping an eye on the place, he thought, this'll be a good opportunity to take a look at it myself. Combine business with pleasure. But he didn't expect it would be much of a pleasure – he just wasn't sure he would be able to relax with her.

Dorothy chatted on breezily, oblivious of his turmoil.

"By the way," she said, "how did you get on with that photo you showed me? The one of the two women. Did you find that other woman I saw at the table with them?"

Jago was relieved that he could talk about the case, not about themselves or the dance. Had she seen him? He thought not, but couldn't be sure.

"Yes, I did," he said. "Cradock and I were just talking about it. A handbag was handed in today, and I believe it belonged to the dead woman. We've found a photo inside it, and I think this may have been the one you saw the woman who was murdered take out of the other woman's handbag."

"I'm getting confused now: too many handbags and photos."

"It's simple. You said you saw Mary, the woman who's been murdered, take a photo out of another woman's handbag. We've now found the woman that photo belonged to – she's called Celia – but it's turned up in Mary's handbag, which confirms what you saw: that Mary removed a photo from Celia's handbag and put it in her own. And here's the handbag, handed in this morning."

Dorothy glanced at the handbag.

"And the photo?" she said.

"Here. It's on the table."

"May I see?"

"Certainly."

He slid the photo across the desk, using his pencil again, and then straightened it so that she could see it the right way up.

"No touching, please," he said. "We don't want to get your fingerprints on it."

Dorothy peered closely at the photo.

"Not a very good snapshot, is it? Not the sort of quality we'd use in the *Boston Post*. But do you know who these people are?"

"I'm not at all sure. If what Celia says is true, that should be her there in the bride's dress. But to me it looks nothing like her. You can't make out her facial features, and the hair is short and looks dark, whereas Celia has long hair, and she's a blonde."

"Do you know when it was taken?"

"She said she got married in February 1938, so if it's her, that's when it was."

"That may explain it, then. That's more than two and a half years ago. I don't know whether you've noticed, John, but women's hairstyles change. I mean, when I was fourteen I had cootie garages. Can you believe it?"

Jago caught sight of Cradock's face and almost laughed. It registered a look of complete bafflement. Jago himself was no wiser, however.

"I'm not sure whether I can believe it," he said, "because I haven't the faintest idea what it means. Is it something American?"

"Cootie garages? Well, a cootie is a slang word. Cooties are lice, the kind you get in your hair if you don't look after it."

"I know all about lice," said Jago. "But garages?"

"A garage is where you park your car. You have them over here, don't you?"

"Yes, but —"

"So a cootie garage is where you park your cooties."

He still looked puzzled.

174

"Okay," said Dorothy. "It was a hairstyle lots of girls went for in the twenties. We rolled our hair round over our ears – it looked like earphones, and people called them cootie garages, as if they might be a good place to keep your lice."

"I see," said Jago. "But what's that got to do with Celia and the photo? She wasn't wearing that style."

"That's my point. Cootie garages were all the rage when I was a kid, but now I wouldn't be seen dead in them. Like I said, women's hairstyles change. Not so long ago the only things girls wanted were bobs and crops and fingerwaves – everything short and close to the head. Women today are going more for long hair and waves, and those old tight crimps are as out of date as Blucher shoes. But a couple of years ago you'd still have seen quite a lot of short hairstyles. If that was Celia in the photograph, she probably doesn't look like that now."

"But what about the colour? She's a blonde, but here in the photo it looks dark."

Dorothy looked at him with surprise.

"Now, I know your police work keeps you very busy, but there are some things going on in the world out there that you really should know about. I'm going to share a women's secret with you. Okay?"

"Of course."

He felt irritated. He wasn't accustomed to being teased in front of Cradock and he wasn't enjoying the experience.

"Here it is, then. There are blondes and blondes in this world. The natural and the not so natural. She may be the peroxide type."

"Now I see what you mean," said Jago. "Peroxide. You're the second person who's used that word with me this week."

"Well, yes, it's what women who want to turn blonde overnight use. Your Celia might have decided she wanted a change. Next time you see her, check her roots and her eyebrows. If they're still dark, she's probably a fake blonde. Millions of women do it."

"Do you?"

"No: I prefer things the way nature intended. I used to do fancy tricks with my hair, but that was before I became a war correspondent. Once I got to Spain I realized it wasn't a place to start messing around with wave sets – the less hair maintenance I needed to put in the better. Since then I've been plain and natural all the way – well, maybe I give nature a little helping hand when I'm in a place where you can get a half-decent perm, but that's all."

"Right. I think DC Cradock and I are better educated than we were about ladies' hairstyles, but I'm not sure we're any the wiser about this case – except that you've helped to confirm that Celia could well be telling the truth when she says this is her wedding photo."

"So what I said was useful?"

"Yes, I think so. But to be honest, all I know is that this photo may have some connection with Mary's death. But equally, it may not."

"Do you have some angle yet on what this case is all about?"

"Not really. All we've got is two sisters who didn't get on, one married, one not – and now one dead."

"Like your Boleyn girls, then?"

"I suppose so, yes – but that's not much help when we're trying to solve a crime in 1940. Peter, I think you and I need to talk to Celia about this photo. Dorothy, we must say goodbye."

CHAPTER 25

Cradock took the wheel for their journey to Ilford, a small Essex town three miles to the east of West Ham. He enjoyed the opportunity to drive the Riley, although the journey itself was undistinguished – Jago's directions took them through the usual sprawl of houses, factories and railway lines that marked London's rapid eastward expansion over the last half-century.

"So she works for Ilford, the film people?" he said as they approached their destination.

"That's what she told me," said Jago. "Said we could meet in her lunch break at twelve-thirty. We're right on time."

"They're a big company, aren't they? Seems odd for them to be in a little place like this."

"I believe the man who started it moved out here because there was no dust in the air – which I suppose makes sense if you're manufacturing photographic plates."

"Right. Not the sort of thing you'd want to try in West Ham – I don't like to think what I'm breathing in down there sometimes. Maybe he thought Ilford was a bit more out in the country and the air was cleaner."

"Yes. Mind you, I met an old girl once who used to work here in the early days and she said the silver they used in the production process made people's skin go blue. Makes you think of the Bryant & May girls and their phossy jaw, doesn't it?"

"Phossy jaw? Was that a case, sir? I think it must've been before my time."

"It wasn't a case, but it should've been. No time for that now, though: we're here."

They had arrived at the company's headquarters, a large brick building in Roden Street. Cradock stopped the car outside it, and the two men got out. It didn't take long to find where Celia worked: a modern two-storey structure had the words "Sales Office" proclaimed in big letters across the front. A woman in a brown coat was waiting by the entrance.

"That looks like her," said Jago.

The woman saw them. She walked along a path round a neatly laid lawn to meet them and shook their hands.

"Hello, Inspector. I'm afraid I haven't got long," she said. "Can we go somewhere away from here to talk?"

"Of course," said Jago. "Where would you prefer?"

"We can go half a mile one way to Valentine's Park, or about the same distance the other way to the City of London Cemetery. It's all the same to me."

"I think the park sounds more attractive," said Jago.

"Okay, then, follow me."

Celia strode away quickly, leaving the men in her wake. Jago increased his pace to catch up with her, studying the back of her head on the way. Dorothy was right. Celia's hair was blonde, but its roots were darker. Fancy her knowing that, he thought.

Within a few minutes they reached the park. Celia led them in past a lake and towards the far side, where a fingerpost sign said the open-air swimming pool was. To his right Jago could see a large area covered in what looked to be the feather-like leaves of carrots.

"The council's turned some of the park into allotments," said Celia without stopping. "Growing vegetables for the war effort. All right for people who've got time for that kind of thing, but I haven't."

"Have you had much bombing here?" said Cradock.

"None in the park itself yet, but we've had a few round Ilford. Not as bad as where you are, though. I go down Canning Town way from time to time – got friends there – so I've a pretty good idea what it's like. See that?"

Cradock followed her pointing hand but could see only grass and the bathing pool beyond.

"No. See what?"

"That's where all those people got killed last year – just a couple of weeks before the war started. It wasn't the Germans, though. More like nature giving us a taste of things to come."

"What happened?"

"It was in August, about five o'clock on a Monday afternoon. I'd knocked off work a bit early and come over here for a breath of fresh air. Ordinary summer's day it was: lots of mums and kids swimming, playing. But then there was a thunderstorm. There was a kind of shelter just over there, and loads of people crowded in under it to get out of the rain – but it was made of corrugated iron and it got struck by lightning. Seven killed, two of them just kids. It was chaos – dead bodies, people with terrible burns, children screaming. Just like we've seen in the air raids. I tried to help, but there was nothing you could do for some of them. I'd never seen anything like it, and it was all over the papers, but now worse things happen every day."

"A terrible tragedy all the same," said Jago. "Now, Mrs Berry, I know you haven't much time, so can we stop here? I just want to ask you a couple of questions."

"Of course."

She stopped in her tracks, and Cradock only narrowly avoided colliding with her.

"We can sit there beside the pool," she said, nodding towards some empty chairs.

They crossed a patch of grass and sat down. Jago pulled a package from inside his coat.

"Since I last spoke to you someone's handed in a woman's handbag, and we've found a photo in it. Can you take a look, please, and tell me if you recognize either item?"

Celia took the handbag and photo from him and gave them a quick glance. She handed the bag back with a shake of her head.

"No."

"Take your time, please."

"I don't think that'll help. I can't be sure whether I've seen it before or not. I don't take much notice of other women's handbags. But that's my photo, and it's my wedding. That's me and Richard. Do you mind telling me where you found it?"

"In Mary Watkins' handbag. It was found not far from her body."

"And you think it's got something to do with why someone killed her?"

"Not necessarily. We're simply trying to find out more about Mary and what might have been on her mind at the time."

Celia was still holding the photo. She looked at it in silence, as if it had sparked some train of thought in her mind. Eventually she spoke, in little more than a murmur.

"It must have been her who took it then, stole it from me. That Mary."

"Do you have any idea why she might do that?"

"No, not really. I remember telling you she looked a bit surprised when she saw it – it was as if maybe she'd recognized someone she knew. The only thing I can think is that she recognized Richard. But she went all serious, like I said. Then she asked me his name."

"When we spoke about this before, you didn't mention her asking you his name. You said she didn't say anything."

"Did I? I must have meant she didn't say anything when she looked at the photo. She asked me his name afterwards."

"And you told her?"

"Yes, and when I told her, she just went quiet again. It was a bit spooky, to be honest. Why do you think she did that, Inspector?"

"I don't know. It may be significant, or it may mean nothing at all."

"I suppose so. I shouldn't read too much into it. And you said before you thought she might have been murdered. Do you still think that?"

"That's what we suspect, yes."

"Well, well. They say your sins'll find you out, don't they?"

"Why do you say that?"

"Oh, I don't know. I suppose I'm just surprised at what some people get up to. Although actually, after having a husband like Richard nothing surprises me."

"Meaning?"

"Let's just say there's a lot of deceit in the world, and sometimes a bit of truth doesn't do any harm."

"When we spoke at the dance, you said you took what your husband said with a pinch of salt – about his wartime service, for example. You said he might have made the whole thing up. Do you have any evidence that he wasn't telling the truth?"

"I can't say, really. I dare say something happened. I just wonder whether he dressed it up a bit, to make it sound grander. Some men do that, don't they? Want to be heroes, especially if they're villains. I don't even know if he was wounded – I mean, I wasn't there, was I? He might've got injured some other way, unless he was born like that. The only thing I know for a fact is that he's missing the last two fingers on his left hand, so something must've happened. Why? Is it significant?"

"Thank you, Mrs Berry, you've been most helpful. We must let you get back to your work, but before we go, may I ask one more small question on a totally different subject? It's a rather personal matter, I'm afraid."

"Fire away."

"I just wondered whether you use anything to colour your hair."

Celia laughed.

"My roots are showing, are they? Very observant of you. Yes, I use a drop of peroxide from time to time, but I must be a bit behind, mustn't I?"

"Is it difficult to get hold of?"

"Can be these days. It's a bit scarce in the shops, but it's not rationed or anything. You sometimes have to shop around to get some, but you can usually find it somewhere. I know girls who pay a bit over the odds for things like that from what you might call private suppliers."

"Do you know of any such suppliers yourself?"

"Oh, Inspector, fancy asking a question like that. A girl's got to have some secrets, hasn't she?"

Celia pulled back the sleeve of her coat and glanced at her watch.

"Oh dear," she said. "Look at the time – I must get back to work. Sorry to rush off."

Before Jago could reply, she was skittering back down the path towards the park entrance.

CHAPTER 26

"Guv'nor," said Cradock, "are you thinking what I'm thinking?"

Jago waited until he had seen Celia Berry disappear from view before turning back to the detective constable.

"Thinking what you're thinking?" he said, pursing his lips and inclining his head a little to one side. "Difficult to say. I often wonder what you're thinking, Peter – it intrigues me. But judging by the evidence to date I would say that the likelihood of our thoughts coinciding is not great. Give me a clue."

"Well, the fingers, of course."

"The fingers?"

"Yes – George Fletcher and Richard Berry's fingers. We've got a case that two men are mixed up in –"

"We don't know that they're mixed up in it. One is married to the victim's sister and the other is the absent husband of a woman who briefly met the victim. That could be regarded as just a tenuous connection."

"Yes, but both of them have got the last two fingers of their left hand missing. That's what Celia said, wasn't it? And it's what we saw when we met George Fletcher."

"The latter we've seen with our own eyes, but the former we haven't. In any case, there are plenty of men of their age with war wounds like that. Could it be a coincidence?"

"Two men in the same town with the same injury, yes, but surely not in the same case. That must be too much to be a coincidence."

"So what are you saying?"

"Well, it's obvious, isn't it? They must be the same bloke."

"What we've heard doesn't quite add up, though, does it?"

"In what sense?"

"Well, Celia Berry says her husband lost his fingers when he was in the Navy, at the Battle of Jutland. What date was that?"

Cradock's face was blank.

"Er, sorry, sir, I don't know. Before my time. Is it important?"

"Yes, it is. The battle was on the last day of May and the first of June in 1916, so that would be the time and place where Richard Berry lost his. But George Fletcher told us he got his wound when he was in the merchant navy, and the merchant navy wouldn't have been involved in the battle. And more importantly, he said he didn't go to sea until 1917, so he couldn't have been there in 1916."

"So do you mean that ruins our theory?"

"No, not necessarily. It would do if both George and Celia were telling the truth, but we can't assume that. And if Celia did tell us what she believed to be true, it would also depend on whether Richard Berry had told her the truth too. But in any case, what she's said is just hearsay, so it's not admissible as evidence anyway."

"But you're saying it's impossible to be sure."

"Yes. Mind you, having met George Fletcher, I wouldn't take everything he says at face value. On balance, at this stage I'd say your theory is an intriguing possibility."

"And it would be an interesting situation, wouldn't it?"

"Yes, but we'd need some stronger evidence to prove it."

Jago began to walk back towards the park entrance. Cradock fell in beside him, striding along eagerly with his face turned towards his boss.

"Just for the sake of argument, though," said Cradock, "supposing it was true. The person in the picture who surprised her must have been Richard Berry. But suppose that wasn't why she was surprised. What if the person she recognized was George Fletcher – her sister's husband? That certainly would've been a turn-up for the book as far as Mary was concerned."

"But everyone's said Mary had never met George Fletcher,

and she didn't go to the wedding. She couldn't recognize George Fletcher if she'd never seen him."

"But what if Mary had actually found out who Susan had married – or maybe she even found out before the wedding. It's possible, isn't it?"

"Yes, the fact that she wasn't at the wedding doesn't necessarily mean she'd never seen him. But the problem is we've no proof that she did, and we can't ask her now."

"All right. But let's say she saw Richard Berry in the photograph and recognized her sister's husband. She'd have just discovered he was a bigamist. That would be more than enough reason to make her look shocked, wouldn't it? And what might she have done with that information? Something that would get her killed?"

"Yes, but that's just supposition."

"You're always telling me to ask the 'What if?' questions. Shouldn't we look into it?"

"Yes, Peter, we should – and your reasoning is good. Now let's see if we can substantiate it. You'd better start by checking the two weddings actually took place. If Mary had discovered some skulduggery going on it would put a very different complexion on things. I'm still wondering what Celia meant when she talked about deceit just now. We've only got her word for it that she was married, and these days a woman might have all sorts of reasons for saying she's married when she's not. Celia told me herself that she wears a wedding ring to keep the men at bay, and that wedding photo wasn't very clear, so you can imagine that if she wanted to deceive them any old photo would do."

"And she didn't even have the same colour hair in that picture as she does now. How do we know she's telling the truth?"

"Steady on, Peter. A woman's allowed to dye her hair if she wants to. That's not a reflection on her character – we can't infer she's a liar just because she wants to look blonde. Now then, I want you to find out what the parish church is for where George and

185

Susan Fletcher live and get over there. Find out if they got married on the twenty-seventh of July – ask the vicar to show you the register and check what names it gives for them. Then get hold of the vicar at St Luke's Church in Wolverhampton on the telephone and ask him to check his wedding register for the seventeenth of February 1938 to see if there's a Richard Berry marrying a Celia whatever her name was then."

"Very good, sir."

"But first I think we'll see whether Mr Fletcher's company can spare him for a little while so that we can have a chat with him and his wife."

CHAPTER 27

A snub-nosed Morris van was parked on the road outside the house. Its freshly washed black bodywork contrasted sharply with the white stripes that had been painted round the edges of its mudguards to comply with the blackout regulations. The words "Empire Office Services" and the company's address were also painted neatly in white on the side panel, together with a telephone number on the Maryland exchange, creating an impression of orderly professionalism far removed from the scene Jago and Cradock had encountered at the company's offices.

"Looks as though George is home," said Cradock.

"Yes," said Jago. "Now, I don't want you asking him whether he's a bigamist or whether he's got two fingers missing because he's really someone else, or any other clever questions like that. We don't want to frighten Mrs Fletcher unnecessarily, and if all that's true I'd like to keep it up our sleeves for the time being. Understood?"

"Yes, guv'nor."

At a nod from Jago, Cradock leaned forward to knock on the door. They heard footsteps pacing down the hall behind it, and it opened a crack to reveal George Fletcher, still in his work suit.

"Come in," he said, looking down the street to left and right. "I hope you won't make a habit of this. The company don't like me taking time off in the daytime, and if the neighbours get wind of the fact that you're police there'll be rumours flying up and down this road like nobody's business. A bit toffee-nosed, some of them. You know the sort."

He ushered them in and closed the door behind them.

"Come on through. My wife will put the kettle on."

"Thank you, Mr Fletcher."

They sat in the living room, on the sofa as before, and waited until Susan Fletcher arrived with a tray bearing tea in dainty china cups and saucers which she set on an occasional table beside them.

"So, what can we do for you?" asked Fletcher. "I'm hoping this won't take long – I've got to get back to work."

"We'll be as quick as we can," said Jago. "We'd just like to ask a few more questions about your sister-in-law."

He took a spoonful of sugar from the sugar bowl and stirred it into his cup, then turned to Susan.

"Very kind of you, Mrs Fletcher. This is such a nice house. Your husband was telling me you inherited it from your parents."

Susan shot a glance at her husband. Jago thought he detected both surprise and irritation in her expression.

"Don't look at me like that," said Fletcher. "He already knew, so I assumed you must have told him."

Susan switched her eyes back to Jago.

"What's that got to do with anything?" she said.

"Not necessarily anything," said Jago. "But is it the case?"

"Yes, if you must know. I told you my parents died three years ago. It was their home, and I grew up here."

"Did they leave it just to you, or to you and your sister?"

"I'm not sure I like what you're implying, Inspector."

"I'm not implying anything, Mrs Fletcher – simply asking."

"They left it to both of us."

"And did you live here alone for three years until your marriage?"

"Yes, but I really can't see what the relevance of all this is."

"I just wondered whether your sister had come to live here with you. After all, a big place like this – she could have lived here for nothing instead of paying rent all that time somewhere else."

"The reason for that is very simple, Inspector. My sister preferred her own company, and she wanted to live on her own, in her own place."

"Did you buy her out? I mean, if she had no intention of living here –"

Susan interrupted him.

"Mr Jago, I was twenty years old when my parents died. What do you think I would have bought her out with? I didn't have any money. Mary was quite happy for me to live here, and she still owned the house jointly with me."

"I see. But now that she has unfortunately died, I assume the whole property belongs to you."

"I suppose so, yes, but I haven't had time even to think about that. It's of no importance to me."

"And strictly speaking, I suppose that now you're married, the house belongs to you and your husband."

Fletcher jumped from his seat.

"Now look here, Inspector," he said. "You've tried that line once already and I told you I didn't like what you were insinuating."

Susan stood too and looked angrily at Fletcher.

"Have you been discussing this behind my back already?" she said.

Jago remained on the sofa and spoke quietly.

"Come now, Mr and Mrs Fletcher, these are perfectly normal questions in an enquiry like this, and I'm not trying to insinuate anything. Please sit down."

The couple complied, but with an air of reluctance. Jago sensed an atmosphere of residual tension between them. Fletcher reached for the silver case in his pocket and selected a cigarette. He lit it and drew in the smoke. As he exhaled, Jago could tell that this time he had chosen one of the Turkish variety.

"Must you smoke those ghastly things, George?" said Susan. "They make the place smell like a – well, like an unsavoury place."

"Brothel? Is that the word you were looking for?" said Fletcher. "Well, you're wrong. These are perfectly respectable in Turkey. I've enjoyed them ever since I first smoked one in a very fine hotel in Constantinople during the British occupation."

He smiled across the room at Jago and Cradock.

"I'm sure the inspector will recall, although perhaps not his colleague, who is probably too young to know about it, like my wife. It was in 1919, after the Armistice of Mudros. That marked the end of hostilities with the Ottoman Empire, and I was on the first of Sir John Ellerman's ships to arrive there –"

Jago judged it prudent to nip a potentially long story in the bud.

"Thank you, Mr Fletcher, but as you said, you do have to get back to work, and I don't want to detain you unduly."

"Of course, Inspector, please carry on," said Fletcher. He gave a casual wave of the cigarette, as if granting permission, and then picked a strand of tobacco from between his teeth and discarded it on the carpet.

"I recall you telling me that you and Mrs Fletcher first met on a blind date," said Jago. "When was that?"

"It was in April," said Fletcher. "Just after we first heard the Germans had invaded Norway. Chamberlain said we were sending the Navy in, and I remember thinking there'd be trouble. It was mad to think we could stop the Germans when their communication lines were so much shorter than ours. We lost a lot of ships, and he lost his job – and that was the end of the poor old Umbrella Man, wasn't it?"

"So something of a whirlwind romance – you and Mrs Fletcher, I mean."

"I suppose it was," said Fletcher. "Wouldn't you say so, my dear?"

Susan seemed to have recovered her composure. She smiled at Jago.

"Yes, I rather think it was. But it's all worked out well, and I've no regrets. You must excuse me though, Inspector, if I sounded a little on edge just now. It's just that I – well, not to put too fine a point upon it, I don't feel safe."

Her eyes darted back to Fletcher, and it seemed to Jago as

though she were hesitant about continuing, but her husband simply stared at her, his face expressionless.

"It's my nerves, you see," she said. "These air raids have affected me, I think. I know we're all going through it, and many people have suffered far worse than I have, but I can't help it. The bombs make me jittery."

"That's perfectly understandable," said Jago.

"I try to keep calm, to pretend there's nothing the matter, because otherwise I'm afraid that I'll go to pieces."

"I noticed that you took the news of Mary's death very calmly when we were here on Friday."

"Yes. That's it, exactly. When people meet me they probably think I'm the picture of serenity, but it's just what I do to hold myself together when I get the jitters. Underneath it's very different."

"How did you get on with your sister? You mentioned before that you didn't see a lot of each other. Was that by choice?"

"I don't know whether it was by choice," said Susan. "It was just something that happened. I think I told you she was older than me."

"Yes – five years older."

"Precisely. That's quite a gap when you're young, you know. I don't recall us playing together. I think my relationship with her was probably the same as it is for any girl with an older sister. She always knew things I didn't know, was allowed to do things I wasn't allowed to do. And then of course it got to the stage where she'd done things that she wasn't allowed to do too – things that I didn't understand. She was a big girl and I was just a kid. Whatever I learned to do, whether it was swimming or riding a bike or my twelve times table, she'd already done it. Sometimes it felt as though I didn't really exist, I was just her shadow. Even the clothes I wore were mostly things she'd already worn and grown out of."

"So you wouldn't say you were close?"

"Close? I don't think there was ever a question of us being close. She was always too far ahead of me. We were in the same house, but it seemed as though she was living in a different world to me, in a place I hadn't arrived at yet. It felt as though I could see her further down the road but would never catch up with her."

"And when you grew up?"

"I suppose I caught up with her then. You might even say I overtook her, when I met George and got married, but it didn't change the way I felt."

Susan got out of her chair and crossed the room to her husband. He stood and put his arms round her as she laid her head on his shoulder. Fletcher spoke over her to Jago.

"You may think this is a nice house and everything's just fine here, Inspector, but as you can see, my wife's life has not been easy. Her mind is fragile. That's why I want to look after her."

Susan eased herself out of his embrace and stood beside him, holding his hand, to face Jago.

"Perhaps I should have burst into tears when you told me Mary was dead, Inspector," she said. "Perhaps I should have screamed. You must think me cold-hearted, but it's not that. It's just that sometimes things happen to you in life, things change. I had plenty of tears to shed when I was a child, but now…"

She sighed. Her face looked tired.

"Maybe we all start with a different number – some people have enough to last a lifetime, others run out when they're still young. I don't think I had many when I started."

Chapter 28

At first Jago wasn't sure he'd heard it, but it sounded like a quiet knock on the CID office door.

"Come in," he said, raising his voice enough to ensure it would be heard in the corridor outside.

The door opened slowly and a head poked round it.

"May I have a word, sir?"

Jago recognized the face of War Reserve Constable Price.

"Yes. Come in, sit yourself down. A word about what?"

Price came in, treading gently on the floor as if he were entering a solemn gathering that would be disturbed if he made a floorboard squeak. He sat down on the vacant chair in front of Jago's desk.

"Thank you, sir. It's to do with the case you're investigating – that woman who was found dead in Tinto Road."

"It was you and Ray Stannard who were first on the scene, wasn't it?"

"That's right, sir."

"He told me you're an old soldier, same as me. Were you in France?"

"Well, actually, sir –"

There was a brief silence. Price seemed to be struggling with something in his mind.

"The thing is, I think I might have misled Ray a little," he said. "You see, I wasn't actually in France – in fact I never left England. I was conscripted in 1916, but when they found out I'd done a bit of boxing before the war they made me a physical training instructor. I'm sure you'll remember the Army Gymnastic Staff, sir."

Jago nodded, recalling endless training in bayonet fighting, but he said nothing.

"So I never got anywhere near the front," Price continued. "My job was to get soldiers fit while they were alive. I never saw any dead ones, and I'm glad I didn't."

Price looked down into his lap. Jago wondered why the man seemed reluctant to catch his eye.

"I see," said Jago. "That would explain why you weren't looking too good on Friday morning after you'd found that woman's body. But there's nothing to be ashamed of – there were plenty of people in the Army in the Great War who never saw a corpse on a battlefield."

Price nodded but did not lift his head.

"Besides, front-line experience or not, no normal person would enjoy finding a young girl like that murdered."

Jago's words seemed to have a physical effect on Price. He jolted, and when he looked up Jago could see his mouth was quivering and tears were welling in his eyes.

"Whatever's the matter?" he asked.

"I-I'm sorry, sir," said Price. "It's just –" He seemed to be struggling again to bring himself under control. "It's just what you said then, about that girl. I've had some terrible news."

He reached into his pocket and pulled out a folded newspaper.

"Have you seen today's papers?" he said, his voice breaking.

"Not yet, no," said Jago.

Price spread the newspaper out on the desk before him. Jago scanned the headline: "83 children die as Huns sink liner in storm".

"See that, sir? Eighty-three children. All drowned. My wife and I had a visit yesterday – a man from the council. He said –" Again Price was unable to continue. He breathed in deeply before speaking. "He said our children were lost – both of them."

Jago leaned forward across the desk and looked Price in the eye.

"I'm so sorry. I had no idea. I can't imagine a worse thing."

194

"Just nine and seven they were, just kids. I'm worried my wife might lose her mind. Do you have children, sir?"

"No," said Jago. "I can't begin to know what it must be like for you. I can only offer you my sincere condolences."

"Thank you, sir."

Price took a couple of deep breaths and straightened himself up in the chair.

"I'll be all right, sir. Just give me a moment. I need to tell you why I came here."

Jago waited until Price regained a degree of composure. The constable dragged the back of his hand across his eyes quickly to remove the tears.

"It's about that woman, the one we found on the bomb-site. I'm sorry I didn't say this at the time, but when I tell you about it I think you'll understand why. The thing is, when I saw her body, I remembered her. What I mean to say is I recognized her. That's why I was feeling queasy. The last time I'd seen her she'd looked so full of life."

"Do you mean you knew her?"

"No. It was her appearance that I recognized. That red hair and the green coat. My mother used to say you should never wear red and green together, but on her it looked very attractive – the time before when I saw her, I mean, not when she was dead."

"When did you see her last?"

Having to concentrate on details seemed to be helping Price to recover.

"I've only seen her once, before the war started, but when I saw her lying there I was sure it was the same woman. I didn't know her name or anything about her, but I'd seen her out walking and it had stuck in my memory."

"When exactly before the war was this?"

"It was last year, sometime in the summer. I can't remember exactly when. She was with a man I used to know slightly, although

195

I'm not in contact with him now. The thing I clearly recall is that they looked on decidedly friendly terms, as you might say."

"His name?"

"It was Robert or Richard or something, but I can't remember his surname."

"What can you tell me about this man?"

"Very little, really. He was one of a few people I knew some years ago in a couple of organizations you might have heard of – one was called the Link and the other was the Imperial Fascist League."

Jago looked askance at Price and raised an eyebrow.

"Yes, yes, I know," said Price. "'Fascist' is a dirty word these days, but it wasn't the same then. People had sincerely held views. I used to believe in some of it myself, but of course I don't now."

"Did this come up when you applied to join the War Reserve?"

"No, they never asked, so I didn't mention it. Later on I kept quiet, because I was worried I might be sacked, but now I realize I have to tell you, because of that poor woman."

"What matters now is that you're a police officer, and by telling me this you're doing your duty. I don't hold a man's past against him. I've never had much time for Mosley myself, but I know there were some in the police before the war who did."

"And why shouldn't they? All this trouble we've got now is because of the way we treated the Germans at Versailles. All those reparations we forced on them after the Armistice – that war was just as much our fault as Germany's."

"I can't agree with you there," said Jago. "If they'd left Belgium alone, there wouldn't have been a war. We didn't intervene when the Austrians attacked Serbia, and we only declared war on the Germans after they'd declared war on France and invaded Belgium."

"I don't want to argue about who started the war – I just thought we could've learned a lot from the way Mussolini and Hitler were solving problems like unemployment."

"Perhaps, but what about that report the Foreign Office published last year? You know the one I mean? The one that said the German government was torturing Jews in concentration camps. I don't want us to learn from that."

"That's just hate propaganda by our government. Why should we believe what they say?"

"Why indeed? You could be right, but time will tell. Time and evidence. Now, leave the history aside and get on with telling me about this man of yours."

"Yes, sir, I'm sorry."

"What did he look like?"

"Tallish, average weight, I'd say. In his late thirties. That's all I can remember, really."

"Hair colour?"

Price thought for a moment.

"Dark, I think."

"Was he married?"

"I don't know. Like I said, we weren't close friends: he was just someone I knew, more like a casual acquaintance."

"That's helpful. There's someone I'd like to eliminate from our enquiries, so would you be willing to come with me and identify him?"

"You mean an identity parade?"

"No, I just want you to take a look from a safe distance and tell me if you know him. He won't even know you're doing it."

"I don't want to get into trouble."

"Yes, but you're a police officer: I'm asking you to come, but if you prefer it I'll order you."

"All right, I'll come."

"Good. Now, if you'll go and wait for me at the front door I'll be with you in a few minutes. I just need to make a telephone call."

***

Ten minutes later Jago was parking his car on a street in Forest Gate. Price was in the passenger seat.

"You stay here and don't show your face if you're concerned about being seen. I'm going to that building down the road there and I'm going to ask a man who works in it to step outside with me for a brief question. You should be able to see him clearly from here. All you need to do is take a good look at him and see if you recognize him. A couple of minutes should be enough, then I'll go back in with him for a few moments before I come back to you. Got it?"

"Yes, sir," said Price.

Jago crossed the road and mounted a few steps to the building's entrance. He disappeared inside and shortly afterwards emerged with another man, as he had said. Price watched from the car, keeping a hand over the lower part of his face in case the man saw him. In due course the detective inspector went back into the building and then re-emerged and returned to the car.

"Well?" asked Jago. "Did you get a good look? Was that the man you were telling me about?"

"Yes, sir," said Price. "Like I said, I haven't seen him for quite a while, but I'm pretty sure it was him. In fact as soon as I saw him his name came back, just like that."

"And what was it?"

"It was Berry. Richard Berry."

CHAPTER 29

The clock on the wall of the CID office showed ten minutes to six when the door crashed open and Cradock bounded back in. Jago looked up from his desk and scrutinized him.

"You look as though you've just tried to beat Sydney Wooderson in a one-mile race. Sit down and get your breath back."

"Thanks, guv'nor," said Cradock, collapsing onto a chair. "I've just run back from the church, hoping to catch you before you went home."

Jago eyed the clock.

"At ten to six? You must be joking. You could have walked it and stopped off for a pint on the way and still found me here."

"Well anyway, sir, I wanted to catch you, because I think I was right."

"Tell me more."

"Well, the place where George and Susan Fletcher got married is Emmanuel Church in Forest Gate, the parish church. The register there shows they were married on the twenty-seventh of July, like he said, so that all seems above board."

"And the vicar in Wolverhampton?"

"Yes, he had a phone, and I got hold of him eventually. He had a look and said there was an entry in the register for Celia and Richard Berry, married on the seventeenth of February 1938. So that means Celia was telling the truth about the wedding, although the vicar did say he was fairly new to the parish and hadn't actually conducted the wedding himself."

"And what did the register say about the groom's job?"

"The vicar said he checked the entry in the Rank or Profession section and it said 'mechanical engineer'."

"That sounds a bit grand for the kind of work George Fletcher said he was doing."

"Does that mean you're coming round to my idea that he and Richard Berry are the same person, then, sir?"

"Hold your horses – we'll come back to that in a minute. Tell me what you've found out first."

"Okay, so Richard Berry put himself down as a mechanical engineer. Now, Fletcher said he's been working as a typewriter mechanic for the last nine years. That's not exactly a mechanical engineer, but if Richard Berry was really George Fletcher, from what I've seen of Fletcher he's not the sort to underblow his own trumpet."

"Peter, I really do think sometimes I ought to write down the things you say."

"Yes, sir. Anyway, I mean he's not one to play down his own achievements. So I wouldn't be at all surprised if he'd decided to promote himself so as to cut a more impressive figure at the wedding."

"Celia told me that when she met Richard Berry in 1937 he was doing some kind of factory job."

"Oh, I see. So could that mean he wasn't a typewriter mechanic? That would rather undermine my case, wouldn't it?"

"I don't know," said Jago. "The way Fletcher describes it, a typewriter mechanic is someone who visits offices in a van, but I suppose they might work in factories too. Don't forget, though: when he told us about his work he said he'd been a typewriter mechanic on and off, with the odd gap. So if you're right, he could have been having one of those gaps when he met Celia. But anyway, at least we now have confirmation that Celia and Richard Berry were married when and where she said they were."

"That's right. But that doesn't necessarily mean they're married now, does it? Supposing they've got divorced since then?"

"I can see why you might imagine that. When I was with Celia at the dance she said she only wore her wedding ring for the same reason that she carries the photo, to fend the boys off – so if she found out he'd been having an affair she might have decided to end the marriage."

"But then even if he was the same man who married Susan this year it wouldn't be bigamy after all, would it? That whole theory would collapse. Shall I go to the district registry and find out whether there's any record of a divorce?"

"No. You'd be wasting your time. Matrimonial Causes Act 1937."

Jago recognized on Cradock's face one of his attempts to make something reassuring out of what was essentially a blank look.

"Sorry, sir, I'm not completely, er... What does it say?"

"No divorce allowed within the first three years of marriage. She can't divorce him until next year, even if she wants to. Celia is still married to Richard Berry, whether she likes it or not."

"Right, I see. Sounds like she'll have grounds for it when the time comes, though."

"Yes, and that time may be closer than we thought."

"What do you mean, sir?"

"I mean that while you've been out I've had a very interesting afternoon. I've had a visit from PC Price."

"The War Reserve fellow who was with Stannard when they found the body? Stannard told me he looked as though he was about to throw up."

"That may be a slight exaggeration, but the poor man was certainly disturbed by what he saw."

"Shouldn't have joined up if he can't cope with the odd body, should he, sir? Some of these War Reserves are a bit of a joke, I think. Would never have got in the force in the old days."

"The old days? You're beginning to sound like Frank Tompkins. And don't be so quick to judge him. He's going through a very difficult bereavement."

"Sorry, sir."

"Anyway, it turned out that it wasn't the fact that he had to see a dead body – it was that when he saw it, he recognized her."

"Really? Now that is interesting. How did he come to recognize her?"

"He'd seen her with an acquaintance of his last year. And here's the really interesting thing: he named that acquaintance as Richard Berry."

"You mean Mary did know Berry? That would explain why she was shocked when she saw him in Celia's photo, then. If she already knew him, it'd definitely be a surprise to find him in a photo that belonged to some woman she'd just bumped into, especially if that woman turned out to be his wife."

"And especially as Price told me that when he saw her with Berry they were out walking and they looked, as he put it, on decidedly friendly terms. Which raises a very interesting possibility."

"What, you mean they were –"

"Yes, it could indicate that Richard Berry was the man Mary had her affair with."

"Did Price say when he saw them?"

"Yes, he said it was last year, in the summer, although he couldn't say more precisely than that."

"So that would tally with what Celia told you, then, that her husband left her in June of last year, and what Angela said about Mary telling her she'd had a liaison that ended when the war started, so presumably in September."

Cradock rubbed his hands together in an expression of glee.

"It's hotting up now a bit, isn't it, guv'nor? Looks like our Mary and that Richard Berry were a saucy pair on the quiet."

"If you can contain your excitement for a moment, there's something even more interesting I can tell you."

"What's that?"

"I then took Price out so he could have a discreet look at a man from a safe distance, and he identified him as Richard Berry – and the man he was looking at was George Fletcher."

"Amazing – so that means I was right about those two blokes, doesn't it?"

"Yes, Peter, it does. You've done very well."

"Thank you, sir. So Fletcher and Berry are the same man. Well I never."

Jago could almost see Cradock's mind working. He smiled to himself as he waited for the next penny to drop.

"But then – oh, my goodness. That means Mary was having an affair with her sister's husband."

"Not exactly: he wasn't Susan's husband at the time of the affair, but even so… In any case, I could kick myself. It was there all along, staring me in the face. I should have listened to Dorothy –"

Cradock's face registered surprise, and Jago hastily corrected himself.

"I should have paid more careful attention to Miss Appleton. She said it this morning, when I told her about the two sisters in the case."

"Said what?"

"She said, 'Like the Boleyn girls, then.'"

"Sorry, sir, I don't get it."

"It means she hit the nail on the head without even knowing it. If I'd thought about those words for a moment I might have cottoned on sooner. Think of it: Anne Boleyn had a sister, Mary – the younger of the two ended up marrying Henry VIII, the man who'd had her sister as his mistress. We've got Susan and Mary Watkins, both in a relationship with George, or Richard, whatever his name is. It's the same in both cases – there was one man in the triangle, husband to one sister and lover to the other. Only in the case of Henry VIII, both sisters knew what had gone before. It seems ours didn't."

"Was Anne Boleyn one of the wives who had their heads chopped off? I can never remember what happened to which one."

"Yes, she was beheaded at the Tower of London – found guilty of adultery, incest, and treason, poor woman."

"So with the Boleyn girls it was the wife who was the traitor, right?"

"Yes."

"But in our case it's not the same, is it? At least, not as far as I can see. It looks like it was the man. Is that why Mary said 'He's a traitor' to Angela? I know you said that was later, not when she was looking at the photo, but if she'd discovered her lover was Celia's husband it would make sense – he'd betrayed his wife. And if somehow Mary knew he was the same man as Susan's husband, she'd have been thinking he'd betrayed two wives."

"That could be it – unless there was also something much more serious going on that Mary knew about."

"You mean if he was a proper traitor, as in high treason and off to the Tower?"

"Who knows? He's clearly a man with secrets who knows how to lead a double life."

"Talk about having your cake and eating it. So where do we go from here?"

"The main question is, did Mary know who her new brother-in-law was? If she really had discovered that George Fletcher was the same man as Richard Berry, how might she have reacted?"

"She could have tried to blackmail him by threatening to tell Susan he was a bigamist, couldn't she? Or perhaps by threatening to tell Celia, now that she'd met her. Or to tell both of them, for that matter. After all, she did say, 'He'll pay for this.' Maybe she meant that literally."

"That's possible. Alternatively, of course, if her dislike for her sister was deep enough, she might have just told her for the spite of it. What if Mary went to her sister and said, 'That man of yours, your husband – I've already had him as my lover'? What would that do to Susan? That might have given Mary real pleasure. How would Susan have reacted to that?"

"You mean Susan might have…?"

"It's within the bounds of possibility."

"Crikey, guv'nor: what a mess!"

"Hell hath no fury, Peter."

"What's that?"

"Hell hath no fury like a woman scorned."

"Shakespeare?"

"William Congreve, I believe, but it doesn't matter. The point is, what Mary knew about George could have been a powerful weapon in her hands."

"Could she have used that weapon against Celia too?"

"I don't see how. If she didn't know Celia before she met her at the dance, there'd be no obvious motive for Mary to want to hurt her. If anything, you'd think Mary might want to blackmail George in some way, because now she could tell him she'd met his other wife."

"So are we going to bring all this up with Susan and George? And what about Celia?"

"No, not yet. I think I'd prefer to keep this to ourselves for the time being. We haven't got many cards to play, and I don't want to show them all this early in the game."

"When you were talking to Celia about the murder, she said, 'Your sins will find you out,' didn't she? What did she mean by that? Whose sins was she talking about?"

"That, I think, remains to be seen."

CHAPTER 30

First thing on Tuesday morning Jago had received a phone call at the station from Dyers, thanking him for their drink on Sunday evening. He would have phoned yesterday, Dyers said, but he'd had a busy day – the Luftwaffe had attacked RAF Hornchurch. He added swiftly that no damage had been done. Jago took this assurance at face value and said he was pleased to hear it, but almost immediately found himself questioning in his mind whether what his old friend had told him was true. It sounded too much like the official reports of air raids in the press and newsreels – always more positive than the evidence of his own eyes.

That was the problem these days – what could you be sure of? He thought of Dorothy, and was troubled once more by what he'd seen at the dance and by what it was making him think. He braced himself in his seat as the underground train rattled deafeningly round a bend in the tunnel, and tried to put the picture out of his thoughts. He needed to keep his mind clear, especially today.

He wondered whether he was becoming too secretive himself. Dyers had wished him a good day today, but Jago had said nothing about what he was doing. He hadn't told Cradock either – he'd just said he'd be out. Perhaps he would tell Cradock later, but it would depend on how things went.

He leafed through the morning paper. Today's news was mixed. RAF bombers had attacked Hitler's invasion bases overnight again, and the special invasion weather forecast said the Channel was calm. The king had broadcast on the wireless from an underground shelter during an air raid to announce a new medal, the George Cross, for civilian bravery. Goebbels had told his own radio listeners that Londoners were running about helplessly in the streets and screaming because of the air attacks. French and British warships had fought each other off the coast of Dakar after the local French authorities refused to surrender to General de Gaulle. J. Edgar Hoover had said there was a Fifth Column already at work in America. Two Japanese consular staff in Singapore had been arrested on spy charges. Local authorities were going to issue free ear plugs to people being bombed. Petrol was up by a penny a gallon from today, and West Ham were playing away to Clapton Orient on Saturday.

He closed the paper. At least no one could say there was no news these days. It was a far cry from the four-line reports on the local magistrates' court proceedings that he'd been learning to write as a boy at the *Stratford Express* before the previous war took him away to be a soldier.

The train came to a screeching halt at Westminster tube station, and Jago got off. The wooden escalator rumbled and clanked its way to the surface and he walked out onto the street, catching the familiar rank odour of the Thames blown off the river by a light breeze. The weather was dry, and the fog that he'd seen when he woke four hours earlier was clearing. No doubt Dyers would be disappointed – he might have been hoping a touch of fog would keep the German bombers away.

It was a short walk to Jago's destination, the distinctive building on the Embankment that had started out as one man's vision for the largest opera house in Europe but had ended with him bankrupt after sinking forty feet of concrete and most of his funds into the foundations. Jago's father had told him how grieved he felt as a singer – no opera tenor but a humble music hall performer – when in 1888 the project finally failed and the uncompleted theatre was demolished. How ironic it was that those costly foundations were the only part to survive, and upon them was constructed a very different establishment – and doubly ironic that while his father's profession had never taken him into the original building, his own had brought him on many occasions into its successor. From what he had heard, the original visionary must have had a sense of irony too – the bankrupt Mr Mapleson had said that with such solid foundations, at least the cells below New Scotland Yard would be dry.

The headquarters of the Metropolitan Police hadn't pleased everyone. According to one member of parliament, in architectural terms it was inferior to the Crosse & Blackwell jam and pickle factory on the opposite side of the river. Soon, however, it had become one of the sights of London. To Jago it seemed a solid and reassuring presence only yards from the heart of government. At the same time, those eye-catching horizontal bands of red brick and white Portland stone gave the building its own separate and unique identity, even through the London grime that coated them, while the round turrets at its corners added a whimsical hint of medieval romance.

There was nothing romantic about the inside of the building. The North Building, where Jago was heading, was a warren of unremarkable offices, many of which had seen better days. Within a few minutes he was at the door of one of these rooms, just in time for his meeting. He tapped on the door, turned the cheap-looking Bakelite door handle, and went in. The room contained several filing cabinets and racks of box files, and in the middle of it was a desk with a telephone, a perpetual calendar, a double inkwell, a desk lamp, and the usual two wooden trays – "in" and "out", the former brimming with papers and the latter less full. Behind the desk Jago recognized the familiar figure of Detective Superintendent Arthur Ford of the Special Branch.

"Ah, welcome, John. Do come in and take a seat, make yourself at home. It must be a couple of years since I last saw you."

"Nearer four, I think: my secondment to the Branch was in 1936."

"It was that arms smuggling business, wasn't it, on the French–Spanish border?"

"Yes, I was acting as liaison with the French police."

"That's right," said Ford. "I can remember being jolly pleased that we'd found you – and that K Division was prepared to release you for six months. We were very stretched then, and there aren't that many coppers in the Metropolitan Police Service who can speak French – not properly, that is. It didn't tempt you to consider a permanent transfer to us, though? We'd have been glad to have you."

"No, sir. It was interesting, but it wouldn't be my first choice for the rest of my career."

"But you helped stop weapons being smuggled into a civil war across the border. You probably saved lives by doing that. That's something to be proud of."

"Yes, I suppose I thought so at the time, but from today's perspective it all looks a bit different. Whatever that Non-Intervention Agreement may or may not have achieved, the end result was that Franco won the war, and we all know how his friends have turned out. If anything I did helped Hitler and Mussolini to get what they wanted back then, I'm not so sure it's something to be proud of after all."

"The important thing is that you served your country and defended its interests."

"And as Lord Palmerston said, 'We have no eternal allies, and we have no perpetual enemies. Our interests are eternal and perpetual, and those interests it is our duty to follow.'"

"Yes, it's a question of being realistic, pragmatic."

"But Palmerston also said, 'The real policy of England is to be the champion of justice and right.' Sometimes that's not the pragmatic route to take."

"Quite, but we have to live in the real world, John. You must know that."

"Yes, I know that only too well, and it's about the real world that I've come to see you. There's a few things I'd like to check with you. I'll understand if you don't want to comment, but you may be able to help."

"Of course, John, you know you're trusted here. What is it you want to know?"

"First of all, I wonder if you can tell me anything about the Radio Security Service. I've heard it mentioned, but I don't know what it does."

"Yes – as far as I'm concerned you're still one of us, and I don't need to remind you you've signed the Official Secrets Act. The whole thing's rather hush-hush, so do please keep it to yourself. The powers-that-be are obviously worried there might be German agents in the country sending secret messages back to Berlin, so our colleagues in Military Intelligence have people looking for suspicious wireless signals – but it's a huge job, so they've set up a network of radio amateurs to help."

"These are the sort of chaps who used to rig up aerials in their back gardens and talk to other amateurs all over the world in the middle of the night, yes?" said Jago.

"That's right," replied Ford. "Of course they had to stop doing that last year because we impounded their transmitters, but they were allowed to keep their receivers. Anyway, discreet approaches were made to them – sometimes through the local police, as I expect you know – asking if they'd be willing to do some radio work for the government in their own time. It's on a voluntary basis, so they're called voluntary interceptors, although you won't read about them in the papers. Their job is to check the airwaves and report anything that might be a coded message. Then if we think someone's making a suspicious transmission we can investigate. Mind you, as far as I know we haven't caught anyone yet. Anyway, the whole set-up's part of the Radio Security Service. I've an idea the intelligence chaps run it from Wormwood Scrubs, of all places – nice strong prison walls to keep the bombs out, I suppose. Don't tell anyone I told you that, by the way. But what's your interest in the whole business?"

210

"It's just that I've got reports that someone is claiming to be one of these people and threatening to report a member of the public unless they give him money."

"Well, when you find out who he is, let me know, and we'll check whether he's a genuine interceptor and get him dealt with. If he isn't, he shouldn't know about it, which will mean someone's been talking, so thanks for the tip."

"I'd like to ask you a question about a chemical too."

"By all means. Which one?"

"Hydrogen peroxide."

Ford laughed.

"Thinking of changing your hair colour, are you?"

"Surprising as it may seem, I'm not," said Jago, "although I'm impressed to discover there seems to be no subject on which you're not well informed. As it happens, I was interested in hydrogen peroxide's other uses. A pal of mine in the RAF told me the Germans had been working on using it as fuel for some kind of rocket plane."

"True enough, as I understand it. I don't think they've got close to anything operationally viable, though. The big potential of hydrogen peroxide is that if it's used in the right way it can release large amounts of energy, because it decomposes into hot steam and oxygen."

"But it can also blow up, right?"

"Exactly, so they've still some way to go."

"I've got a local engineering company that's had some of its hydrogen peroxide go missing. I'm assuming it must be just plain pilfering, but is there any way that this substance could be useful to an enemy?"

"Not if it's just the chemical itself, and in small quantities. What might be of more interest to the enemy is what the company's doing with it."

"I see. They haven't told me that, of course."

"Quite right too. What's their name?"

"Everson Engineering."

Ford nodded.

"Does that mean you know them?"

Ford simply smiled, his facial expression indicating that he was waiting for Jago's next question.

"If they're doing secret work for the government, is there any way it could be significant that hydrogen peroxide is going missing?" said Jago.

"On the face of it, that seems unlikely. If a design or a component for a device using hydrogen peroxide as a fuel went missing it would certainly look suspicious, but it's difficult to imagine what the enemy might be able to infer from a sample of the substance itself. After all, as far as I know, hydrogen peroxide is the same compound here as it is in Germany. Unless…"

"Unless what?"

"No, I'm letting my imagination run away with me. Just keep me informed of any further developments in your investigation, will you?"

"Of course."

"Is that all?"

"No, I've got one more question. It's about valves – as in wireless valves."

"Right, those are much more interesting. They're crucial in radio location work, for example."

"Locating radios?"

"No, it's a way of detecting enemy aircraft before they get here."

"Ah, you mean those big concrete ears I've seen down in Kent?"

"No, those are sound mirrors – they're meant to pick up the engine noise of approaching enemy aircraft. Radio location is quite different and far more efficient."

"How does it work?"

"That I can't tell you, but I do know that it depends on valves, and that a lot of work's being done to develop new types of valve. It's essentially about making them smaller and more powerful. If we can do that, one day we might be able to put the equipment in the aircraft itself."

"Which would be an obvious advantage, I suppose."

"Yes, and I'll tell you something else. Before the war started we were having trouble manufacturing a particular part for a new type of valve, and we had to import them from a big manufacturer in Holland."

"I think I can guess who you mean."

"Maybe you can. But then it became clear the Germans were going to invade Holland, and it looked like we'd lose the supply. At the last minute, just hours before the Nazis overran the country, we managed to load the valves and the machines for making them onto a truck and got it back here. Now they're being made in this country."

"Are you saying Everson Engineering could be making these valves?"

"I'm saying nothing of the sort. I have no idea where they're being made."

Jago eyed him suspiciously. Here was someone else who might be leading him up the garden path.

"The thing is, you see," he said, "they've had valves go missing too."

"It may mean nothing," said Ford. "I think it'll depend on what kind of valves they are. If they're just for domestic wireless sets they might make someone a few bob on the black market but they won't be of any military importance – they're too big and too weak. But if they're some of the more advanced kind, a sample or two could be of great interest to the enemy. And in that case your investigation would in turn become of great interest to the Branch."

Jago decided it was time to be on his way. He stood and extended his right arm to shake Ford's hand.

"Thanks very much," he said. "You've been a mine of information. But if it's not a silly question, how do you know all this stuff?"

"That's easy," replied Ford. "How do you know every crook in West Ham who's ever robbed a till? Because it's my job to know. The government believes we face a major threat from Fifth Column saboteurs, so we need to know what their potential targets might be, and that takes us down all sorts of unexpected alleys."

CHAPTER 31

Jago came out of New Scotland Yard and walked up Derby Gate towards Whitehall. There to his right, in the middle of the road, was the Cenotaph. The sun was high, and it cast no shadow. In just twenty years this monument to the dead of the Great War had become an established feature here on one of London's most famous thoroughfares. A wry smile crossed his face as he recalled why Westminster City Council had opposed the location in 1919 – because it would create a safety hazard for members of the public crossing the busy road to pay homage. More safety than any serviceman ever knew, he thought.

He paused to gaze at the memorial, the faces of friends he had lost drifting through his mind. Even in the midst of the great stone-clad offices of government, it had its own imposing dignity. He appreciated its restraint – no statuary, no romanticized imagery of battle, just the stark whiteness of the stone. No words except "The glorious dead". What a price they had paid, he thought, and how inglorious the death of those he had seen falling beside him.

What would they think, those glorious dead, if they knew this empty tomb of theirs had not stood here two decades before Britain and its empire were again at war with Germany? How many more dead would join them? Even this, the visible emblem of their nation's sorrowful respect, might be blasted to dust and ashes tonight, tomorrow night, or whenever the bombers next flew this way. And yet he was pleased to see that the Cenotaph was unprotected. No wooden boards or steel plates to shield it, no sandbags heaped around it. That gave it another dignity, he thought, as if those who had lost their lives in that war – his war

– were still defiant in the face of death's new offensive. He would like to bring Dorothy here – but no, he pushed the idea out of his mind.

He crossed the road and headed up Whitehall towards Trafalgar Square, passing the Home Office on his left, and then the Colonial Office on the corner of Downing Street, where two Home Guard volunteers with rifles stood on the pavement beside a sandbagged guard post. For a moment he considered turning in to Downing Street to take a look at Number 10, but decided there was only a door to stare at, so why bother? He crossed the prime minister's side street and continued on past the Treasury Buildings. He imagined the civil servants inside, separated from him by no more than the glass of a window and yet invisible, living in a different world. They probably think they run the country, he thought. Control what happens out here. Maybe that's what Arthur Ford thinks too, in his way. If they spent less time in Whitehall and more in places like West Ham, Liverpool, Bristol or anywhere else getting a taste of Hitler's fury at the moment, they might be in for a shock.

He was starting to feel hungry.

He walked up to Trafalgar Square and on a little farther to the corner of Craven Street and the Strand, where he got a decent lunch for half a crown at the Lyons Corner House. He thought he would then take a stroll up the Strand and catch a District Line train at Temple station, but remembered this would take him past the Savoy Hotel, where Dorothy was living – along with what seemed like half the American press corps. He noticed his own unwillingness to risk bumping into her on the street. Perhaps he was just nervous about unplanned meetings with her. Perhaps he wanted to avoid complications. He wasn't sure, but he decided to steer clear of the area and get the train from Charing Cross instead.

***

Jago returned to West Ham police station to find Cradock waiting for him. There had been another phone call from Everson Engineering.

"It's Miss Hornby again, guv'nor," said Cradock. "She wants to see us."

"About what?" asked Jago.

"She didn't say. But she sounded agitated, as if it wouldn't wait."

They drove to the company's premises. Miss Hornby took them to her office and closed the door behind them.

"Thank you for coming, Inspector," she said. "Something's gone missing, and in view of what happened on Friday it seems too unlikely to be a coincidence."

"What is it?"

"It's a personal file on one of our employees. Confidential, of course."

"Can you tell me who the member of staff is?"

"Yes, it's Miss Cartwright, the young lady I brought to see you on Sunday – Beatrice Cartwright."

"When did it go missing?"

"That's difficult to say. I've only just discovered we don't have it, and it's weeks since I last referred to the file myself. It could have gone missing at any time since then."

"Who's authorized to have access to these files?"

"Only those of us whose job involves maintaining and managing them."

"And who would those people be?"

"Just me and Miss Watkins. We are the department, effectively – or we were."

"And no one else?"

"No. Except Mr Everson, of course: he has access to them. After all, he owns the business, so they're his property. But I can assure you there's no laxity in our procedures, Inspector. Mr Everson is most particular in these matters."

"Have you told him the file's missing?"

"Yes."

"And he hasn't got it himself?"

"No. He told me that immediately, and he was also most concerned that I should not feel there was any failing on my part. Such a caring man – I sometimes think that if there were more like him in the world it would be a much better place."

"I can see you hold a high opinion of Mr Everson."

"Oh, yes. I couldn't wish for a more considerate employer."

Jago walked to the office window and looked down at the street below.

"I understand that his wife is an invalid," he said, without turning round.

"Yes," said Miss Hornby. "She's in a nursing home, poor woman. He's devoted to her, of course."

Jago turned back to face her.

"Would you say Mr Everson is the kind of man that women might find attractive?"

Miss Hornby looked surprised, and Jago thought he saw a hint of a blush in her cheeks.

"What a question to ask," she said. "The short answer is I have no idea, but I'm sure he would never do anything to encourage such feelings."

"How long have you known him?"

"For fifteen years – since I came to work here."

"And would you say he's popular with the staff?"

"I think they see him as a fair man."

"How would you describe Miss Cartwright's relationship with him?"

"I'm not sure: in her position she wouldn't have had much contact with him."

"People these days are sometimes a bit more free with their seniors than they were when I was a young man."

"Yes, I know what you mean. Miss Cartwright is young, of course, and probably a typical girl of her age – thinks she can do anything but isn't old enough to know her limitations yet. You know what young women are like these days. I'm afraid I find them altogether too forward. Too many of them seem to think the world owes them a living. It wasn't like that in my day – we had to fight every inch of the way to be accepted in companies like this. Now they just waltz in and expect everything to be handed to them on a plate. They don't know they're born, some of them. Look at the way some of them dress, too: it's simply not appropriate for a place of work."

"You're talking about Miss Cartwright?"

"I'm talking about young women in general. But yes, there have been occasions when I've had to have a word with her on the subject. She would come to the office dressed in a way that would not have been acceptable when I was her age, and I got the impression she was perhaps doing it for Mr Everson's benefit."

"You mean he wanted her to?"

"Not at all. I mean it seemed to me that perhaps she was trying to make an impression on him."

"Trying to turn his head?"

"That's not what I'm saying. I'm simply observing that I thought she was perhaps endeavouring to catch his eye. She may well have assumed that arousing his personal interest might serve to advance her career. I'm afraid that's just the way some young women are today."

"So are you suggesting there may be some kind of emotional relationship between them?"

Miss Hornby lowered her voice.

"These are delicate matters, Mr Jago. I'm not in a position to comment on such a possibility, and even if there were such a relationship I would not have the wherewithal to prove it. All I can say is that I get the impression Miss Cartwright would not be averse to the idea, if you know what I mean. Mr Everson is a remarkable man, Inspector. He's doing important work, and one day this country will be grateful to him. His mind is entirely on his business, but I worry that he may be vulnerable to the charms of a wily young woman."

"You feel you need to protect him?"

"Where it is within my power to do so, yes. Mr Everson has had a hard life; he's suffered, and I don't want to see him suffer more. He doesn't need to be distracted by young women who only want to get their hooks into him."

"Is that what you think is happening?"

"No, no. I'm speaking generally, you understand. I just think that Miss Cartwright may not be as innocent as she appears to be."

"And what about Mary Watkins?"

"In what sense?"

"She was a young woman too. Was she the sort of woman who might have found it in her interests to catch Mr Everson's eye?"

"Really, Inspector. Is that any way to speak of the dead? I have no evidence that Mary Watkins made any advances to Mr Everson, and if she did, I'm sure he would have ignored them or if necessary repulsed them. Mr Everson is an honourable man, not the sort to fall for the guile of a young woman."

***

Jago and Cradock took their leave of Miss Hornby and walked back to the car.

"What do you make of that, then, sir?" said Cradock as soon as they were out of earshot. "Do you think there's been something going on between Everson and one of these women? Maybe he's not as pure as the driven snow after all, despite what Miss Hornby says. And she didn't exactly spring to Mary's defence when you suggested there might have been a bit of eye-catching going on, did she?"

"Maybe it's just as she said – she sees it as her job to protect him," said Jago. "She seems very loyal."

"Or she might think she has a special place in his affections, mightn't she? If that were the case, younger women like Beatrice or Mary could seem like rivals."

They reached the car and got in. Jago sat at the wheel, giving Cradock's ideas a moment's silent consideration.

"We've been thinking that liaison of Mary's last year was with Richard Berry," he said, "but maybe we've been looking in the wrong direction. I think we need to have another word with Angela, see whether she can remember Mary saying or doing anything that might suggest that. I'll visit her this evening while you're out sampling the ales at the Railway Tavern."

He was about to turn the ignition key when Cradock jumped round in his seat.

"Sorry, sir, that's just reminded me. There was another call while you were out this morning. It was from Beatrice Cartwright. She said that man Smith has told her to meet him at a phone box in Prince Regent Lane."

Jago turned to face him.

"When?" he asked.

"Eight o'clock – tonight."

CHAPTER 32

Cradock felt uneasy as soon as he entered the Railway Tavern. It was a working man's pub, the kind of place where every head turned to look at you as soon as you crossed the threshold. Checking to see whether you were a local or a stranger, insider or outsider, threat or mug. He could tell from the suspicion in their eyes that they'd got him marked down as a stranger in two shakes of a lamb's tail. No hesitation. He considered trying on a little self-protective bravado, maybe just a hint of a swagger, but then a vivid image of fists flying and glasses smashing flashed through his mind. He thought better of it. Besides, tonight it was his duty to come across as a mug.

It was a little before six o'clock when he arrived. The pub had been open since five, and the public bar was filling with early-evening drinkers hoping to get a couple of pints in before the blackout. The air was warm, stale, and heavy with cigarette smoke, and the harsh hubbub of men's voices was spiked by outbursts of raucous laughter. He eased his way through the press of bodies, making sure not to jostle anyone's drinking arm – they didn't look as though they'd take kindly to having their ale spilled.

The beer was a bit cheaper here than in the adjoining saloon bar, but Cradock also reckoned it was where he was more likely to find opportunities for illicit trading. He walked up to the bar and rested one foot on the brass rail that ran along it near the floor. Catching the barman's eye and getting service was going to be tricky, and he didn't have much time. Probably just as well, though – DI Jago wasn't going to be pleased if he'd done too much drinking.

The barman's face was pockmarked and lumpy – it looked as though he'd been breaking up fights since the Battle of Verdun.

He was rolling a cigarette at the far end of the counter. He kept an eye on Cradock while he licked the edge of the paper, pressed it between his fingers to seal it, and pinched off the excess tobacco hanging from the ends. He placed it behind his left ear for later use and approached his customer.

"And what'll it be for you?" he growled.

"Half of mild, please," said Cradock. "I need a bit of Dutch courage."

"You won't get much of that out of a half of mild," said the barman.

"All the same, that's what I'll have – for starters."

The barman pulled on the hand-pump and delivered a half-pint of ale into a glass. He set it down on the counter before Cradock.

"That'll be fourpence, please."

Cradock reached into his trouser pocket and pulled out a handful of change. He picked out a threepenny bit and two ha'pennies and pushed them across the mahogany counter. The barman gathered them up and then leaned forward with a confiding look on his face.

"What's up then, mate?" he asked. "Wife just found out?"

"No," answered Cradock, trying to look morose. "No wife – not yet, anyway. It's the girlfriend. I'm supposed to be seeing her tonight and I've forgotten it's her birthday. Haven't got her a present. There'll be hell to pay, if I know her."

"You should've made that a pint then, lad. Sounds like you'll need it."

The barman gave him a crooked smile that suggested man-to-man sympathy, then wandered away to drop Cradock's coins into the till.

A man in an ill-fitting dark suit appeared at Cradock's side and leaned his back against the bar. His eyes flitted round the room. He turned to face Cradock, one elbow on the bar counter.

"I, er, couldn't help overhearing you, squire," he said. "What you said about your girlfriend. It so happens that I might be able to help you out. How about giving her a nice pair of silk stockings for her birthday? She'll love them. Like gold dust they are, these days – they're using all the silk for parachutes."

He produced a packet from an inside pocket and teased out a small piece of material from it.

"Look at that," he said. "So sheer you can see right through it. Really glamorous. She'll go crazy for these."

Cradock rubbed the fabric gently between his finger and thumb as if he could tell one silk stocking from another and gave an appreciative murmur.

"Finest quality," the man continued. "You could spend a week going round the shops looking for stockings like this and you won't find them, but I can let you have a pair for twelve and six."

Cradock winced at the price, and at what Jago might say if he bought them. He made some further appreciative but non-committal noises, then continued.

"Actually there's something else I think she'd appreciate more," he said. "Maybe you could help me with that."

"Of course. I can get you anything. Cigarettes, booze, ladies' underwear, you name it."

"She needs a light bulb for her torch."

"What? Is that your idea of a romantic present? That poor woman needs her head seeing to – and so do you. Anyway, I haven't got any right now."

"How about batteries?" asked Cradock, wishing the ordeal were over.

"A right little Rudolph Valentino you are. But you're in luck tonight. Torch batteries I can do you – one and nine a go."

"One and nine? They were only fivepence farthing last time I bought one."

"That must've been before the war, mate. You can't get them for love nor money now – although from what I can see, you're not going to get very far with love anyway."

"How about this, then?" said Cradock. "She likes her hair blonde but she isn't a natural, and she said she was trying to get some stuff you could buy to do it but the shops didn't have any."

"You mean peroxide?"

"Yes, that's the stuff."

"You should have come to me before," said the man. "I haven't actually got any on me right this moment, but there's this mate of mine who can get hold of it. His work takes him here and there, and he sometimes comes across merchandise that's fallen off the back of a lorry, if you know what I mean. He lives just round the corner – I'll nip down there and see if he's got any. You stay here, or come back in about twenty minutes."

"Right you are, then," said Cradock.

The man tipped his hat to Cradock and moved towards the door. As soon as he had left, Cradock slipped out after him. He followed him as closely as he dared, anxious not to lose sight of him in the blackout. After a couple of turnings he saw the man stop outside a house and knock at the door. It opened, and he disappeared inside. Cradock crossed the road and took a closer look at the house – but he already knew who lived there. He made his way quickly back to the Railway Tavern so that he'd be ready to buy his bottle of peroxide when the man returned.

He chuckled at the thought of what Jago would say when he reported the address the shady dealer had visited. Forty-seven Hemsworth Street. The residence of one Harry Parker.

CHAPTER 33

Angela had a flat in Chadwin Road, not far from Everson Engineering, and it was after blackout time when Jago got there. He resigned himself to the usual complications. Like probably everyone living in a street like this she wasn't on the phone, so he'd had to go on the off-chance that she'd be in. The last time he'd called at her home was when he drove her to RAF Hornchurch, and then it had still been light. Even if he found the right house again in the dark there'd be no tell-tale lights visible to show she was at home. And he'd have to remember not to get so absorbed in finding her that he walked into a tree – the white rings the council had painted round the tree trunks weren't as effective a safety measure as they'd claimed.

He peered at the number of the first house he came to, then counted along the roofline silhouetted against the night sky, chimney pot by chimney pot, until he got to roughly where hers should be. Stepping close to the front door, he pulled out his flashlight and switched it on and immediately off again to find the number that confirmed he was at the right place. Even for this brief moment he shielded the flashlight with his hand, but that was more to avoid attracting the attentions of the local ARP warden than out of fear of betraying his location to the German air force. The thought that one flash of his hand-torch could bring a torrent of high explosives down from the skies and onto Angela's flat was ridiculous, but there was something about the blackout propaganda that seemed to have made everyone edgy about the slightest hint of light – that and people being fined a pound for striking a match on the street during the blackout. He found a doorbell button for the downstairs flat and pressed it.

Angela looked surprised to find Jago on the doorstep but welcomed him in. She closed the front door behind him and pulled the blackout curtain across it, then switched the light on. There wasn't much to the flat – Angela took him into a small living room with a kitchen opening off it at one end, and he guessed there would be one bedroom, possibly two. He glanced into the kitchen and glimpsed a pile of dirty dishes beside the sink before she closed the door on it and motioned him towards a faded brown moquette sofa under the window. He sat down and felt the lumpy cushions sag beneath him.

"You must excuse the state of this place, Inspector," said Angela. "I've been so busy at work these last few weeks – rush orders, extra hours. I normally try to keep it a bit tidier, but you know what they say – there's a war on. Care for a drink?"

Jago noticed there was a tumbler half full of a clear liquid that he suspected would be gin rather than water.

"Not for me, thank you very much," he said.

"Suit yourself. I was just having a little one to keep me company. It can seem very quiet when you get home from work if you live alone. Are you a married man?"

"No, I'm not, as it happens."

"You'll know what I mean, then. Are you sure you won't have a drink?"

"No, really, it's most kind of you, but I won't. I just want to ask you a few more questions, if you don't mind."

"I see. Well, fire away, then, although I'm sure I've told you everything I can."

"I'd like to ask you about the liaison you said Mary had mentioned – the relationship she had with a man last year. I know she didn't tell you who the man was, but it's been suggested to me that it could have been someone at Everson Engineering. What do you think?"

"It's possible, I suppose. I mean, as far as I could tell she didn't see much of Everson people outside work, apart from me. She never mentioned any other friends, either, and never brought anyone else along when we had our nights out. But on the other hand, she didn't seem to have anything to do with her family – well, with her sister, anyway, since there didn't seem to be any other family. So if she did meet a man, the most likely place would have been at Everson's."

"Do you think it could have been with Mr Everson himself?"

Angela laughed. She sipped her drink but laughed again and began to choke. She put a hand to her mouth and brought the coughing under control before speaking.

"Now there's a possibility I hadn't considered, Inspector. An affair with the boss. Well, she wouldn't be the first to pursue her career in that direction, would she? He's living on his own now, worth a bob or two and maybe looking for a bit of warmth and company. He may not be a bachelor but he's certainly eligible, to some girls at least."

"Was Mary that kind of girl?"

"I honestly couldn't say. If she did fancy him, she never let on to me. But she could be a dark horse, that one."

"So what do you think of the suggestion that it was Mr Everson she was referring to when she mentioned her liaison, as you called it?"

Angela pursed her lips in thought before replying.

"Now you mention it, I must admit the impression I had when she talked about the affair was that it might have been a married man. Nothing I could put my finger on specifically, you understand – just the way she talked. But no, I can't imagine her and Mr Everson being like that. I don't know him well, but I've heard he's very kind to his poor wife, makes sure she gets the best care and all that, you know."

"Could Mary have found him attractive?"

Angela's expression suggested that this was a very debatable question.

"Who knows why anyone finds a man attractive?" she said. "Sometimes it's just baffling – but in this case, no, I don't think so. She was young and liked a laugh. He's old and serious." She laughed again. "No, if there's anyone with a crush on him, I reckon it'll be that Miss Hornby. She's a funny old stick. Looks like butter wouldn't melt in her mouth, but I could imagine her swooning like a schoolgirl if Mr Everson so much as looked at her. They're much the same age, too, I would think."

"Are you aware of any other married men that Mary could have been in such a relationship with?"

"No. But then she didn't give anything away. It could have been anyone."

"Do you think there could have been any significance in the photo that the woman you met at the dance – Celia – showed to Mary?"

"If I knew what it was a photo of I might be able to say, but I was too far away."

"In that case it may interest you to know that when I spoke to Celia after you'd brought her to me at the dance on Saturday, she told me it was a picture of her and her husband at their wedding. She also told me that when Mary saw it she seemed surprised. She even used the word 'shocked'. What do you make of that?"

"I see… Yes, that begins to make sense, doesn't it?"

"What do you mean?"

"Well, look at it this way. Mary sees Celia's husband and recognizes the man she'd had her affair with. Even if she knew he was married at the time, she wouldn't necessarily ever have seen his wife. So that would be a shock, yes. And that would explain why Mary was quite different by the time I got back to them. I'm not surprised she wanted to go home – she wouldn't want to hang about with Celia any longer if that was going through her mind. Mind you, I'm only guessing – I mean, Mary never said anything to me that would prove it was Celia's husband she'd been carrying on with."

229

"I understand. But there's one small point that I don't understand, and perhaps you can help me with that too."

"Of course. Anything I can do to be of help."

"On that night at the dance you were too far away to see what was in the photo, so you didn't know until I told you just now, yes?"

"That's right. I was dancing with a young airman."

"But when I mentioned that to Celia, she said that wasn't the case. She said you were still sitting at the table with her and Mary when she showed Mary the photo."

"Did she? I see."

"Is her recollection correct?"

Angela averted her eyes and nodded.

"Yes, it is. I'm sorry, Inspector, I was mistaken."

"Mistaken?"

"Well, not exactly mistaken. You see, I was at the table and I did see the photo, but to tell you the truth it put me in a rather awkward position."

"Please tell me more."

"Well, when Celia showed it to us she said it was a picture of her wedding. The photo wasn't very clear, but I thought I recognized the man in it."

"You recognized her husband?"

"Yes. I didn't know he was her husband until I saw it, of course, but he looked like someone I'd met."

"And why would that have put you in an awkward position?"

"Well, you see, if it was who I thought it was, he was someone who'd come up to me in a pub one night and paid me what you might call unwanted attentions. I didn't want anything to do with it – I'm not that kind of woman – so I told him where he could get off. In no uncertain terms."

"And was that the end of it?"

"As far as I know, yes. Some other people came in and he cleared off. I didn't hear from him again. But when I saw him in that photo and Celia said he was her husband, I thought it would be a bit embarrassing if it came out that her old man had been up to no good in that way and that I was the one who'd been on the receiving end of his advances. Besides, the photo wasn't clear enough for me to be sure. So I decided to keep out of the whole thing."

"And made a false statement."

"I didn't think it would make any difference whether I'd seen the photo or not. And I didn't want to get mixed up in someone else's marital problems either. In any case, I still can't be sure it was him. You won't mention this to that Celia, will you?"

"Only if it's necessary for the purposes of our investigation. I can't promise not to mention it. It would have been helpful if you'd told us this earlier."

"I'm sorry. I didn't think it was important, and I didn't want to hurt Celia if it turned out I was mistaken."

"Any detail is potentially important in a case like this. What's his name, this man who was troubling you?"

"I can tell you the name he gave me, but I don't think it's going to help you much."

"Just tell me."

"All right, he said his name was Smith. But then again, his sort often do – that or Brown or Jones. He probably didn't want me to know who he really was."

"And when did this happen?"

"It was a week or so before the dance."

"You also told us that after the incident with the photo, Mary said, 'He'll pay for this. He's a traitor.' Is that true?"

"Yes. The only thing I told you that wasn't completely true was what I said about seeing the photo, and I've just explained why that was. What Mary said was nothing to do with that."

"At the time, you implied that you didn't know what she meant by those words. If I asked you now why you think she said that, what answer would you give?"

"Well, yes, of course, knowing that Mary had just been looking at a photo of Celia's husband, I did think it must be something to do with that. But I'm still not sure what she meant. What I mean is, who was he a traitor to? If Mary had known he was married when she had the affair with him, she'd already know he'd betrayed his wife, so why react like that? Unless she didn't know he was married. Perhaps that's it – although if the relationship was over, as she said, why would she care?"

"Could she have meant he was a traitor to someone other than his wife? Or even a traitor to his country?"

"I've no idea."

"Let me ask you one last question about something else, to do with your work. Are you aware of any pilfering going on at Everson Engineering?"

"No. Pilfering of what?"

"Just pilfering of property belonging to the company."

"No, I'm not. But that happens everywhere, doesn't it?"

"Did Mary ever say anything to suggest that she knew it was happening?"

"No, I don't think she did. Not that I can recall, anyway."

"That will be all, then, Miss Willerson. And if you do think of any other way in which your recollections may have been inaccurate, please let me know."

CHAPTER 34

Jago drove slowly south from Chadwin Road down almost the whole length of Prince Regent Lane, the car's hooded headlight picking out only meagre detail in the darkness. He turned left into Maybury Road and parked by the kerb. It was a short street, and unless Smith actually lived on it he would be unlikely to approach from this direction and spot the car, since the road and the turning off it led only to the new primary school and to the playing fields. Cradock was due to turn up by a quarter to eight. The detective constable had briefed Beatrice that she was to do exactly as Smith told her – bring the money, meet him at the phone box on the corner as he had said, and let him take it. Then he and Jago would take over. They would be in place close to the phone box before eight o'clock – close enough to watch what was happening and apprehend Smith, but not close enough to be seen.

The air-raid siren had already sounded, and overhead the searchlights traced their criss-cross patterns in the sky. Jago craned his neck to look up through the windscreen. He couldn't see any enemy planes caught in the beams of light, but the anti-aircraft fire was projecting its deafening volleys into the night regardless. Somewhere in the distance he could hear explosions.

It wouldn't be easy to see Smith clearly in this darkness, but on the other hand, he would be equally unlikely to spot them. And he would be at a disadvantage, because he didn't know they were there. Even if he suspected a trap, he wouldn't know where they might come from, whereas they knew exactly where his designated meeting place with Beatrice was.

Jago heard a finger tapping on the car's side window. Cradock opened the door and slid into the passenger seat. His breathing was laboured.

"Sorry, sir, hope I'm not late."

"Only one minute," said Jago.

"Right. I'm a bit out of breath – had to run all the way from the Railway Tavern."

"They were chasing you?"

"No, sir. I meant I had to run to get here on time. It was an interesting experience."

"Tell me later. Get your breath back – you'll need it if Mr Smith turns up."

Cradock sat back in the chair and took deep breaths.

"Okay now, sir," he said. "Ready for action."

The explosions were getting closer. Fires were starting somewhere not far away, and the black night began to lighten a little as the flames took hold.

"Follow me," said Jago, getting out of the car. He led Cradock a few yards down the road, to the junction with Prince Regent Lane. Where the houses ended there was a patch of wasteland. The two men ran across it and crouched behind a clump of bushes from where they had a good view of the street and the phone box.

Before long they saw the figure of a woman approaching, clothed in a coat and a headscarf. She was carrying a large handbag. There wasn't enough light to see her face, but it could only be Beatrice, they assumed.

She took up her position, as agreed, beside the phone box. Cradock had told her to stand between the phone box and the inside edge of the pavement, to restrict Smith's potential escape routes.

It was eight o'clock. As if intentionally marking the hour, a fire engine thundered by, its bell ringing. If Smith was here, thought Jago, that might hold him back, increase his caution. But even as he considered this possibility another figure appeared. From the size it looked like a man, in a dark jacket and trousers and with a cap pulled down over his face. Jago nudged Cradock in the ribs to make sure he'd seen too.

The man approached Beatrice and stood close to her. There was presumably some brief exchange of words which the detectives could not hear – the only sound was the continuing crump of bombs and the pounding of the anti-aircraft guns.

"Let's get him," said Jago.

He got to his feet and began to run towards the man, followed by Cradock. As they crossed the short stretch of wasteland the suspect turned and saw them. He grabbed the handbag and dashed away, into the road.

Jago and Cradock gave chase. He was heading north up Prince Regent Lane. He'd already made twenty yards on them, running with long strides down the near side of the deserted roadway. Jago pushed on as fast as he could, but Smith seemed to be at least their match in speed. He was holding them off, possibly even gaining ground.

A shape appeared in the gloom ahead. It was a vehicle of some kind, a dark shadow on darkness. It was heading towards Smith, who was running towards any oncoming traffic. Its dim lights drew near. It was a truck.

"Watch out, you fool!" Jago shouted. At the last moment Smith swerved out of the way, onto the other side of the road, and it was the pursuers' turn to dodge the lorry. Jago and Cradock lunged out of its way and followed him on the opposite side of the road. Now there was a new danger – any traffic would bear down on them unseen, from behind.

"Pavement!" shouted Jago to Cradock.

They both jumped onto the pavement and continued in hot pursuit. The blast of a nearby bomb jolted the ground. A car sped past them and pulled round Smith just in time to avoid hitting him. Jago saw him leap onto the pavement too, still at least fifteen yards ahead of them.

"We're gaining on him," he shouted to Cradock. "Come on!"

He heard something else approaching behind him. Another vehicle. The engine was loud, a deeper growl than the car, and a sound he knew well. He looked over his shoulder just as it passed them – a double-decker London bus, the dim blue wartime-regulation lights in the lower saloon glimmering through its side windows. In a moment it was ahead of them, gaining on Smith.

Their quarry was now no more than ten or twelve yards ahead. Smith must have heard the bus approach, because he turned round to look too. Jago shouted a warning to Cradock, but they could run no faster. Smith stepped into the road as the bus passed him, ran three or four steps behind it, then jumped onto the back platform and grasped the vertical handrail. They saw him turn towards them. He clung to the handrail with his left hand, leaned out at an angle and waved to them casually as the bus pulled ahead and gradually disappeared into the darkness.

Jago and Cradock stopped in their tracks – there was no catching him now. They hunched over, hands on their knees, and fought to get their breath back. A few moments passed before either could speak.

"He's pretty fit," said Cradock at last.

"Fit and lucky," added Jago. "That bus saved his bacon. He'll be well away by now."

"With the money, too."

"You don't need to remind me. We'll have to make our apologies to Miss Cartwright."

They trudged back down the road, the air around them still ringing with gunfire but now also bitter with the smell of smoke. When they reached the phone box they leaned against it, neither of them speaking.

"Where is he?" said a voice behind them. "Where's that man?"

It was a woman's voice. They both turned towards its source and recognized Beatrice emerging from the shelter of a shop doorway. When she got close they could see the anxiety on her face.

"I'm afraid he got away," said Jago. "He managed to hop on a bus as it was passing – too fast for us."

"You let him escape? How could you?"

"Don't worry, we'll track him down."

"But what about me? What happens if he tracks me down first? He'll know I went to the police now, and he said he knows where I live."

Beatrice's voice was trembling. She looked down the street as if expecting the man to appear out of the darkness.

"What am I going to do? I can't go home. He'll find me."

"We'll make sure he doesn't," said Jago. "I have a friend who'll be happy to put you up for the night – a lady friend. She's called Rita. We'll take you home to pick up some things, then drive you to her place. It's not far. Then tomorrow we'll find you somewhere a bit further away where no one knows you, so you can lie low for a couple of days."

"I've got a cousin in Chigwell, sir," said Cradock. "A female cousin, that is. I'm sure Miss Cartwright could stay with her for a while, out of harm's way."

"Does that sound all right, Miss Cartwright?" asked Jago.

"I don't care, as long as that man can't find me," said Beatrice. "Did he get away with my money too?"

"I'm afraid so, but we'll do everything we can to recover it."

"Did you see his face?"

"No, it was too dark."

Beatrice wiped her eyes and composed herself.

"In that case, I've got something that might help you."

She returned to the shop doorway, picked up an object and brought it back to Jago. He strained his eyes through the gloom and then saw it was a man's cloth cap.

"I think this is his," she said. "I found it on the ground as soon as he'd dashed off. I thought perhaps it would give you a clue or something."

Jago took the cap, turned it upside down and peered inside it, shifting his position to try to capture any tiny scrap of light that might help him.

"Thank you, Miss Cartwright," he said. "I think you may be right."

CHAPTER 35

The next morning Jago and Cradock collected Beatrice and drove north towards the small rural town of Chigwell. Beatrice sat in the front next to Jago, while Cradock and the small suitcase she had packed on the way to Rita's were relegated to the back. She seemed to have recovered from her fright of the previous evening. Rita had been very kind, she told them, and she had slept surprisingly well. Cradock's private observation from the back seat was that she looked a sight fresher than either him or his boss.

"What I still don't understand," said Beatrice as they bowled along the main road into the Essex countryside, "is how that man Smith, or whatever his name really is, knew all that information about me."

"You're sure he's not someone you've seen before – someone at Everson's, for example?" said Jago.

"I'm as certain as I can be, but then I've only met him twice, once in the blackout and both times with that cap over half his face. Why do you mention Everson's?"

"It's just that it seems to me it might have been passed on to him by someone who has a connection with you through your job. I want you to think, Miss Cartwright – how much of what he knew about you would have been known to Everson Engineering?"

Beatrice sat in silence, head down, counting off the fingers on her left hand with the forefinger of her right as if working through a list in her mind. She looked up.

"From what I can remember him saying, all of it, I reckon. It's the sort of thing that would probably be in my personal file. Why do you ask?"

"Because I think that's where our Mr Smith may have got it from. Is it possible someone could have gained access to it?"

"I suppose it's possible. Certainly Miss Hornby could have – she's the head of personnel, so she's in charge of all the files. But how would I find out? I mean, if I thought someone had got hold of my file who shouldn't have and I wanted to enquire about it or make a complaint, the person I'd have to go to is Miss Hornby. But if she's the one who's taken information out of it and given it to a criminal she's not going to tell me, is she?"

"If you felt uncomfortable about taking the matter to her, could you raise it with Mr Everson? He's the only person in the company who's senior to Miss Hornby."

"Are you joking?" said Beatrice. "I don't think so. Have you seen those two together? They're like a couple of love birds. You couldn't get a cigarette paper between them sometimes. I'm sure there's something going on, now his wife's out of the way. While the cat's away, you know. I think she's got him wrapped round her little finger."

"In that case," said Jago, "I think you'd better leave this matter with us. Stay out here where you're safe until we contact you."

"All right, I will. But I want you to catch that man, and I want my money back."

***

Cradock's cousin proved to be a good choice. She lived in a dilapidated but clean cottage just outside Chigwell on the road leading to the RAF barrage balloon depot and the River Roding, and she and Beatrice seemed to hit it off as soon as they met. Jago and Cradock left them chatting and began their return journey to West Ham.

"Interesting, isn't it, guv'nor?" said Cradock, now promoted back to the front seat.

"What is?" asked Jago.

"The difference between the generations. I mean, there's Beatrice Cartwright saying to our faces that the two senior people in the company where she works are like love birds, while old Miss Hornby witters on about 'delicate matters' that she'd rather not talk about, but in fact she's doing the same thing as Beatrice – they're both insinuating the same about each other."

"They can't both be right, then."

"Not unless Mr Everson's got more time on his hands than he lets on," said Cradock. "By the way, sir, I noticed you didn't tell Beatrice that Miss Hornby's already told us her file's gone missing."

"Yes, that was intentional. For the time being I think it's best that not everyone working at Everson's knows everything we know."

"What I'm thinking is why would Miss Hornby bring it to our attention? If she's the one who passed the information to Smith, whoever he is, surely it would be in her interests to keep the fact quiet?"

"But equally, if she's up to something it could be a bluff. She's the only person who definitely doesn't need to steal the file in order to get the information out of it. So if it is her, it would make a lot of sense for the file to go mysteriously missing – then it could be anyone who took it. And she puts herself in the right by reporting it to us."

"So what we need to do is find this Smith fellow."

"Yes, exactly. He seems a slippery customer, but when we get our hands on him we'll know how he got the information. And speaking of information, how did you get on at the Railway Tavern?"

"It was really interesting. There was a bloke in there selling silk stockings and what have you, on the quiet."

"Did you buy some?"

"Really, sir – what would I do with a pair of silk stockings?"

"I don't know. Save them for a rainy day?"

"I'm not sure it'll ever get that rainy. He wanted twelve and six for them. Anyway, I didn't buy them, but he did say he could get some of that peroxide for dyeing your hair, only he had to nip round the corner to get it from his mate. I kept an eye on him as he went, and you'll never guess whose house he went to."

"Surprise me."

"Harry Parker's."

"That's not a big surprise. So he's the source of your man's hydrogen peroxide. We'll have a word with Harry, then."

"And you, sir?"

"What about me?"

"You haven't told me yet what happened when you went to see Angela Willerson."

"Ah, yes, that was most interesting too," said Jago. "To put it in a nutshell, it turned out she wasn't quite telling us the whole truth when she said she hadn't seen that photo of Celia's at the dance."

"Do you know why?"

"Yes, because she says when she saw the man in the picture, she recognized him."

"Who was he?"

"You'll like this, Peter. An intriguing coincidence. She said he was a man who'd paid her what she called unwanted attentions, and she'd had to send him packing. She didn't want to mention it, because she thought it might embarrass Celia. And what's more, she said he'd called himself Smith, but she wasn't convinced."

"So that would mean the man who was pestering Angela and calling himself Smith was actually Celia's husband. Could he be the same Smith who accosted Beatrice too?"

"A Smith here, a Smith there... These types don't have much imagination, do they?" said Jago. "It's possible, but on the other hand you could probably walk down the street today and meet at least two Mr Smiths, so I'd keep an open mind on it."

"But even so, sir, that means –" Cradock broke off, catching up with his thoughts, then smacked his hand against his thigh. "Yes, that's it! Angela's Mr Smith is really Richard Berry, and we know he and George Fletcher are one and the same. So if it turned out

Angela's Smith was the same man as Beatrice's Smith, they'd both be George Fletcher!"

"Quite possibly," said Jago.

He gestured to a buff-coloured envelope poking out of the cubby hole in the passenger side of the dashboard.

"That cap Beatrice says she picked up last night after Smith lost it is in there. Take it out and have a look inside."

Cradock followed his instruction and examined the inside of the hat from every angle.

"Nothing as far as I can see, except for the manufacturer's label."

"But that's the whole point. Who's the manufacturer?"

"It says Herbert Johnson, hat and cap maker, Bond Street."

"Correct. And if you knew anything about hats you'd know Herbert Johnson makes top quality ones. Worn by the crowned heads of Europe, that sort of thing. This one looks fairly new, and it may have been bought locally, so I want you to start by checking the local gents' outfitters. There won't be many shops round here that sell pricey items like this. If you don't get any joy here, try their own shop in Bond Street. Find out if anyone remembers selling it, and to whom."

CHAPTER 36

The boot was on the other foot. Jago was accustomed to questioning suspects whether they liked it or not, but now it felt as though he were the one assisting Dorothy with her enquiries. He'd promised to take her to the Railway Tavern on Wednesday evening so she could sample the kind of haunt where black market trading went on, and possibly even see some of it in action, and Wednesday evening had now come. He'd asked her to arrive by six, so that they'd stand a chance of avoiding the evening air raids, but she'd been late. Now it was almost blackout time. He hoped she'd be able to absorb as much of the atmosphere as she needed for her article before the bombs started falling.

He ushered her in through the entrance. Inside there were doors marked "Public Bar" and "Saloon Bar".

"Which one?" said Dorothy.

"They're not used to seeing women in the public bar," said Jago. "It might overexcite them. We'll take the saloon bar. Even so, stick close to me."

The saloon bar was crowded, but he spotted one small table at the far end that was unoccupied and asked Dorothy to sit at it and keep his chair while he went to the bar in search of drinks. Dorothy asked for an orange juice but they didn't have any, so she settled for a lemonade, to the apparent disgust of the barman. Jago got himself a pint of bitter and joined her at the table.

"How did you get on in Liverpool?" he asked, taking his seat.

"That trip was a real eye-opener," said Dorothy. "I've seen what's happening to London, but they're getting it up there too. Terrible bombing, people suffering."

"Because it's a port, I suppose. Biggest on the west coast,

main port for North American shipping, it's bound to be a major target."

"Yes, like here – the Germans need to destroy the ports, but the civilians are getting bombed too. The destruction is as bad as anything I've seen down here. Even the prison got bombed, just a few days ago – Walton Gaol. Twenty-two prisoners died, they said. I saw a destroyer bringing in survivors from a passenger ship that had been torpedoed too – the *City of Benares*. Just kids, they were: children being evacuated to Canada. It would break your heart."

"One of our men came to see me a couple of days ago. He lost both his children on that ship."

"I'm so sorry."

"This war spares no one. But I'm glad you were there to see what was happening. You know more than I do about how things are up there."

Jago glanced over Dorothy's shoulder towards the other end of the saloon bar. Without a word he slumped down into his chair, held his glass in front of his mouth and used his free hand to obscure the upper part of his face, as if resting his head on it.

"What's the matter?" asked Dorothy. "Are you okay?"

"I'm fine, thank you, but all of a sudden I don't want to be seen. You're interested in crime, aren't you? That's why you're here?"

"Well, yes, I suppose so."

"I've just spotted a man I'm planning to question about some potentially criminal activity he may have been involved in. Don't turn round. I don't want him to know I'm here, but I want to keep an eye on him."

Dorothy resisted her instinct to look over her shoulder.

"Okay. Just let me know if you want me to move or anything. Everything in me wants to take a look and get the story, but I won't get in your way."

"Thanks," said Jago.

He was concentrating on what Harry was doing. Not much, it

seemed. He hadn't bought a drink, and wasn't talking to anyone. He kept glancing at the door, as if he were waiting for someone. A couple of minutes passed. The door opened, and the person who came in scanned the room cautiously, then approached Harry.

Jago almost spilled his beer.

"Good heavens," he exclaimed, his eyes fixed on the new arrival.

"What's happening?" asked Dorothy. "I can't bear the suspense."

"The man I'm watching is called Harry Parker, and I suspect him of selling scarce items on the black market. Someone's just come in who's the last person I'd expect to see in a pub like this, and especially meeting Harry. They seem to know each other."

"Who is he, this other person?"

"Not he. It's a she. She's a very respectable lady, and her name is Miss Winifred Hornby."

The name meant nothing to Dorothy, but she could tell from Jago's face that the woman had captured all his attention.

"What are they doing?"

"Wait a moment and I'll tell you."

Jago didn't take his eyes off the couple as they got into a conversation.

"They're talking about something," he said, "but she looks a bit frosty, and he's got his hard face on. It doesn't look like a friendly chat. But not an argument either, more like business. She's running her eyes round the room, looking furtive."

"Can she see you?"

"I don't think so. Now she's getting something out of her handbag. It's a purse. She's opened that now and she's taking something out – a banknote, I think. I can't be sure, but it looks mauve from here, so that would make it a ten bob note."

"A what?"

"Ten shillings – two dollars in your money. She's giving him a few coins too. Now he's putting his hand in his pocket. Maybe he's got something to give her. Let's just – yes, he's passing her a small package, she's taking a look inside. Now she's moved. I can't see what he's doing – she's got her back to me and she's blocking my view. But it looks like they've finished whatever it is they're here for anyway. She's leaving – probably can't wait to get out of a dive like this. What's Harry going to do? He's waiting… Yes, it looks like he's just waiting for her to get away – now he's making for the door too."

Jago waited for a moment in case Harry should return, then relaxed. He took a sip of beer and put his glass down on the table.

"Well, that was a surprise," he said. "It was worth coming here tonight just for that, whatever they were up to."

"I was kind of hoping it might have been worth your while coming here tonight to see me too," said Dorothy.

"Yes, of course, obviously I –"

He felt he was about to run out of words, but was spared when Dorothy continued.

"You see, I've got a surprise for you too."

"Really? What is it?"

"You can't have it just now – I didn't bring it with me. Someone else is bringing it. You just have to wait a few minutes."

CHAPTER 37

Ten minutes or so passed while Jago tried to make conversation with Dorothy by asking her more about her visit to the north-west of England. She kept checking her watch, and soon began glancing towards the door every time she did so.

"Whoever's bringing my surprise had better get here soon," said Jago. "If he doesn't get a move on the Luftwaffe will be here first, and they usually bring some very nasty surprises."

"Oh, don't worry," said Dorothy. "He won't let them interrupt anything."

She looked at the door one more time, and this time it opened. Jago saw a look of excitement flash across her face.

"There he is," she said.

Jago looked too. He was about to share in her obvious pleasure when he saw the man enter the pub. He was a tall young man in RAF uniform, with one ring on his tunic cuff.

Jago felt an unfamiliar mix of emotions welling up in his chest. Disappointment, sadness, and a curious sense of defeat. So what was the surprise? Were they going to announce their engagement to him? His mind spun briefly as he struggled to bring his feelings under control.

The man strode across the room to Dorothy, placed his hands lightly on her shoulders while she was still seated, and planted a quick kiss on her left cheek. She turned to Jago with a wide smile. He wasn't sure what to say.

"Is this my surprise?" he said at last.

"Not entirely," replied Dorothy. "This is part of it. This gentleman, as you can probably tell, is in the Royal Air Force."

The man put out his hand and gave Jago's a firm shake.

"Pleased to meet you, sir," he said.

Jago didn't know whether this was what she had referred to, but he was indeed surprised to hear what sounded like a North American accent.

"You too," he said. "Are you Canadian?"

The man laughed.

"Everyone says that. I guess it's entirely understandable, though. After all, the Canadians are in this war with you, and we're not."

"You mean —"

"You got it. I'm American."

"Fighting for us?"

"One of a very select few, yes."

"But how —"

Dorothy stood and interrupted them.

"Now, now, boys. Before you get busy talking about the war, there's my surprise to think about."

"So he's not your surprise?" said Jago.

"He's part of it," said Dorothy. "But I said he was bringing it too."

Whatever he was bringing must be pretty small, thought Jago. He clearly wasn't carrying anything, and the pockets on his tunic were flat.

"So what is it?"

"The surprise is something he couldn't help bringing with him — it's his name. Allow me to introduce you. Detective Inspector John Jago of the Metropolitan Police Service, this is Pilot Officer Samuel J. Appleton of the Royal Air Force."

"Appleton…" said Jago. "You mean you're related?"

"You silly boy, John. Haven't you worked it out yet? He's the one I told you about. You remember, when you took me to lunch the other week and we had that pie and mash thing? You asked me who else was in my family."

"Yes…"

"Well, this is the one I said I'd tell you about later. But then I thought, I can do better than that – I'll introduce him in person."

"You mean –"

"Yes," said Dorothy. "This is Sam – my brother."

* * *

It took a little while for Jago to regain his composure. He was now filled with a sense of embarrassment and guilt for what he'd been thinking about Dorothy. His first response was to mask his state of confusion by going to the bar to fetch a drink for Sam and taking his time about it. He soon realized, however, that even fiddling round in his pocket for the exact change could only buy him a few extra seconds. He returned to the table, where Sam had now pulled up an extra chair.

"If you'll excuse me," said Dorothy. "Now you're back I think I'll go powder my nose. Is that safe here, John? I know you're concerned for my safety."

"It should be okay now you've got the RAF here," he said, in an attempt at light wit.

"Okay, well you boys can get to know each other while I'm away."

She disappeared across the bar, leaving the two men alone. Jago raised his glass.

"Cheers. I hope you don't mind the beer being warmer than you're used to."

"Cheers," said Sam. "No, that's fine. I'm getting used to it now."

Jago gestured at the ring on Sam's sleeve.

"So you're a pilot officer, then. What do you fly?"

"Fighters."

"Really? Fast work, then?"

"Yes, I fly Spitfires, and they're very fast."

"How is it you're an officer in the RAF when you're American? I didn't know that was allowed."

"Well, it's a long story, but essentially you're right – it was actually illegal for an American citizen to go to another country to enlist in their armed forces. If we wanted to join the RAF, the quickest way was to cross over into Canada, but if the US authorities caught us trying, they could jail us for three years – we'd be breaking the neutrality laws. But once France fell this year the government seemed to turn a blind eye."

"Did many Americans try?"

"I don't know how many, but quite a few, I'd say. Our air force has got all the pilots it needs, and we're not fighting a war. There's a lot of guys who know how to fly but can't get a job. And who'd pass up the chance to fly a Spitfire? It's the best plane in the world."

"But if you join the RAF, don't you have to swear allegiance to the king? Surely that'd be a bit steep for a true-blooded American, even if it did mean you got a chance to fly a Spitfire."

Sam laughed.

"Absolutely – we don't get along with kings too well where I come from, especially when they're called George. But someone worked out a way round it. Instead of pledging allegiance to the king, all we had to do was pledge to obey the orders of our commanders and we were in."

"And did you come through Canada?"

"Yes. I arrived here and joined my squadron at the beginning of August. That was a Sunday, and on the Monday I was in action against a bunch of Me 109s at ten thousand feet over the Channel. That was an exciting introduction, I can tell you."

"And this may sound like a crazy question, but why do it? Why volunteer for another country's war when you could sit tight at home?"

"Well, you know, I don't want to sound too serious about this, but I was raised to do what I thought was right. I look at the world and I see a country in Europe doing bad things to people. That makes me think I want to stop them doing that. My country doesn't want to do that, but yours does, so I decided to come here and do my bit, as you all say. It's as simple as that. If you know my sister, you'll know the way I think."

If I know your sister, thought Jago... He was beginning to wonder whether he knew her at all. He had some making up to do, even if she didn't know what he'd been thinking.

"So which squadron are you in, if I'm allowed to ask?"

"I'm in 41 Squadron, but I heard just the other day there are now enough American pilots in the RAF to form an all-American squadron, so I may find myself getting transferred soon. I'm kind of hoping that won't happen, though, because where I'm stationed now I'm very close to the action."

"Where are you stationed, if I may ask?"

"I'm not far from here, actually – at RAF Hornchurch."

Jago saw Dorothy approaching. She rejoined them at the table and sat down.

"How are you boys getting along?"

"Fine," replied Jago. "Your brother was just telling me he's stationed at Hornchurch."

"Yes," she said. "That's why I couldn't tell you why I was at that dance – the one where there was that business of the women and the photograph. I'd gone to see Sam, but if I'd told you it would have spoiled my surprise. I'm so proud of what he's doing, I wanted to introduce you to him in person rather than just tell you about him."

Sam was beginning to look puzzled.

"I'm getting lost," he said. "What's all this about the dance at the station and a photograph?"

"Do forgive me, Sam," answered Dorothy. "I should have explained. John is investigating a murder case at the moment, and it seems to have some connection with RAF Hornchurch."

"Murder? Anyone I know?"

"I doubt it," said Jago. "It's a Miss Mary Watkins."

"Mary Watkins? You don't say…"

"You mean you know her?"

"No, I can't exactly say I know her, but I did dance with her – at the station, a couple of weeks ago. I remember her name – I knew a girl at home who looked a little like her called Mary Watson, almost the same, so I guess that's made it stick in my mind."

"That's very interesting. Did you just dance, or did you have a conversation?"

"We did talk a little, yes."

"What did she say?"

"I remember some of what she said. It's always the same with your English girls – it's like a language lesson. She said something was giving her gyp, and I had to ask her what it meant. I think she said it means it was giving her a hard time or giving her pain. She said she was glad to get up and have a dance and a move around at last, because she'd hurt her back and it was giving her gyp."

"Do you recall anything else she said?"

"Yes, I remember her commenting on my accent. Just like you did, really, because of the uniform. As soon as I opened my mouth she assumed I must be Canadian, then when I said I was from the USA she was really surprised, and she said what on earth was I doing here fighting someone else's war."

"A reasonable question: I asked it myself."

"Yes. I said it was because I thought it was my duty, and I'd been brought up to do my duty. But that seemed to set her off. She said she'd had enough of duty. She'd been a dutiful daughter, a dutiful sister, a dutiful employee, a dutiful everything, she said, but from now on the only duty she was going to do was to herself. I tried to keep it light, and said something like, 'Not planning to become a dutiful wife any time soon, then?' – just to make conversation, you understand – but that seemed to set her off again. She said, 'No, my sister's the one playing that game. Just to spite me, I wouldn't be surprised, the smug little madam.' 'You don't get on, then?' I said, and she said, 'Too true, matey.' That's another word I love – it's so British."

"Did she happen to say why they didn't get on?"

"No, she just said, 'I'm going to wipe that smirk off that sweet little holier-than-thou face of hers. I'll teach her to look down on me.' I remember that, because it didn't sound like a very sisterly thing to say."

"Anything else?"

"No, that's all I remember. By that time I was thinking this was all a bit serious, not something I wanted to get involved in at a Saturday night dance. So I confess I just finished that dance and said 'Thank you, ma'am', and then avoided her for the rest of the evening."

CHAPTER 38

The next morning was an early start. Jago had written down a list of people and given it to Cradock, saying these were the people they needed to see during the day. He planned to catch Susan Fletcher and her husband at home before George left for work. Cradock was still suppressing a yawn when they arrived at the front door.

Jago knocked, and it opened.

"Good morning, Inspector," said Fletcher. "Up with the lark today, eh? I'm still eating my breakfast, so please excuse me. Was it my wife you wanted to see, or me?"

"It's both of you, actually. It won't take long."

"I should hope not – I've got to be off to work in about twenty minutes."

"It's just a brief word with you. I'll do my best not to detain you."

"Mind if I finish my toast while we're talking, then?"

"Of course, please do."

They went into the house and found Mrs Fletcher already sitting in the living room. She wasn't eating.

"Good morning, Mrs Fletcher," said Jago. "I'll come straight to the point, if you don't mind. The last time we met, you seemed a little agitated. You talked about the gap between you and your sister, and the difficulties that it caused in your relationship. Was there any animosity between you?"

"Animosity? No, I wouldn't say I felt like that. It was just difficult."

"And did you feel that your sister harboured animosity towards you?"

"No. Why are you asking this?"

"We have a witness who says he met your sister and had a conversation with her in which she talked about you."

"Is this someone I know?"

"No, I've no reason to believe you know or have ever met this person."

"Talking behind my back to strangers then, was she?"

"It was only a few passing remarks, as far as I know, but nevertheless they do seem to have been addressed to a stranger."

"All right, what did she say?"

"I'm afraid what the witness reported hearing wasn't very pleasant. I'll paraphrase it – she said you looked down on her, and that you'd only got married to spite her."

"Well maybe I do, and maybe I did. That's not so terrible, is it? I don't find words like that very offensive."

"But if you'll pardon me, I'll quote some other things our witness reported."

He took out his notebook, flipped to the right page and read from it.

"The person in question reported that your sister called you a 'smug little madam' and said she would 'wipe that smirk off that sweet little holier-than-thou face'."

Susan looked shocked and remained silent.

"Do you have anything to say?"

Susan shook her head, avoiding his eyes.

"This perhaps sheds some new light on why your sister wasn't at your wedding, does it not?" said Jago.

Susan shrugged, still silent.

"Mrs Fletcher, there's a discrepancy between what you said on that subject and what your husband told us. You said Mary wasn't able to come to the wedding, which implies that she had an invitation but was unable to attend. But your husband told us she wasn't there because you hadn't invited her, and he suggested Mary didn't like you. He didn't know why you hadn't invited her, because you refused to discuss it."

Susan flashed a look at her husband that to Jago spoke louder than words.

"All right," she said. "If you really want to know I'll tell you. I didn't like my sister. You hear me? I didn't like her, and I'm pretty certain she didn't like me. If you've got any doubts about that, I think those words you've just quoted prove it."

"That's only hearsay, not proof."

"It sounds very much like what I'd expect her to say, especially if I'm not there to hear it. We may have been sisters by blood, but that's the only thing we had in common. I know that's not the way it's supposed to be, but that's how it was."

George sat down beside her and took her hand in both of his. He squeezed it gently, but she looked away. Jago couldn't tell whether he was expressing sympathy or trying to get her to stop talking.

"My wife has been under a lot of strain," said George.

"What do you know about what strain I'm under?" she demanded. "Why don't you just leave me alone? I can't breathe without you fussing all over me."

Susan yanked her hand away from his. Without another word she jumped to her feet and walked over to the living room door. She held it open and stood beside it, facing Jago and Cradock.

"So there you are, Inspector. You wanted to know, and I've told you. Is that enough for you? I think you'd better go now."

***

The second name on Jago's list was Winifred Hornby. The two detectives drove to Everson Engineering and found her at work in her office.

"I'm sorry to interrupt you, Miss Hornby, but there's a small matter we need to clarify with you."

"By all means, Inspector. I'll do my best to be of assistance."

"Were you at the Railway Tavern public house in Scott Street yesterday evening?"

Miss Hornby's eyes widened and she looked from Jago to Cradock and back again.

"How —" She seemed to think better of whatever she'd been about to say and started again. "Well, yes, Inspector, as a matter of fact I was."

"And what time would that have been?"

"I don't recall precisely — I wasn't checking my watch. It must have been sometime between half past seven and eight o'clock, because the blackout started just as I got there."

"And what were you doing there? You don't strike me as the kind of lady who'll go out for a drink in the evening in a place like that."

"Certainly not. I was there only briefly — I was meeting someone, and he had said he wanted to meet there."

"So you were meeting a gentleman?"

"Now hold on, Inspector, this is not what you're thinking."

Miss Hornby's pale cheeks had begun flushing. She looked round again anxiously, as if someone else might be in the room and witnessing the scene.

"Don't you worry, Miss Hornby, I'm not thinking anything. What was the name of the gentleman?"

Her voice dropped to a half-whispered tone of resignation.

"He's called Harry Parker."

"And what was the purpose of your meeting?"

"I, er… that is to say he… He does some window cleaning for us at Everson Engineering."

"How interesting. Do continue."

"I normally pay him from the petty cash when he's done them, but on this occasion I wasn't able to, so I said I'd pay him in the evening. I don't think he's very flush with money."

"At the Railway Tavern?"

"Yes. I said I'd take it to his house, but he said he and his wife would both be out, so I asked him where he'd be. He said the Railway Tavern and told me where it was, so I said I'd drop it in there. I had no idea, of course, what kind of establishment it was until I got there. 'Tavern' sounded like a nice, homely place to me."

"I'm sure it would. How much did you pay him?"

"I gave him twelve shillings and sixpence, then got out as quickly as I could. That's all there is to it, Inspector."

"I don't believe that's the case. I believe there is something more to it – he gave you something in exchange for that money."

"I don't know what you mean."

"Miss Hornby, are you familiar with section two of the Prevention of Crimes Amendment Act 1885?"

A look of alarm crossed her face.

"No, of course I'm not. What are you talking about?"

"It is an offence to wilfully obstruct a police officer in the execution of his duty. I shouldn't like to have to charge you with that offence, Miss Hornby, but I must have the truth from you. What was in that package?"

Miss Hornby crumpled. Her voice was almost inaudible.

"Stockings."

"I beg your pardon?"

She looked at him and spoke a little louder.

"Stockings. If you must know, I was buying silk stockings from him. I needed them, and he told me he had a pair he could let me have. You just can't find them in the shops, you know."

***

The third name Jago had written on his list was Herbert Johnson, but this did not require a visit.

"So," he said as he started up the Riley's engine, "did you get anywhere with that cap?"

"I did," said Cradock, "and I didn't even have to go up to the West End. The fourth place I checked was a gents' outfitters in Stratford Broadway, and they had a record of selling it five weeks ago. They said the customer paid with a cheque."

"And the customer's name?"

Cradock stared ahead through the windscreen and grinned.

"You'll never guess."

CHAPTER 39

The ARP depot had been a school until September 1939. Jago had last visited it twelve years ago, when an anxious headmaster had discovered damage suggesting someone had broken into the premises during the night. On that day the playground had swarmed with boys playing improvised games of football, but now there was not a child or a teacher to be seen. The pupils had long since been evacuated to safer parts of the country, and the place where they had stood in neat lines ready to return to their classrooms after playtime was now occupied by a stack of timber props and three sets of ladders. Through a window in what looked like the gymnasium he could see stores of tools, buckets, stirrup pumps, and other paraphernalia for dealing with air raids.

The playground itself presented a curious sight. It was now a parking space for vehicles. They were clearly all serving one purpose – Air Raid Precautions – but unlike a commercial or council yard, where he was accustomed to seeing a fleet of identical vehicles in identical livery, this was a hotchpotch. Civilian saloons of various makes that had been converted into stretcher carriers for rescue parties stood alongside lorries borrowed from local firms, now loaded with ARP equipment but still bearing their owners' names in smart lettering. On the other side of the playground he saw a couple of Tilly vans, some motor cycles, and a heavy lorry with a crane mounted on the back. Somewhere among these, he assumed, would be the truck Harry was driving on the night of the murder.

Cradock found a man in bluette ARP overalls and wellington boots who took them to the depot superintendent. The superintendent confirmed that Harry Parker was there and offered the use of his office for their conversation.

Ten minutes later Jago and Cradock were seated alone with Harry in the office.

"I know you're on duty, Harry, so I'll be brief," said Jago. "What were you doing at the Railway Tavern last night?"

"Railway Tavern? I think there must be a mistake."

"I saw you there, Harry."

"What? Oh, you mean that Railway Tavern. I thought —"

"Cut the nonsense, Harry, and just tell me what you were doing."

"Having a drink, of course."

"You weren't having a drink when I saw you. You were talking to a lady."

"Was I? Well, I do sometimes talk to ladies. If I did talk to one last night I don't know who she was."

"You do know her, Harry. Miss Winifred Hornby."

"Oh, yes, now I remember. Tall, with glasses."

"I saw money changing hands between you, and I'd like to know what that was for."

"Money? Oh, that… Yes, I'd, er, cleaned some windows for her, at her house, and she was just settling up."

"I wish I could believe this charming story, Harry, but I'm afraid I know it's not true. We've already spoken to Miss Hornby, and she's told us you were selling her silk stockings. Is that true? I was watching you, remember."

Jago watched Harry's eyes. He seemed to be weighing up his options, as if trying to work out whether further denial would mean deeper trouble.

"All right, yes, I was. Just helping her out, you know – only one pair. A harmless little spot of private enterprise, that's all."

"And does your range extend to other products? Hydrogen peroxide, for example?"

Harry's expression turned to astonishment. Now he looked like a man in a music hall audience who'd just had his mind read.

"How did you know —"

"By keeping my eyes on you. You must have walked under a ladder, Harry. Your luck's just run out."

Harry's shoulders slumped.

"You've had a little scheme working at Everson's, haven't you?" said Jago.

Harry nodded, his eyes down.

"Tell me how it worked."

"Okay. It was nothing big, you know. Just a little bit of stuff here and there. My missus cleans for them, and she'd sometimes come across a bit of this or that, so I told her to put it out near the dustbins by the back door where I park my barrow while I'm doing the windows. Then I'd come along and put them in the barrow — just had to make sure I got to them before the dustmen came to empty the bins and cart the rubbish away."

"And what made you think you were entitled to do this?"

"I got the idea from someone who worked there. I was cleaning their windows one day and this person asked after the wife, as you do, and I said well, we're usually a bit short at the moment, so she's still charring, but it's bad for her knees. Then she says something like it's not surprising some people help themselves to a few bits and pieces and find good homes for them, especially when they can see their loved ones suffering for lack of a bit of cash."

"You said 'she' — so this was a woman?"

"Of course it was. She virtually told me to help myself. She said there's gallons of peroxide lying around and doing nothing when there's plenty of women who'd be glad to get their hands on it for their hair. I asked, casual like, where they kept it, and it turned out it was in a place my Flo cleans in the mornings before the staff come in. I thought she was a bit dim to give away information like that, but I suppose she didn't think of me as someone who might nick the stuff. Then I thought maybe she's dropping some kind of hint. Either way, it all looked too easy, so I did it."

"Including valves?"

"Valves? No. A few batteries, but no valves. What kind of valves?"

"Never you mind. And this woman who spoke to you: would that be Miss Hornby?"

Harry hesitated.

"No. It was someone else who worked at Everson's. That other lady, the one we found on the bomb-site – Mary Watkins."

CHAPTER 40

Jago and Cradock sat in the Riley outside the ARP depot. Jago pulled his sleeve back and checked his watch.

"We've still got some calls to make, and I want to finish them before blackout time."

"I thought we were going to arrest Parker for pinching that stuff," said Cradock. "Did you change your mind?"

"There's no time to get him back to the station if we want to finish our calls. Harry won't go anywhere. He's an old-timer – the sort that knows when the game's up and takes the consequences. Doing time is just part of the job for a man like him."

"So are we going to see Mr Everson and tell him we've found his pilferer?"

"No. I still need to see some people about a murder, and I want to see them tonight. Besides, we still don't know who's been taking the valves. I can't see why Harry would lie about that if he's admitted taking the other stuff."

"Yes, obviously the murder's more important, but what Harry said about Mary – couldn't that be about the murder too?" said Cradock.

"What do you mean?"

"He's as good as said she talked him into doing that pilfering. What if she was the brains behind the whole thing?"

"Possible, I grant you. She's on the inside, knows where everything is. I certainly don't think Harry has brains to spare."

"So then what if there was some reason why he had to silence her? Supposing she'd threatened to shop him or something, or tried to blackmail him into doing something else for her? He'd have had a motive to kill her, wouldn't he?"

"All theories for which we have absolutely no evidence," said Jago. "What's more, we've only got Harry's word that Mary said any of what he claims she said – there was only him and her there, and now she's dead. She may have put some pressure on him, but Harry's always been content with relieving other people of their property, not taking their lives."

"Every murderer starts somewhere, though, sir. We've been taking Harry's account of finding Mary's body at face value – but is it true?"

Jago was looking in the car's rear-view mirror while they spoke. As Cradock reached the end of his question, Jago opened his door.

"Here's someone who may be able to help us," he said, and got out of the car.

Cradock strained round in his seat, but could see no one. He followed Jago onto the pavement just in time to see him walking back towards the car with Harry's colleague Stan Jenkins.

"Jump in the back and let Mr Jenkins have a seat in the front, please, Peter, will you?" said Jago.

Jenkins settled into the front passenger seat, with Cradock behind him, and Jago resumed his place at the wheel.

"Mr Jenkins, I'd just like to check one or two details with you," he said. "Please tell me again what you can remember of the night you found the body."

"It's like we said," Jenkins replied. "We were on duty, searching that bomb-site. That poor woman who was killed wasn't there at ten o'clock, but when we came back next morning, there she was."

"So what exactly did you do when you finished searching the site at ten?"

"It was a bit before ten, I reckon, but I couldn't tell you the exact time. We'd looked all over the site, we'd established there were no cellars in those houses, and we'd listened out in case anyone was buried under the wreckage. We'd checked with the air raid warden that no one who lived there was unaccounted for. We'd

265

done everything we're supposed to do. So then we loaded all our gear back onto the lorry and I drove the lads down the road to get a cup of tea from the WVS mobile canteen."

"You drove the lorry?"

"Er, yes."

"But Harry told me he was the only member of the squad with a licence to drive that lorry."

"Well, technically, yes."

"So you don't have a licence?"

"Strictly speaking, no, I suppose I haven't. But driving tests and licences were all suspended when the war started, weren't they?"

"Yes, but it was Harry's job in the rescue squad to drive the lorry, wasn't it? Why wasn't Harry driving?"

"He was, er, taking a break. He likes his food, does Harry, and he gets a bit hungry. He said he was going to nip home for a bite to eat. His house was only about ten minutes' walk away, but the opposite way to the canteen, so he said he'd walk – didn't want to waste government petrol on a lift, I suppose."

"So he went off on his own while the rest of you drove off for your cup of tea?"

"Yes, that's right. I do know how to drive a lorry, though. I've just never got the licence. I thought it wouldn't matter, just popping round the corner."

"And at what time did you next see him?"

"When we got told to go to another site. We drove round and picked him up on the way. It must have been about half past eleven."

"Thank you for your time, Mr Jenkins," said Jago.

Jenkins got out of the car and continued on his way to the ARP depot's entrance, where he turned in and was lost to sight. Jago sat in silence for a moment without starting the engine.

"So what do you think?" he said.

"I'm thinking Harry didn't tell us about taking that little break, did he?" said Cradock.

"Indeed. Popped home for some of his wife's good cooking, it seems."

Cradock took his notebook from his pocket and flipped back a page.

"Yes, from what Jenkins said, they left the Tinto Road site at about ten, and Harry went off home to his missus – about ten minutes' walk away. If we assume he helped the rest of the squad load their gear back onto the lorry first, that would get him home sometime between a quarter and half past ten."

Jago turned the ignition key in the lock on the car's dashboard.

"I think we need to add another brief call to our itinerary," he said. "I'd like to drop in on Mrs Parker and find out from her what time her husband got home that night."

CHAPTER 41

Despite a number of encounters with Harry Parker over the years, Jago had never met his wife. As he and Cradock waited on the front doorstep of number 47 Hemsworth Street he was curious to meet the woman who'd taken on the challenge of marriage to Harry.

The door was opened by a short, stout woman dressed in a flowery cotton pinafore over a brown woollen dress, with sturdy lisle stockings in the same colour and a pair of old green slippers. Her hair was streaked with what looked like the early stages of greying, and her eyes were tired.

"Detective Inspector Jago and Detective Constable Cradock, West Ham CID," said Jago.

"Oh aye, what's he done now, then?" she said, her voice weary. "You'd best be coming in."

"Thank you," said Jago, stepping into a dark and narrow hallway. "Mrs Parker?"

"That's me, for my sins."

"I don't believe we've met before."

"I don't think we have, but I've met one or two of your boys in blue over the years. Come and take a seat. You can call me Flo – everyone else does. Cup of tea?"

"No thanks," said Jago. "We won't be staying long."

She led them into a cramped kitchen with one small window. Jago noticed the glass was grimy and admitted little light.

Flo followed Jago's eye.

"I know what you're thinking, Inspector. A window cleaner with filthy windows. Like cobblers' children, isn't it? Never have shoes. He's always been so busy cleaning other people's windows he's not had time to do ours."

"And he's had other things keeping him busy of late too, hasn't he?"

She eyed him warily.

"Other things?"

"I mean his work with the heavy rescue squad."

"Oh, that. Yes, that's his new hobby. He's always been full of surprises, my Harry."

"How long have you been married?"

"Seven years," she said. "And before you say anything, yes, I did marry late in life."

"Judging by your voice, it sounds like you're not from these parts."

"That's right. I come from a place most people down here have never heard of – the Isle of Lewis. It's in the Outer Hebrides, and Londoners seem to think that's some kind of joke, as if I were saying I'm from Timbuctoo. It's a beautiful place, but a hard life, Inspector."

"What brought you down here?"

"I'd like to say it was love, and in a way it was, but it was the sorrow of love."

"What do you mean?"

"I was walking out with a young man, but he was taken away to the war, to be a sailor in the Navy. We got engaged before he went."

"Was he lost in the war?"

"No: that's the sorrow of it. He got through the whole thing, but never made it home. Have you heard of the *Iolaire*?"

"I think so. Was it a shipwreck?"

"Yes, New Year's Day 1919. Two hundred and eighty Lewis men coming home from the war – all they had to do was cross the Minch from the mainland to Stornoway, but there was a storm. Their wee boat ran onto the rocks just outside the harbour. All those men, but just two lifeboats and eighty lifejackets. More than two hundred of them drowned just twenty feet from the shore, and my fiancé was one of them. They say there was a radio aboard but there was water in the batteries and the telegraphist couldn't signal for help, and the rockets they fired were too late."

"That must have been a terrible shock."

"My mother told me people had seen deer on the island that night, and deer are an omen of death. Harry's always saying I'm too superstitious, but I've got good reason to be."

"So was that when you moved away?"

"That's right. To get away from the memories – and the work."

"What work was that?"

"I was a herring girl – gutting fish every day. That's what you did if you were a woman in Stornoway, and it was hard work. Look at these hands."

She held out her hands towards him, palms up. They were criss-crossed with scars.

"Those are the marks of a herring girl. From the knife we had to use – the *cutag* we called it in the Gaelic. A vicious thing, and working in brine made the pain twice as bad. You have a think about that next time you have kippers for your breakfast."

"So you moved down here and met Harry?"

"Yes, a bit late in life, but I got married in the end. When I was young a fortune-teller told me I'd marry a tall, dark foreigner, and I did."

"I believe Harry was on duty with the rescue squad last Thursday night. Is that your recollection?"

"I think so, yes, on a night shift."

"Can you tell me what time he came home that night?"

Flo looked wary again, as if unsure which answer to give.

"Well, I remember he popped in for a bit, quite late. Said he was hungry. He's always hungry, that man – he says it's my cooking's to blame, but I reckon it's his eating. Anyway, I remember now, he got in at five to eleven. I was a bit cross – I char, you see, so I have to be up early. I go to bed early and don't appreciate being woken up once I've gone. I don't care whether it's my Harry or Hitler, I need my sleep."

"Weren't you in a shelter?"

"No, I can't sleep in those things. It's the damp, you see, and being shut up like that halfway underground. It makes me think about those poor men drowning. When all these raids started I decided that if I had to die, I'd rather be cosy in my own bed than down in some cold, damp hole in the ground. I haven't been killed so far, touch wood."

She reached towards the cupboard door and tapped it as she spoke.

"So anyway, I heard him come in through the door downstairs and I remember looking at the clock and shouting out, 'What time do you call this, Harry Parker? It's eleven o'clock at night.' He said he was hungry, so I told him where he could find some cold meat and bread, then I turned over and went back to sleep."

"How long was he in for?"

"I haven't a clue – I went straight off to sleep. Harry always was a bit of a night worker, as you may recall, Mr Jago. I know he spends half the night digging people out of bomb-sites now, but as far as I'm concerned, whatever else he might want to get up to is his own business. And now, if you'll excuse me, I have to get his supper ready."

CHAPTER 42

Cradock shooed away a couple of boys who were peering curiously into Jago's car as they drew near. It was the only car parked in the street, and therefore presumably an object of unusual interest. Evening was approaching, and some mothers were calling their children in for tea, but farther down the street he could see a group of girls playing a skipping game. They had a rope stretched from one side of the street to the other and were taking it in turns to dance in and out and skip, as one at each end held the rope and swung it round. He could just make out the sound of their voices chanting "salt, mustard, vinegar, pepper", and it reminded him of being a boy, always trying to spoil the girls' games and usually being chased away by them.

He pointed them out to Jago.

"Takes you back, doesn't it, sir?"

"Yes," said Jago. "Shame we have to grow up, really. But at least I had a proper childhood. These poor kids have got nothing but bombs to look forward to."

"They should have been evacuated, shouldn't they?"

"What the government says people should do and what they actually do are two different things. I can't say I blame the parents who've decided to keep their kids. Some of the ones who've gone have ended up in more danger, so who's to say what's best?"

"I suppose nowhere's safe at a time like this," said Cradock. "A bomb could fall anywhere."

"Including on us, so let's not hang around too long. Blackout's at twenty past seven tonight, and we've still got work to do."

They got into the Riley.

"They've dropped him right in it, haven't they?" said Cradock.

"Who has dropped whom?" said Jago.

"Stan Jenkins and Flo Parker — they've dropped Harry in it."

"Explain."

"Well, until this afternoon we'd been assuming the rescue squad were together all that night — you'd think they would be, wouldn't you, if they're on duty and there's air raids on? But if Harry sloped off on his own for a bit, that blows his alibi out of the water."

"The timing's a bit tight, though, isn't it?"

"I don't know. If what Jenkins said is true, Harry should have got home between a quarter and half past ten, but Flo says he got in at five to eleven. That leaves anything up to forty minutes unaccounted for. What was he doing? Playing skipping ropes with his mates?"

"So you're saying he could have been murdering Mary in that time."

"I think it's possible, yes."

"But how would he know where she'd be?"

"I don't know. But what if he just ran into her, unexpectedly? It could happen. She liked going out for a drink, and it was getting on for closing time, so she could have just been walking home and they bumped into each other."

"And?"

"Well, they had a row. Maybe it was something about the pilfering racket, or about something else, or maybe she threatened him. He got angry —"

"Or scared?"

"Yes, angry or scared, or whatever, and he attacked her, got carried away, and before he knows it he's strangled her, and she's dead. He dumps her body, then runs off home."

"He certainly hasn't got much by way of an alibi — Flo's just seen to that."

"Yes, which makes it more likely he just came across her by accident and acted on impulse. If he'd planned it he'd have been more careful."

"Somehow I don't see Harry masterminding a cast-iron alibi."

"He doesn't need to, though, does he? Not if there are no witnesses. If he had to explain that time gap away, he'd probably just say something like he stopped off for a drink in a pub where no one would remember him, or he stopped to help someone who twisted their ankle, or he thought he saw something suspicious on another bomb-site and went to have a look. He could make up a thousand excuses and we'd never be able to prove him wrong."

Jago pursed his lips in thought.

"I'm still not sure," he said. "I've known Harry a long time – he's a petty thief and a failed burglar, but I don't think he's a killer. A man's entitled to be delayed on his way home." He looked at his watch again. "And I don't want to be late home either. Time to get moving – there's someone I want to see on the way."

***

Even at the best of times the back streets of Canning Town could be confusing. Short roads packed closely together at every imaginable angle meant you had to know your way around – a driver new to the area would soon get lost without a street map. Jago knew the streets, and in days gone by, having his own car at his disposal had enabled him to nip from one side of the borough of West Ham to the other without difficulty.

But now there was a war on. Every night the German bombers wreaked their destruction on the people and buildings below, and every morning the workmen were out on the streets repairing water mains, gas pipes, electrical wires, and telephone cables. Drivers had to take more and more circuitous routes as streets were cordoned off. Jago did his best not to show his annoyance as he wove his way through the maze.

He brought the car to a halt.

"Right, here we are," he said.

Cradock peered out of the side window.

274

"This is where Angela Willerson lives, isn't it? Is she the person we need to pop in on?"

"Correct," said Jago, getting out of the car. "Step lively now — we haven't much time."

He walked briskly to the door, followed by Cradock, and rang the bell. Angela opened it.

"Good evening, Miss Willerson. I'm sorry to disturb you, but I need your help with a loose end that I'm trying to tie up."

Angela looked surprised, but moved aside to let them in. As they entered she stepped in front of them, just enough to stop them continuing into her flat.

"The thing is," she said, "I've got a visitor with me."

No sooner had she said this than a familiar figure emerged from the living room into the hall.

"Mrs Berry," said Jago. "How nice to see you. I didn't expect to see you here."

Celia Berry gave him a polite smile.

"It's my first visit, actually. I only arrived a few minutes before you. There was something I wanted to ask Angela about, but it can wait."

Angela looked from Jago to Cradock and then back again.

"Celia and I have met up once or twice since that dance at Hornchurch."

"Yes," said Celia, "I suppose you could say we've become pals, haven't we? I hope I won't be in the way, Inspector. Would you like me to leave?"

"No, not at all," said Jago. "In fact it could be rather convenient that you're here. But if you can give me a moment alone for a quick word with Miss Willerson I'd be grateful."

"Of course," said Celia. "I'll wait in the kitchen."

Angela took Jago and Cradock into the living room.

"How can I help you?" she said.

"I'd like you to come with me and meet someone," said Jago.

"It's not far from here in the car, and the meeting shouldn't take more than half an hour, so I'll get you back here in good time before the blackout."

"Of course. If it'll help you. But hang on – it won't be dangerous, will it?"

"No. Detective Constable Cradock and I will be with you at all times."

Cradock was listening carefully, wondering where his boss was heading in this mysterious visit.

"There's just one other point," Jago continued. "Since Mrs Berry's here, I wonder if she would come too. Could you bring her in?"

Angela walked down the hall and called out in the direction of the kitchen.

"You can come out now, Celia."

Jago heard the sound of a chair scraping on linoleum in the kitchen, and a moment later Celia Berry appeared in the doorway.

"The inspector wants to take me out for half an hour or so," said Angela, "and he wants to know if you'll come too."

"How exciting," said Celia. "Of course. I'm sure we'll be safe with a policeman." She glanced at Cradock. "A policeman each, in fact, if this young dear is coming too."

Cradock looked at Jago with a face that betrayed his bafflement at what was going on.

"In that case," said Jago, "if you ladies can get your coats we'll be off. I should warn you that my car can sometimes be a little draughty, even with the roof up."

They went out into the street, and Angela closed the door behind her. Jago ushered the two women into the Riley's back seats, then took his place at the wheel, with Cradock seated beside him. He pulled away from the kerb and joined the traffic.

CHAPTER 43

Jago could feel his heart beating faster as he urged the car on. This final leg of the journey was longer than the one he'd just done, and he was surprised by the anxiety he felt. Perhaps it was the risk of being caught in an air raid, growing greater with every minute. He thought he'd beaten that old ghost, but maybe not. Or perhaps it was tension, even excitement, as he sensed he was closing in.

There were few vehicles moving on Prince Regent Lane, and he drove almost the whole length of it faster than he should. It was only forty-eight hours since that night's quarry had eluded his grasp, and he didn't want to be reminded of it. He was almost at the northern end of the road. He took a turning to the left for a more direct route, the car lurching on its springs as it rounded the corner. Then he saw. He shouted to his passengers to hold on, and slammed on the brakes. They responded with a squeal and the car stopped just in time. A pair of wooden poles had been stretched across the road with a red road lamp positioned in front of them, and in the middle stood a small wooden trestle sign painted with the words "Police Notice. Unexploded Bomb".

He reversed the car past the last turning, selecting first gear as he went, and braked to a halt, then pushed the change pedal down and stabbed at the accelerator. The car lunged forward into its new route with an angry snarl that seemed to give voice to the urgency clenching his stomach.

Cradock steadied himself with a hand on the dashboard. He was still puzzled about Jago's intentions, where they were going and why he had the two women in the back. He didn't ask, for fear of saying something that might compromise his boss's plans. He glanced over his shoulder. It struck him as odd that despite the apparent friendliness of the two women, not a word had passed between them since they'd started the journey. Angela was staring out of the side window, while Celia was facing straight ahead.

Then he remembered – Angela had said the man in the photo had paid her what she'd called unwanted attentions. Whatever she meant by that, knowing that this man was Celia's husband, she might be wondering why Celia had come to see her. And as she'd said, she didn't want to mention his behaviour to Celia because it might embarrass her. Maybe Angela just wanted to avoid having to speak to Celia. But why was Celia keeping silent too, if they were friendly enough for her to visit? He couldn't think of an answer to that question.

It was a full twenty minutes before they arrived. Jago pulled up in front of a house, and when Cradock saw it he began at last to get some inkling of what might be in Jago's mind.

Jago turned round in his seat towards the two women.

"Miss Willerson, would you mind coming with me now?"

"Of course. If you can let me out of this contraption."

"And Mrs Berry, would you be so kind as to wait here for a little while?"

Celia pulled her coat a little closer round her shoulders.

"By all means, if you insist, but please don't be long. I don't want to sit around out here on my own for too long, thank you very much."

"I'll be with you as soon as I can," said Jago.

He strode towards the front door, followed by Cradock and Angela, and knocked.

It was opened by Susan Fletcher.

CHAPTER 44

The house was silent as they entered. Jago asked Susan if her husband was at home and she said yes, they had just eaten and were planning to be in for the evening. She was in the middle of drawing the blackout curtains. She seemed nervous to Jago, perhaps as the prospect of another evening air raid drew closer. He also sensed a coldness in her manner, and wondered whether she felt she had revealed too much of her fragile nerves the last time he'd seen her. He noticed that she didn't offer them a drink, and also that she showed no curiosity when he didn't introduce Angela.

"I have a few more questions to ask you and your husband," he said.

"Oh," she said, "I see."

There was a silence. She struck Jago as tired and subdued, like a patient who's been told the disease they feared has been confirmed.

"You'd better come in here, then." She opened the door to the living room.

Jago entered the room first, then Cradock showed Angela in. Before Susan could say anything to her husband, he sprang to his feet. A look of alarm flashed across his face.

"Here, what's going on?" he said to Jago. "What's that woman doing here? Who told you you could bring her to my house?"

"George, what do you mean?" said Susan. "Do you know this woman?"

"No, I don't, but he's up to something, and I want to know what."

Angela walked up to him, stood before him and looked him in the eye.

"You bastard," she said.

She turned to Jago.

"It's him, Inspector – the one I told you about, the swine."

"The man you said had been paying you unwanted attentions?" asked Jago.

"George?" said Susan. She looked from one to another in the group, as if she was the only one who didn't understand what was happening.

"Worse than that," said Angela. "He's been trying to ruin me."

She burst into tears and fumbled for a handkerchief in her sleeve.

"How could I be so stupid?"

Susan seemed even more confused, and this time she raised her voice.

"I demand to know what's going on here."

Jago spoke quietly.

"I suggest we all sit down and calm ourselves."

George, Susan and Angela obeyed him and took their seats silently.

"Now," said Jago. "Miss Willerson, perhaps you could tell us what you're referring to."

"I told you someone had been pestering me," said Angela, "but that wasn't the whole story. I was trying to keep out of this."

"I think now you should tell us what happened."

"All right, I will. It was like this. I was having a quiet drink in the pub one evening, by myself." She shot a glance at Cradock. "And before you start jumping to conclusions, Constable, I'm not the kind of woman who goes into pubs on her own every night. It was my local, and I wanted some time to myself."

Cradock tried to look as though that was the last thing he'd been thinking. Angela turned away and faced Jago.

"This man came in and sat down at my table. He used my full name, Angela Patricia Willerson, which not even my friends know

– my middle name, that is – and said he needed to talk to me. I told him to clear off, but he said he was on official business and I had no choice. All right, I said, but keep your voice down. So he did, but what he came out with got me really worried."

"What did he say?"

"He said he was something called a voluntary interceptor, whatever that is, and he worked for the security service. He said he'd been investigating me. At first I thought he was having me on, but he knew everything about me – not just my name, but where I was born, my parents, where I live, where I went to school, people I'd worked for, everything – he even knew this was my local. What he said next really put the wind up me – he said MI5 were tracking people who were using wireless equipment to communicate with the enemy. He said he'd been watching me and had evidence that I was involved in that."

"Was that true?"

"Of course not, and I told him so, but he wouldn't have it. He started saying I was part of the Fifth Column, that I had links to Nazi sympathizers, and that I had a choice: to cooperate or go to prison. I was getting worried now. He didn't look like the kind of man who'd take no for an answer: he was strong, forceful. I said there'd been some mistake, but he said no, there hadn't, and then he started demanding money to keep quiet about it."

"Thank you," said Jago. He turned to George.

"Is this true?"

"Why are you asking me?" said George. "It's nothing to do with me. I don't know what she's going on about."

"It's just that you seem to have a way with women. What can you tell me, for example, about another young lady, Miss Beatrice Cartwright?"

"Never heard of her."

Jago pulled a buff envelope from his coat pocket, opened it and took out a man's cap.

"Is this yours, Mr Fletcher?"

"I don't know."

"I think it is, and I congratulate you on your taste in hats. It's an expensive piece of headgear – not the sort of thing many people in West Ham buy. But then I can imagine you have expensive tastes. It's almost new, too. We have a local gents' outfitter who says he's only sold one of these in the last five months, and the person he sold it to was you."

"I don't know what you're talking about."

"You seem not to know what anyone's talking about, but perhaps you'll understand this simple fact. We found a couple of hairs inside the cap. I very much suspect that if I ask the pathologist to compare them with a sample of yours under a microscope, he'll find that they correspond in all their natural characteristics."

Susan interrupted.

"Why have you got George's hat, Inspector, and why are you talking about hairs? What is this all about?"

"Shut up, you stupid woman," hissed George.

"Mr Fletcher," said Jago, "we're here to find out why Mary Watkins died and who killed her, and I think you can help me."

"But I've never met her," said George. "If you want to know about her, it's my wife you want to talk to, not me. Or that lying witch over there." He pointed at Angela.

"So you do know this lady," said Jago.

His next words were overwhelmed by a noise that came from outside the house and displaced every other sound in the room – the rise and fall of the air-raid siren's wail.

Susan looked anxious.

"Quick, everyone," she said. "We must go down to the cellar – we use it as our shelter. Follow me."

As she moved across the room there was a pounding at the front door.

"Stay where you are," said Jago. "I'll see who that is."

"But the bombs!" said Susan.

"Just stay there for a moment," said Jago.

As he approached the front door the pounding continued. He opened it, and Celia half fell through the doorway, her hair slipping down over her face. She stumbled to a halt in the hall.

"Didn't you hear the siren?" she said. "You can't leave me sitting out there in that little car with an air raid on! I don't care what you're up to in here, I'm coming in. Where's the –"

Her voice trailed off, and a bemused smile flickered across her face. She seemed to forget the sound of the siren.

"Well, would you believe it?" she said. "No wonder you wanted me to stay outside. You never told me that lying rat would be here."

Susan followed the new arrival's eyes to the hunched figure of her husband. He looked shocked.

"George," she said. "Who is this woman?"

Fletcher stared at the new arrival and gave no reply.

"Inspector Jago," said Susan. "Who is this woman? What's she doing in my house?"

"Mrs Fletcher, I think we need to get to the shelter," said Jago. "We can continue this conversation there."

"Yes, yes," said Susan, casting a suspicious glance at Celia. "Come this way."

She took them into the hall, opened a door and led them down a staircase to the cellar that lay beneath the house. She flicked a switch and two electric light bulbs came to life, revealing a neatly arranged room fitted with props of six-by-six timber to reinforce the floor above. There were five chairs and a small table, mattresses and blankets on the floor, a wireless set, oil lamps, torches, buckets of water, an electric kettle, and what looked like a generous stock of dry foods. A selection of books stood in a neat row on a shelf, together with a pile of magazines. Jago wished he had something like this at home instead of his Anderson shelter. He could imagine getting some sleep in a set-up like this.

Susan tried to speak confidently, but there was a tremble in her voice that she seemed unable to control.

"We'll be as safe here as in any Anderson shelter, but with plenty of space, and we'll be dry, too."

"And if there's a bomb with our names on it we'll be blown to pieces just the same," muttered Celia.

Susan rounded on her, barely restraining herself from shrieking.

"If you want to come into my house and use my shelter, will you please mind your tongue? Some people don't find these air raids amusing." She seemed to hear the harsh edge in her own voice and dropped it to a calmer tone. "Now, everyone, please make yourselves comfortable."

Five of the six people in the room sat down. Seeing there was no chair left for him, Cradock shrugged his shoulders and sat on the stairs.

"I'll ask you once again, Inspector," said Susan. "Who is that woman?" She shot another cold glance at Celia, who responded with a sneer.

"Allow me to introduce you," said Jago, rising from his chair. "This is Mrs Celia Berry, wife of Richard Berry, known to you as George Fletcher."

The siren had stopped, and now there was silence in the shelter. It was broken by Susan, her voice barely more than a whisper.

"What?"

Celia replied, the sneer still lingering in her response.

"Sorry, dear, I got him first," she said. "We got married in 1938, and we still are."

"You mean –"

"Yes, dear. I believe the word is bigamist – that's the polite term for a man like him, but I can think of others."

Susan shook her head slowly.

"I don't believe this."

"You can believe it or not, dear," said Celia, "but it's true. Ask your husband – or to be precise, ask mine."

Susan turned to George, but he would not meet her eyes.

"I'm afraid your husband has not been a model of fidelity, Mrs Fletcher," said Jago.

"Are you all trying to humiliate me?" said Susan. "Why? And what's any of this got to do with my sister?"

"It's very much to do with your sister," said Jago. "I suspect there may have been a liaison between your husband and Mary."

"No!" said Susan. "I don't think I can take any more of this. George?"

George grasped her hand.

"It's not true, it's not true," he said. "You know yourself I've never met your sister. You haven't seen her yourself since heaven knows when. Don't listen to him, Susan. And you, Inspector, stop making foul accusations when you have no proof. I told you, I've never met her."

"But I have a witness who saw you and Mary together last year," said Jago. "So you had met her. What's more, she told Miss Willerson here that she'd had a liaison with a man in the past, and I believe it was only when Mary saw a photograph of you in a different context that she realized who you were."

"What photo?" said Susan.

"This one," said Jago.

Susan sprang to her feet. She grabbed the photo, studied it for a moment, then thrust it towards George and stabbed at it with the forefinger of her other hand. George stood up and faced her.

"It's not true," he shouted. "They're making it all up."

Anything he might have said after this was drowned by the crash of a bomb. To Jago it didn't sound very close, but it was close enough. He saw Angela clutch her chest and give an anxious gasp, but what surprised him was that Susan seemed impervious to the noise. She stared coldly at George, turned her back on him and

285

walked away. She stood at one side of the basement room, facing the wall and hugging both arms close to her body.

Jago spoke to her back.

"I'm afraid the truth is your husband is a bigamist, a blackmailer, and in all likelihood an adulterer. Two of those are matters for me, and the last is for you, or perhaps" – he turned to Celia – "perhaps you, to deal with."

Susan swung round to face Jago. He could see she was beginning to tremble, but still she said nothing.

"If he's convicted of bigamy and demanding money with menaces," he continued, "you won't be seeing him for some time."

He now turned his attention to George.

"But there's another and more important question for you, Mr Fletcher. Are you a murderer? You stood to gain from Mary's death, because it meant this house would pass entirely into Susan's hands, and thus effectively into yours – provided you could continue to convince her and the world that you were her husband. It was essential for you to maintain that pretence."

"Hang on," said George. "What do you mean, 'pretence'? How dare you accuse me –"

"I say pretence, Mr Fletcher, because not only were you already married to someone else, but to add insult to injury you'd also had a relationship with Mary before you met and married Susan. Was that how you found out about the house? I don't suppose you wanted news of that liaison to reach Susan's ears. And if Mary recognized you in that photo, standing alongside Celia as her lawfully wedded husband, did she threaten to tell her sister that her husband was a cheat and a liar and her marriage a sham? She might have relished the opportunity to put Susan in her place. You're not the only one who knows how to demand money with menaces, and a threat to reveal that information would be quite a menace. Mary had the power to ruin your plans, and you had plenty of reason to want her dead."

George leaped to his feet. His face was contorted with anger. "It's all lies!" he shouted.

He took a step forward, jabbed his right hand into the inside pocket of his jacket and produced a flick knife. Snapping it open, he lunged towards Angela, who was cowering in the chair beside him. She clutched her hands before her and screamed. George grabbed her by the shoulder with his free hand and yanked her to her feet. In an instant he had pulled her back onto his chest and put his arm round her neck, holding the knife to it.

She looked down at the blade pressing against her throat and whimpered.

"Stop him, please. Don't let him hurt me."

CHAPTER 45

Fletcher grasped Angela tighter and began to drag her across the room, backing away from Jago. He turned towards the stairs that led up from the cellar, pulling Angela round with him. Cradock got to his feet, apprehensively.

"You, get out of my way!" said George.

Cradock took a step down the stairs towards him. George dragged Angela back a pace, his eyes flitting between Cradock to his right and the rest of the room to his left. He twitched the knife against her throat and shouted at Cradock.

"You let me go, or so help me I'll –"

Angela let out a tearful moan.

Jago was positioned six to eight feet away – too far to attempt to rush Fletcher. He stood still and spoke quietly.

"Put that knife down, Mr Fletcher. I asked you a question – are you a murderer? You have a choice to make: you can do the wrong thing now and put your head in a noose, or you can be a sensible fellow and calm down."

George held the knife firmly in place and turned slightly towards Jago.

"But you said –"

Before Fletcher could complete the sentence that was forming in his mind, Cradock plunged down the remaining couple of steps and rammed him sideways against one of the timber props. Fletcher let out a cry of pain as his face slammed into the rough timber, and Angela slipped out of his grasp. Cradock grabbed the man's right arm and forced it up his back as far as it would go. Fletcher screamed and dropped the knife. Cradock kicked it across the floor to Jago, who stopped it with his foot and picked it up.

Cradock forced his captive down onto a chair. Jago pocketed the flick knife, then pushed a pair of handcuffs onto Fletcher's wrists, screwed them shut and put the key in his pocket.

"Thank you, Detective Constable," said Jago. "Now, Mr Fletcher, you sit still and don't think about moving. Any trouble you're in is of your own making, and I would advise you not to compound it by any more rash actions."

Fletcher's shoulders slumped.

A second bomb landed somewhere outside. This time it was closer. Jago felt the blast transmitted through the ground and into his feet. A scattering of dust fell from the cracks between the floorboards above his head. He brushed it off his shoulder and continued.

"You're not the only person here that I want to hear the truth from, Mr Fletcher." He looked round the room. "Here in this cellar we have a sister, a friend, and two betrayed wives. Jealousy is a very powerful emotion, and so is a sense of betrayal."

Susan spoke for the first time since Fletcher's attack. Her voice was subdued and her gaze fixed, as though she were struggling to control her emotions.

"You're saying one of us killed my sister?"

"I'm saying that is possible," said Jago. "But first there are one or two facts I would like to establish."

He turned to Angela. She was rubbing her neck.

"I have a question for you, Miss Willerson. Do you need a little time to recover?"

She stopped rubbing, wiped her eyes and began to pat her hair back into shape.

"No, I'm all right. Carry on."

"You were telling us that Mr Fletcher here had demanded money from you by threatening to report you to the security service as a Fifth Column spy."

"Yes, that's right. That man is evil, Inspector. Believe me, he's the most wicked man I've ever met."

"So he claimed you were a spy. Is it true?"

"Of course not. The whole thing's nonsense."

"I have no knowledge of whether you are a spy or not, so let's assume for the time being you're not."

"Very generous of you, I must say."

"But if that's the case, what did you have to fear? Why not just call his bluff?"

Angela hesitated before replying.

"It was something else he said – something he knew."

"Something he knew about you that was true and that you didn't want other people to know?"

"Yes. I was afraid."

"Afraid of what?"

"Afraid I'd lose my job."

"And why was that?"

"It's because of my work, the work we do at the company. It's war work. Secret war work. I can't tell you what it is – I had to sign the Official Secrets Act."

"I wouldn't expect you to tell us what it is. But if you had a personal secret that you didn't want your employers to know, one that made you fear for your job, I shall have to ask you to tell me what that secret was."

Angela seemed to be weighing up the risks in her mind, unsure whether to speak.

"I belonged to the Link. Do you know what that was?"

"I do."

"This was before the war, you understand. I had views, you see – views that it doesn't pay to have now. The Link was a kind of Anglo-German friendship society, but there was a bit more to it than that. They said the only way to have peace in the world was for Britain and Germany to be friendly and cooperate. Then when there was that business with Czechoslovakia they said the Munich Agreement was only putting right a terrible injustice that we'd all done to Germany in the peace treaties at the end of the Great War."

"You mean it was Nazi sympathizers?"

"Some people might say so, but that wasn't against the law in 1938. I was a bit young and naïve. They had a branch in Ilford, and I went along to some of their meetings. I thought German people were nice and we ought to be friends with them, and I agreed with what some of those Link people said about the Jews controlling everything and needing to be sorted out. I've never told anyone I was mixed up with it, and if my employers knew I reckon I'd be out of a job. I don't know how he found out."

"I think the answer to that may be quite simple," said Jago. "Mr Fletcher, I've been told by another witness that you were a member of the Link yourself. Is that true?"

Fletcher nodded silently.

"And you somehow knew of Miss Willerson's past involvement with it?"

"Yes."

"How was that?"

"I remembered her name from the membership list. It's an unusual name."

"I see."

Jago turned back to Angela.

"And you say the prospect of being dismissed worried you."

"Yes. That job's everything to me. I haven't got a husband, I've no family – my job's all I've got. I have to pay my own way. So when he mentioned the Link, that was the last straw. I knew he'd found out everything about me and was about to ruin my life."

"So then what happened?"

"He said he'd give me two days to think it over, and not to try anything funny, because I was under surveillance. He said I mustn't tell anyone what he'd said, or I'd be in trouble with the law, because of the Official Secrets Act. Those two days were the worst of my life."

"And did he come back after two days?"

"Yes."

"How much did you pay him?"

Angela gave a bitter laugh.

"Everything."

"What do you mean?"

"This time he came to my flat. It was just as the sirens were going off for an air raid, but he wouldn't let me go out to the shelter. He kept me there in the flat. I got emotional and begged him not to report me, not to tell anyone about my past, and he seemed to soften up. He said he didn't want me to go to prison, he liked me, and he'd be prepared not to report me, but he'd be taking a big risk himself, so I'd have to give him an assurance – a 'deposit', he called it. I was getting worried about the bombs coming, so I said what do you mean, and he said it would be like bail, a sum of money to ensure I behaved myself in future. When I asked him how much, he said seventy pounds. I couldn't believe it. I've never had that much money at one time. I started crying. Then he got all sympathetic and kind, and said I could give him a different kind of guarantee: he'd see to it that I wasn't arrested if I was nice to him."

"And would I be right in thinking –"

"Yes, Inspector, you would. You probably think I'm stupid, but I was so worried, I didn't know what to do. He was there in the flat, the bombs were starting to fall outside, and he was threatening to expose my past or even have me arrested. So yes, like a fool I was 'nice to him', right there in my own flat. Then he went. I felt ashamed, filthy, disgusted with myself. I was broken."

Angela pointed an accusing finger at Fletcher and seemed to struggle to control her feelings as she spoke.

"You need to arrest that man and send him to prison. He's a criminal."

A silence followed. Angela began to weep quietly into her handkerchief. When she spoke, her voice was muffled.

"Can I ask you something?" she said.

"Yes," said Jago.

"When Mary was... When Mary was attacked, did she die quickly?"

"She died of strangulation. That doesn't kill immediately, but I understand from the pathologist that she would have lost consciousness within a few seconds."

Angela nodded slowly.

"That's good. So she didn't suffer?"

"I cannot say that, Miss Willerson."

CHAPTER 46

Jago left Angela to her thoughts and took a few steps across the room to Susan. Her back was pressed against the wall, and there was still a distracted look in her eyes.

"I realize the last few minutes must have been distressing for you, Mrs Fletcher," he said. "But I need to ask you about Mary."

Susan's body twitched, as if she were waking from a sleep. She nodded silently, then met his gaze and stood straight before him.

"Go ahead. Ask me anything you like."

"When we spoke to you this morning you said you didn't like your sister and you had nothing in common with her. Is that a matter of regret to you?"

"Regret?" said Susan. "What is there to regret? She had her life and I have mine – or had it, until you turned up here." Her voice faltered, but she wiped her eyes and continued. "Listen, Inspector, it isn't always all sweetness and light having a sister. There were plenty of times when I wished I didn't have one. I'd have been happy enough on my own."

"You suggested before that you found it difficult having a sister who was older than you. Is that what the problem was?"

"Some girls manage. If they have a big sister they look up to her, they want to be like her, but I never did. Mary never gave me any reason to. I think she resented the fact that I'd come along. You know what it's like – there's an only child and it's used to getting all the attention, and then suddenly there's this new baby. The older kid gets jealous. I think that's what happened with Mary, only she never grew out of it."

"So how would you describe your relationship with Mary?"

"Non-existent," said Susan. "It was like I didn't exist. Even when we were little she ignored me, and as we got older she froze me out of her life. I used to get her hand-me-down clothes – I felt as though I was just a kind of dustbin for any old rubbish she didn't need or want any more."

"But then you both grew up. Did it change when you weren't children any more?"

"When you've had that kind of treatment all your life, you don't change just because you've reached a certain age. Even when I got married I thought she'd probably just sneer at me. It was always the same with boys – if there was one I liked she'd say nasty things about him. She'd say, 'Oh, yes, he used to ask me to walk out with him and I said no because I didn't think he was good enough, but he might do for you.' Anything to make me feel inferior, a failure compared with her."

"So you feel better off without her?"

"You tell me – you're the detective. But if you're thinking I killed her, you can think again. I told you before, I was at home here all that night, and my husband can confirm that."

"So you said, Mrs Fletcher," said Jago. "But I'm afraid your husband is hardly in a strong position to act as a reliable witness at the moment."

"I don't care," said Susan. "I'm not a murderer."

She gestured in the direction of Celia.

"You can send him back to her, for all I care. If she had him first she's welcome to him. Look at her – I can see why the stupid old trout lost him in the first place."

"You watch your tongue," said Celia, half rising from her seat.

"That'll do," said Jago, positioning himself between them. "Mrs Berry, you met Mary, didn't you, and you told her about your husband?"

"Yes," said Celia. There was a note of wariness in her voice.

"Did you know at that point that your husband had married for a second time?"

"Of course I didn't."

"And did you have any reason to believe Mary had had an intimate relationship with your husband?"

"No – he kept that a secret. Seems he was good at doing that."

"So she was just a stranger you happened to meet at a dance."

"Yes."

"And you didn't know anyone else who knew her?"

"That's right."

"But you did get to know Angela Willerson that night at the dance, didn't you? And she was a friend of Mary's."

"Yes."

"And you told me today that you and Angela have become friends since then."

"Well, yes, I did, but what's that got to do with anything?"

"I'm just wondering whether Angela knew who it was that Mary had that liaison with – or at least had a strong suspicion. So if you and Angela became pals, maybe she told you what Mary had been up to. And I'm wondering whether you then decided Mary had destroyed your marriage. It's not something she could have gone to prison for, but perhaps you decided to impose your own form of punishment. To take revenge on her and your husband. They'd betrayed you together – and the penalty for traitors is death."

Celia gasped.

"That's outrageous!" she said. "How dare you? It's a pack of lies from beginning to end. Who put that idea in your head?"

She rounded on Angela.

"Was it you? Speak up, woman."

Before Angela could reply, there was a deafening explosion as another bomb landed. This time the whole room shook. The water in the buckets slopped over onto the floor, and the books and magazines slid off the shelf and landed in a clumsy heap on the floor. Susan Fletcher clutched her head and began to weep quietly.

Jago waited for the noise to die away. The electric light had flickered, but it stayed on. He was relieved that the power supply had not been cut off by the explosion – he was anxious to keep an eye on everyone in the room.

He turned to Angela.

"And you, Angela," he said. "You knew Mary, you know Celia, and you've just told us that you've had a very unpleasant contact with George Fletcher. Did Mary know about that? She was your friend, after all."

Angela closed her eyes tight, as if in pain, and slowly shook her head. Then she looked up at the ceiling, saying nothing. It seemed to Jago as though she were trying to see through it to another place, perhaps another time. Finally she lowered her gaze and spoke.

"My friend? No, Inspector, she wasn't my friend. She was the one who betrayed me."

Jago squatted before her, looked her in the eye and spoke quietly.

"Mary betrayed you?"

"Yes. You're right, of course – she was my friend, my best friend, the only real friend I had in the world. That's what I thought, but what I didn't know was that all the time she was betraying me, selling me. More fool me." She gestured with her head towards the handcuffed Fletcher. "I couldn't understand how that swine over there knew so much about me – not just the business about the Link, but all the other stuff, personal stuff, that convinced me I must be under some kind of official surveillance. I thought he could really get me into trouble. It never crossed my mind that she... Not until that night."

"Which night?"

Angela sobbed.

"The night she died."

"What happened?"

"We went out for a drink together, and by the time we set off home it must have been getting on for half·past ten. We were both

297

a bit tipsy – her more than me. We got to a place where the houses had been bombed, and it was all just a pile of rubble and wreckage. I said something like the whole country was going to pot these days, and before long it'd all be smashed to pieces like this, and the way things were going I wouldn't be able to afford to go out for a drink soon. She said, 'It's all about number one, Angela,' said you've got to look after yourself, because no one else is going to look after you. Then she started telling me about this thing she'd been doing at work – said she was making a bit of cash on the side."

Angela wiped her eyes with a handkerchief and continued.

"I asked her what she meant, and she said, 'Supply and demand, my girl.' I didn't know what she was talking about, but she said there was this man who wanted information about people – not big secret information, not like a spy, just ordinary personal information. 'That's what we call demand,' she said, and then she said something like, 'So I just give him some ordinary bits of information from the personnel files at work – that's what we call supply. And he gives me money, so everyone's happy.' Then she laughed, like it was some big joke."

"Did she say who this man was?"

"No, but I wasn't so tipsy I couldn't put two and two together and make four. I could see it, plain as day – it must be the bloke who'd been trying it on with me. That would explain how he knew so much about me. She'd just got my file out and told him what it said."

"So what did you do?"

Angela's expression grew hard, and she spoke through gritted teeth.

"I got angry – said, 'How could you do this to me? I'm your friend.' That sort of thing. She just said, 'You poor naïve little kid,' and laughed in my face. I felt so angry. All that time I'd thought she was my friend, and she'd betrayed me, made a fool of me. I could see she was wobbly on her feet because of the drink, so I pushed her. I couldn't get over the fact that she'd betrayed me to that man. I grabbed a piece of wood and swung it at her."

"Did you hit her?"

"I was so mad I didn't know what I was doing. I wasn't even aiming – I just sort of lunged at her with it. It caught her on the side of her head. She went flying backwards and landed on her back on this pile of bricks. I got down beside her. It was too dark to see properly, but it looked like I'd knocked her out cold. I put my hand over her mouth and I could feel she was still breathing. Then I panicked. I knew if she told anyone what had happened I'd be in trouble and it would all come out. I knew no one would see us in the blackout, so I just held her down and put my hands round her throat and squeezed as hard as I could. Then she stopped breathing."

Angela began to cry. When at last she spoke through her tears, her voice was hushed, but it had the intensity of a scream of anguish.

"I didn't mean to kill her."

Jago got up and stood before her. He laid his hand on her shoulder.

"I'm arresting you on suspicion of murder. You are not obliged to say anything, but anything you say may be given in evidence."

Angela collapsed back in her chair and raised one arm to cover her eyes. Her body shook as the tears welled up from somewhere deep inside her.

She seemed oblivious to the bombs which continued to crash to the earth, their blasts now thuds receding gradually into the distance. A silence fell on the room.

CHAPTER 47

It was Friday morning, and Jago felt as though some of the weight had been taken off his shoulders, at least for the time being. He took the two steps up to the front door of West Ham police station in one stride and greeted Sergeant Tompkins with a broad smile.

"Morning, Frank."

"Morning, sir. You're looking pleased with yourself."

"That's because it's Friday, and tomorrow it'll be Saturday, and then it'll be Sunday and I can have a whole day off."

"You mean you won't be sneaking in just for a few hours?"

"No. I intend to have a day off, and I'm thinking of telling young Cradock to do the same."

"He'll think you're going soft – soft as a mop."

"I think we both deserve it."

"You got your man, then."

"In a manner of speaking. We got one man, but the main man we got was a woman."

"Well, they do say we're living in tumultuous times, so I suppose nothing should surprise us."

"No, this really was a woman."

"Whatever you say, sir."

"What's the matter, Frank? You sound a bit down in the dumps. What's up?"

"I've got to work an extra shift on Sunday. At my age. It's bad enough being hauled out of retirement because of staff shortages, but then they go and get more shortages and I have to work extra hours. It's not right."

"I expect your wife will see the bright side of it."

"I'm not entirely sure what you mean by that. Actually, I reckon she'll go on about it. She'll say she's managed to get a bit of beef for a roast on Sunday and now it'll go to waste. She'll say that, even if she hasn't. You know what women are like. And how's that –"

Jago held up his hand.

"No more questions, Frank. I must get down to work. Any messages? Does DDI Soper want me to join him for a celebratory drink?"

"Yes, sir, and no, sir. Mr Soper hasn't mentioned that to me, but there's one message. It's from Detective Superintendent Ford – he says you're to go and see him at the Yard as soon as you come in. I'm sorry if that prevents you catching up with your work today, but it's the world we live in, as they say. Perhaps you can get it done on Sunday."

***

Within an hour Jago was back in Ford's office. The detective superintendent gave him a warm welcome, as on his previous visit.

"I expect you'll be wondering what this is all about, me dragging you back here," said Ford.

"Yes, I am, rather," said Jago.

"Well, it's a bit off your normal beat, as it were, down in West Ham, but there's a connection."

"I assumed there must be."

"It's about Japan, you see."

"Ah, now that is not something I assumed. We don't have a lot to do with Japan in West Ham."

"It's not top of our list at the moment either, with Hitler threatening to break down the door and help himself to everything in the house. But better minds than mine in the government have their concerns. Did you hear about the Tientsin Incident last year?"

"I read a few bits and pieces in the paper, but I can't say I know much about it."

"To be honest, there's not much to say. Tientsin is one of those treaty ports in China dating back to the Opium Wars, on the coast up Peking way, and some local unpleasantness in June of last year ended with the Japanese Navy blockading the British concession. I daresay you and I had never heard of the place, but I can tell you we came very close to war with Japan – the last thing we wanted, given what was brewing in Europe."

"It obviously didn't come to that, though."

"No. It seems the Foreign Office managed to smooth things out, but the government's still anxious. And now there's this business with the Japanese invading French Indo-China and squaring up to the Americans. There's trouble ahead, and if the Americans get sucked into any kind of war with Japan they won't be able to spare anything to help us. There's no doubt the Japanese have their minds set on expansion. We've got enough on our hands trying to keep Hitler out of Kent, so it leaves us very vulnerable in the Far East. What they've been doing in China is bad enough, but if they ever start looking beyond that the consequences are unthinkable. Imagine if they set their sights on Malaya, or even India. If they start trouble there we might as well shut up shop."

"That I can understand, but what's it got to do with me?"

"Well, it's not quite from the sublime to the ridiculous, but the fact is that ever since Tientsin we've been asked to keep an eye on one or two characters from the Japanese Embassy here. A couple of our men were watching one of them last night. He was in a café up west with a woman they didn't recognize, and it appeared she was trying to pass him something in exchange for cash. When she left they picked her up and brought her in for a chat. She's here now, helping us with our enquiries, and I think you might like to meet her. You might be interested to see this, too."

He opened a drawer in his desk and took out a woman's handbag.

"This is hers. And look what we found in it."

He opened the bag and put in his hand, then withdrew it.

"There we are."

"A wireless valve?"

"Indeed. The very thing you were asking about on Tuesday. Come with me."

CHAPTER 48

They entered the interview room, where a woman was sitting at a table with her back to the door. At the sound of their arrival she turned round. Her eyebrows arched in surprise.

"Mr Jago," she said. "What are you doing here?"

"I might ask the same question," he replied. "Since I'm a policeman and this is Scotland Yard, it's perhaps less of a surprise for you to see me here than it is for me to see you, Miss Hornby."

Ford and Jago sat down on the other side of the table. Ford put the handbag on the table, took out the valve, and placed it in front of her.

"Miss Hornby," he said, "I'd like you to tell my colleague here exactly what you were doing discussing one of your employer's products with a Japanese diplomat last night, and to answer any questions he may have."

Miss Hornby shifted on her chair to face Jago. It was difficult to interpret her expression, but he read it as reflecting a kind of embarrassed hopelessness.

"The short answer, Inspector Jago, is that I've been a fool," she said. "I've no idea what that valve thing is for, but I knew we were making them for the War Office and the job was very urgent and secret. I thought it might be something important."

"So you phoned an acquaintance who just happened to be a Japanese diplomat?"

"No, of course not. It was he who contacted me. The Japanese gentleman was a pre-war customer of ours – he'd visited Everson Engineering in 1938. He seemed to know we were manufacturing valves for the government and he asked me to get him a couple of samples. He said he might buy some if they were interesting enough."

"And you thought this was above board? You didn't think it was suspicious that a representative of a foreign power was asking you for something that our government had said was a secret project?"

"But they're not an enemy, are they? We're not at war with them. And in the last war Japan was on our side."

"So was Italy, but that didn't stop them declaring war on us three months ago when Mussolini could see that France was finished."

"Be that as it may, Inspector, I just thought I'd take a few of those things for myself."

"Mr Everson told me those valves were behind some heavy crates and he thought they'd have been too heavy for a woman to move on her own. Did you have someone to help you?"

"Yes, I did, actually. I persuaded Mrs Parker to help me. She does some cleaning for us. There was no reason for her to think there was anything suspicious about pushing a few crates to one side, and between us we managed it."

"Were you aware of the scheme she and her husband were running to pilfer various items from the business?"

"Yes, I was. As you know, I was one of Harry Parker's customers. I bought silk stockings from him, but I know other women got hydrogen peroxide, batteries and so on from him – things which tallied rather closely with what I'd heard was going missing from Everson Engineering."

"You knew who was stealing these things and you didn't tell Mr Everson?"

Miss Hornby gave a shrug of the shoulders as if to say there was nothing she could have done about it.

"No, I thought Harry's activities would provide a useful cover for what I was doing. If the disappearance of the valves came to light I could always give an anonymous tip-off or do something else like that to point you in the direction of the Parkers."

"Harry Parker said it was Mary Watkins who put the idea of

helping themselves to a few odds and ends into their heads. Is that true?"

Miss Hornby hesitated.

"I'm sorry. I know it wasn't right, but it was I who told Harry to say that. You must think I'm an awful person, but I'm afraid in the heat of the moment I thought, 'Mary's dead, so she won't be able to deny it, and also no one will be able to punish her for it, so why shouldn't I?'"

"And you were prepared to sell the Parkers down the river just to protect yourself?"

Jago could see the distress creeping into her face as she spoke.

"I didn't want to go to prison, Mr Jago. I knew that Mr Parker had already been to prison, so I thought he would be used to it, and in any case generally their class of person is more accustomed to imprisonment than mine, so I thought it would simply be judicious to cast suspicion in their direction if the need arose."

"And what about Mr Everson? I thought you were one of his most trusted colleagues. Weren't you concerned about jeopardizing his business?"

Miss Hornby looked down at the table. When she spoke, her voice was softer and quieter.

"Yes, I realize that. As I said, I've been foolish. The more I think about it, the bigger fool I think I've been." She paused, as if struggling to find the right words. "I just wanted him to… to notice me. All these years… I felt taken for granted. Oh, yes, it was always Miss Hornby, very efficient, a model employee, nobody more reliable than her. But he never even looked at me. I wanted him to – I wanted him to look at me… in that way. But he didn't."

"So you decided enough was enough?"

"Yes. It all just got too much." Her voice broke. "The truth is I wanted to hurt him. I know it doesn't make sense. Why would I want to hurt the man I – the man I respect?" She took a handkerchief from her sleeve and delicately blew her nose. "Now you can see,

Inspector – I'm just a foolish woman. Why is it we hurt the people we hold dearest?"

Jago did not respond to her question. His face was an impassive mask.

Miss Hornby crumpled the handkerchief in her hand and dabbed at the corners of her eyes.

"What will happen to me now?"

"That's a question for my colleague here – not me, I'm afraid."

"What will Mr Everson say?"

"I expect that will rather depend on whether he manages to keep his contract with the government. If he does, you may be able to prevail upon him to vouch for your previous good conduct."

Detective Superintendent Ford rose from his chair.

"Stay here please, Miss Hornby. Detective Inspector Jago and I are just stepping outside."

In the corridor, Ford closed the door and motioned Jago a few steps away to get them out of earshot.

"So what are you going to do with her?" said Jago.

"Actually, John," said Ford, "I was rather thinking you might like to take her away with you. Put her up before your local magistrates if you like. I don't think she's of any great interest to us – the Japanese fellow didn't take the valve. I doubt whether she knew whether it was technically significant or not. I'm no expert, but it looks like the kind of thing you'd put in an ordinary domestic wireless set to me, so she may have taken the wrong sort – in which case the diplomat may have spotted that for himself. Either way there's no harm done to national security."

"She's a lucky woman, then. She could have been facing a hefty stretch of penal servitude for assisting the enemy."

"Yes, but she said it herself: we're not in a state of war with Japan, so they're not strictly the enemy. You could charge her with larceny, but that's more in your line of work, not mine. My advice is take her away and give her a stern talking to. Have a chat with her employer and see what he wants to do." He paused and leaned forward in an air of mock confidentiality. "And when you've done that, perhaps you should find her a good man to occupy her thoughts."

Jago smiled.

"I think I may already have done that."

CHAPTER 49

When Jago returned to the station he opened the door of the CID office to find the divisional detective inspector's back filling most of his view. Over Soper's shoulder he could see Cradock on the far side of the room. The detective constable's face reminded him of a cornered cat trying to calculate an escape route. A wave of relief seemed to pass over Cradock's face as he saw Jago enter the room.

Soper turned round on hearing the rattle of the door handle.

"Ah, good morning, John," he said. "I was just asking Constable Carruthers here about your murder."

Cradock half opened his mouth, wondering whether he should attempt to correct the DDI, but caught the look in Jago's eyes and thought better of it.

"Yes, sir," said Jago. "DC Cradock has been of great assistance to me on this case."

Soper eyed Cradock sceptically, as if finding this claim implausible.

"Very good. And what about that fellow from the hospital – the pathologist? When we were at the mortuary he seemed to know all about what had happened to that Watkins woman – was he anywhere close to the mark?"

"Spot on, actually, sir," said Jago. "The suspect we've arrested told us she hit the victim with a piece of wood, then held her down and strangled her, which is what Dr Anderson had deduced from his examination. I'd say he was pretty impressive."

Soper made no comment, maintaining his sceptical expression as he digested this response.

"And it wasn't a robbery?" he continued. "What about that handbag you said was missing?"

"Harry Parker brought that in – claimed he'd found it and was returning it as lost property. Turns out he did us a favour. The bag contained a photo that was a valuable piece of evidence."

"So what does he want? A special award from the commissioner for assisting the police?"

"No, sir. It also turns out he's been doing some informal trading in ladies' silk stockings and other things that he shouldn't have been, so he'll be receiving some rather different attention from us."

"Good. And what about that American woman? Have you managed to keep her out of trouble?"

"She got back from Liverpool in one piece, although that's no thanks to me. I think what she saw there will help her to write for her newspaper in a way that's helpful to our war effort."

"She's definitely on our side, then?"

"I'm not sure I could speak for her views that categorically, sir, but I think I can say she's on the side of the things that this country says we're fighting for."

Soper gave him a quizzical look.

"I'm not sure I know what you're talking about, but I take it you're satisfied she's not one of those Fifth Column types. Is that right?"

"Yes, sir. I don't think we've anything to fear in that regard. Mind you, I think the whole thing's a bit exaggerated. Don't you?"

"To be honest, I don't know what to think," said Soper. "But as long as she's not getting under your feet I don't mind. Is she happy with the information you're giving her?"

"As far as I can tell, sir," said Jago. "There's always the risk of misunderstanding, of course, but I'll be meeting her soon. I'm planning to bring her up to date on a few points of interest."

***

Jago thought Cradock looked relieved to have been rescued from Divisional Detective Inspector Soper's clutches, and headed off with him in the direction of the canteen. On the way they met Sergeant Tompkins.

"Ah, there you are, sir," said Tompkins. "I was looking for you. Could you just pop along to speak to someone? They say it won't take a minute."

Jago went with him, with Cradock following in their wake. At the front desk a woman was waiting. Jago didn't recognize her, but he did know the man standing just behind her – it was War Reserve Constable Price, but not in uniform.

Price hastened over to Jago.

"I'm sorry to disturb you, sir," he said, "but I wondered if we could have a brief word with you. I'm off duty, as you can see, but we had to see you."

Price turned back, took his wife by the arm and led her forward.

"This is my wife, sir – Mavis."

"Pleased to meet you," said Jago. "Now, tell me what this is all about."

"We've had a telegram," said Price. "From Cunard."

"Was the *City of Benares* one of their ships?"

"Yes, that's right. It came at lunchtime. It said some more survivors had been found, so we went to the post office on the corner and phoned them – they agreed to reverse the charges, of course. They said that three days after that man came to tell us our children had been lost when it sank, an RAF plane had spotted another lifeboat – it seems there was one that got away that no one knew about. The people in it were picked up by a destroyer that got in to Scotland yesterday."

"That's wonderful news," said Jago. "Does that mean your children are safe?"

Price's face told him this was the wrong question to ask. Mrs Price began to weep quietly, holding on to her husband's arm. Price was clearly labouring to bring his emotions under control.

"No, sir. They said our daughter Gracie was in the lifeboat, but

311

they had no word of our son. They said we must assume he was definitely lost."

Mavis Price gulped for air and swallowed hard, then spoke.

"So you see, Mr Jago, it's not the best news, but it's good news – better than it was when Gordon came to see you on Sunday. We thought we'd lost both of them, but now we've got a daughter again. It's like she's come back from the dead. We had to let you know. We're going to bring her home and keep her safe with us, or get her to somewhere safe in the country."

"I'm so glad for you," said Jago. "And thank you for telling me."

"You were very understanding when I spoke to you last weekend," said Price. "I didn't know what to do. Everything in my life has changed – for the worse, and now for the better."

"I hope your memories of your son will be some comfort to you."

"They will," said Mavis. "But I can't keep sitting in the house thinking about Tom."

She turned to her husband and wiped her eyes with the back of her hand.

"And I don't want the Germans here… I've got to do something, Gordon, whether you approve of married women working or not. I want to get a job in a munitions factory and help sink those U-boats, or join the WVS and look after children who've lost their parents, or parents who've lost children. I don't care what it is, I just need to get out there and do something."

Price nodded, putting his arm round his wife.

"And you?" said Jago. "What about your job? Are you going to carry on?"

"Yes, sir," said Price. "I'd like to stay in the police until we win this war – and maybe even after it, if they'll have me. I don't want anything else from life, not now I've got Gracie back. I just want to see her grow up – and one day when all this is over, I'll walk her down the aisle. I'll be the proudest man in England."

CHAPTER 50

They met at Westminster Abbey. It was Dorothy's suggestion – a high explosive bomb had fallen during the night and smashed its Great West Window, and she wanted to see the damage before darkness fell again. Jago repeated his journey to Scotland Yard, except that this time when he came out of Westminster tube station he turned right instead of left and took the short walk down towards the abbey. The weather was fine, but the clouds gathering in the sky hinted at rain to come.

It was two days since he'd last seen Dorothy, but it seemed longer. That was Wednesday, when he'd sat with her in a seedy saloon bar in Canning Town, more on duty than off. That was also when he'd met her brother. He still felt a surge of shame when he thought of the conclusions he'd jumped to. Now it was Friday, and for the first time since this case had begun he felt there was enough space in his mind for him to think it through properly. He was definitely off duty, and it was time for him to treat Dorothy to a proper meal.

As he approached the abbey he glimpsed her in the distance, walking towards him. She was wearing a blue coat that he didn't recall having seen before, but he recognized her more by her confident stride than by her clothes. She saw him and waved. Watching her approach, her heels tap-tapping on the paving stones, Jago tried to interpret the way she was walking, the movement of her arms, for clues about how to greet her, but he had no idea whether she would shake his hand or fling her arms round him. Everything about her seemed relaxed, open, and free – or in other words, unpredictable. He stood awkwardly, waiting for her with his hands behind his back, like a naughty schoolboy. She came to a halt in front of him, the hem of her coat swinging round her knees.

"Hi," she said, a little breathlessly. "You made it!"

He nodded and gave her a hesitant smile.

"You too."

"Okay – to Westminster Abbey."

She turned round, took him by the arm and began to march him in the direction of the abbey.

"Is this so you can write about it?" said Jago.

"Correct," she said. "A bomb hitting Westminster Abbey – that's a story."

"Will they let you?"

"You mean the censors?"

"Yes, I mean the abbey's a national institution. Won't they say it'll be bad for public morale to report it?"

"They'll let me write something, just not everything," said Dorothy. "I'll probably have to say the damage was minimal and easily repairable, that kind of thing. They can't very well say nothing, because thousands of people can walk past every day and see it, even go to services."

"Are they still having services?"

"Why? Do you want to go to one? If you do, you're out of luck – I heard they still hold a morning service, but the evening one has been suspended."

"Same as the theatres, then."

"I guess so. A cathedral isn't the safest place to be in an air raid."

"It's not a cathedral – it's a royal peculiar."

"You're kidding. That sounds like some crazy old king."

"I suppose it does. We've had a few – not least the one who lost the North American colonies and then went mad. But it doesn't mean that."

"So what does it mean?"

"It means the dean who runs it is accountable directly to the king, not to any bishop or archbishop. But don't ask me why – I haven't the faintest idea."

"It sounds like most things in this country: you do all sorts of weird things, and no one knows why. It's like you make it up as you go along."

Jago did not demur.

They arrived at the abbey, and Jago watched while Dorothy set about her work amidst its sandbagged treasures. She surveyed the site, checked its surroundings, and scribbled in her notebook. It reminded him of himself, examining the scene of a crime and trying to piece together what had happened. Within a few minutes she was folding her notebook closed and putting it in her handbag.

"All done?" he said.

"Yes, that's all I need."

"In that case, would you like to eat? It's a little difficult these days – so many of the small places are closing early so their staff can get home before the blackout, and who can blame them? But I know a little French restaurant in Horseferry Road – it's a family business, and several of the staff sleep on the premises."

"I didn't know you were an expert on restaurants in this area."

"I'm not – but I used to work near here, and someone recommended it to me."

He hoped she wouldn't ask questions. His time with Special Branch at Scotland Yard was something he wasn't at liberty to discuss. He'd dined once at the restaurant during those days, and didn't know any others near Westminster Abbey. It was certainly a far cry from any of the eating places he knew in West Ham, and considerably more expensive, but then London SW1 was a different world. He wondered what Rita would think of the prices. He couldn't afford to eat in such a place regularly, and in truth he preferred Rita's more homely establishment, but he'd felt in some ill-defined way a need to do penance for not having trusted Dorothy, for having judged her on superficial evidence.

"Actually," said Dorothy, "would you mind if we didn't go to a fancy restaurant? I've spent all day indoors and I'd like to spend a little more time out in the open before we all have to get in our shelters. Can we just get a coffee or something?"

Jago felt an unexpected sense of relief. Moving about outside and chatting with Dorothy seemed a more manageable prospect than trying to explain himself at a table in a public restaurant. He walked her back towards the river, passing the House of Lords on the opposite side of the road. A bomb had narrowly missed it the previous night. The House was still standing, but all its windows facing the road had been shattered, and the area in front of it was strewn with broken glass and rubble.

"So the Home Secretary was right," said Dorothy.

Jago gave her a blank look.

"About those little strips of brown paper on your windows not being very effective against bombs after all," she said. "They'll believe him now."

"Ah, yes, I see," said Jago. "But look at that." He pointed to an equestrian statue still standing in the middle of the debris. "That's Richard the Lionheart, another of our crazy old kings. The bomb's bent his sword, but he's still holding it high. I like that."

They walked on and turned the corner, and soon found a coffee stall near Westminster Bridge. Jago bought them a mug of coffee and a hot meat pie each and got change from a florin. Rita would approve of that.

He handed Dorothy her coffee and pie.

"I've told him I'm a police officer, so he's going to trust us to bring our mugs back. Let's find somewhere to sit."

The light was beginning to fade and the air chill as they walked slowly back to Parliament Square and found a bench. Ahead of them ranged the gothic splendour of the Palace of Westminster, with the clock tower housing the Big Ben bell outlined against the sky above it. The tower seemed to Jago to stand guard over parliament, as it had done all his life, the only change being that now it had to comply with the blackout, so the lights behind its clock faces would soon be turned off.

"You know what I can't get used to with these air raids?" he said.

"Tell me," said Dorothy. She was clutching her coffee with both hands for warmth, and he felt her slide a little towards him on the bench so that they were almost touching.

"It's looking at a place like the Houses of Parliament over there – it's been standing there all my life, governing the country and a quarter of the world besides while the river flows quietly past, and yet in a couple of hours a hundred planes could come over and bomb it to kingdom come. Nothing's certain any more."

"Was it ever?"

"I don't know. I know it wasn't when I was fighting in France, but then we came home, and I thought life would never be that fragile again. I thought I'd spend my life as a policeman, keeping everything in order, but now it's all gone mad again. Sometimes I wonder what's the point? I mean, why have I just used all my time and energy to solve a murder when a hundred times as many innocent people will be killed in their beds tonight?"

"Because it's your job, that's why, and you do it well. No one else can be you and do your job, so you have to do it, just like I have to do mine. It's not your job to bring Hitler to justice, but if someone takes another person's life on your precinct it is your job. If you didn't do it, you'd be giving in to evil."

"Do you believe in evil? I'm not sure it's an entirely fashionable concept these days."

"I don't know how anyone can live in this world with their eyes and ears open and not believe in evil. I believe it exists, and I believe we have to fight it wherever we are with whatever abilities we have. When you find your murderer and send them to court, you're demonstrating that evil exists and that there's a justice that exposes and judges it. If I didn't think that was possible I'd go crazy."

"Eat your meat pie," said Jago. "It'll go cold."

Dorothy laughed.

"Back to earth again. You really do keep your feet on the ground. So, tell me about your case. Did it have anything to do with the Fifth Column?"

"There was a man who accused a couple of young women of spying for the enemy, but it turned out he was an imposter."

"And what did that have to do with the woman who was murdered?"

"It looks as though Mary was taking information from their personnel files at work and passing it to the man. All we know is that one of those files went missing when Mary was still alive, so she could have taken it and let him see it, but unless he tells us that, it's only a suspicion."

"So who killed Mary?"

"It was the other woman he'd tried to blackmail. She discovered Mary had passed him information about her and she felt her friend had betrayed her. She hit her with a piece of timber and then strangled her."

"Will she hang?"

"That's for the court to decide. If she'd only hit Mary she might have got off with manslaughter, but the fact that she then decided to strangle her means that she had time to think about it and acted deliberately, and that makes it murder."

Dorothy shivered.

"Are you cold?" said Jago. "Perhaps we should take our mugs back and go."

"I'm okay. It's the thought of one woman killing another in cold blood. But we should probably go anyway – it'll be blackout time soon."

"I've just had an idea," said Jago. "Have you ever had a ride on a London tram?"

"No, I haven't."

"Well, now's your chance. Another London experience for you. We can get one just over there."

He pointed in the direction of Westminster Bridge and jumped to his feet, cramming the last remaining piece of his meat pie into his mouth while Dorothy wiped a crumb of pastry from her lips. This time Jago offered her his arm, and she took it.

CHAPTER 51

They had to wait for a while, but eventually a Number 33 tram came into view, heading towards them across the bridge from the other side of the Thames. It turned into the Victoria Embankment and stopped with a piercing squeal of its brakes. They got on and Jago paid the conductor tuppence for two tickets, then led Dorothy up the steep half-spiral staircase.

"This one's come across from Kennington, where Charlie Chaplin comes from, and it goes up into North London," said Jago as they got to the top. "Go down the front there."

He followed her along the narrow gangway in the centre of the upper deck, and they sat on the curved seat at the front, above the driver.

"Do you have these in America?" he said.

"Sure – we call them streetcars. Boston's full of them, except ours are single-deckers and run on overhead wires. We have the El too – that's the Boston Elevated Railway, and it runs through the city twenty feet up in the air."

"Trains in the air? That sounds dangerous."

"No, it's not a railroad, it's streetcars. We don't have as many as we used to, though. They're being replaced by buses and trackless trolleys now – what you call trolleybuses, I think."

"Same here – there's hardly any trams left in London, and most of those are south of the river. The last ones in West Ham stopped running in June."

The tram began to move, the whirring hum of its electric motor rising as it picked up speed, and the wheels below them squealed on the rails, steel grating sharply on steel. The river was dark and sluggish on their right as they bumped and swayed along the Victoria Embankment.

"You were talking about evil, and bringing people to justice," said Jago. "I think the biggest thing for me is that I just can't bear the thought of them getting away with it. I mean, why should a man who murders a girl live to a comfortable old age with his grandchildren on his knees? It's not fair. I don't want that to happen – I want him to face justice. I feel the same way about this war. The Nazis have got away with it in Czechoslovakia, in Poland, in Belgium, France, Norway and more besides, and I don't want them to get away with it here. I want us to fight them with everything we've got. Even if we lose, at least we'll have tried. I can't bear the thought of criminals escaping justice."

"I was brought up to believe that we'll all be judged when we die."

"Do you believe that? I'd like to, but I don't. What if we all just live and die, and then there's nothing? There has to be justice before death, otherwise they've got away with it."

"I don't believe there's just nothing after death. I can't prove it, but I do believe there will be justice. You believe in truth, don't you?"

"Well, we can't always tell what's true, but if I didn't believe that truth exists regardless of whether we can discover it I wouldn't be able to do this job. So yes, I do."

"I do too, but I believe justice is a consequence of truth, so if there is truth after we die, there will also be justice. I can't believe Hitler's going to be sitting there in heaven, patting his favourite dog. So I guess I'm like you – I don't want anyone who does evil to get away with it. But that means I mustn't expect to get away with it myself."

Jago twisted round on the seat and looked ahead.

"I can see Waterloo Bridge," he said. "We're almost at your hotel."

The conductor called out the stop. They descended the narrow staircase and stood on the platform until the tram came to a standstill, then climbed down onto the road.

"Mind the traffic," said Jago.

They waited until a car passed, its single headlamp shedding a dim light on the roadway, and then crossed to the pavement.

"I'll walk you to the Savoy," he said.

Only a few days before, he had avoided this area because he'd been wary of bumping into Dorothy. Now, he realized, he had no desire to avoid her, but he knew there was still something he had to say.

They turned into Savoy Place. They were only yards from the hotel.

"Let's stop for a moment," he said.

She stopped, and he turned towards her. Behind her the windows of the hotel were already darkened, but he could half see her face as the first of the moonlight broke through the clouds.

"There's something I need to tell you," he said. "If we both believe in truth, I don't want you to think I'm more than I am."

"Why would I think that?"

"That night when you introduced me to Sam — it wasn't the first time I'd seen him. I was at RAF Hornchurch last week, at that dance, and I saw you with him, saw him kiss you. I didn't know he was your brother. It was stupid and childish of me, but I assumed he was someone that you were — well, to put it simply, you could say I put two and two together and made five."

"Or maybe even six or seven?"

"Yes, that was very foolish of me. I've thought about that a lot since Wednesday, and I can only apologize. I'm sorry."

"Thank you."

"I think it must be something to do with what happened all those years ago in France, when I knew Eleanor."

"You don't mean it's my sister's fault?"

322

"No, not at all. It's my fault, but I'm trying to understand. I think it's because when I developed that affection for her and it came to nothing, I felt I'd failed – with women, I mean. I thought if I played that game I was bound to lose. So I concluded that that part of life was not for me, and I suppose from then on I avoided women – in the sense of relationships, that is. I didn't want to go down that path again. By the time the war ended, I don't think there was enough left in me emotionally to take it on. I was exhausted."

"Did you wish she hadn't gone away?"

"At the time I did, yes. I felt that she'd let me down."

"Like I did?"

"If I'm brutally honest, then yes, that's how I felt in that moment when I saw you. When I saw him kiss you, I felt as though you'd betrayed me in some way. I know that's stupid – I have no claims on you – but I was surprised by how painful it felt."

Dorothy put her hands on his upper arms and looked him in the eye.

"I guess what you saw that night at the dance touched a nerve that you weren't expecting to be touched – that you maybe thought wasn't even there any more," she said. "That's natural. It's just one of those things. You can put it behind you now."

"Thank you," said Jago. "It was only when we were sitting on that tram just now that I realized what was happening. It's as though I've been running on tramlines. But a tram can only take you to one place. If you want to get to somewhere interesting down a side road you have to get off and make your own way. And when I saw you with a handsome young man in an RAF pilot's uniform I could think only one thing. I'm ashamed to say that's one of the oldest tramlines in the world."

"I understand," said Dorothy. "Thank you for being honest with me."

He felt her grip on his arms release, and then she took both of his hands in hers. He flinched at the unfamiliar touch, but then relaxed. He held her gaze.

"The answer's simple, then, isn't it?" he said. "I think it's time I changed – it's time I got out of the tramlines."

"I like the sound of that," said Dorothy. "It could be a much more interesting journey, don't you think?"

Jago nodded. A cloud drifted in front of the moon, but in the momentary fading of its light he thought he saw her smile.

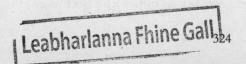

ACKNOWLEDGMENTS

As in *Direct Hit*, the first of the Blitz Detective novels, I've tried to ensure that the historical events that form the backdrop to the murder mystery are portrayed as accurately as possible. Some readers have asked me whether specific incidents mentioned in *Direct Hit* really happened – for example, the demonstration at the Savoy Hotel – and the answer is yes.

The event that sparked *Fifth Column* was real – a trial in December 1939 in which a London man was convicted of attempting to extort money by threatening to accuse someone of spying for Germany. This started me thinking about how and why such a crime might occur, and the entirely fictional case which Detective Inspector Jago investigates in *Fifth Column* is the result.

I would like to thank two of my former BBC colleagues: Richard Measham for his helpful advice on the wartime Radio Security Service, and Dave Crisp for explaining the inner workings of 1930s wireless sets. Thanks to author Richard C. Smith for helping me with some details of RAF Hornchurch. I'm also grateful to Barry Scrutton and his team for literally opening doors for me in Canning Town, and to local residents Alma Clunn, Doreen Fox, and Molly Morgan for sharing their memories of the old days with me.

I'm once again indebted to Richard White, Rudy Mitchell, and Roy Ingleton for their help with details of the Riley Lynx, the American aspects of the story, and wartime policing respectively.

As ever, my thanks go to my family for encouraging me, and to my wife Margaret for supporting me during the long writing process and for her invaluable critical scrutiny of the finished work.

To find out more about the Blitz Detective and to contact the author, go to

www.blitzdetective.com

Fifth Column is the second book in the

BLITZ DETECTIVE

series

Don't miss the first in the series…

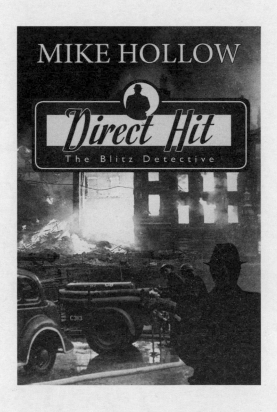

Direct Hit

FRIDAY 6 SEPTEMBER 1940

He was alone, and there was no one to help him. Trapped in the silent space between two rows of graves, he heard every rasp of the madman's breath. The reek of stale beer soured the air between them as the dark figure grabbed his lapels and pulled him close. The attacker's face was vicious, and the cap yanked down onto his forehead was shabby. No witness could have identified him, even if there had been one in this gloomy wilderness of the dead. But Hodgson knew him well enough, and wished they had never met.

It was absurd. There were houses just a hundred yards away. He could trace the outline of their roofs and chimneys against the night sky to his right. But in the depths of the blackout, with not a light showing anywhere, he might as well be on the moon. The only people out at this time of night would be the ARP wardens and the police, and he could hear no sound of them. They would have plenty of things to attend to.

He knew he was trembling, but could not stop it. He was out of his depth, overwhelmed by a familiar surge of panic. His father used to say dogs and horses could smell fear, so maybe people did too. He remembered the two women who'd stopped him on Stratford High Street in the autumn of 1916 and given him a white feather. Perhaps they could smell cowardice on him. He could have made an excuse: he'd been officially ruled unfit for military service in the Great War because of his short-sightedness. But no, he just took the feather without complaint and went on his way. He knew they were right: he was a coward through and through.

Now he heard himself babbling some futile nonsense about reporting this to the police. The man released his hold on one lapel, but only to slap him in the face. The sting bit deep into Hodgson's cheek, and his glasses rammed painfully into the bridge of his nose. He wanted to cry. It's just like the way gangsters slap hysterical women in the pictures, he thought. He knows that's all it takes with someone like me.

"Not so high and mighty now, are we, Mr Hodgson?" his tormentor snarled. "I think it's time you started putting a bit more effort into our little arrangement. Don't you?"

He flung Hodgson back against a gravestone. Its edge cracked into his spine and he slumped to the ground.

Humiliation. Again. All through his life. His wife might like to think he had some status because he worked for the Ministry of Labour and National Service, but he knew his post was shamingly junior for a man with twenty-four years' service. After all this time he still wondered if she knew what kind of man she had married. But *he* knew, only too well. He saw himself, eleven years old, and the gang that set about him on his way home from school, older boys looking for fun in their last term at Water Lane. His West Ham Grammar School uniform made him an easy target. When they snatched his cap and tossed it onto the roof of the nearest house, he understood for the first time in his life that he was a victim. They were just a bunch of fourteen-year-old boys, but he was outnumbered and powerless. Now he was outnumbered by one man.

"I will, I will," he said. "It's just difficult. You don't understand."

"Oh, I understand all right," said the man, hauling him back onto his feet.

Hodgson pushed his glasses back up his nose to straighten them. Now he could see the scar that ran three inches down the side of his assailant's face, just in front of his ear. The man didn't look old enough for it to be a wound from the last war, and not young enough to have been involved in the current one. He tried not to think how he might have got it.

"You just look here, Mr Hodgson. You're a nice man, so I'm going to give you one more chance."

The sneer in his voice made his meaning clear. He pulled a crumpled piece of paper from his trouser pocket and stuffed it into the inside pocket of Hodgson's jacket, then patted him on the chest in mock reassurance.

"Right, Mr Hodgson, you just sort it for this little lot, and there's a pound in it for you for each one. Mind you do it right, though. If you don't, I'll shop you, or worse. Now you won't forget, will you?"

Hodgson hurried to give his assurance, relieved that the ordeal was over. Before the words were out of his mouth, he felt the first blow to his stomach, then a second full in his face, a third to the side of his head and another to his stomach. After that he lost count.